**"*WARHEAD* IS AN
EXPLOSIVE NOVEL OF
ACTION AND INTRIGUE.
I COULDN'T PUT IT DOWN."**

J.A. Jance, author of *Skeleton Canyon*

COUNTDOWN

*The drone was moving eastward at a mile and
a half per minute, flying blind. It would barely
miss colliding with the narrow spire of the
Washington Monument. But as it raced over the
Mall it wouldn't miss the Capitol Building.*

*The drone was heading toward the central dome.
It would impact the cupola slightly right of
center, about thirty feet below the bronze statue
of a woman.*

*The sword that Lady Freedom grasped was a
symbol of America's strength. But she was
powerless to stop the evil that was bearing down
on her.*

Other Avon Books by
Jeffrey Layton

BLOWOUT

WARHEAD

JEFFREY LAYTON

AVON BOOKS NEW YORK

This is a work of fiction. Names, characters, places, and incidents either are the product of the author's imagination or are used fictitiously. Any resemblance to actual events, locales, organizations, or persons, living or dead, is entirely coincidental and beyond the intent of either the author or the publisher.

AVON BOOKS
A division of
The Hearst Corporation
1350 Avenue of the Americas
New York, New York 10019

Copyright © 1997 by Jeffrey Layton
Published by arrangement with the author
Visit our website at http://AvonBooks.com
Library of Congress Catalog Card Number: 96-95172
ISBN: 0-380-79154-4

First Avon Books Printing: May 1997

AVON TRADEMARK REG. U.S. PAT. OFF. AND IN OTHER COUNTRIES, MARCA REGISTRADA, HECHO EN U.S.A.

Printed in the U.S.A.

WCD   10 9 8 7 6 5 4 3 2 1

This novel is dedicated in the memory of my father,
Raymond E. Layton

ACKNOWLEDGMENTS

I would like to extend my gratitude to Alice Volpe, Northwest Literary Agency; and Tom Colgan, former editor at Avon Books, who gave me a chance; and to Peter Buck, Al Hoviland, Patricia McShea, Daryl Petrarca, Ian Sayre, Bill Schilb, John Sell, Stan Stearns, Jeanette Stephenson and Tony Urban for their encouragement and support. Thanks.

AUTHOR'S NOTE

WE ALL KNOW THAT NUCLEAR TERRORISM IS THE stuff of great fiction. What I, personally, didn't know until doing my research on *Warhead* was how terrifying the reality is: namely, that it will be nearly impossible to avert a nuclear catastrophe unless a radical change is made in how humanity confronts the risk. What I dread is that this change will take place only after we receive the worst of all wake-up calls. According to the experts, we are already living on borrowed time.

When the Cold War ended, the West's knee-jerk reaction was to breathe a sigh of relief. Why? Because the big bad enemy was gone. But what are we facing instead? In many respects, we are in more peril now. Perhaps it might be better to have a strong enemy.

The former Soviet Union had the money and the resources necessary to safeguard its vast nuclear arsenal, and for over forty years it retained absolute control over its nukes. Yes, they aimed their missiles and bombers at us, and we aimed back. But no one pulled the trigger; the nuclear nightmare never happened. However, now that a nearly bankrupt Russia has inherited over 30,000 nuclear weapons, the risk of nuclear nightmare is greater than ever before.

Every day, as the Russian Mafia gains strength, the threat increases. Reports of missing atomic materials and smuggling of nuclear high technology are now rampant. The potential payoffs from illicit nuclear trading are so astronomical that it has become a growth industry. Legions of Russians—from petty street criminals to laid-off H-bomb designers—are entering this new black market

If Russia were strong, then she might have a chance of maintaining control over her nuclear stockpiles. Unfortunately, she can barely house and feed her own people. It will be decades before she has enough resources to provide proper security. It is much more likely that weapons-grade plutonium or uranium, in the wrong hands, will be detonated, either accidentally or on purpose.

To complicate matters, we too are part of the problem. Alarmingly, our free society has generated an enormous amount of technical data on nuclear weapons; this information is readily available in our libraries, universities and on the Internet.

Where did these nuclear-bomb primers come from? A lot of it is provided by our own government. Over the past several decades, hundreds of documents dealing with nuclear weapons research have been declassified and then released into the public forum. The technical data in these publications make dandy reference tools for the world's would-be bomb makers.

The American print and broadcast media are also part of the problem. Yes, you will occasionally see a cover story or a feature TV report sounding the alarm over Russia's "loose nukes." But when it comes down to giving thought, column inches and sound bites on how to realistically deal with the problem, the media fall short. The effective solutions aren't popular with most journalists. Spending large sums on our civilian and military intelligence services, as well as possibly restricting certain personal freedoms, goes against their political grain.

And then there's Hollywood. The recent motion pictures about this subject universally gloss over the real horror of what might happen if a nuclear bomb were actually detonated in an American city. Arnold Schwarzenegger, Steven Seagal and Christian Slater will be around to save the day.

Our national security forces certainly know the risks concerning nuclear terrorism. Some have been speaking out. In one interview, an expert on terrorism was asked this question: "What is the likelihood that in the remaining years of this century terrorists will assemble a nuclear weapon and then detonate it?" His answer came without the slightest hesitation: "One hundred percent."

So we leave the arena of chance and enter that of certainty. The only questions are who, where and when.

What can we do?

First, we need to spend whatever it takes to help Russia secure her nuclear stockpiles. It will require billions of *our* own dollars. With Congress in a budget-cutting mode, any new funding for foreign aid–related projects will likely meet stiff opposition. But what choice do we have? How much will it cost to replace Manhattan? Or Dallas? Or San Francisco?

Second, we need to expand our intelligence-gathering services with the specific goal of intercepting would-be nuclear terrorists long before they ever get a chance to set off a bomb. This will also cost plenty to implement.

Third, we have to be willing to temporarily suspend some of our own personal freedoms in order to aid our security forces in ferreting out the bad guys. This will not be popular with most of us.

Fourth, we need to impose a cap on the dissemination of our nuclear secrets. We should keep our secrets secret!

Finally, we all need to change how we personally view the threat of nuclear terrorism. For too long we have had our heads buried deep in the sand.

There is no guarantee that if we implement the above countermeasures, a catastrophe will be averted. However, if we do not, a nuclear nightmare is a dead certainty. Let's improve the odds for the sake of our children.

Jeffrey Layton

PROLOGUE
PANDORA'S BOX OPENED

"I HATE WORKING ON THESE OLD DINOSAURS," THE SENIOR engineer said. "They're unpredictable as hell. You just can't trust them."

The middle-aged man stepped away from the countertop, using the back of a gloved hand to wipe the sweat from his brow. Although the laboratory chamber was slightly chilled, his insides were sizzling. Fiery adrenaline pulsed through his blood vessels.

"What's the yield on this one?" asked the assistant engineer. The young woman stood next to the man. She was as cool as glacier ice.

"Should be around eighteen kilotons, maybe a little more." He then reached up with his hands and massaged the back of his taut neck. A few seconds later he turned to face his assistant. "Get me a ten-millimeter socket," he ordered. "It's time to remove the core."

"Yes, sir."

The two Russian engineers were deep underground. The disassembly chamber was only eighty feet square, but it was part of a much larger complex. The secret military laboratory was hidden away east of the Urals, near Kasli.

Located throughout the compartment was a series of waist-high, stainless steel counters, each one about four feet wide and ten feet long. Built into the base of the counters was a variety of electronic instruments: oscilloscopes, volt and amperage meters and numerous other calibration devices. A TV-sized computer screen, positioned on the right-hand side of each counter, displayed the graphic and digital output from the diagnostic tools.

In the past, the compartment had been filled with dozens of

technicians and engineers, but today just the two persons were working. The male-female team stood side by side at a workstation near the back of the room. They were dressed in one-piece, head-to-toe white garments. Gauze masks covered their mouths and noses. Latex gloves protected their hands. Clear plastic safety glasses guarded their eyes. White head caps concealed their hair. They looked like surgeons operating on a patient.

The two Russian engineers were indeed in the middle of a surgery. But their patient wasn't human. It was about four feet long and eighteen inches in diameter. The cylindrical steel casing had already been gutted, its side access panel removed an hour earlier. A myriad of its electromechanical components was scattered across the plastic-coated, antistatic countertop.

The heavy-set male now had his hands deep inside the cylinder. He was working with something heavy. "All right," he said, "I've got it free. Have you got the cradle?"

"Yes," replied the female. She slid a salad bowl–sized fiberglass container to the opening, right under the man's outstretched arms. She then connected a pair of steel rods from the cradle to the lower edge of the opening in the cylinder. "It's ready now," she said.

The man carefully extracted his hands from the interior of the steel casing, rolling a metallic ball onto the guides and then into the center of the cradle. The cradle's molded polyurethane foam padding fit the lower hemisphere perfectly.

The purple-black globe was about the size of a bowling ball. It wasn't a perfect sphere, though. There was a sizable hole through its center. And it was backbreakingly heavy, weighing just over a hundred pounds.

The senior engineer stepped away from the counter, flexing his hands and arms to increase circulation. His fingers were almost numb from tension. He sighed and then said, "I'm glad that thing is out of the way."

The woman nodded and reached up with her right hand, stroking the ball. It was glass-smooth to the touch. She turned to face her companion. "Alexi, are you going to remove the projectile now?"

"Yes, but before I do that let's isolate the core. No sense in taking any unnecessary risks."

The woman again nodded and then walked a few steps to

her right, stopping beside a handcart. It looked like the kind of cart used in grocery stores except that a metal box occupied the basket area. One side of the box was already open, its heavy door swung to the side.

She rolled the cart next to the workstation, lining up the bottom edge of the cart's container with the countertop. She then turned a plastic knob on the side of the cart, locking its four wheels into place.

"All set," she said.

"Good, let's do it," he replied.

They both reached for the cradle containing the sphere and carefully slid it across the countertop and then into the interior of the box. The man swung the heavy lid shut.

"That'll do it," he said.

The woman released the cart's wheel locks and pushed it toward the workstation immediately to her right. When she returned, the man had once again inserted his hands inside the steel casing. This time, however, he didn't have any trouble removing the next component. The metallic plug was about the size of a large soup can.

He used both hands to hold up the hunk of dark metal. Like the sphere, it was heavy for its size. "Well, this one's neutralized so I think it's time to quit for the day." He paused, eyeing his companion. "Now, how about having dinner with me tonight?"

"I'd like that," replied the woman, meeting his eyes. She smiled, but the mask hid her attractive face.

The man stared back. Although she was young enough to be his daughter, his heartbeat accelerated as his imagination set to work. Despite the bulk of her protective garments, underneath was a supple, well-curved female body. He had been attracted to his new assistant from the first time he had met her, five weeks earlier. And now, finally, she had agreed to a date. He could hardly wait.

"Good," he said. "Let's clean up and then we'll go."

The man turned away and set the metallic plug on the tabletop. Then, while he started to clean up the various tools lying around the steel casing, the woman silently opened a drawer on her side of the table. She inserted her hand, searching for an object that had been planted hours earlier. *Got it!*

she thought as she gripped the handle. She peeled off the tape that held it to the side wall.

The man had just turned back to face his assistant when he spotted the pistol. She gripped the nine-millimeter semiautomatic with both hands. It was aimed at his chest.

"Irina! " he called out, his voice shrill. "What are you doing?"

"Sorry, Alexi," she said, her voice steady.

And then she pulled the trigger.

The only sound was a dull *zap* as the bullet exited through the suppressor. The hollow point bored a pencil-thick hole in his sternum and then ripped into his heart.

The woman watched as her coworker collapsed. She felt little remorse for the man; he had been just another obstacle to overcome. There would be more before she finished her work.

She set the pistol on the countertop and grabbed the metallic plug. After wrapping it with a thin layer of sheet lead, she slipped it into a pocket near the waist of her anticontamination suit. She then picked up the pistol and triggered the magazine release, verifying that it had been fully loaded. The remaining fourteen rounds would be more than enough to finish her mission.

She slipped the weapon into another pocket and then walked back to the cart containing the metallic sphere. She avoided the blood that was pooling around the corpse. As she began to push the cart toward the doorway, she mentally rehearsed her next series of moves. There were only three guards between her and freedom. And not one of them would be expecting trouble from the pretty blond engineer.

PART ONE

COLLISION COURSE

ONE
THE CLIENT

"DAMN!" THE DRIVER SHOUTED, SLAMMING HIS FOOT ONTO the brake pedal. The high-performance automobile skidded evenly, its tires screaming in protest. The Corvette came to a stop just inches behind the vehicle in the same lane.

If the driver had hesitated at all he would have plowed into the rear of a full-size Ford pickup. The F250 had stopped right at the peak of the bridge span and there was no shoulder to run off onto.

What the hell's going on? thought the driver as he strained to look past the truck. A moment later he saw the problem. About half a mile ahead, down the elevated span and on the floating bridge section, was a cluster of flashing blue and red lights. *Oh, great,* he said to himself, *another frigging wreck. I should have taken I-Ninety.*

The driver checked his wristwatch. It was ten to ten; he would never make his meeting on time. He reached into his coat pocket, retrieved a tiny cellular phone and pushed the power key, waiting for the digital readout to materialize. Nothing. He keyed the switch again. The phone was stone dead. *That's just great, you turkey!* he thought, now disgusted with himself. He had forgotten to charge the battery overnight.

He prided himself on being punctual, especially at a first meeting with a new client, and he really needed this new assignment. But there was nothing he could do about it now. Until the wreck cleared, he was a hostage, just like all of the other hundreds of drivers stranded in the middle of Lake Washington.

The driver switched off the engine, resigned that he was going to be late. He removed a cigarette from his coat pocket and pushed in the dashboard lighter. It popped out a few seconds later. As he lit up he automatically rolled down his window. Before the cigarette smoke completely overwhelmed his nostrils, he caught the pungent odor of burning rubber. He was thankful that he had bought the new set of Michelins the previous week.

The driver took another deep drag and exhaled. The nicotine was working; he felt better already. He had been smoking for over twenty years now—all of his adult life. The pleasure was genuine. He had no interest in stopping.

In spite of his nicotine addiction he kept in shape through a rigorous program of running and exercise. He ran a six-minute mile and could still play a mean game of racquetball.

He settled back in the bucket seat, glancing to his right. A color snapshot of a little girl was mounted on the dashboard next to the radio. He smiled as he thought of his daughter. He then reached forward, switching on the radio. It was the original and it still worked. His 1965 Corvette fastback coupe was in prime condition. The classic automobile was worth a small fortune to the right collector; it was also the driver's only hard asset, and he would never sell it.

He tuned the radio to a local station. A golden oldie was playing—one of the Beach Boys' hits. He smiled as the fast-paced tones and high-pitched vocals brought back a flood of memories. He had grown up in the Bay Area and used to surf at Santa Cruz.

The driver took another drag on his Marlboro and then glanced over the passenger's seat, looking beyond the guard-rail. There was a speedboat running southward along the Seattle shoreline, towing a water-skier. Farther lakeward he spotted several Jet-Skiers tearing across the placid water. *Gotta be kids on their summer break. Must be nice out there.*

It took twenty minutes before the wreck was finally cleared away. He restarted the V-8 and then slowly began to work his way east.

He arrived at the Redmond office park at half past ten. It took him another few minutes to find a place to park. He wouldn't take just any spot; he preferred one that provided the most protection for his Corvette, preferably one that was away from transient traffic.

The driver really hadn't paid any attention to the building until he began walking up the entry ramp. And then it hit him.

Geez, this place is huge! He was entering the ground floor of a modern two-story building. It was spread out in two wings on a campuslike setting. As he reached the doorway he noted that there was only one name on the marquee: NORDSOFT.

He pushed open the swinging glass-panel doors and walked into the lobby. It was modern and elegantly appointed, matching the exterior. Already he was impressed. He walked up to the reception desk. A pretty redhead sat behind the counter. She was in her early twenties. The name tag on her silk blouse read: Marisa. She wore a headset with a tiny boom mike. Marisa was speaking on the phone.

He waited.

When she finished the call she looked up, quickly scanning the stranger. He was a good-sized man, over six feet tall with a medium build. His face had a clean but noticeably rugged look to it. She guessed he was in his late thirties. There was no potbelly, no graying or balding hair, no glasses. His suit was well-cut and his tie colorful.

"Yes, sir, how may I help you?" she asked. Her face was neutral.

He smiled, the best he could manage. "Hi, Marisa, my name's Parker, Tom Parker. I was supposed to meet with Linda Nordland at ten but I got caught in that mess on Five-Twenty. I hope I'm not too late to see her."

Marisa smiled back. She was impressed that he had used her name. Most first-time visitors never did that. Besides, he was cute, even for an old guy. "I've heard that the bridge was just horrid this morning," she replied.

"Oh, it was brutal—sat there for a half hour without moving." Tom flashed another smile. It was working.

"Why don't you have a seat and I'll check for you. I know Linda has some kind of meeting going on right now so it might be a while."

"No problem. I'm the one that's late."

"Would you like some coffee?"

"Love some. Black would be fine."

"Coming right up."

He had been waiting just long enough to finish the coffee when a tall, slim woman approached.

"Mr. Parker, I'm Linda Nordland," she said.

Tom stood up, surprised that the owner of the company had

come into the lobby to personally greet him. He extended his hand and she reciprocated.

"I'm sorry I was so late," Tom offered.

"Oh, don't worry about it; I know what it's like trying to get here from Seattle. Why don't we go into my office?"

"Great."

As Linda led the way past the reception counter, Tom winked at Marisa. She smiled back.

A minute later Tom was seated in front of a freestanding black marble table desk across from Linda. The backdrop was a floor-to-ceiling glass wall that looked out over a beautiful garden setting. It reminded Tom of a finely detailed Japanese garden, but instead of following an Asian theme, the plantings were all native to the Pacific Northwest.

The phone rang and Linda looked at Tom as she reached for the handset. "Excuse me a moment," she said. She then picked up the phone with her left hand.

When Linda started speaking she swiveled in her chair so that she was looking off to the side. That gave Tom a perfect opportunity to view her.

He liked what he saw.

Linda Nordland was a few years younger than Tom. She had honey-blond hair that just touched her shoulders. Her facial skin was lightly tanned, with no visible wrinkles. Although she wasn't drop-dead beautiful, Linda was certainly attractive enough to turn more than a few heads in a crowd. Especially his own.

She wore a pale red lipstick. Her eye shadow was barely visible. The eyeglasses she wore were custom designed and matched her face perfectly—you hardly noticed them at all. And there was no wedding ring. Her only jewelry was a necklace with a tiny gold cross.

Her dress was professional and elegantly cut. Her shoes were simple flats, but of top-of-the-line quality.

At five foot nine, Linda was tall. Her figure was slim, maybe 130 pounds. She was nicely curved at the hips, and her bosom was ample.

Very nice, Tom Parker thought, *very nice, indeed!*

Linda hung up the phone and turned back to face her guest. It was time to get down to business.

"Well, Tom, since our last telephone conversation, I take

it you've had a chance to review all of that information I sent to you.''

''I sure have. And I have to admit it, I don't think I've ever had a client supply me with so much background data before. I was impressed.''

''Well, it wasn't really hard for me. I've been after this jerk for years now, and besides, I have a lot of resources to call on.''

No kidding! thought Tom. He had heard that Linda Nordland was wealthy, but he had no idea. Nordsoft was one of the leading software development firms in Silicon Valley North, and she owned most of it.

''Your friend,'' Tom said, ''the one that spotted the subject, is she still convinced that it was him?''

''Yes. As you asked, I called her again. She only saw him once, but she's as certain as she can be that it was him.''

Tom nodded. ''Okay, good. Then, assuming he's still there, we have several approaches we can take. First . . . ,''

For the next half hour Tom and Linda discussed the pros and cons of each alternative plan that he had prepared in advance of the meeting. Tom was surprised at how quickly Linda took it all in. He never once had to repeat anything; she had an amazing memory, almost like a computer. She was so quick it was scary.

At the end of the discussion, Linda leaned back in her chair with her arms around her neck, stretching. He had never seen a woman do that before, only men. He found it seductive, in a strange way.

Linda leaned forward and returned her arms to the desktop. She had made her decision. ''Okay, Tom, let's go for the grand prize. When can you set it up?''

Tom shifted in his seat to hide his astonishment. She had just surprised the heck out of him. He had been certain that she would select one of the less risky scenarios.

''Ah, it'll take me about a week to clear my calendar and prepare everything.''

''Okay, but if you can do it quicker, I'd really appreciate it. He could disappear again.''

''Right. I'll see what I can do.''

Tom started to stand up but Linda raised her hand, signaling him to wait. ''Just a sec,'' she said. She turned toward a file cabinet at the side of her desk. Opening a drawer, she removed a sheet of paper. When she turned back she handed it to him. It was a signed engagement letter on Tom's letterhead—and clipped to the letter was a personal check for $20,000. It was made out to Parker Investigations.

"I assume that's a sufficient retainer to get you started. Your letter didn't specify an amount."

"Yes, that's more than adequate. I'll bill against it with my hourly rate and expenses."

"Fine."

Tom couldn't believe his good luck as he scanned the check again. He was going to ask for only half the amount that she had offered.

Linda was now standing. For the first time, she smiled. "Tom, I know all of this must sound strange to you, but that man really hurt me. Until he's paid for what he's done, I'm just not going to be at peace."

Tom nodded. "I understand. This case will be my highest priority."

"Thank you."

TWO
ADVENTURES IN PARADISE

THE AIR WAS STILL. THERE WASN'T A HINT OF A BREEZE. AND it was hot—stinking hot. At half past midnight it was still ninety degrees.

The sky was as black as India ink on this moonless night. Far off to the south, at the foot of the bay, a summer lightning storm continued its spectacle. For just an instant the bolts of fire would silhouette the peaks of the jungle mountains, revealing their majestic slopes as they thrust from the sea.

The speedboat rocked gently as the swells rolled in from the west. Its powerful engine was silent. It was drifting with the current. There were no running lights, just the red glow of a lit cigarette.

Two men were seated in the open cockpit of the twenty-eight-foot Donzi. They were both in their mid-forties. The man behind the wheel stood six foot three and weighed a solid 225 pounds. He wore knee-length shorts and leather sandals. His well-muscled torso was cloaked in an oversized T-shirt. Printed across the chest were the words *Puerto Vallarta— Mexico's Pacific Playground*. A half-spent Camel hung from the corner of his mouth and a nearly full bottle of ice-cold *Corona Clara* rested between his legs. Four empty bottles littered the water around the boat.

The man sitting in the passenger seat was a mere bantamweight compared to the behemoth behind the helm. A head shorter and rail-thin, he looked like a bag of bones in his loose cotton trousers and open-collar shirt. Sweat streamed off his forehead, dripping onto his neck and shoulders. The humid heat was miserable, but it was only part of his problem. He was scared—gut-wrenching scared. Spasms of fear periodically gripped him, causing his legs to tremble. He locked his knees together and sipped sparingly from a can of Coca-Cola, hoping it would calm the churning sea that raged inside his stomach.

"Do you think they'll show up?" asked the skinny one. His voice was a little strained in spite of his best efforts to sound calm.

"Hell, I don't know. No telling what those gook bastards are up to." The helmsman took a long pull from the beer bottle and then belched. "They're supposed to show up tonight, but they could just as easy be a week late."

"You mean we might have to come out here again, if they don't come tonight?"

"Yeah. I guess so. They sure as hell aren't going to look for us at the resort."

"Shit," muttered the passenger.

The man behind the wheel turned to look at his companion. For the first time he noticed the man's distress. "Jesus, Pete, you look like shit. You gettin' sick or something?"

"This rolling around is getting to me," he lied. "I should have taken some of those seasick pills you have." He was too proud to admit his fear to anyone.

"Well, it's too late for that now. They won't do you any good unless you take it before you get on the boat."

"Yeah, I know that. I'll just tough it out."

The big man turned around in his seat and reached into an ice-filled cooler. He grabbed another *Clara*. After removing the cap he handed it to the passenger. "Here, suck on this—it'll calm your belly."

"I don't know about that, Dave. I think I'll just stick with the Coke."

"Shit, that's for pussies. Try the beer. It'll help."

"All right, I'll give it a try."

The passenger took a sip. The twang of the Mexican brew was surprisingly refreshing. He took another sip and then a longer one. It helped. *Maybe I'll be all right, after all,* he thought.

Captain Yook Ku-Ho leaned against the guardrail, resting his forearms on the polished oak top rail. His slight body was barely noticeable on the starboard bridge wing as the 260-foot-long ship slipped through the night. The *Korean Star* was blacked out: no pilothouse lights, no running lights, not even a masthead light on top of the radar dome. It was like a ghost passing invisibly over the night sea.

Captain Yook could see the lights of the city far in the background. Puerto Vallarta was ablaze with activity. The high-rise beachfront hotels were bathed in floodlights, the airport tower's beacon rotated with clockwork precision, and the lights from the constant stream of vehicles racing along the coastal highway blended into long, narrow streaks of white and red.

Yook was young for a full captain. He was only thirty-six, but he had the experience of a man twenty years his senior. His father had been a master mariner, commanding a succession of commercial vessels, and young Ku-Ho had accompanied him on many voyages. He was only twelve years old on his first outing. The three-month trip through the Aleutians, dragging for pollock and other bottom fish, had been especially grueling. But the boy-sailor took to the routine with relish. Like his father, the sea ran strong in his veins.

Captain Yook pulled up a pair of binoculars and searched the black waters ahead. Nothing. *So far, so good,* he thought.

He then walked back into the enclosed pilothouse.

The *Korean Star* was a state-of-the-art vessel. She was designed to collect and process fish anywhere on the world's oceans. Powered by huge diesels, she could charge through the sea at twenty knots for days on end. Packed with the latest electronics, she had every conceivable gadget aboard: sophisticated fish-finding sonar systems, four different radar units, two global positioning satellite navigation systems, and a multitude of communication radios, ranging from VHF to a high-seas satellite system.

In addition to the sophisticated electronic systems, the *Korean Star* was also equipped with a computer-controlled ballast system. Water-level sensors located throughout the ship's various cargo holds and ballast chambers were linked to a minicomputer located on the bridge console. When the ship's holds were filled with tons of fish, the computer automatically monitored the ship's overall trim. If the vessel was loaded unevenly, causing it to lean or list excessively in one direction, then the ballast control system would automatically compensate by flooding various ballast tanks with seawater or high-pressure air. The system was designed to prevent the top-heavy vessel from capsizing.

Yook didn't own the vessel. It belonged to a *kye,* a consortium of individuals back in Pusan. They put up the money to purchase the ship while Yook managed it. He was the *kye*'s highest-paid employee.

Although Captain Yook was well compensated, he didn't plan to stay with the *Korean Star* for much longer. He was too impatient to work for others for the rest of his life. Soon he would have enough money to purchase his own ship. And then he would truly be his own master.

Yook walked over to the main radar console, a few steps away from the ship's helm. He nodded to the twenty-three-year-old mate monitoring the ship's controls.

Captain Yook glanced down at the Furuno radar display. Banderas Bay was lit up with a dull fluorescent green. Several bright spots—blips—blinked near the shoreline of downtown Puerto Vallarta. Small boats from the local marina were enjoying the late evening. But five miles ahead, in perfect alignment with the radar's track line, was another blip. It was northwest of the harbor entrance, a little over a mile from shore. Yook checked the coordinates of the contact, aligning the radar unit's electronic cursor over the blip. A few seconds later the target's latitude and longitude were computed by the ship's GPS-linked navigation computer and displayed on the radar screen. Yook smiled as he read the coordinates. *Right on target,* he thought.

"You hear something?" asked the passenger in the speedboat.

"What?"

"It's like a dull rumble—sounds mechanical."

The man behind the wheel turned to his side, cocking his right ear seaward. "Yeah, I hear it now. Diesels."

"Is it them?"

"Hell, I don't know. I can't see shit out there."

And then they saw it. The giant processor was almost on them. The white foam of its bow wave gave the vessel away.

"Jesus, it's going to run us down," cried out the pilot as he hit the ignition key. The Donzi's engine blasted to life. He shoved the throttle forward and the boat blasted ahead.

The desperate maneuver wasn't needed. The *Korean Star* was already backing down, its momentum slowed by reversing the pitch of the twin propellers. Captain Yook had timed his rendezvous perfectly. After traversing more than five thousand miles of the Pacific, he took pride in arriving at the designated coordinates precisely on schedule: 1:00 A.M., local time.

The Donzi headed south for half a minute and turned around. The processor was barely moving now. "Damn," the pilot said. "I thought that sucker was going to nail us for sure."

"How'd they stop so quick?" asked his companion.

"Beats the hell out of me. Someone up there must know what they're doing."

"It's got to be the one, don't you think?"

The pilot glanced at his watch. He then looked back at the giant hulk looming in the distance. "Yeah, that's got to be it. Right size and it's dead-on-time."

"What do we do now?"

"I'll send the signal and see what happens." The pilot picked up a flashlight and aimed at the ship's bridgehouse. He flipped it on and off six times.

Twenty seconds later the signal was answered: four quick flashes from the ship.

"Okay, Pete, it's showtime." The pilot looked his friend straight in the eye. "You going to be okay with this?"

The passenger nodded his head. "Yeah, I'm okay, now."

Despite the man's acknowledgment, he was still nervous. His knees were no longer shaking, but his stomach felt like a Maytag on the wash cycle. *What the hell am I doing out here? Fucking Dave is crazy!*

The Donzi pulled up to the starboard side of the ship, near the bridge house. An articulated ladder had already been lowered over the side from the main deck. The speedboat's fenders scraped against the gray steel of the processor. The hull plates near the waterline stank of algae slime.

Two crewmen aboard the Korean vessel dropped mooring lines down to the Donzi. The men in the boat secured the lines to bow and stern cleats. The man who had piloted the speedboat moved aft toward the ship's ladder. His partner slid into the seat behind the wheel.

Before climbing onto the bottom rung, the man looked back at his partner. "Okay, Pete, you just sit tight. This shouldn't take too long."

"But what about the money?" The passenger looked down at the Samsonite suitcase wedged into a storage compartment under the instrument panel.

"I've got to check out the merchandise first. If it's okay, then we'll give it to 'em."

"Okay, I'll be here."

The passenger watched as his friend started to climb up the steep ladder. Dave Simpson's bulk filled up the aluminum stairway. When he reached the halfway point, an errant breeze blew the tail of his shirt up for just an instant. The handle of a nine-millimeter pistol flashed momentarily into view. Its barrel was stuffed under the man's waistband,

Dammit, Dave. Why the hell did you have to bring that? Pete Chambers' gut tightened another notch at the appearance of the weapon. His partner had assured him that the entire transaction would be safe. "Hell, Pete," Simpson had said, "you don't have to worry about this deal. These guys in Pusan are all first-class. There won't be any of that TV bullshit about deals turning sour at the last minute. This one's in the bag!''

Pete Chambers watched his friend step aboard the main deck of the *Korean Star*. A nearby hatchway gave just enough light to see him by. Simpson towered over the two crewmen who met him. They exchanged words for a minute. Chambers couldn't hear anything; the rumble of the ship's engines masked the voices.

While Chambers watched, Simpson turned away from the Koreans. He leaned over the steel railing and looked down at his partner. "Hang in there, buddy," he yelled. "Everything's cool." A moment later Simpson was heading into the interior of the ship, following one of the crewmen. The other man trailed behind.

Pete Chambers looked down at the suitcase near his legs. *God, I hope all this crap is worth the risk.*

Dave Simpson was now in Captain Yook's stateroom. The compartment was spacious for a commercial fishing vessel. An elegant metal dining table with four chairs was located near the center of the room. A thick beige carpet covered the entire steel deck. On the far side of the compartment, next to the double-berth bed, were a built-in hardwood desk and a leather-lined swivel chair. The bulkhead wall next to the desk was crowded with instrument readouts. There was everything from a Fathometer display to a TV monitor that allowed Captain Yook to check on a dozen remote cameras located throughout the ship. If he were ever injured or ill, the system was designed so that he could command the vessel from his bed.

Yook and Simpson were seated at the table. The two men had been chatting for a few minutes, checking each other out. Neither had met before; the entire transaction that was about to be consummated had been orchestrated through other parties.

The captain sipped at his mug of tea. Simpson declined the drink. He was still full of beer and wished that he had urinated before climbing aboard.

"Well, Captain," Simpson said, "I'm amazed at your seamanship. You were right on time—almost to the damn second."

Yook grinned a little. "It is my business to be punctual."

"Yeah, I guess so." Simpson paused. He was tired of the

small talk. It was time to get down to business. "I assume the transfer went as planned?"

"Yes. We picked up the merchandise without incident."

"So you've got it aboard!"

"Of course," Yook said. He looked Simpson directly in the eyes. "And you have the money?"

"That's right—it's nearby."

Yook was familiar with the routine; this was his fifteenth transaction. It was useless to ask the Americans to produce the money until he had shown them the contraband. "Then I assume you want to see it first."

"You got it."

"Very well, follow me."

Pete Chambers' stomach was still churning. *Dammit, Dave, what's taking you so long.*

For the moment, Chambers' fear was under control. The only thing that kept him going was thinking about the reward. If everything went right, he'd net about $1.5 million from the deal. *Jesus Christ, one point five mill! Tax-free! I'll never have to work a day again.*

He looked down at the suitcase again. It was stuffed full with thick bundles of cash: twenties, fifties and hundreds. Pete had "borrowed" the money and he had another month or so to replace the missing funds. He wasn't worried about making up for the missing money, though. In just a couple of days, he and Dave would have more money than they'd ever dreamed.

Captain Yook and Dave Simpson were deep in the bowels of the *Korean Star*. The main freezer compartment was chock-full of frozen fish. The vast hold contained tons of pollock, tuna, cod and halibut. The processor had collected the fish from dozens of smaller vessels during its voyage across the Pacific.

Yook led the way as the men moved around and over the frozen blocks of fish. Both men were now wearing parkas and gloves. They expelled thick plumes of foggy breath as they walked. All thoughts of the outside tropical air were gone.

"Dammit, Captain," Simpson said, "it's colder in here than a witch's tit in January."

Yook just smiled as he continued aft.

About a minute later Captain Yook stopped. He knelt down and began to pry away several cardboard boxes stuffed with frozen fish. "Ah, here it is," he said as he uncovered another box. This container, however, was filled with forty kilos of pure heroin. Grown in the temperate regions of Central Asia and smuggled across Mongolia and China to the port city of Shanghai, the narcotic was far more valuable than its weight in gold.

Captain Yook slid the box to the top of another fish-filled container. He unfolded the cardboard flaps.

Simpson looked into the box. It was crammed with dozens of clear plastic bags, each one filled with a pale white substance. Yook started to hand Simpson one of the bags, but Simpson declined. Instead, he reached into the box with his own gloved hand, digging deep until he gripped a tube near the bottom. He pulled the package out and examined it.

The elliptically shaped package was frozen solid. It felt and looked like a giant version of one of those colored ice sticks that kids like to eat. "This shit's brick-solid," Simpson said. "I can't test it this way."

"All right then, let's head back to my cabin. I've got a microwave there. You can defrost it and then test it."

"Okay, that'll work," answered Simpson.

Yook reached down and started to lift the heavy box.

"Hey, let me do that," Simpson said as he moved to the tiny Korean's side. The burly American lifted the ninety-pound box like it wasn't there. Just as he started to move forward he noticed another box just like the one he was holding. It was partially covered by frozen fish.

"You got more of this stuff aboard?" he asked as he nodded toward the second box.

"Sorry, that's not part of your property," Yook replied. He grabbed a tuna and tossed it over the exposed edge of the box. He would have to be more careful in the future. The box did not contain any drugs. It was mostly filled with lightweight packing materials and a few salmon fillets. But hidden in the bottom were half a dozen ten-pound bars of pure gold. It was part of Yook's personal stash.

*　　*　　*

While the transaction between the Americans and the Koreans entered its final phase, a third party arrived on the scene. The boat was small, only about twenty feet long, but it was fast and its engines were quiet. Had the *Korean Star's* watch officer checked the radar display, he would have seen the boat approaching from the northeast. But he was too busy fiddling with the bridge television. He wanted to see what Mexican TV was like.

The new vessel slipped alongside the aft port side of the processor at 1:32 A.M. No one aboard the *Korean Star* was aware of its presence.

It didn't take long for Simpson to verify the purity of the test sample. The heroin was uncut and absolutely top quality. "Okay, skipper," he said, "looks like we got ourselves a deal."

"Excellent. Let's conclude our business. I need to get underway as soon as we finish."

"Heading back out so soon?" asked Simpson.

"Yes, I've been away too long. The ship's owners think we're offshore of Panama. I've got a lot of running to do in order to get back on schedule."

Yook was telling Simpson only part of the story. He was far from his normal area of operation; that was true. But what he didn't say was that he had another illicit transaction to complete before he could leave Mexican waters. The following night the *Korean Star* was scheduled to make another secret rendezvous, this time offshore of Cabo San Lucas. If Yook ran the ship at flank speed and the weather remained good, they'd make it to the tip of Baja on time.

"Okay, skipper, I understand. I'll be right back with the money."

Five minutes later Simpson returned to Yook's cabin. He placed the heavy suitcase on the table and opened it.

Captain Yook thumbed through the bundles of cash.

"It's all there," Simpson said. "One point two mill, just like we agreed on."

Captain Yook didn't reply. Instead, he methodically checked randomly selected bundles. He didn't doubt that the full amount was there. He was checking, however, to make sure the money was legitimate. There was no way he'd get stuck with counterfeit greenbacks.

Ten minutes later Captain Yook was satisfied. The cash was legit.

"All right, my friend," Yook said, "everything looks good here."

"Then we're done," Simpson replied.

The intruders didn't have any trouble climbing aboard. The plastic-coated grappling hooks hardly made a sound as they hooked onto the guardrails near the ship's fantail. The four men pulled themselves up, easily scaling the high sheer of the *Korean Star's* hull. Nine-millimeter submachine guns were suspended across their backs. They all wore black from head to toe, and each one had a dark scarf across his face.

Three minutes later the intruders burst into the ship's pilothouse without warning. Startled, the watch officer reached for the ship's main alarm. He never made it. One of the gunmen drilled him with half a dozen rounds from an Uzi.

The *Korean Star's* only armed crewman was standing on the starboard bridge wing when the roar of gunfire spurred him into action. He too ran into a wall of lead.

Yook and Simpson were just about to leave the captain's cabin when they heard the gunfire. It was loud, like firecrackers going off.

"What the hell was that about?" asked Simpson. He now had his Beretta out. It was aimed right at Yook's belly.

"I don't know," the captain answered. His eyes were glued to the ugly pistol. He was slightly faint.

During his previous drug transfers, there hadn't been a hint of trouble. Everything had been businesslike and proper. He gave the shore contact the heroin and he received the money in return. He then hid the cash in a secret compartment built into his cabin. Once the ship returned to Pusan, the cash was turned over to the customer, minus a transaction fee. Yook and his Pusan-based partner shared the fee. The system had worked like clockwork—until tonight.

"Are your people armed?" asked Simpson.

"Only one. One of the deckhands that helped you aboard, that's all."

"You trust him?"

"Yes, he's been with me for years."

"Well, then someone else must be shooting up your bridge."

"But who?" asked Yook. He was just as flabbergasted as Simpson. And then his eyes flashed as a new thought popped into his head. "Let me check the console." He pointed to his desk. "There's a remote camera in the bridge."

"Do it," commanded Simpson. He kept the pistol aimed at the captain.

Twenty seconds later the color monitor snapped on. The watch officer's bloodstained corpse was in the foreground. Four gunmen were standing around it as if it wasn't there. Their bandannas were now removed, exposing their faces. They all had long straggly black hair, thick mustaches and very brown skin.

"Son of a bitch," Simpson shouted.

"Who are they?" demanded Yook.

"Pirates," answered Simpson.

"What?"

"I'll bet my bottom dollar, those pricks are Mexican drug pirates." Simpson paused for a moment. He was now scared. "I've heard about 'em but never believed the stories—until now."

"Pirates?"

"Yes. They're here for your drugs and my money."

"But how could they know?"

"Someone talked, but that doesn't matter now. They're all stone-cold killers, and unless we stop 'em they're going to kill everyone aboard and sink your ship. They don't leave witnesses."

The intruder who had killed the watch officer turned to face the young crewman manning the helm. "Where's your captain?" he asked. His English was poor, heavily accented with his native Spanish.

"He's in his cabin—with the American," answered the frightened helmsman. His English was excellent.

"Where?"

The man turned his head and looked down a long companionway. "Second door on the left, at the far end."

The lead intruder ordered one of his men to remain on the bridge. He then headed aft with his other two companions.

Pete Chambers almost had a heart attack when he heard the gunfire. It wasn't loud, but he heard the shots from the bridge-house. *Oh, shit. Now what do I do?* He felt like throwing up.

Just minutes earlier, everything was going great. When Dave Simpson returned to retrieve the money he was all smiles. "Stop worrying, partner. It's a done deal," he had said when he climbed back up the ladder with the suitcase.

Chambers hit the starter button and the Donzi came to life. He reached forward and released the bow mooring line.

"Is there another way out of here?" asked Simpson. He no longer pointed his pistol at Captain Yook.

"There's a small fire escape hatch in the head. It leads into a storage locker."

"Good. Now, have you got any more weapons in here?"

"I've got a shotgun in a hidden locker." He pointed to a wood-lined bulkhead next to the bed. "It's behind a false panel over there."

"Get it, man. We haven't got much time."

The three pirates moved softly down the tile companionway. So far, their carefully planned operation was working well. All they had to do was find the master. The money and drugs wouldn't be far behind.

The lead intruder stopped by Captain Yook's cabin door. He touched his right ear to the wood door. He could hear muffled voices from inside.

He smiled at his comrades. "They're in there—get ready," he whispered.

Captain Yook had just enough time to hide the suitcase full of money, but the box of heroin was too heavy for him to move alone. It remained on the table.

Yook's eyes were now glued to the TV monitor. A new image was on the screen. Another camera mounted in the over-head near the bridge was monitoring the long companionway outside his quarters. He could see the three men preparing to assault his cabin. He ignored the chatter from the radio that played in the background. Simpson had told him to turn it on when he crawled through the hatchway.

Captain Yook pulled the twelve-gauge up to his shoulder and aimed it at the wood door. A second later he pulled the trigger.

The first charge of double-ought buckshot blasted a fist-sized hole through the doorway. It caught the lead intruder in the stomach, almost tearing him in half. The second and third blasts missed the other two men as they dove to the deck. And then, as Yook studied the camera, selecting his next shot, both pirates fired into the cabin door, spraying their weapons back and forth as if they were hosing down a fire.

The first casualty was the cardboard box of drugs. It was peppered by machine-gun fire. The nine-millimeter rounds shredded the frozen plastic bags, blasting debris out of the open lid.

Captain Yook was hit next. The ricochet was half spent when it ripped into his neck, but it had more than enough momentum to sever his carotid artery. The young captain collapsed to the floor in shock. An uncontrollable torrent poured from the ugly wound.

Dave Simpson had managed to crawl through the storage locker and onto an exterior catwalk when the shooting restarted. A few seconds later he entered the bridge just as the guard who had been left behind turned to look down the corridor at his companions.

Simpson killed the man with a single shot. He then dropped to the deck and slithered along the tile until he was next to the companionway. He snapped his head into the opening for a quick look. The two surviving intruders were reloading their weapons, preparing to again pepper Yook's cabin.

Got to do it now, he thought. He rolled onto his side and let loose with the Beretta. He emptied the clip and then rolled back. His firing had been so rapid that he didn't have any idea if he had hit the men or not.

Dave Simpson had hit them both. One was killed instantly, the bullet ripping his heart apart. The lone survivor felt the searing pain of the three bullet holes in his chest. He ignored the pain as he struggled to reach his shoulder harness. A second later he tossed the grenade. It rolled down the long hallway like a bowling ball.

Simpson watched in horror as the grenade slid past. He was now standing, preparing to peek down the corridor at his victims. He didn't think; he just reacted. He ran through the open bridge door and leaped overboard. The weapon detonated before he hit the water.

The blast shattered the pilothouse as if a tidal wave had hit it. All of the windows blew out and fires started in half a dozen locations. The only surviving bridge crewman, the helmsman, had ducked behind his console when the grenade exploded. But the shelter didn't help. The concussion scrambled his brains.

The ship's nerve center was now in shambles. None of the electronic controls worked, except for one device: the computer that controlled the ship's internal ballasting system was still functional. However, the shock of the explosion had upset its delicate sensors. A bogus signal was now telling the ship that it had a stability problem. Consequently, thousands of gallons of seawater were flooding the port ballast tanks while the starboard tanks were being emptied with high-pressure air.

The 2,500-ton vessel took on a noticeable list within a minute.

Most of the *Korean Star's* crew had been asleep when the gunmen attacked. Unsure of what was happening, many remained in their cabins with their doors locked. But now that the gunfire had stopped, a few ventured into the companionways, trying to find out what had happened. No one was yet concerned about the tilting deck.

The problem with the ship's computerized ballast system would not have been so critical if the hull's watertight integrity had been maintained. However, because of the oppressive tropical heat, cargo hatchways located on each side of the hull near amidships had been opened. The cross ventilation through the two openings helped vent the ship's steaming interior. Normally, these eight-foot-high by ten-foot-wide hatches would remain sealed while the *Korean Star* was at sea because they were located just six feet above the ocean's surface. Only when the ship was docked would they be opened. But earlier in the evening, when the ship had passed into the calm seas offshore of Puerto Vallarta, they had been opened. And now, as the computer-induced list increased, tons of seawater began to pour through the port hatchway, cascading into the ship's interior.

It took only a few minutes for the *Korean Star* to exceed the hull's stability limits. And then, without warning, it capsized. With most of the crew still belowdecks, it turned turtle in just a matter of seconds. It was like riding on a slow-motion roller coaster. The trapped men couldn't believe what was happening to them.

When the ship capsized, it took the pirate's boat with it. Mooring lines and grappling hooks anchored the tiny boat to the larger vessel. Before the speedboat's remaining occupant could release the lashings, the giant ship rolled. It squashed the fiberglass runabout as if it were a bug. The sixteen-year-old tender jumped overboard just in time to save his life.

The *Korean Star* floated upside down for about twenty minutes before it sank. The current carried it a little closer to shore so that when it finally went down, the water depth had shoaled to a hundred fathoms. None of the ship's thirty-eight crewmen made it out. They were all trapped inside the upside-down hull.

Pete Chambers spotted Dave Simpson when he jumped overboard. Within a minute he had plucked his partner from the sea. And then, from a safe distance, they watched the *Korean Star* die. They never saw the pirate boat.

When the ship finally submerged, Dave guided the Donzi slowly over the grave site, more out of curiosity than anything else. He saw nothing of interest and promptly turned the boat around. He then shoved the throttle to the stops. They would be back in P.V. in minutes.

Just before the Donzi blasted off, it passed within fifty feet of the remaining survivor of the ordeal. The Mexican teenager had a death grip on a seat cushion from the sunken speedboat. He was too scared to call out for help, fearing that he would be shot on the spot.

Dave and Pete never saw him. Just a mop of black hair projecting out of the water, it looked no more conspicuous than the other flotsam and jetsam that had surfaced after the ship went down.

As the Donzi sped away, the teenager pushed the seat cushion under his chest and began to kick. He was a poor swimmer and struggled to keep his head above the water.

THREE
THE SURVIVOR

IT WAS LATE MORNING. THE SUN WAS HIGH OVERHEAD IN THE cloudless sky. And it was still hot. A tiny whisper of a breeze from the ocean helped, but the heat would have been unbearable if the palm trees hadn't provided the shade.

The poolside patio cafe was not yet jammed with the lunch crowd. That would change in about an hour. Until then, the dozen patrons sitting at the open-air tables could enjoy their breakfasts in relative peace.

Dave Simpson and Pete Chambers sat well off to the side to avoid the other occupied tables. They were both drinking coffee. Chambers was still picking at his omelet. He hadn't touched the *frijoles*. Simpson's plate was clean; he had inhaled the half dozen hotcakes and a side order of *tocino*.

"You going to eat those *frijoles* or what?" asked Simpson.

Pete Chambers looked up at his friend and then pushed his plate forward. Simpson began to scoop up the beans.

"Jesus, Dave," Chambers said, shaking his head, "how can you have such an appetite after last night?"

Simpson smiled as he took his first bite. "It ain't going to do you any good worrying about that shit. It happened and there's nothing you can do about it." He stopped momentarily to swallow. "You still gotta eat."

"Yeah, well, that's easy for you to say. Your butt's not hanging out there like mine."

"You mean the money?"

"Of course I mean the money. If it isn't returned next month, my ass is going to be cooked for sure."

"Fuck it—you never liked being an attorney anyway. You can stay down here and sell time-shares with me. The cops won't bother you here."

"Bullshit. You ever hear about extradition? With over a million bucks missing, you can be sure they'll come after me."

"They never bothered me," Simpson said. He then drained his coffee cup.

"Yeah, well, all you're wanted for is forgery and some other minor stuff. No judge is going to bother sending down U.S. Marshals to pick you up." Chambers paused a second to push his chair away from the table. "Hell, I'll bet everyone up north has forgotten about all those cons you pulled."

Simpson grinned. "Yeah, that may be true about the Feds, but I've still got a couple of ex-lady friends who would like to burn my butt. None of them have forgotten me."

Chambers didn't reply. Instead, he stared at the nearby pool. There were several attractive women sunbathing at the water's edge. He wasn't enjoying the view, though. His mind was racing. *What the hell am I going to do now? If I don't return the money, I'm finished. I'll go to jail for ten years. And Laura—she'll dump me like a piece of garbage. What will my parents think about . . .*

Chambers' thoughts were abruptly interrupted by Simpson's voice: "Pete, I think we've got a shot at getting it back."

"What?"

"I think I know how we can get your money back."

"How?"

Simpson leaned over the table, his voice a little lower. "I know about this guy in Manzanillo. He's got this . . ."

Dave Simpson outlined his plan for the next five minutes. Pete Chambers repeatedly asked questions. He was skeptical at first, but slowly the merits of Simpson's plan began to gel. When both men stood up to leave, Pete felt better. *Maybe this'll work out after all,* he thought.

Juan Diaz looked like a corpse. His emaciated body was bleached white by the ocean waters. Now clad only in his tattered underpants, he was a pitiful sight as he lay curled up on the bank of the river. The thick shrubs and billowing mangroves protected his exposed skin from the ravages of the sun. The vegetation also isolated him from the herd of longhorn cattle that grazed in the pasture adjacent to the river.

The sixteen-year-old was exhausted. After struggling all night, he had managed to make landfall at the mouth of the Rio Ameca. Normally, the muddy river flowed strong, its dirty plume spreading far offshore into Banderas Bay. But it hadn't rained in the upland watershed for several weeks and its flow had dropped off to a dribble. Juan had beached himself just before sunrise and had pushed inland, following the riverbank for almost a mile until he finally collapsed. He then rolled onto his side and closed his eyes. He planned to restart his trek after a short nap; Instead, he fell into a deep sleep.

Juan had been asleep for nearly four hours now. His weary body had completely shut down. He wouldn't awaken until late afternoon.

He was tired of waiting. He had been sitting in the cockpit seat for nearly five hours now. The sun would be rising soon. *Dammit,* he thought, *where the hell are you?*

Once again he stood up and peered over the windscreen of the flying bridge. He looked south toward the open sea. It was black. There wasn't a hint of light on the invisible horizon.

Stan Reams sat back down on the foam cushion and, for the eighteenth time that night, lit up a cigarette. As he inhaled, he glanced down at the global positioning system monitor. The GPS earth coordinates of the yacht were updated every few seconds. Despite the persistent onshore breeze and the long rollers from the southwest, the sixty-five-foot yacht was still on target. The autopilot and twin turbocharged diesels were in perfect sync.

Reams turned around and looked aft over the stern. In the distance, he could see the city lights of Cabo San Lucas. The Mexican town was located at the southern tip of Baja California. Even though it was early August and the heart of the off-season, the Cabo resorts were surprising full. He would have to return the boat to its berth within the hour. He had an all-day charter with four businessmen from Vancouver and he had a lot to do to get ready. They were going after marlin.

Reams waited another twenty minutes before finally giving up. He flipped the spent butt overboard and stood up. At five foot eleven and 175 pounds, he looked fit and trim in his white

T-shirt and matching Bermuda shorts. Although he was in his early fifties, his full head of brownish-blond hair and his fair complexion presented the appearance of a much younger man. And the reading glasses he sometimes wore hardly detracted from his good looks. Women of all ages still found him attractive. Many thought he looked like Robert Redford.

Reams disengaged the autopilot and took manual control of the yacht. He swung the wheel hard to starboard and advanced the throttles. The Hatteras convertible charged ahead. Half a minute later it was on a heading of due north. It would take only fifteen minutes to reach the outer channel of the marina.

After sleeping for hours alongside the riverbank, Juan Diaz restarted his homeward trek. He walked for miles along the dirt road that paralleled the Rio Ameca before managing to hitch a ride on an empty farm truck. At sunset he eventually reached his shack on the northeastern outskirts of Puerto Vallarta.

The one-room adobe hut was about twenty feet square and it had a flat tin roof. There were no windows, only holes in the walls that were partially covered with worn-out screens. An army of scrawny chickens, led by an ornery Bantam cock, picked at the dirt around the yard. A couple of mangy dogs and one goat also roamed the grounds, scrounging for anything edible. And buzzing around all of the animals were legions of flies. It seemed that every living thing around the shack was hungry.

When Juan arrived, the shack was unoccupied. His uncle was out for the evening. Juan was so tired that he didn't bother with a meal. He didn't have the energy to start the cooking fire. Instead, he flopped down on his sleeping mat and instantly fell asleep.

Juan finally woke up a few minutes before eleven the following morning. He would have slept longer if the woman hadn't started screaming.

Juan turned on his side and looked across the room. In the opposite corner was an ancient four-poster metal frame bed. It belonged to Uncle Ernesto.

The 42-year-old man had returned around three in the morning. But he wasn't alone. The whore he had bought for the night was young, just a few years older than Juan. Both had been so liquored up that when they staggered through the doorway, arm in arm, they failed to see tiny Juan curled up on the floor in the corner. It wouldn't have mattered anyway. Ernesto had been bringing women home ever since Juan could remember.

Ernesto and his woman had peeled off their clothes and crawled onto the bed. The mattress sagged like a camel's back as they began to couple. However, after a few minutes of halfhearted kissing and fondling, they rolled apart. Ernesto was too drunk and Maria was too tired.

The couple slept until late morning. When Ernesto finally regained his consciousness, his strength also returned. He was again 100 percent—everything worked.

Ernesto was on top of Maria when her fake orgasmic shrieks woke Juan. Juan studied the flurry of motion on the ancient bed. It rocked and rolled, it squeaked and creaked. The wood flooring under his mat vibrated like a racing train. And then his uncle finally bellowed out his conquest and Maria shut up.

Good, thought Juan as he shut his eyes and rolled onto his side. *Maybe now I can sleep some more.* Juan shut his eyes and drifted back to sleep. His siesta, however, would be short.

"Hey, boy? What's wrong with you?" asked the gravelly voice.

Juan's subconscious heard the voice but it hadn't really registered yet. He was still asleep. He woke up instantly, however, when a hand gripped his exposed shoulder and pinched it with a plierlike grip.

"What do you want, Uncle?" Juan asked as he sat up, blinking his eyes and rubbing his shoulder with his fingers.

"When did you get back?" asked Ernesto Diaz. He was squatting barefoot on the floor next to Juan's head. He was wearing a pair of tattered knee-length shorts and a shirt that had once been white but was now a dull gray. The stench of tequila diffused from his mouth.

"I got back yesterday, late."

"Well, where's the money?"

Juan looked toward the bed for an instant. The whore's feet hung over the end of the mattress. A white sheet covered her backside and she appeared to be fast asleep. He turned to face Ernesto. "I don't have any."

"What?"

"I never got paid. Something went wrong." Juan stood up and for the next ten minutes he relived the terror of the previous night.

"The Korean boat sank and Paco and the others are dead?" shouted Ernesto, bewildered.

"Yes, I think I was the only survivor—except for the *gringos.*"

"The *gringos?*"

Yes, two *norteamericanos,* I'm sure of that. They took off in a speedboat."

"Where'd they go?"

"I don't know—probably Vallarta."

"Did you see them up close, enough to identify them?"

"Yes, their boat passed close by—they didn't see me. The first one was big, like a mountain, and the . . ."

While Juan continued his description, Ernesto listened carefully. Although Juan's uncle had only a sixth-grade education, he was cunning. He never forgot anything. And as he digested Juan's incredible tale, a new idea began to form.

FOUR
THE HUNTER

HE FIDGETED IN HIS SEAT. HIS PULSE RATE ACCELERATED. HE even mumbled a few words. All of the warning signs were there; his body sensed what was coming. But he was powerless to stop it, just like all the other times.

He was back inside the house, the revolver glued to his right hand.

He had walked right in—the front door had been unlocked. That had been the first warning.

He couldn't see anything as he entered the living room. The darkness shouldn't have been a problem; he had resided in the house for over a year now. But then he tripped over some-

thing, some unseen object that shouldn't have been there. That was the second warning.

He picked himself up, his heart now thundering in his chest like a racing locomotive. He found a wall switch and flipped it. The ceiling light illuminated the room. It was a war zone: furniture overturned, paintings and photographs ripped from the walls, bookshelves tipped over.

"Jesus," he muttered, "what's happened?"

He ran down the long hallway and pulled open the door to the first bedroom. He looked inward, not knowing what to expect. A moment later he stepped inside. There was a tiny night-light in one of the electrical wall sockets. He leaned over the crib. Thank God! *he thought.*

He quietly backed out of the room, gently closing the door. He then walked to the end of the hallway and stopped opposite another doorway. He took a deep breath before turning the knob.

Unlike the first bedroom, the master suite was blacked out. He could see nothing. He felt for the lamp switch on the dresser by the doorway. He found it.

And then his world shattered.

"No! No! No!" shouted the passenger. "Dear God . . . please . . . stop this . . ."

"Sir! Sir! Are you all right? Sir, what's wrong?"

It took nearly half a minute for him to wake up. It was like coming out of surgery.

The flight attendant looked down at the man in 21A. He was covered in sweat and his face was beet-red. Even his hands were trembling.

"Sir, are you sick? Can I get you some water?"

Tom Parker sat up, rubbing both temples with his hands. "I'm okay, miss. Just a bad dream." He shook his head, trying to clear his brain of the awful memories that haunted him. "I'm sorry if I disturbed anyone."

Tom deliberately didn't look around. He could feel the stares of the other passengers. *They must think I'm nuts.*

"Are you sure you're all right, sir? You don't look too good."

"Thanks. I'll be okay. This has happened to me before." He paused while shifting his legs, trying to get comfortable. And then a lightning spike of pain surged through his gut.

For a moment he thought he might vomit. But it passed, just as quickly as it had come. He finally looked back up at the young woman. "You know, a little water does sound good."

"Certainly, sir. I'll be right back."

Almost an hour had passed since the nightmare. Tom was back to normal—as much as anyone would be after such an experience. He had traded the water for a glass of champagne. It helped.

Tom cocked his head to the right, scanning the aisle. The MD-80 wasn't very crowded. There were maybe sixty passengers aboard. *Alaska isn't going to make much on this run,* he thought.

Almost five hours earlier he had boarded the Alaska Airlines jet in Seattle, settling in for a long journey. The plane had landed in San Francisco first. And after waiting for over an hour, it had taken off for points south.

Tom stretched his arms out and rotated his head from side to side. He had plenty of room to move; he was the only passenger in his row. After completing his mini-exercises, he stood up and stepped into the aisle. He opened the overhead locker above his seat and began to search through his carry-on bag.

Tom found the yellow pad of legal-size paper and closed the locker. Before sitting down, however, he turned around and scanned the aisle. *Ah, there she is,* he said to himself. The flight attendant with the champagne bottle was a few rows back, heading his way. *Might as well have one more.*

Parker sipped his second glass of bubbly and then began to make notes. He started with the woman who had just served him: *Subject 1: Alaska F. A. Early 20s. Blond—pageboy cut. Hair an inch below ears. Real cute. Tall and slim: 5' 10", 120 pounds. Swedish-Nordic bloodlines. Not tan like other stews—alabaster-white skin. Face a little oblong. Scars from teenage acne. Makeup does a good job of covering but . . .*

Parker completed his first description and then turned to a new subject. It was the woman sitting on the aisle two rows up. He had been watching her all morning. *Subject 2: Passenger. Female. Late 30s. Traveling alone? 5' 5", 160+. Plain-Jane face—a touch of lipstick and way too heavy eyeliner (green). Brunette. Short hair, cut like a poodle. Could have a pleasant face with right makeup and hair combo. Pear shape.*

Heavy thighs. Large bust. Waddles down aisle with huge purse hanging from left arm. Green stretch pants way too tight for her butt. Looks like she's a mom, but no kids around. Already made three trips to the head.

Tom Parker continued his character sketches for the next thirty minutes, randomly picking out passengers and then carefully describing their physical characteristics. It was an old habit he had picked up when he was in the Army. Through the years this simple exercise had helped to hone his observation skills. He needed only a brief look at a person—just a few seconds—and then he could provide a detailed description, ranging from the tiny scar next to the left ear to the type of laces on the shoes.

Parker had found his observational skills to be especially helpful during surveillance operations. No matter how crowded an area might be, he could quickly isolate the target from the background. Even when they tried disguises or other camouflage, he could see through them. He always found his man—or woman. That's what made him so good at his profession.

A private investigator, Tom Parker lived in Seattle but traveled the world. His specialty was finding persons who did not want to be found.

Tom was on his way to Mexico. The subject he was charged with finding had recently been spotted in Puerto Vallarta.

FIVE
MOBILIZATION

THE LAW FIRM TOOK UP THE SIXTEENTH AND SEVENTEENTH floors of a high-rise located near the water. Most of the perimeter offices had commanding views of San Diego Bay and Coronado Island. They were reserved for the partners and the up-and-coming associates, allocated by a rigid system of seniority and performance. And of those power offices, the premium corner slots were forever reserved for the firm's senior partners. The other offices, on the non-water-view side of the building, were allocated to the attorneys fresh out of law school and the not-so-hot associates.

Pete Chambers' office was located on the sixteenth floor. His vista was dominated by a massive shopping center surrounded by acres of asphalt parking.

Pete was leaning over his desk, staring at a computer screen. He was reviewing the balance sheet for the Julia Harris account. He was the trustee for the teenage girl whose parents had been killed in an airplane crash several years earlier. The insurance proceeds had been deposited into a trust account for the girl's benefit, and Pete had complete control of the money. Pursuant to the parents' wills, his task was to guard the funds until she turned twenty-one. When she came of age, the money would be turned over to her. Until then, for all practical purposes, it was his.

Pete scrolled a new sheet on the electronic ledger. The net value of the trust was currently $1.5 million. A month earlier it had been nearly twice that amount. And within the hour, the account would be further eroded.

Pete and his partner needed cash, and lots of it. If they were going to have any hope of making up for the $1.3 million they had already stolen, most of which was now resting on the bottom of Banderas Bay, they had to take more. Pete didn't have any real money himself, only twenty grand in a CD. Dave Simpson was always broke. So once again Pete decided to raid the unsuspecting teenager's inheritance. The third quarterly report wouldn't be sent out to Julia's grandfather for another six weeks. That's how long Pete had to make up for the shortage.

There was no time to hide the transaction, as he had done in the past, so Pete decided to execute a simple wire transfer. He had just finished a telephone conversation with the brokerage firm that held the trust's assets. As trustee, Pete had absolute control of the account so there had been no questions raised when he made the request. The $100,000 had been sitting in the firm's Ready Assets Fund and was instantly available.

Within the hour the money would be wired to the account

of a real estate development firm in a San Diego bank. This account, however, was nothing more than a paper holding company that was used to transfer funds. Pete controlled the account, but under an alias. Early next morning the funds would be wired to another account in the Bahamas. From there the money would be immediately transferred once again.

By the end of following afternoon, the hundred thousand dollars would be on deposit in a bank in Puerto Vallarta.

Pete could have taken more from the trust account but he deliberately limited the amount. He had learned his lesson. Dave Simpson had a tendency to spend every extra dollar that Pete contributed to their venture.

Pete and Dave had met three years earlier, in San Diego. It had been strictly a social occasion: Pete's wife, Laura, an aspiring socialite, managed to finagle an invitation to a celebrity fund-raiser for disadvantaged children. Pete had no interest in the media event but she dragged him along anyway. After the perfunctory introductions, Pete retired to the bar while Laura mingled. That's where he met Simpson.

Dave was in a similar fix. At that time he was dating a rich widow who happened to spend much of her time in Puerto Vallarta. Her principal residence, however, and most of her money, remained in La Jolla. She had convinced Dave to fly up for the evening event. He had been nervous about reentering the States—he still had several warrants out for his arrest—but he breezed through customs and immigration without a problem.

Normally, Dave would have mixed well with the high-end crowd, yet he elected to maintain a low profile at the party. Although his problems were back in the Pacific Northwest, there was always a chance he'd be recognized.

While standing at the bar, he and Pete began to chat. It was mostly small talk, and they had little in common until it came to fishing. Pete was a recent convert; Dave had been fishing for years. After spending nearly two hours together, occasionally interrupted by their female companions, the two men bonded. That's when Dave invited Pete to visit the resort. The offer was too good to turn down.

Pete flew down the following month. Laura and the kids were visiting her parents in Denver at the time. Airfare was all it cost him; Dave took care of the room and meals and everything else.

Dave Simpson was the senior time-share salesman for the resort. He had a huge promotional budget to milk and he used it to cover Pete's visit. Dave didn't spend a dime out of his own pocket during those five days.

Marlin were not yet in season but Dave and Pete caught a boatload of yellowfish and dorado. It was best vacation Pete had had in years. He had a ball.

At the end of the trip, Dave Simpson knew much about his new friend. Pete had opened up several times, especially after a bellyful of beer. He freely admitted his disdain for the legal profession; the failure to win partner drove his bitterness. And then there was the problem with Laura: she was a big spender. She spent nearly every spare dollar of his $150,000 annual income. Between the IRS and Laura, Pete was always short. He'd never get ahead.

Dave recognized an opportunity, deciding that the friendship with the lawyer might come in handy in the future. As a consequence, he maintained contact with Chambers, inviting him down every six months or so for fishing. Their friendship blossomed.

After taking up residence in Mexico, Dave Simpson eventually tuned into the fact that vast sums of money were being made in the drug business, right in his backyard. But like most everything else, it took money to make money. And by that time he had managed to blow most of the funds he had embezzled. He needed a new partner to bank his plans. That's where Pete came in. The trust accounts he controlled were a potential gold mine.

Dave's campaign took a couple of years to complete but he was patient, and events played right into his hands. Pete was again turned down for partner and Laura was pressuring him to move to another firm where he could earn more.

Dave's suggestions were never overt; they were always disguised in some form of a story, as though he were repeating gossip that he had heard. Pete eventually succumbed to the subtle indoctrination. It was the money that did it. When Dave told him about a couple of L.A. businessmen that had netted three million after a week's work in P.V., Pete's ears really perked up. In the end, Pete actually suggested that they work together, just as Dave had planned.

While Pete Chambers set about replenishing their money supply, Dave Simpson was working hard to spend it. He was aboard a 120-foot work boat at a marina in Manzanillo, about 130 miles down the coast from Puerto Vallarta. The skipper of the salvage vessel wouldn't take anything but cold, hard cash. And he wouldn't even think of pesos; it had to be Yankee dollars.

"Shit, twenty grand just to get mobilized. That's highway robbery," shouted Simpson.

"Well, you can take it or leave it, buddy. That's the way I work." The tall, bearded American seaman took one final puff on his cigar and then flipped the butt overboard.

Simpson was expecting the runaround on price. It was the same everywhere now. Everyone, even the expatriates, expected you to bargain for almost everything. Only the dumb tourists paid the asking price.

"I'll give you ten grand, that's it."

"Twenty big ones, *amigo*. And up front, or this lovely lady doesn't leave the dock."

"Ten now and five when you arrive in Puerto Vallarta."

The skipper nodded. "And you pay for the fuel up front, round-trip?"

"How much will that be?" Simpson asked, the expression on his face telegraphing annoyance.

"Say, five hundred gallons of diesel—it's damn expensive down here, you know?"

"Yeah, I know."

"Okay, that'll make it an even fifteen hundred."

"Done," Simpson answered.

The skipper smiled. "Good, then we'll get underway as soon as you bring the green."

"All right. I'll have it for you by tomorrow. You can pick it up at my bank."

"What bank?"

Simpson gave him the name of a Manzanillo bank. It was affiliated with the bank that he and Chambers used in Puerto Vallarta.

"Shit, I don't like banks," the vessel owner said. "Too much red tape with those bastards." What he really objected to was the possibility of having the funds taxed. He hadn't paid income taxes to anyone—U.S. or Mexico—for over ten years.

"Don't worry about it. Just ask for Señor Sanchez. He's my *banko personal*."

"Your personal banker?"

"Yeah, just like back in the States." Simpson was grinning. "He's on my payroll for this job."

The seaman smiled, now understanding. Some Mexican banks, really only a few, provide very special personalized services for their customers. For a fee, usually a few points on the transaction amount, and with no questions asked, the personal banker will arrange for the delivery of cash funds to a designated recipient. A code name or a number series is usually employed to guarantee a proper transfer.

"Well, that should be all right then. All I have to do is go see this Sanchez guy?"

"That's right. Just tell him that you're Mr. Wainwright from Portland."

"That's the code?"

"Yep. All you'll have to say is Wainwright and Portland. Then he'll give you the money. It's that simple."

"Good, that'll work." The captain, however, had no intention of picking up the money himself. He would send his two crewmen for that job—one to pick up the money, the other to make sure the first one brought it back to the ship.

Simpson and the captain shook on the deal. Dave then climbed down the boarding ladder and headed down the long float back to shore.

As Simpson walked he couldn't help but think that he had bargained well. Unbeknown to the American skipper, Dave would have paid $50,000 to get the boat. It was the only vessel within a thousand miles that could do the job he had in mind.

As Dave Simpson walked along the long pier, he was carefully scrutinized by another man. The man stood on a public boardwalk about five hundred feet to the north. The telephoto on his Canon easily captured Simpson's tan face. The powerdrive whirled as he finished the last few frames of the roll.

Tom Parker had been following Dave Simpson for nearly twenty-four hours now. He had spotted Simpson just a few hours after arriving in Puerto Vallarta. The encounter was purely accidental. Tom had been sitting in the resort's garden bar, enjoying a beer, when Simpson and two women wandered in. They had sat down at a nearby table. The bar was crowded with guests and the noise had prevented Tom from hearing the trio's conversation. Nevertheless, he discreetly watched. They seemed to be celebrating something—all three were in obvious good spirits.

Simpson had stayed for nearly an hour and then left. Tom had followed.

Parker was thankful that he had had the foresight to rent a car when he arrived at the airport. Normally, he would not bother driving in Mexico; the drivers were crazy and the cops were especially tough on *gringo* drivers. But he had had a feeling that he might need to be mobile. He was right.

Simpson headed to the parking lot near the main entrance to the resort and jumped into his Ford Explorer. A few minutes later he was on Highway 200, heading south.

Parker was right behind in his Jeep Wrangler. The road was slow. They drove until late evening, finally reaching Manzanillo. Simpson stayed in an expensive resort that bordered the Bahía de Manzanillo; Tom dozed in the rental.

The following morning, Tom followed Simpson to the boat. He had been staked out on the boardwalk for over an hour now. It was almost noon. *What the hell are you up to?* Tom wondered as he watched Simpson walk from the float to the shore. Dave then made a beeline for his Explorer.

Five minutes later Simpson pulled out of the parking lot and began to head north. Tom followed.

SIX
SURVEILLANCE

THE WATER FELT WONDERFUL. IT WAS STEAMY HOT, JUST THE way he liked it. He never wanted to come out.

Tom Parker had been in the shower for almost half an hour. After the long drive back from Manzanillo, he had followed

Simpson for half the night as the man barhopped through the *cantinas* and resort bars in downtown Puerto Vallarta. He was amazed at the man's stamina; he hadn't appeared to be tired while Parker was on his last legs. And the women Simpson knew—they were everywhere he went. Most had approached him, flashing their white teeth and tan bosoms as they competed for his attention.

Parker had seen the phenomenon before—only a couple of times in his life. Just a few very special men seem to have that something extra that attracts women like nothing else. Simpson was handsome all right, and well built, but that was only part of it. There was more. It was as if he radiated an invisible sixth sense that let the opposite sex know when he was ready and willing. Males would never understand it, but some females sure did.

Simpson had had his pick that night. And he'd taken his time. The women all had that hungry look in their eyes, like they were hoping to win the grand prize. To the last one, they were attractive—not a dog in the group. They were young and not so young. And he didn't discriminate. Mexican nationals as well as American expatriates had competed for his attention.

Finally, after seven smoky barrooms and at least a dozen contacts, Simpson had found what he was looking for. He and his pickup had then retired to his suite at the resort.

Parker felt the first change in water temperature. It was a tiny spike of cold. A few seconds later, a real chill hit him. Other guests on his floor were now using their showers. It was time to get out.

After shaving, he slipped on a pair of tan cotton shorts and a Seattle Seahawks T-shirt. He then walked onto the deck of his hotel room. When he pulled back the sliding glass door, the ovenlike blast of humid air hit him with a vengeance. It was August and the tropical sun was once again slowly baking the Mexican Riviera.

He stood by the railing, looking west at the turquoise ocean. He was on the ninth floor of the fourteen-story building. The narrow sandy beach at the base of the building was crowded with sun worshippers. And offshore there were dozens of Jet Skis, catamarans and sailboards. A powerful speedboat towed a para-glider near the shoreline.

Parker could feel sweat dripping down from his armpits. He had showered just fifteen minutes earlier and already he was perspiring like he had jogged five miles. *Damn, this sucks,* he thought. He then stepped back into the air-conditioned room.

He checked his wristwatch. It was 11:20 A.M. *Might as well do it now.*

Two minutes later he placed his call.

"Nordsoft," answered the receptionist.

"Ah, hello. Is this Marisa?"

"Yes."

"This is Tom Parker. Remember me? I was the one who was really late last week."

"Oh, sure. Hi, Tom. What can I do for you?"

"I'm calling for Linda Nordland. Is she available?"

"Just a moment while I check."

Tom Parker could picture the young woman's pretty face in his mind. One of his long-standing rules was to always make friends with a client's receptionist. You never knew when you might need help.

"Good morning, Tom," said a new female voice.

"Hello, Linda."

"I assume you're in Mexico?"

"Yep. I arrived in Puerto Vallarta two days ago."

There was a slight pause before the woman responded. "Well, did you find him?"

"Oh, yes. He's right here at the resort, just like we had hoped. And he doesn't seem to be a bit bothered about maintaining a low profile."

"What's he been up to?"

"I'm not really sure. Yesterday, I followed him down the coast to Manzanillo. He met with some guy on a boat and then . . ."

For the next few minutes Tom continued to report his surveillance observations, including Simpson's carousings of the previous night. Linda listened quietly, occasionally asking for clarification. And then, just after Tom finished his report, she lost her self-control: "Damn him to hell!" she said with her teeth gritted. "That son of a bitch will never change."

Tom didn't respond to his client's outburst; he was too

stunned to comment. It was the first time he had ever been around Linda Nordland when she was angry. Normally, she was easygoing and nonconfrontational. But there was something about Simpson that cut right to the bone with her.

Linda recovered her composure in a few seconds. "Please excuse my language, Tom," she said, knowing that her outburst had been uncalled for. "It's just that I can't stand the thought of that man living free like that. He's such a disgusting beast!"

"Hey, no problem. I understand what you've been through with that turkey." Tom paused a moment. "You know, Linda, if you still want to go ahead, it can be done—just like I planned. He's a sitting duck."

"Do you have what you'll need to do it?"

"Yes. I brought everything I'll need—except for the bait." Linda remained silent for a few seconds. "Okay then, let's do it."

For the next five minutes Tom Parker and his client discussed the details of the next phase of the operation. It would be risky and expensive.

"What do you mean you haven't heard from it?" asked Stan Reams. He had a telephone handset glued to the right side of his head as he lay in the middle of a king-size bed. A four-armed brass ceiling fan whirled away above him. The cool down-rush of air helped, but the migraine that hammered away inside his skull still tainted every thought.

"We've heard nothing for four days so far," answered the voice. The man's English was good, but he had a pronounced Asian accent.

"Nothing?"

"That's correct. At first we thought they might have had some kind of weather-related problem. But now we think it might be the ship's radio systems. We've had problems like this before."

Reams slipped his long legs over the edge of the bed and stood up. He was wearing only a pair of Jockey undershorts. "Well, you damn well better figure out what happened to that boat of yours." His anger was rising by the second. "I paid you a shit-load of money up front and you owe me big-time."

"I know that. It's just going to take time. I'm sure we'll be hearing from Captain Yook any day now. If he has to, he'll pull into port somewhere and phone in his report."

Reams walked to the end of his second-story bedroom and looked seaward. The sun was high overhead and the Pacific was almost at his doorstep. The sliding door to his deck was wide open. The six-foot breakers pounded the white sands of his beach with a relentless rhythm. The noise was oppressive, but he was immune to it. Since he'd lived on the beach for several years, the sea sounds had been naturally programmed into his brain.

"All right, Kim," Reams said as he walked outside onto the timber deck, "it's time to quit screwing around. I want you to locate the *Korean Star* and tell that Captain Yook of yours that if I don't get my merchandise by the end of the week, I'm going to personally fly to Pusan and find his wife and kids. And then I'm going to kill 'em!"

The man on the other end of the line, over five thousand miles away, could hardly believe what he had just heard. The American had always been friendly during their previous conversations, but now he was talking like a lunatic. "That would be a very regrettable action, Mr. Williams," he replied, addressing Reams by one of his many aliases.

"Look, you little bastard, I'm beginning to smell a setup here. And if I find out you're behind it, then I'll be after your ass too."

My God, what's the matter with this man? thought the Korean merchant. He was not used to having any person—Korean or otherwise—talk to him like that. "Mr. Williams, you're not being set up! I do not know where the *Korean Star* is right now. It should have arrived offshore of Cabo San Lucas four nights ago. That was the schedule, but obviously it has been delayed."

"Well, it sure as hell didn't arrive when it was supposed to, nor did it show up on the following days. I've been out there every fucking night."

"I'm working on the ship's whereabouts right now. Hopefully, I'll have an answer for you in the next day or so."

"I can't wait that long. I need my stuff."

"I know that, and believe me, I'm working on it."

"All right, Kim, I'll give you another day. But I need to

know for sure when that boat of yours is going to show up. I'm getting sick of waiting offshore night after night.''

''I understand and I should have some answers by tomorrow. Call me this time tomorrow and I'll let you know.'' He hung up before the American could reply.

It was a bright sunny morning in Pusan, Korea, but Kim Hyun-Jae didn't know it. He was inside a windowless office located in one corner of a huge, forty-year-old ex–U.S. Army warehouse. The building stank with mildew. Massive wooden boxes and truck-size shipping containers filled most of the storage area located outside the office.

Kim was the only person in the office section of the Yellow Sea Shipping Company's central warehouse. His office employees had not yet arrived for work. He leaned back in an old wooden swivel chair, placing his feet on top of an equally ancient oak desk. He was still smarting from the verbal lashing he had just taken. *Why is Williams so nervous about the bout being late?* he wondered. *I told him before that our schedules were sometimes delayed. And what could be so valuable in the box to make him act like a madman?*

Kim had set up the deal with Williams several months earlier. The $25,000 down payment that had been advanced by the American had been too much to ignore. At first, Kim thought that Williams had wanted to smuggle drugs on the *Korean Star*, like his other customers. But when the timber crate containing the sewing-machine-sized stainless steel box had mysteriously arrived at the wharf in Pusan, he decided that drugs were out. After opening the crate and inspecting the contents, Kim had realized that whatever was inside had to be worth a lot more than the amount of cocaine or heroin that could fit inside.

Both he and Captain Yook had tried to open the heavy steel box—it weighed about 125 kilos—but it had been sealed shut. The steel lid had been continuously welded to the case. The only way to open the container was with a blow torch, and that would have left unmistakable traces of tampering.

As curious as Captain Yook and he had been, they had decided to let the box be. They made their money by transporting a customer's product, not by stealing it. As a consequence, Captain Yook and Kim had returned the box to the timber crate and placed it inside a secret storage locker that was built in the captain's stateroom.

Kim shook his head back and forth. The mysterious American could be real trouble if he didn't find his merchandise, and soon. He reached for his phone. He was reluctantly going to contact the owners of the *Korean Star,* masquerading as a relative of Captain Yook. His story line, worked out long ago with Yook, would alert the captain to call him after the company headquarters radioed the ship.

Something had gone wrong. That he was certain of.

Tom Parker had just returned to his hotel room. It was almost midnight, and he had spent most of the evening following the subject. It was a repeat of the previous night's surveillance.

Dave Simpson had made the same rounds again. This time he'd made his pickup in Pablo's Place, a garden bar just a few blocks away from the resort. Dave and the redhead from Dallas were now in his one-bedroom suite, five floors below Tom's studio unit. They would be busy all night.

Tom was in the bathroom, brushing his teeth. He was leaning against the sink, staring at himself in the mirror. His eyes were slightly bloodshot, the result of minor jet lag and too little sleep. *Geez, you look like crap, buddy. You better get some rest while you can. No telling what that turkey's going to be up to tomorrow.*

He rinsed out his toothbrush and then reached for his toilet kit. The black leather case was sitting on the shelf next to the mirror. While he was searching for the dental floss, it hit with the impact of a magnitude-seven earthquake: *Damn, I completely forgot!*

All thoughts of the floss container evaporated as he continued to probe the kit, frantically looking for something else. *Where the hell is it?*

He gave up on the kit and headed back into the bedroom. His suitcase was propped open on a portable stand next to the dresser. That search proved just as fruitless.

After looking over the rest of the room, he finally surrendered. *Oh, shit, I must have left it at home. Now what am I going to do?*

Tom had forgotten his medication. The innocuous plastic bottle of green-and-white capsules was back in his Seattle apartment, sitting on a nightstand next to his bed.

At first the doctor had prescribed two capsules a day. It took a couple of weeks before Tom noticed any difference. And then he began to feel better—much better. Later the dosage was cut back to one per day. Tom continued to do well. And now he was taking just one capsule every other day. The goal that his doctor had recently set for him was to be completely off the drug in six months.

Tom had been taking the medication for almost two years now. The antidepressant had probably saved his life.

Tom sat on the edge of the bed. His initial panic was over. *The hell with it,* he thought. *I'm doing fine right now. I'll just tough it out. Besides, I need to ween myself off 'em anyway. This way I'll just do it a little sooner.*

Five minutes later Tom was in bed. The clean sheets felt cool next to his body. The lights were out and he could barely hear the beat of the surf over the drone of the air conditioning. Just before drifting off, he thought about his seven-year-old daughter and his own mother, both back in Seattle. He missed them—a lot.

SEVEN
ARRIVAL

THE WAITING AREA AT THE AIRPORT'S INTERNATIONAL TERMINAL was chock-full. About a hundred people, mostly Mexicans with a smattering of Americans, were waiting for the passengers to clear customs. Tom Parker was one of them.

Three flights from the States had just arrived: two from L.A. and a nonstop from Seattle. The airport terminal was a madhouse. Hundreds of passengers poured out of the jets, all heading to Mexican customs.

Tom Parker watched the spectacle from an open observation area next to the customs loading area. He had arrived early, parking himself by the gate in an effort to find some relief from the heat. What little breeze there was washed through the opening. It didn't help much; he was still sweating.

As another group of passengers filed into customs, Tom lit up. The Marlboro tasted good, even with the heat. For the next few minutes he watched the throngs of passengers milling about. And then he spotted her.

The young woman was dressed for the heat: sleeveless yellow-and-white cotton dress with an open neck. Her bosom wasn't large but was nicely proportioned, complementing her trim waist and the curves of her hips. The hem on her dress stopped a couple of inches above her knees. And the leather sandals on her feet were comfortably worn; she was used to warm climes.

The strap of a brown leather handbag rested on her right shoulder. She carried a professional briefcase with her left hand.

Tom Parker watched as she worked her way through the crowded baggage-claim area. She eventually found her suitcase and lined up behind one of the half dozen Mexican customs inspection stations. The stoplight display at the front of the counter was used to randomly inspect entering passengers. As long as the light remained green, one could walk right into the main lobby without being stopped. But if the light changed color, then you were detained by the inspector and your luggage was searched. Linda Nordland made it through without incident.

Tom Parker was waiting for his client as she officially entered Mexico. "Hi, Linda," he said as he reached for the suitcase.

She handed it over without question. "Hello, Tom."

"How was your flight?" he asked automatically.

"Good. I really like that nonstop run. It sure beats waiting in L.A. or San Francisco."

"Yeah, too bad they're not all like that. I had to wait over an hour when I came down."

Tom and Linda made their way through the still-packed lobby, heading for the parking lot. Five minutes later they were inside Tom's rented Jeep, heading south toward the city center.

"I've got you a hotel room at the resort like you wanted," Tom said as he pulled up to an intersection. The light was red.

"Good. And I assume Simpson's still around."

"Oh, yeah. He's hasn't gone anywhere for the past couple of days," Tom said while turning his head to steal a quick look at his passenger. "This morning I spotted him in the sales center with a young couple." He then glanced at his watch; it was almost two o'clock. "In fact, I bet he's still working on them right now, trying to close the deal."

"Yeah, I know," replied Linda. "He's very good at that."

Tom turned away, now facing forward. The stoplight switched to green and he let the clutch out. The Jeep charged forward. Tom waited a minute before speaking again. "Linda," he said, briefly turning to once again face her, "you still want to go through with this thing?"

"Absolutely. I want that bastard."

Tom turned back to face the road. He wasn't concentrating on the traffic, however. His mind was running a mile a minute. *Dammit, she's really serious about this thing. What the hell did I get myself into?*

A little over an hour after Linda Nordland's aircraft touched down at Puerto Vallarta International, another jet landed. The Mexicana Airlines 737 from San Diego was a quarter full. Pete Chambers breezed through the now-deserted baggage-claim area, but was stopped at the customs station. Yet he wasn't a bit concerned as the young Mexican woman searched his briefcase and carry-on bag. He had nothing to hide. The money he had embezzled from the Julia Harris trust had been electronically wired to his P.V. bank account two days before.

EIGHT
DEEP RECOVERY

THE SEA WAS GLASS-SMOOTH AND THERE WASN'T A BREATH of wind. The sliver of moon cast just enough light on the ocean's surface to reveal the blacked-out vessel. It was half past two in the morning.

The 120-foot-long craft was about a mile offshore, anchored in 100 fathoms of water. Four mooring lines, one from each quarter point, held the salvage ship in place. The *Pacific Salvor* had arrived over the wreck of the *Korean Star* four hours earlier. It had been easy to find; it had sunk within 200 meters of the rendezvous coordinates. The salvage ship's side-scan sonar had spotted the wreck during the first transect. The hull jutted up from the bottom like a mini mountain. After dropping through 600 feet of water, the processor had landed on its keel.

Dave Simpson and Pete Chambers were standing in the main salon of the twenty-two-year-old salvage ship. The owner of the *Pacific Salvor*, a burly fellow with a thick beard and long black hair, was leaning over the galley table, fiddling with a television set. After adjusting the fine-tuning controls, he turned to face his customers.

"Okay, it's working now."

Simpson leaned forward, staring at the black-and-white screen. All he could see were differing shades of gray. "You sure that's it?" he asked.

"Yep, we're right over the bridge now," replied Captain Einar Osterback as he pointed to the center of the screen. Osterback was an American but his roots extended back to Europe. Both of his parents had emigrated from Finland.

Simpson focused on the TV display. He could see a vague

rectangular shape but couldn't make out any details. "Can you get closer? I still don't see much."

"Yeah, sure." Osterback turned to his right and addressed one of his crewmen sitting at a console. "Bill, work her down a little, say about ten feet above the deck."

"Okay, Skipper," replied the man as he began to adjust a hand-held control. It looked like a Nintendo joystick. The device transmitted electronic signals through a fiber-optic cable to an underwater vehicle that was hovering over the ocean floor.

The ROV, or remotely operated vehicle, was about four feet long and eighteen inches in diameter. It looked like a beer keg on its side. Thick aluminum tubes framed the exterior of the core, forming a protective cage. A television camera with floodlight was mounted to the top side of the frame, providing a real-time video link back to the *Pacific Salvor*. Four ducted propellers, one on each corner of the frame, propelled the vehicle. The drives could be operated together or independently, allowing the ROV to hover, dive or climb, much like a helicopter.

Attached to the forward end of the ROV's aluminum frame was a mechanical arm. The robotic device could reach outward four feet. A viselike hand at the end of the arm was designed to retrieve underwater objects.

Electrical power for the ROV was supplied by a cable that was attached to the fiber-optic control tether. A five-foot-diameter drum located aboard the salvage ship held over a mile of the tether.

A tiny computer and a series of other electronic sensors and controls were housed inside the ROV's steel cylinder. The pressure casing was designed for a working depth of ten thousand feet.

After the ROV had descended fifteen feet, the resolution of the television screen improved dramatically. The top of the *Korean Star's* pilothouse looked completely normal. All of the radio and radar masts were intact. A limp Mexican ensign hung from one of the lanyards.

"I'll be damned!" Simpson said. "Now I can see it." He was impressed.

"That look familiar to you now?" asked the salvor.

"You bet. That's gotta be the sucker." Simpson turned to

face his partner. Pete Chambers had remained silent during the ROV's descent. "Pete, you agree?" he asked.

Chambers nodded. "Yeah, it sure looks like it."

Simpson turned back to the captain. "Okay, Skip, what do we do now?"

"Well, I suggest that we head inside the wheelhouse and start looking."

"Let's do it," replied Simpson.

It took a half hour for the ROV to work its way into the bridge house, swim down a long corridor that led aft, and then enter the stateroom. Along the way, the ROV encountered a myriad of debris, everything from half a dozen grotesquely bloated corpses and assorted body parts to a barrel-size semi-buoyant fire extinguisher, reams of free-floating waterlogged Korean newsprint, and a pot full of *kimchi*.

The ROV was now inside Captain Yook's cabin. Its flood-light lit up the compartment as if it were high noon. The once orderly and well-appointed stateroom was an absolute shambles. When the ship capsized, everything had been turned inside out. The stainless steel dining table and its metal chairs were flipped over. A bulkhead-mounted shelf next to the door was broken. And Yook's body hugged the overhead, along with a collection of other buoyant litter.

Dave Simpson was the first to react to the chaos. "What a fucking mess."

"Do you see your suitcase?" asked Captain Osterback.

Dave Simpson stared at the screen, squinting his eyes. The black-and-white images were murky, almost opaque. "It was on the table when I left. That's all I remember." He paused momentarily. "Maybe Yook hid the damn thing."

"In the cabin?"

"Hell, I don't know."

"But what about the heroin, then?" Osterback asked.

"Oh, yeah. It was on the table too. It was inside of a . . ." Simpson stopped speaking as he stared at the screen. "There it is," he yelled.

"Where?"

Simpson pointed to the lower right-hand side of the tele-vision screen. "That's the cardboard box—on the floor. The dope's inside. In a bunch of salami-size plastic bags."

The ROV operator maneuvered the robot until it was just

two feet away. He then reached out with the mechanical arm and pulled up one of the waterlogged flaps. The soft material ripped away and the box opened up. A white cloud of fluid poured from the opening.

"Open up that sucker all the way," demanded Simpson.

The ROV operator peeled the box apart. More whitish material diffused into the compartment, partially reducing visibility.

Once the turbid cloud dispersed, the camera zoomed in on the contents. Except for a stack of deflated plastic bags, the box was empty.

"Oh, shit," moaned Simpson.

"What's wrong?" asked Captain Osterback.

"The dope's all screwed up."

"You mean it's gone?"

"No, it's in the ship all right, but it's dissolved and washed out of the bags."

"How could that happen?"

"Hell, I don't . . ."

"Look at this," interrupted the ROV operator. He held up one side of the cardboard box. The perforations from the bullets were clearly visible.

Simpson stared at the screen. A sickening feeling jolted his stomach as reality hit home. "Jesus!" he shouted. "Those bastards must have shot the shit out of the box. The bags are all torn apart and the dope's gone."

"You mean there isn't any more heroin aboard?" asked Captain Osterback.

"That's right. Everything was in that . . ." Simpson stopped as a new thought popped into his mind. "Hey, wait a second. I remember seeing another one of those cardboard boxes in the hold. It was right next to this one, buried under a bunch of frozen fish."

Osterback's eyes widened at the news. "Then maybe we can get that one. I'll have Bill work his way aft and then we . . ."

"No way!" yelled Pete Chambers. "Dave, you're not going on any fishing expedition—at least not until we've recovered the money. And dammit, I mean it!"

Simpson stared at his partner. He had never seen Chambers so upset. "Okay, Pete. Just take it easy. Me and the cap got a little carried away about the dope. We'll find the suitcase now.''

Simpson turned toward the ROV operator. ''Can you pan that thing around a little? I'm sure it's somewhere inside the cabin.''

The man nodded. A moment later the images on the TV screen began to change as the ROV pivoted in place. For nearly ten minutes the underwater robot surveyed the cabin's interior. The debris and upturned furniture made it difficult to see. The ROV operator was just about to suggest that they restart the search when the camera focused on the forward end of the compartment. Part of the mahogany paneling had peeled away. There should have been a solid steel bulkhead under the paneling. Instead, the camera revealed a dark shadow. There was a cavity behind the wall.

''Hey, what's that?'' asked Simpson.

''Looks like it might be hollow behind there,'' answered the ROV operator.

''Check it out,'' ordered Osterback.

The ROV operator maneuvered the robot closer and extended the articulated arm.

As the arm pulled the paneling away, Captain Yook's secret storage compartment was completely exposed.

''There it is!'' shouted Simpson.

''Where? I don't see anything,'' responded Chambers. Pete was standing next to Simpson, staring at the black-and-white image. All he could see were varying shadows.

''There, under the crate.''

''I don't see it,'' Pete replied, twisting his head for a better view. His heart was almost in his mouth. *Please, God, let it be there!*

Simpson pointed to the screen. And then Pete saw it. The gray suitcase was almost invisible because of the background blackness. But there was just enough light reflecting from its chrome trim to reveal its presence. It was wedged into a recessed compartment that was built into the bulkhead next to the cabin's head. When the ship rolled over, the false wood panel covering the opening had separated, revealing Captain Yook's secret nook.

The ROV swam forward until it was just a few feet from the opening. The suitcase was clearly visible now, and crammed next to the plastic-sided case was a wooden crate. It was about four feet square and three feet high.

"Can you grab it with that robot arm of yours?" asked Simpson as he faced the technician.

"I don't think so. That crate's right in the way and it looks like it's jammed up against it pretty tight."

Pete Chambers commented next: "Well, can't you just move the damn box?" He was getting impatient at the delay. His salvation was inside the suitcase. All he cared about was getting the stolen money back into the trust account.

"I'll give it a try," replied the ROV operator.

A minute later the ROV's articulated arm was fully extended and latched onto one of the crate's rope handles. The robot's thrusters were all operating at maximum power, trying to pull the box out of its storage compartment. It wouldn't budge.

"Sorry, gents," the ROV tech said, "but there's no way we're going to move that thing with the ROV. That crate must be loaded with rocks."

"Shit," muttered Chambers.

"Damn it!" Simpson said.

The salvage skipper studied the video image. He was more than curious as to what might be stored inside the crate. *Loaded with rocks? Not likely,* Osterback thought. But whatever was inside was damn heavy, that much he knew. His mind had begun to wander with possibilities when the brainstorm hit. He smiled for just a second before turning away from the TV screen. He faced the technician. "You know, Bill, we just might be able to move that thing if we attach some bags to it."

The young man's eyes lit up as the idea struck home. "Yeah, Skipper, I see what you're getting at. That just might work."

"Bags? What the hell are you guys talking about?" asked Simpson.

"It's really simple. We've got these inflatable bladders that we use to lift sunken objects, like downed airplanes and artifacts. We attach them to the object to be removed and then fill 'em with compressed air. Once they're neutrally buoyant, we can move them around with ease."

"Great. Let's do it, then."

"Okay, but we'll have to bring the ROV back up and rig it with the inflation gear."

"How long will that take?"

Osterback unconsciously scratched his scalp. "At least a couple of hours."

Simpson checked his watch. It was 4:03 A.M. "Shit, the sun'll be up by then."

"Yep. So what do you want to do?"

Simpson faced Chambers. "Pete, I think we should come back later this evening. We're too damn close to Vallarta. If someone sees us working out here they might figure it out."

Pete Chambers wasn't ready to quit. He was so close to deliverance that he could taste it. "No way. I want to get this fucking thing over with—today!"

Simpson's face telegraphed his displeasure. "Pete, those suckers that screwed us over are still out there. I can feel it." He paused for a moment. "If any of those pirates see a salvage ship moored out here, it won't take a rocket scientist to figure out what we're doing. And you can bet your last buck, they'll come looking for us again."

Pete Chambers remained silent for a few seconds. He had ignored the Mexican outlaws and their savage attack on the *Korean Star*. All he could concentrate on was recovering the $1.2 million inside the suitcase. But Simpson's logic made sense. It was, indeed, too risky to continue in the daylight. "Okay, Dave," he said, "but we come back tonight, come hell or high water. I want this frigging disaster over with."

Simpson flashed a smile and turned toward the *Pacific Salvor's* master. "Tonight okay with you, Skip?"

Captain Osterback's face masked his anticipation. "I don't know. If the weather holds, and if we come to the right arrangement, it might work out."

"What the fuck you talking about? Arrangements?"

"Hey, buddy, you never said anything about pirates when we made the deal. You just told me that you wanted some drugs and money recovered from a ship that went down. You never told me that it was scuttled by a bunch of seagoing *banditos!*"

"But what does that matter? The ship's where I told you it would be and the money's there."

"Yeah, that's all true, but I live down here. And I haven't

had any trouble with those pricks. But if they get wind that I'm involved with you guys, they'll come after me, sure as flies on shit.''

This bastard's up to something, thought Simpson. The man was holding back. "Okay, just what do you want?"

The captain rubbed his beard with his right hand. *Got 'em,* he thought. "Well, for starters, my fee's doubled because of the risk factor."

"Doubled! Now *you're* the damn pirate!" shouted Pete Chambers. The normally mild-mannered lawyer was beside himself. He and Dave had already paid the salvor $16,500 up front and would owe him another twenty grand plus expenses when the job was complete.

Simpson turned to his partner. "Cool it, Pete. Let the man finish."

The captain continued, stating that in addition to his fee and operating expenses, he wanted another $25,000 for relocation expenses. He explained that he would have to head back north to the States until it was safe to return to Mexico.

Simpson remained stone-faced as the captain made his demands. *This guy's got us by the balls and there's nothing we can do about it.*

At the conclusion of his demands, the captain offered a carrot. "Now, I just might be willing to waive the extra fee if we can come to an agreement on the salvage rights."

Salvage rights? thought Simpson. "Just what did you have in mind?" he asked.

"We recover the heroin from the hold and . . ."

"No way!" interrupted Chambers. "We just want the frigging suitcase. If we try to get the dope, that could take forever."

"Sit tight, Pete," commanded Simpson. He turned to face Osterback. "Please continue, Captain."

"Yeah, like I was saying, we recover the smack and I get half. You guys do what you want with yours and I'll take mine."

"Okay, that'll work."

Simpson had just started to turn toward Chambers when the captain spoke again.

"And there's one more thing"

"What now?" asked Simpson, the look on his face soured.

"I want whatever's inside the crate."

So that's it, thought Simpson. *That's what this has been about.*

It would have been easy for Dave Simpson to agree to the last demand, but he had been dealing with characters like the captain for years. If he gave in to everything, the man would just invent more ways to bleed him.

"Well, Skipper, I'm kind of interested in what's in that secret box too. You know those Koreans—they're real tight with their money, don't believe in banks. For all I know that damn thing just might be chock-full of silver coins, maybe even some gold bars."

Shit! thought the captain. The man had read his mind. "Well, I really doubt that," he replied. "Anyway, I want it."

Simpson looked the man right in the eyes. It was time to close the sale. "After we've recovered our suitcase, we share fifty-fifty in everything we bring up—the dope, any extra money we find and whatever's in that box."

The captain stood silently for a few seconds before his bearded face broke into a wide grin. "You got yourself a deal!"

NINE
FAMILY CHRONICLES

TOM PARKER USUALLY DIDN'T EAT MUCH FOR BREAKFAST. A cup of coffee and a slice of toast were his normal fare; but this morning he was famished. He had just consumed a fat *torta de huevo.* The Mexican omelet was mixed with garlic, onion and chili. It was tasty and tolerably spicy.

Tom was seated at a small table in a corner of a tiny street cafe, about a block from the resort. He was now drinking his second cup of coffee. Sitting across from him was Linda Nordland. She was enjoying the last few slices of fresh fruit from her continental breakfast plate.

"Well, how was your room?" Tom asked as he took a sip from his cup.

"Fine. It's really a nice place."

"Yeah, it is. Despite all the crap you hear about time-shares, some of them are okay."

Linda nodded and then popped an apple slice into her mouth.

Tom stared at his client for a moment. She had pulled her hair back into a ponytail and her sunglasses were dangling around her neck, suspended by a nylon cord. The tails of her white cotton shirt were drawn tight and knotted at waist level. It amplified the swell of her breasts. *God, she looks good!*

"Tell me, Tom," Linda said, "how'd you ever get into this business?"

He leaned back in his chair. "I guess you could say it all started when I joined the Army."

"When was that?"

"Back in the late seventies."

"You were an officer?"

"Yeah, eventually. After enlisting and going through basic training, I applied to OCS."

"OCS?"

"Officer Candidate School."

"Oh, I see. Like ROTC?"

"Yeah, it's kind of like that but only when you're already in the service, rather than in college."

Linda nodded. "My ex was in Naval ROTC but he never finished." For just an instant Linda pictured Don's face. *You bastard! I hope you rot in hell!*

They had married while at Stanford. She was a senior in computer science; he was a third-year law student. It was a huge mistake. After he beat her up the second time, she threw him out of the apartment. She ignored his repeated pleadings for another chance, refused to attend counseling sessions, turned down all of the flowers and gifts. He no longer existed as far as she was concerned. Once a wife-beater, always a wife-beater. When the divorce was final, she held a terrific party.

Linda refocused on Tom. "You must have gone through college before joining the Army."

"Right. I had a BS in law enforcement and had planned to attend law school. But I was tired of school at that time so I took off for a year, bumming around the world. I had a great time but I also blew all of my remaining money."

"So you joined the Army instead?"

"Yeah. I planned on serving for only a couple of years as a grunt and then using my educational benefits for law school. It would have been a good deal."

"What happened?"

"I got sidetracked. When I finished basic training, I was offered an OCS slot. It looked like a good move so I signed up. After receiving my commission I was then assigned to a Military Police detachment in South Korea. I served a two-year tour there."

"You got out then?"

"No, not quite. I still had another year to serve—the price you pay for becoming an officer. I was transferred to a CID section at one of our bases in Germany."

"CID! What's that?"

"Sorry. CID. It stands for Criminal Investigation Division—I was an Army detective."

"Wow!" she said with a smile. "If you were in Europe at that time, then you must have been checking up on all of those Russian spies."

Tom grinned back. "Well, I did do a little of that, but my main job was to track down some GIs that were suspected of stealing supplies."

"Did you catch them?"

"Yeah, it took a while but we nabbed 'em, red-handed."

"What did they take?"

"They were stealing diesel fuel."

"Diesel?"

"Yeah, fuel's really expensive in Europe, especially back then. Anyway, these ding-a-lings were part of a supply section that delivered fuel to our units in the field—you know, tanks, trucks and so on. Well, they'd take a tanker out from the fuel depot every day and . . ."

Tom spent the next ten minutes explaining the caper. Linda was fascinated with the story, especially the electronic surveillance measures he had used. "So you finally got them?" she asked.

"Yep. We nailed the whole crew, including the owner of the trucking firm. Our boys still have five more years to serve in Leavenworth. I think the guy in Munich gets out next year."

Linda Nordland was impressed. Tom got results. "So how long were you in the Army?"

"Almost fourteen years. I remained with CID, serving all over the world, even including the war in the Gulf."

"Why'd you get out?"

"It was after Desert Storm. I'd just been promoted to Lieutenant Colonel, but I could see the writing on the wall. The Soviet Union had just fallen apart, the Cold War was over and the Army was beginning to downsize. I could tell there wouldn't be any future for me."

"Why was that?"

"I wasn't a West Pointer—worse, I was an OCS puke. That's about as low as you can get in the Army's officer hierarchy."

"Hmm," Linda said, signaling her empathy.

"Anyway, I resigned my commission and headed back to the Bay Area—Palo Alto. That's where I grew up. I landed a job with a PI firm in Oakland. I spent about half a year working there, and then they sent me up to Seattle on a case. I really liked it there so I stayed."

"That's when you started your own business?"

"Yeah—not by plan, though. The Oakland firm laid me off; they didn't have any more work for me after the Seattle job. So I started looking for a new job up there." Tom paused to take another sip of coffee. "What I really wanted was to work for some big company as a chief of corporate security—watching over the company bigwigs, setting up electronic security screens for corporate computer systems, that kind of stuff. But things were really tight back then and there weren't any jobs. So, by default, I ended up going into business for myself. I got my PI license and opened shop in a crackerbox-size office in Pioneer Square."

"What kind of work did you do back then?"

"Mostly small stuff: petty theft, shoplifting in stores and, of course, divorce work."

Linda smiled. She knew about the divorce work. Tom had quite a reputation for finding husbands that cheated on their wives. One of Linda's best friends in Seattle, a single woman who had inherited a fortune, had hired him to check up on her fiancé. It turned out that the man was a hustler, but he was careful. It had taken Tom almost a month to discover the deception.

The thief had another girlfriend who lived in Kirkland; they had been lovers for years. She was a newly hired attorney with a large Seattle law firm. The firm represented Linda's friend in various business matters, and the twenty-five-year-old woman attorney happened to see her file one day. With a net worth of almost twenty million, and still not married, she was a perfect target.

The plan had been for the boyfriend to marry her and then take control of her business affairs. With help from his lawyer-mistress, he would drain off income from her investments and carefully transfer control of key assets to his own account. At the appropriate time, he would then skip town, disappearing with most of the money. His attorney-partner would wait a respectable time period and then quit. They had planned to live in the south of France.

But Tom Parker had put an end to their trickery. Tom's damning videotape of the man and woman in bed was all it took. The raw images of the two were bad enough for Linda's friend, but the afterglow talk was the worst: they had openly discussed how they were going to spend her money.

Linda's friend was forever grateful to Tom Parker. He had saved her a life of misery and probably several million dollars. So when Linda told her about her own problems, she naturally recommended Tom.

Linda sipped the last of her coffee and set the cup on the table. Tom reached for the coffeepot. ''Care for some more?'' he asked.

''Sure.''

As Tom refilled her cup she glanced at his face. He was an attractive man. His short, dark hair and rugged tan complexion created a striking appearance. She wondered if he was married. There was no wedding ring—no rings at all. She decided to find out.

''Do you live in Seattle?'' she asked.

"Yeah, I rent a small condo on Queen Ann."

"Oh, that's a nice area. I used to live in Magnolia."

Tom nodded as he returned the pot to the table.

"Your family still down in the Bay Area?" she asked.

"My brother and his family still are—they live in Piedmont. He's an attorney; a partner with a firm in Oakland. My dad passed away ten years ago." He sighed. "Mom moved back to the Northwest a few years ago. She now lives on Bainbridge. That's where she grew up."

Tom did not volunteer anything else.

He's not telling me everything, Linda thought. She decided to continue her probe: "It must be nice, having your mother close by like that."

"Yeah, she's a wonder. I don't know what I'd do without her."

Linda thought that his statement was a little leading. "Oh, how's that?"

"Sometimes I have to go out of town on extended assignments—like this one. Mom always takes care of Keely for me when I'm gone."

A pet? she wondered. "Keely?" she asked, smiling.

"Yeah, my daughter." His face lit up with delight. "She's seven. A real beauty, just like her mom."

Linda's face mirrored her confusion. *He never said anything about a wife. There's no wedding ring. Is he married? Divorced? What?*

Tom recognized the questioning look. He'd seen it before. "I'm a widower. Keely's mom died three years ago."

"Oh, I'm so sorry. I had no idea." She blushed, embarrassed at her intrusion into his privacy.

Tom shrugged his shoulders. "Thanks. It was a long time ago."

Linda sensed that there was more to Tom's saga but decided she'd probed enough for the time being.

She was right. There was more—much more.

"Tell me, Linda," Tom said as he stretched his arms out, flexing his hands, "your friend that spotted Simpson down here—how'd that happen?"

"She saw him sitting in a bar with some woman. Nicole was a good friend of my mother. She remembered meeting him at a party at Mom's house."

Parker shook his head. "That's amazing. He took off—what was it—five, six years ago."

"Over six years."

Linda remembered the exact length of time: six years, two months and twenty-one days. That's how long it had been since Dave Simpson, a.k.a. David Alexander, raided Marsha Nordland's stock brokerage account. The fifty-one-year-old widow was in California at the time, visiting her ailing sister. And her new younger lover, the handsome and dashing David, had the run of her elegant Magnolia home.

The theft had been simple. Simpson didn't bother with any of her equities or bonds; her broker would never have sold them without Marsha's direct involvement. But the cash account was another matter. Marsha had recently sold off several real estate holdings and had temporarily deposited the money in the account's ready-assets ledger. She hadn't yet decided where she would invest the half-million dollars.

Using a stack of brokerage checks he had found in a locked cabinet, Simpson had written seven checks, forging Marsha's name on each one. The checks were made out to dummy companies that Simpson had set up in advance, all with the words "development" or "real estate" in their names so that when the checks passed through the brokerage firm's banking section they would appear to be for normal purchases. Marsha Nordland had purchased several pieces of property in the past, using the excess cash in the brokerage account to pay for them.

The deception had worked perfectly. After the checks cleared the brokerage account, Simpson had immediately transferred the stolen money to other local accounts, eventually depositing all $500,000 to an untraceable account in the Bahamas. He had also timed the forgeries so that he could intercept the monthly statement summarizing the transactions before Marsha returned. And then, the weekend before she was scheduled to fly home, he had visited her in L.A. He'd explained that he was going on an extended business trip and wanted to be with her before leaving.

By the time Marsha had returned to Seattle, she had had no reason to suspect anything. The doctored brokerage statement that Simpson had left behind with the stack of mail had looked normal. However, about a month later, she'd received the shock of her life. That's when the next monthly statement had arrived. Lover-boy Simpson had left a paltry five thousand in her cash account.

"That whole thing must have been tough on your mother," Tom said as he took another sip from his coffee cup.

"It was—I'm sure it's what killed her."

Tom didn't respond. He let Linda continue. There was a lot of anger to vent.

"When that bastard took off, it tore my mother apart. Stealing the money was only part of it—that hurt real bad because he stole almost a third of her net worth and she only got part of it back from the brokerage firm. But the worst part was the betrayal. She really loved that prick and when she discovered that her money was missing, she refused to believe that he had anything to do with it. But when he never returned from his so-called business trip, reality finally set in."

Marsha Nordland had become so depressed from the embarrassment that she had started drinking again. And within a month she had managed to kill herself, driving her Cadillac over the ravine near her house and crashing onto the beach below. The medical examiner's report indicated that she had been borderline intoxicated at the time and ruled her death an accident. Linda hoped that the report was accurate. She hated to think that her mother had committed suicide.

Three years before Marsha met Simpson, her husband of twenty-seven years had died from a sudden heart attack. Marsha had always been so dependent on Dan Nordland that the shock of being alone was too much for her. Her friends and family had helped at first, but when they all left and Linda returned to her job, Marsha had found herself alone in that big house that overlooked downtown Seattle and Elliott Bay. She couldn't stand the isolation, but she eventually found a way to cope. Her evening cocktail, a ritual she had religiously shared with Dan, turned into two drinks, and then three, and eventually another one or two for a nightcap.

It took only a year for Marsha to get hooked. Luckily Linda, along with her aunt, rescued her in time. With the best professional help money could buy, Marsha dried out nine months later.

To this day, however, Linda Nordland blamed herself for

not recognizing the warning signs the second time around. *After that prick walked out on her I should have known she might start drinking again. The doctors all warned me that a severe emotional trauma could cause a setback.* But Marsha had hidden her addiction well. No one had suspected that she had once again turned to the bottle—until it was too late.

"What the heck do you think he did with all that money?" asked Parker.

"Lord, I don't know. My best guess is that he blew it gambling and living high."

"You never met him, face to face?"

"No. I never met him and Mom hardly talked about him."

"So you're sure he doesn't know you."

"Yes. He may have seen some of my photographs back then, but that's it."

"That's good," Parker said. He pulled out a pack of cigarettes just as a waitress began to remove the plates and utensils from the table. He offered one to Linda. She accepted and he lit her Marlboro. After inhaling on his own, he once again continued with his questions. "So how'd this bastard get away?"

"At first he didn't. About six months later he was arrested in Miami on a federal warrant. Besides forgery, he was charged with mail fraud because of the way he used my mom's brokerage account. Anyway, he was extradited back to Seattle to stand trial. He hardly spent any time in jail before they let him out on bail. Somehow, he convinced a bail bondsman to post the quarter-of-a-million-dollar bond. Apparently, he gave the guy fifty thousand in cash and pledged a two-hundred-K CD as security for the rest."

"Let me guess. He jumped bail."

"That's right. Two days before the trial he disappeared."

"The bondsman couldn't find him?"

"Nope. He had people out looking for him but never found him. Eventually he forfeited the bond and had to cash in the CD to recoup his losses. But the attorneys for Mother's estate interceded, claiming the funds for the CD were stolen from my mom. It took months to resolve, but the bondsman finally got his money."

Tom shook his head. "Well, he's still a fugitive, and the fact that he jumped bail is just another nail in his coffin. If he ever steps back into the U.S. and is spotted, they'll lock him up and throw the key away.''

"Yeah, but he's not that dumb. From everything I know about him, he's real careful.''

"Do you think he has ever come back into the States?''

"Oh, sure. It would be too tempting for him not to try—especially with California so close.''

"What about Seattle?''

"No way. Too many of his victims are still up there. He'll never ever go back there.''

"Maybe not on his own." Parker grinned. "But with a little help, he just might be convinced to do the right thing.''

"Do you still think it might work?''

"Oh, yes. In fact, I suggest we try tonight.''

"Tonight!'' Linda paused for a moment. "Everything's set up?''

"Yep, all we need is for him to show up.''

Linda smiled. The decision was easy. "Good. Let's do it then.''

TEN
DEADLY DECOY

KIM HYUN-JAE WAS UNEASY. AFTER REPEATEDLY TRYING TO make radio contact with the *Korean Star*, he finally gave up. It was as if the 260-foot-long vessel had never existed. The ship should have arrived in Mexican waters over a week earlier, but Kim hadn't heard a word from Captain Yook. And now the vessel's owners were getting anxious. The fish-processing ship had failed to rendezvous with a couple of company trawlers operating four hundred miles offshore of Panama. *Something must have gone wrong in Puerto Vallarta,* he repeatedly told himself.

Only Kim knew Captain Yook's agenda. They were partners in the smuggling operation. Kim lined up the deals and Yook executed them. Kim received only a third of the action, but it was fair compensation. The captain was exposed to most of the risk. After fourteen successful operations, both men were convinced they had a developed a foolproof system. But it now looked as if Yook's luck had run out.

Kim spent most of the morning covering his tracks. There would certainly be a government investigation into the loss of the *Korean Star* and he had to make certain that there was nothing in his company's records that would implicate him. He even purged all of his carefully coded computer files regarding Captain Yook and their financial transactions. The computer security system was supposed to be unbreakable— the best system money could buy—but Kim erased all of the files anyway. He would leave nothing to chance. Besides, with the two million he had stashed away in Tokyo and Switzerland, he didn't need to work any longer. He would abandon the smuggling operation and sell his business. He would live like a king!

But Kim had two problems to solve before he could retire. First, the heroin that had been stashed in the *Korean Star's* freezer compartment had to be accounted for. Kim and Yook never purchased drugs. Instead, they functioned as intermediaries. They would transport a client's property, make the exchange and then collect the money. Once the ship returned to Korean waters, the cash, less Kim and Yook's twenty-five-percent commission, would be turned over to the client. It was an efficient operation that appealed to both seller and buyer. By having an intermediary exchange the cargo for the cash, there was virtually no risk to the seller. And the buyer, knowing that he wasn't likely to get ripped off by an agent, approved of the system because he never had to deal directly with the seller. Like in the movies, most drug deals turned sour when the buyer and seller tried to consummate the transaction.

Kim and Yook, both careful and conscientious men, had anticipated that they someday might lose a client's property. Fear that the ship might sink was always there, but a more likely scenario was a raid by the authorities resulting in a confiscation of the property. As a consequence, Kim and Yook had set aside a contingency fund to cover legal expenses, should they need to defend themselves, and to replace their client's property. The last thing they wanted was an irate customer demanding his property back.

Kim and Yook had slightly over eight hundred and fifty thousand dollars in cash set aside. By adding fifty thousand of his own money, Kim could pay the owner of the heroin in full. That was the easy problem to solve. The other one wasn't.

Kim worried about the American called Williams. The man continued to hound him on the phone, demanding to know when the *Korean Star* would arrive in Cabo San Lucas. He had a bad feeling about the man—there was something very wrong with him.

Kim finally decided that he would have to inform Williams that he feared the ship had gone down. He would offer to return the down payment plus fifty thousand dollars in compensation to settle the man's losses. He doubted that it would be enough. Whatever was hidden inside the steel box in Captain Yook's cabin was of momentous value to Williams. He was fanatical about receiving it.

Juan Diaz spent most of the morning scouring Puerto Vallarta's beachfront resorts. He was tired of looking, but his uncle demanded that he continue. While Ernesto stood on the beach, Juan would walk through the pool and outdoor court areas of the hotels and condominiums. He was looking for the *norteamericanos* he had seen on the *Korean Star*.

Juan didn't look anything like his normal self. He was scrubbed clean, his once-shaggy hair was trimmed neat and proper, and he was dressed in new and expensive clothing. He wore a blue-and-white polo shirt, tan knee-length shorts and a pair of Nike running shoes. The disguise worked perfectly. No one paid the slightest attention to him, not even the pesky Mexican security guards.

Juan looked like just another one of the rich kids that visited the resorts with their parents. Even his very brown skin didn't raise eyebrows; many prosperous Mexicans stayed at the resorts and they often brought their families with them during the summer holidays.

Uncle Ernesto had arranged for the clothing and shoes—they were stolen from the airport. A Canadian family had departed earlier that morning. However, when they finally arrived in Toronto they would discover that their sixteen-year-old son's suitcase was missing. One of Ernesto's cronies worked in the baggage terminal, and for the price of a six-pack of beer would take custom orders.

Juan walked slowly through the poolside area of the seventh resort. It was crowded with sunbathers, like all the others. There were all kinds: fat ones, skinny ones, white ones, brown ones and even a few black ones. He couldn't understand their incessant ritual of exposing themselves to the murderous sun, slowly roasting like pigs on a spit.

Juan was sweating too. The noonday sun was directly overhead and it was almost a hundred degrees. And there was hardly any breeze. The only relief came from the forest of towering palm trees that surrounded the courtyard.

As he moved forward Juan spotted a young couple at a well-shaded table. They were just leaving. And the woman had left a half-full bottle of Coca-Cola on the tabletop. Juan made a beeline for the table, claiming it before any of the busboys had a chance to remove the bottle.

The Coke was still cold and tasted wonderful. He nursed it for about ten minutes, thankful to be sitting down and out of the sun.

Juan was just thinking of heading back to the beach when he spotted the man. He walked by his table, just a few feet away. It was one of the *norteamericanos,* that he was certain of.

Dave Simpson didn't pay the slightest attention to the boy sitting at the table. He was too busy talking with the dumpy-looking blond. He had been working on the prospect all morning. He would close the sale on the time-share unit after lunch.

Juan watched as the tall American walked into the lobby of the hotel's poolside cafe. It was time to find Uncle Ernesto.

Linda Nordland toyed with her drink, just sipping at the salty brim. Her first margarita had gone down much too fast. *Slow up,* she repeatedly told herself. It would have been easy for her to let go but she couldn't afford to lose her wits tonight. She needed to remain sharp.

Linda turned away from the bar, eyeing the rest of the lounge. It was swiftly filling with tourists, and many of the regulars had already staked out their favorite tables. A *mari-*

achi band played in one corner of the garden bar, filling the surrounding courtyard with fast-paced tones. At a quarter to midnight, Pablo's Place was just warming up.

Linda was dressed to the hilt. Diamond stud earrings accentuated her soft blond hair and there was just a hint of pale lipstick on her full lips. Turquoise-tinted contacts replaced her prescription sunglasses—they matched the color of her eye shadow. Her sheer silk blouse clung lightly to her skin; whenever she moved, her breasts quivered, just enough to reveal that she wasn't wearing a bra. Her hip-hugging skirt, fire-engine red and cut four inches above the knee, highlighted her long tan legs. They seemed to stretch on forever as she sat perched on the bar stool. Her black high heels were sling-backs, each laced around the ankle and tied off with a neat bow. A thin gold ankle bracelet on her left leg completed the disguise. If ever there was a woman who looked like she was on the make, Linda was it.

Linda opened her purse and pulled out a pack of Merits. She had just slipped the cigarette between her lips and was fumbling with her own Bic lighter when a gold-plated Zippo magically appeared in front of her face.

"Allow me," said a male voice.

Without looking at the man, Linda leaned forward and ignited the Merit. She then took a long drag before turning to her right. The man standing beside her was in his early thirties—a couple of years younger than Linda. He was about six feet tall and had a slim build. He wore tan slacks with an open-collared multicolored Hawaiian shirt. A heavy gold chain was wrapped around his neck. The top two buttons of his shirt were deliberately left open; thick grayish-black chest hairs erupted from the gap. His neatly combed and not-too-long hair was jet-dark. Although his face was lightly pockmarked, remnants of a bout with teenage acne, he was still pleasant to look at.

Linda made eye contact. "Thanks."

"My pleasure." The man then lit up his own cigarette. "I'm Jeff," he announced.

"Linda."

"Can I buy you another drink?"

"No, thanks, I'm fine."

He inched closer. "You been down here long?"

"Just a couple of days."

"Me, too. I'm from L.A."

Linda just nodded, not volunteering any more information than necessary. She knew exactly where the conversation was going to end up. The man standing by her was the fourth one who had tried to pick her up during the last hour. She really couldn't blame them; her bait was deadly effective.

"How long are you staying?" he asked.

"Maybe a couple of weeks."

"Wow, that's nice. I've got to fly back this weekend—business."

Linda nodded again and took another sip from her drink.

"Say, Linda," the man said, "I was thinking about heading out to a little place I know down the street to get a late dinner. Would you care to be my guest?"

At least this guy is polite, Linda thought. The last one, a sixty-five-year-old fossil from New York City, had offered her $500 for the night. She had been tempted to throw her drink in his face. Instead, she simply told him to "go screw yourself." He had melted into the crowd without another word.

"Gee, thanks, Jeff. But I really can't. I'm just waiting for my date to finish up with a meeting upstairs and then we're going out."

"Oh, I thought you were alone."

Linda smiled. Her teeth were perfect. "Sorry."

The man returned the smile and then stepped away.

Linda looked at the clock behind the bar counter. It was now midnight. *Dammit, that SOB should have been here by now!*

Linda was waiting for Dave Simpson. This was his favorite watering hole and he almost always made an appearance between eleven and midnight. But tonight he was a no-show.

Linda was staring at her drink, trying to decide what to do next, when someone else moved up on her right side. She didn't look. *Oh, shit, here we go again,* she thought as she began mentally preparing herself to fend off another hustle.

"Linda," the voice said in a whisper, "I don't think he's going to show tonight."

Linda turned. Tom Parker was sitting on the bar stool next to hers, a long-neck Bud in his right hand. She looked back down at her drink. "What should I do?" she asked softly.

Parker looked straight ahead. He could see her reverse image in the bar mirror. The CEO of Nordsoft looked like a high-priced whore. He very much liked what he saw. *Sleaze with class. What a combination!*

Tom hadn't felt like this in months—years. Something was happening. The longing, the stirring of his manhood, so long dormant, as if buried deep underground, was once again surfacing, seeing the light of day.

Tom took a sip from the bottle and then responded. "Let's give it another half hour. If he doesn't show up by then, we'll call it a night."

"All right, but I'm getting tired of all these guys hitting on me. There's gotta be a better way than this."

"Just hang in there. You're doing a great job. I know this is a hassle for you but it'll work out if we give it enough time."

"Okay."

At 12:40 A.M. Linda finally walked out of the bar and returned to her room at the resort. Tom Parker left five minutes later. It took all of his willpower not to knock on her door.

ELEVEN
CRITCOM

CAPTAIN OSTERBACK HAD HAD IT. FOR THE PAST THREE hours he and his crew had worked like coolies trying to reanchor the salvage ship over the wreck of the *Korean Star*. But they had failed. The sea was too rough. Whenever they did manage to deploy one of the four anchors, it either dragged on the bottom or the load cell connected to the anchor line indicated that the cable tension exceeded the normal working limit. The *Pacific Salvor's* mooring tackle was just too light for the rough water.

Knowing it was useless to continue, Osterback finally decided to throw in the towel. He was inside the rolling bridge house, sitting in his pedestal chair adjacent to the helmsman. Pete Chambers and Dave Simpson were standing beside him. Both men braced themselves against a brass handrail that ran under the bridge windshield.

"I'm sorry, gents," Captain Osterback said, "but I'm calling it a night. It's just too damn nasty out here."

"Yeah, I guess you're right," replied Simpson. He turned to his partner. "You agree, Pete?"

Chambers nodded his head but didn't say anything. He was more than relieved that the boat would be returning to the calm waters of the harbor. His upset stomach continued to churn away in response to the rolling swells.

"Okay, Captain, we agree." Simpson paused as a new thought developed. "But what about tonight—can we go out again?"

"Maybe. There's a storm a couple of hundred miles out that's been generating this crap. The last weather report I got indicated that it might blow itself out early today. If it does, then the swells might be a little more reasonable."

"All right. I want to try again, assuming the weather breaks."

"Okay by me," replied the captain.

Dave Simpson looked at his partner. "Pete, that okay with you?"

"Yeah, fine," lied Chambers. He absolutely dreaded the thought of coming out again, even if the waves were smaller. But he really didn't have a choice. He had to recover the money—whatever it cost him physically. And there was no way he was going to let Dave Simpson get hold of the money without him being there. He knew Simpson too well to trust him with that much cash.

"Good," Simpson said as he flashed a smile at his partner. He turned to face the Captain. "Okay, Skip, let's head back in so we all can get some rest."

"You got it."

Stan Reams was in the living room of his condominium. The sliding glass doors to the balcony were open. The breeze flowing into the apartment was refreshing but the noise it carried was deafening. Just fifty feet away, ten-foot rollers crashed onto the white sands, one after another. The same tropical storm that hammered Banderas Bay, causing the *Pacific Salvor* to abort its mission an hour earlier, was also pounding the beaches of Cabo San Lucas.

Stan ignored the roaring surf. He was too furious to notice. "You're out of your fucking mind!" he screamed. A second later he slammed the phone receiver down, cracking the plastic cradle on the desk. Reams was livid. His conversation with Kim Hyun-Jae had just confirmed his worst fear. *They lost the damn boat—what a bunch of idiots!*

The Asian exporter had just informed Stan that the owners of the *Korean Star* were now officially listing the vessel as "missing and presumed sunk." The families of the ship's crew had been notified and the owners were in the process of filing a claim with the vessel's casualty insurance carrier.

For all practical purposes, the multimillion-dollar fish processor was being written off as a total loss. It only existed on paper for now. And there wouldn't be a search; no one had a hint of where to look. The ship had vanished somewhere in the central Pacific. The loss would be chalked up as another unsolved mystery of the sea.

The shock of learning that the ship had been declared a loss was bad enough. But what really set Stan off was Kim's offer of compensation: Kim had promised to return Stan's $25,000 down payment and an additional $50,000 for the loss of his merchandise.

Stan Reams was still fuming as he thought of the offer: *That little bastard—I oughta snap his neck! Fifty grand for my stuff! Hell, it's worth a thousand times that!*

Stan was incensed with the Korean merchant—and for good reason—but he was also furious with himself. *I should have just sent it in the damn shipping container, like I originally planned. It would have worked—I know it!*

Stan was now on the lanai, sitting in a deck chair. He looked out blindly into the blackness. He ignored the churning surf. He was locked in a brutal bout of self-criticism and defeatism. It was another low point of his life.

The trouble had started half a dozen years earlier. Back then, Stan was on top of the world. He had everything: a prosperous company, a profession he loved, a beautiful home and, most importantly, a wonderful family. But he managed to lose it all.

In the space of just a few years, he had plummeted from the crest of the wave to the bottom of the pit. It started with the divorce; then his business floundered; and finally his legacy was foreclosed. To say that Stan Reams was bitter was an understatement.

Stan wanted to cry as he thought back to those tumultuous years. The worst part of the whole ordeal was losing contact with his daughters. He hardly knew them anymore.

Stan stood up and stepped next to the deck railing. The strong onshore breeze ruffled his hair. *At least I've got this place,* he thought.

Stan hadn't quite lost everything. He had salted away slightly over a half-million dollars in cash years earlier. His ex-wife's attorneys never knew about the emergency fund. And the court-appointed bankruptcy trustee suspected that Stan had more resources than he admitted to but could never prove it.

After his corporate and personal assets were liquidated, Stan disappeared. He was too embarrassed to face any of his friends or business associates. To Stan, the stigma of bankruptcy was worse than any disease.

Stan had been living in Mexico for almost three years now. About every six months he would return to the States to visit his children. His ex had moved back to her native L.A. She had no idea that Stan was living in Baja.

Stan reached into his shirt pocket and pulled out a Winston. He lit up, cupping his hand over the lighter to shelter the flame from the breeze. He inhaled deeply. *What the hell should I do now?* he wondered. The *Korean Star* was missing. All he had was Kim's acknowledgment that it had been scheduled to arrive in Puerto Vallarta the night before it was due at Cabo.

Stan remained on the deck for five more minutes until he finally made the decision. *I've got to go,* he said to himself. *I have no choice now—it's all that's left.*

Stan took one last puff before flipping the spent butt over the rail. He turned around and walked back into his condominium. It was time for sleep. He needed rest before starting the trip.

*   *   *

The National Security Agency night-watch duty officer stared at his computer monitor. He was in a huge secret complex at Fort Meade, Maryland. A new Critical Intelligence Communication System (CRITCOM) message was coming in via satellite. The top-secret encrypted signal originated from an American electronic listening post at Misawa, Japan. An NSA signals intelligence (SIGINT) unit at the U.S. Air Force facility had intercepted another Russian radio transmission. The military communication had used a code word identifier that, when translated into English, was equivalent to the word "firewatch."

All intercepted FIREWATCH communications were automatically upgraded to CRITIC status. The messages were immediately decoded at the intercept point and then instantly reencrypted using NSA's most sophisticated cipher system. The repackaged message was then transmitted back to NSA headquarters and the White House via military satellite system.

The Russians expected that the United States might intercept their most secret communications. But they were not overly concerned; all of these messages were encrypted. They never imagined, however, that the NSA would manage to decipher one of their key code systems.

The duty officer scanned the message on his screen. It was an internal communication between a special military intelligence unit operating in the Far Eastern Territory and the Federal Security Service, a branch of the former KGB, headquartered in Moscow. The main body of the decoded text read:

CHELYABINSK SEVENTY THEFT STATUS.
VLADIVOSTOK SEARCH TEAM REPORTS NO PROGRESS IN LOCATING MISSING HEU. NOW SUSPECT THAT MATERIAL HAS BEEN EXPORTED. RECOMMEND CONTINUE OPERATION CHOSON.
ADVISE AS HOW TO PROCEED.
KIROV.

Operation Choson, thought the duty officer. *What the hell is a Choson?*

TWELVE

GUADALAJARA DON

"HI, SWEETIE. HOW YOU DOING?"

"Good, Daddy. When are you coming home?"

"Oh, in a week or so."

There was silence for a few seconds and then: "I miss you."

"I miss you, too. How's your kitty?"

"He's fine. Oscar likes it here. He likes to play with Grandma's doggie. They're friends."

"Good, I'm glad he likes Barney." A brief pause. "Now, Grandma told me that you went to the aquarium with her yesterday. Did you have fun?"

"Oh, yes! We saw some otters and seals and . . ."

Father and daughter continued to talk for the next ten minutes. Tom Parker thoroughly enjoyed the conversation. Keely was exceptionally bright for her age—just like her mother had been. He loved her more than anything. She was the light of his life.

"Okay, honey. You have a good day, now. I love you."

"Love you too, Daddy." Keely then handed the phone to her grandmother.

"Tom, everything okay down there?"

"Yeah, fine, Mom. Except it's too darn hot." Tom looked out toward the balcony of his hotel room. It was mid-morning. There was no wind and no cloud cover to filter the brutal tropical sun. Puerto Vallarta would be an oven by noon.

"Well, just make sure you keep covered up—you know how easy you burn."

"Yep, I've got a big bottle of sunscreen. I'll be careful."

"Don't forget to call us, now. We worry about you."

"I won't. And thanks a million for helping me out. I don't know what I'd do without you."

"You just take care of yourself down there. And hurry home."

"I will."

The late morning air had a cool, crisp bite to it. Ernesto Diaz welcomed the mild climate. Back in Puerto Vallarta it was already in the low nineties.

It had taken Ernesto all morning to make it to Guadalajara. He had left at sunrise, hitching a ride on an empty produce truck. The driver had dropped him off on the outskirts of town. Ernesto had been to Guadalajara many times before so he knew the giant city well. It would take him about half an hour to walk to his destination.

With a population of over two million, Guadalajara is Mexico's second largest city. It is also the capital of Jalisco State. Located a mile above sea level, the city has a dry and balmy climate, making it a popular health resort area. The rich soils of the region support an impressive farming community, and the numerous manufacturing and assembly plants that ring the city have transformed Guadalajara into one of Mexico's most important economic powerhouses. The city's excellent collection of universities, museums and art galleries has also made it the cultural hub of the region.

Guadalajara is also well known for one other distinction: it is the drug capital of Western Mexico. Vast amounts of marijuana, cocaine and heroin move through the city on a daily basis, smuggled into the country from South America and Asia. Guadalajara functions as a clearinghouse, sorting and repackaging the illicit drugs for eventual transport to the United States.

Dozens of small-time drug traffickers were based in Guadalajara but there were only a handful of major-league players. And just one of those was the reigning kingpin. Arnaldo Rodriguez ran the largest smuggling operation in Western Mexico. And he was the man that Ernesto Diaz had traveled so far to see.

Ernesto walked along the narrow dusty driveway. Barbed-wire fences ran along both sides of the dirt road. Dozens of longhorn cattle grazed on the scrub grass to the north. A couple of thoroughbreds pranced to the south. The quarter-of-a-mile-long drive terminated in a small compound consisting of four one-story brick and mortar buildings positioned in a U-shaped formation.

When Ernesto walked into the courtyard fronting the compound he was met by a mangy dog. The creature looked like it was starving but seemed to have plenty of energy. It repeatedly barked and snarled at the intruder.

Ernesto ignored the animal as he proceeded onto a brick walkway that led toward the center building. There were two vehicles parked by the building: an ancient Toyota pickup with badly rusted wheel wells and a brand-new Mercedes sedan. Thirty seconds later he was knocking on the front door.

The door opened. A heavy-set man, about forty years old, filled the doorway. He was dressed in bib overalls and wore sandals. His potbelly bulged outward; it looked as if he was pregnant. The stub end of a fat cigar hung out of the corner of his mouth. He was clean-shaven but his long black hair fell almost to his shoulders. "What do you want?" he asked in Spanish.

Ernesto smiled. "I've come to see Señor Rodriguez."

"What for?"

"I have personal business with him."

"Well, he's busy right now. You'll have to come back later." The fat man started to shut the door, but Ernesto stepped forward, blocking him. "No, I must see him now. I've come from Vallarta with important information."

The man started to push Ernesto out of the way when a voice from behind interrupted him. "Who is it, Pepe?"

The fat man turned to look back inside. "It's some dirty peon. I'll get rid of him."

Ernesto recognized the voice. He pushed harder against the door and started shouting. "Don Arnaldo Rodriguez, it is Ernesto Diaz from Puerto Vallarta. I have news for you about that ship." Ernesto's use of the title "Don" was a sign of respect for the man he wished to address.

A moment later the door opened and Ernesto was led inside. The interior of the building was nothing like its plain exterior suggested. The tile flooring was Italian marble, the modern Spanish furniture rich and warm, and the artwork on the walls was a combination of contemporary Mexican and ancient Indian.

Ernesto was led through the foyer into a large office. An eight-foot-long oak desk, the centerpiece of the office, was positioned next to a window wall. The view of the rolling pasture and grazing horses was spectacular. A four-arm ceiling fan located just forward of the desk whirled away, broadcasting a soft swishing sound.

The man sitting behind the desk was in his mid-thirties. He wasn't very big; he was only five and a half feet tall and weighed at most 140 pounds. His brown hair was cut close and his mustache was neatly trimmed. He was dressed in a silk shirt and white cotton trousers. His only jewelry was a Rolex watch.

Arnaldo Rodriguez stared at the peasant standing in front of him. The man looked like he was on his last legs. And he could smell the stench. "What's this information you have about a ship?" asked Rodriguez.

Ernesto smiled. "Don Arnaldo, I worked for you once, about a year ago, when you brought in that fishing boat near Las Hadas."

Rodriguez nodded. The man's face did look familiar now. He had hired a dozen laborers to help unload the tons of hashish that had been brought in by the Chinese trawler.

"Sir, my nephew, Juan, was with your men when they raided the ship."

"What are you talking about?" Rodriguez asked, trying to test the man. None of his men had returned from the operation. He had assumed they were all killed.

"The Korean ship. The one with the heroin."

"Go on," commanded Rodriguez.

"Juan was the cabin boy on the boat your men hired. He went with them." Ernesto paused. The cool air from the ceiling fan felt good. "Juan told me that something went wrong. The ship capsized and fell over on the boat. They both sank."

Rodriguez sat up straight in his leather chair. All along he had assumed that the Koreans had taken out his men. "How could that ship sink?"

"I don't know. Juan told me he heard gunfire and several explosions. And then it just rolled over on its side, crushing the little boat."

Rodriguez shook his head in disbelief. He had gotten wind of the drug transfer through one of his contacts in Puerto Vallarta. At that time, all the man knew was that a ship from Korea was to transfer several dozen kilos of heroin. The informant knew nothing about the recipients—only the location and approximate time of the transfer.

The information had been especially vital to Rodriguez. He controlled the Mexican coastline from Manzanillo to Mazatlán, and anyone wishing to smuggle drugs or other contraband through his territory had to first deal with his organization. The fee for operating in his backyard was a modest ten percent of the gross value of the commodity. Most paid the tribute, knowing that it was worth the cost in order to avoid trouble. But once in a while someone would try to cheat.

The Asian ship that was scheduled to off-load at Puerto Vallarta had not followed the rules. Rodriguez intended to make it a case example. His men were charged with confiscating the money and the drugs and were ordered to execute the principals from both sides. The ship would then be allowed to return to Korea. Rodriguez wanted the surviving crew to tell their story of terror. The whole operation had been designed to discourage future unauthorized encroachment on his territory. But something had gone terribly wrong. Not one of his men had made it back alive.

"Your nephew, Juan, he survived the sinking?"

"Yes, sir. He managed to swim ashore. He then told me what happened."

"Did anyone else survive?"

"From the Korean boat, no. But the two *gringos* did. Juan saw them leave in a speedboat."

Rodriguez's attention spiked. "*Norteamericanos*—are you sure?"

"Yes, and we know where one of them is staying." Ernesto reached into the right rear pocket of his jeans and removed a Polaroid snapshot. "I took this picture of him." He placed the wrinkled color print on the desktop.

"Tell me more," Rodriguez said as he stared at the photo of Dave Simpson.

An hour later Ernesto Diaz was on an air-conditioned bus heading back to Puerto Vallarta. His pockets were full of American greenbacks. The trip had been well worth the effort.

*   *   *

It was a few minutes before 1:00 P.M. and it was hot. The overhead sun was once again broiling Puerto Vallarta. Tom Parker was now camped out by the resort's pool, reading a day-old issue of *USA Today*. He wore a pair of blue cotton shorts with an orange tank top. His exposed skin was covered with the oily sheen of a sunscreen. A Seattle Mariners baseball cap shaded his face, and his sunglasses were the mirrored kind. They allowed him to stare without being seen.

The chairs and reclining lounges surrounding the huge pool were filled with over a hundred resort guests. There were all kinds: old men with potbellies, young women with firm rears and ample breasts, pear-shaped mothers watching over their flocks of children in the water and worn-out dads trying to catch a nap in the shade of the poolside palms. The constant din from the nearby pounding surf helped to mask the noise from the screaming kids and chattering women.

Although Tom's attire was simple and inexpensive, it did him justice. His well-muscled arms and legs, along with his flat belly, turned more than a few female heads as they paraded by. Tom ignored the stares. He was too busy working.

Tom had staked his claim a few hours earlier, ensuring the perfect surveillance point. He had a commanding view of the resort's main lobby as well as the concrete walkway that led to the time-share sales center.

Although the resort was operated as a hotel, it was really a time-share condominium. There were a total of five hundred units. The studio and one- and two-bedroom apartments were sold off in weekly increments. Those time slots not sold or not used by their owners were available for rent through the resort's hotel division. To date, about one-third of the time slots had been sold. The resort's developer maintained a large sales staff to sell off the remaining inventory. As an incentive to stimulate sales, the developer offered a forty percent sales commission.

Tom watched the constant stream of traffic into the sales center. So far, there had been the usual procession of staff as they led their victims to the boiler room. He recognized most of the hustlers. He had seen the same group of men and women for several days now. They all looked alike: slick, flashy and sexy.

The sales center was now filled and the high-pressure pitch was in full swing. Everything was normal, except for one element. The master salesman, the man the rest of the staff admired—and in some cases hated—was a no-show.

As Tom Parker paged through the newspaper he wondered where Dave Simpson could be. The man had never made it to the bar the previous night and now he failed to make it to work the next day. Tom was beginning to fear that Simpson had somehow stumbled onto the surveillance operation. If he had, then he and Linda Nordland's carefully thought out plan was ruined.

Tom decided to wait another hour. He would then have to tell Linda the bad news.

While Tom Parker remained staked out by the pool, Linda Nordland was in her suite, eight stories above the beach. The sliding glass door to the balcony was wide open and the two ceiling fans in the living room whirled away at a furious rate. Linda didn't like air-conditioning.

She was sitting cross-legged on a couch that faced the ocean. She wore a skimpy bikini—the kind that she would never wear in public. It exposed too much of everything. But in the privacy of her room it was perfect. She could stand the heat without having to be totally nude.

Linda had the handset of her phone glued to her left ear, and a thick three-ring binder was perched on her lap. She was wearing her spectacles, not yet bothering to slip in her contacts. Nordsoft's senior vice president was on the other end of the line. In spite of her vendetta, she still had a business to run.

"How about our contract with Packard-Bell?" asked Linda. "Have they signed the change order yet?"

"Yeah, we got the fax copy this morning."

"Great. Then let's get Martin's group working on that ASAP."

"You got it, boss."

"Okay, now what's the status of our contract with IBM?"

"We're right on schedule. We should be able to deliver version three point O by the middle of next month. I've got Wendy starting the . . ."

Linda Nordland was pleased with the report. It looked like Nordsoft would have another banner year.

Linda Nordland's wealth was multiplying each year—she was now worth twenty-five million. If her company continued to prosper, she might really make it into the big leagues.

Linda had started her software development company five years earlier. After rising to a midlevel manager's position at Microsoft, she had quit the software giant to start her own business. Using her half-million dollars of Microsoft stock options as collateral, she had secured a loan to start Nordsoft. To her amazement, and that of her banker, she had paid off the $450,000 note in just eighteen months. It was her new CAD program called *Nord-Draw* that did it.

Linda had toyed with the advanced computer-aided design concept for several years but could never generate any interest at Microsoft. The new application didn't fit in with the company's current development plans. Convinced that her idea would work, she had left her very secure position to pursue her dream.

So far, Nordsoft had sold a quarter of a million copies of *Nord-Draw*. It was immensely popular with engineers and architects, primarily because of its simplicity. The software actually allowed one to turn a rough, hand-drafted sketch into a finished drawing with a minimum of effort.

Another Nordsoft product was also selling well. *Nord-Draw Junior* was designed for kids. It allowed children to create their own custom drawings and sketches. It was a real hit in grades seven through nine.

Linda Nordland's company was a rising star in the world's software business. If Nordsoft continued to grow, she eventually planned to take it public.

"Okay, Bill, sounds like you've got everything under control. Keep up the good work."

"You bet, Linda." The man paused for a moment. "By the way, are you planning to return later this week?"

"I don't know yet. Why do you ask—is there a problem?"

"No, no. It's just that Sally and I are throwing a party on Saturday night, and we hoped that you might be back in town so you could join us."

Linda smiled. She liked Bill Sullivan. He was a loyal friend and a good family man. She couldn't have picked a better corporate executive. "Well, Bill, I've got a few more meetings down here before I can return so I don't know yet. If I get back in time, I'll be there."

"Oh, that would be great. But don't rush back just for that. You should take a few days off and enjoy yourself down there."

As far as Bill Sullivan and the rest of Nordsoft's 180 employees knew, Linda Nordland was in Mexico meeting with several potential customers from South America. Linda had created the ruse to quell the office rumors that she had a new lover and was taking off for a week-long rendezvous. Ever since her last romance, almost two years earlier, any man that she showed the slightest interest in was automatically pegged as her next husband.

Although Linda had an army of potential suitors back in Seattle, romance was the furthermost thing from her mind. She had only one goal for the trip: *put that bastard Dave Simpson out of business for good!*

"Well, Bill, maybe I'll sit in the sun for a few days if I finish early. Anyway, thanks for the update. I'll give you a call in a couple of days."

"Okay, Linda. Enjoy yourself."

"Thanks—I will."

Linda hung up the phone and walked to the balcony. She looked out toward the ocean. She wondered if Tom had spotted Simpson yet.

Tom Parker was discouraged. Simpson was still a no-show. He would remain at his post for another half hour but guessed that it was a waste of time. *Dammit,* he thought, *where the hell is that SOB?*

Dave Simpson was still in his condo suite, four floors above the pool level, sleeping like the proverbial baby. After the failed attempt to anchor over the *Korean Star* during the previous evening, Simpson hadn't made it home until 5:00 A.M. He had then collapsed on his water bed and fallen fast asleep. He wouldn't wake up until three that afternoon.

THIRTEEN
RED PORT ONE

WHEN THE JET FROM CABO TOUCHED DOWN IN PUERTO VAL-
larta, Stan Reams didn't have a hint about where to start his
search. He had never visited the popular resort community and
he knew absolutely no one there.

After taking a cab to a downtown hotel and checking in, he
sat on the tiny deck that projected from his fourth-floor room.
He sipped an ice-cold can of Pepsi while scanning the hotel's
Guide to Puerto Vallarta. It contained the usual stories: a few
paragraphs on the history of the city and its Mexican culture
followed by dozens of paid ads glorifying local restaurants,
nightclubs and golf courses. Like Cabo, Vallarta was geared
for the foreign tourists, especially Americans. Everything ad-
vertised revolved around sun, sand and sex.

Stan tossed the hardback guide onto the deck table. He liked
Mexico yet he still found himself occasionally longing for the
cool rainy days of his native Northwest. But he would never
see them again. It would hurt too much to return to Anacortes,
knowing he had lost his grandfather's legacy. A brand-new
fifty-unit luxury waterfront condominium project now occupied what had once been the family homestead.

Stan stood up and walked back into the living room of his
hotel suite, his mind now refocused on the task at hand. All
he had to work with was Kim Hyun-Jae's sketchy claim that
the *Korean Star* was scheduled to call on Puerto Vallarta before heading north to Cabo San Lucas. But the ship had disappeared.

How am I ever going to find out what happened to it? Stan
wondered as he paced back and forth across the tile floor. It
would have been easy for him to just write off the whole

venture to bad luck, but he couldn't let it go. He had invested too much of himself in the project. He had to know, one way or the other.

Stan was still drawing a blank when a new idea suddenly developed. *Yes, that just might work.* He walked over to the small desk by his bed and began rifling through its drawers. He found the phone directory a few moments later. It was the tourist edition; everything was written in English. It wouldn't have mattered to Stan if it had been in Spanish. He had mastered the language during his first year in Mexico.

Stan opened the back of the directory and began to search through the Mexican equivalent of the Yellow Pages. He soon found the heading he knew would be there: *Marinas and Yacht Services.* There were dozens of listings. He ripped out the tissue-thin pages and once again searched through the desk drawers. He found a map of the city and then set about locating the various marina and yacht businesses listed in the directory. Finally, he had a way to start his search.

Long ago, when Stan had worked at his grandfather's boat-yard, he had learned that the best way to locate a yacht whose owner had skipped out on paying his repair bill was to personally walk the docks of the local marinas and repair yards. The people who service the yachting and fishing industries are generally a tight-knit group that keep to themselves. However, they will usually loosen up if approached correctly. And Stan Reams knew exactly how to prime the pump.

By talking with the deckhands of other vessels, as well as the owners of the small businesses that serviced the yachts and ships, one could obtain a wealth of information. Invariably, someone would remember something about the boat or yacht in question. It might be as simple as a harbormaster who happened to recall seeing the vessel "running north." And sometimes you got real lucky, like when a crew member left his forwarding address with the pretty fuel-dock girl.

All Stan needed was a start and then he would track down the *Korean Star* and his missing cargo. He could not rest until he found her. He had been through too much to give up now.

The seed that had blossomed into Stan's fixation had been planted earlier in the year. Back then, he had been residing south of the border for almost two years. Although San Diego was a short flight away, he had avoided the States through a self-imposed exile. He ventured north only a couple of times a year, and then only to see his children. The rest of the time he wanted nothing to do with the U.S.A. He had even changed his last name, adopting Williams as his Mexican alias.

Stan's malice over the bankruptcy of his business and the foreclosure of his personal assets was like a cancer that attacked his soul. Every day it gnawed away at the good memories, leaving only the bad. Stan now loathed the system that had allowed him to prosper for so long but then had brutally pulled the rug from under his feet. His hard-earned wealth was gone, ripped apart by an act of Congress and then looted by the scores of greedy lawyers that fed on the remains. He would never forgive them—never.

When Stan first moved to Mexico, he had accepted his fate. Sure, he was bitter at what had happened but he blamed himself for most of the problems. He just wanted to forget about the bad times and start over with a clean slate.

About a month after arriving in Baja, Stan decided to make Cabo San Lucas his new home. He liked the fishing-village character of the harbor area, and the local marina was packed with boats. Because of his family background, he could pilot just about any type of yacht and had no trouble landing a job as a charter boat skipper. He was hired by a California-based investment group that owned three yachts. Each one of the sixty-five-footers was outfitted for deep-sea fishing.

After securing the job, Stan purchased a two-bedroom waterfront condominium near the marina. At the time, it was cheap and it suited his needs.

Stan enjoyed cruising in the Pacific and the Sea of Cortez. The warm waters and clear skies made the days go fast. And the fishing was good. It didn't take him long to learn the tricks of the trade. The other skippers helped, but it was his natural skills that made the difference. Within just a few months of starting his new career, he became one of the top marlin skippers in Baja.

Most of Stan's regular clients were American men, and many of those were Californians. They were all successful, ranging from world-class heart surgeons to Hollywood movie moguls. Quite often they would fly down from San Diego or L.A. on a Friday afternoon for a quick weekend of fishing.

They would then head back to their families and businesses on Sunday evening. Generally, the charter trips were an all-male affair. But once in a while his clients would bring their girlfriends with them.

Stan welcomed the females. They were usually a lot of fun. Most were in their twenties or early thirties, and every one of them was attractive. While their dates sat in fighting chairs on the stern, waiting for the elusive marlin to strike, the women frequently sunbathed topless on the foredeck. Stan, perched high up in the flying bridge, had a commanding view of the spectacle.

As much as Stan relished gazing at the women, he really didn't have much interest in them. It seemed that all of the romance had been drained out of him. Sure, he had an occasional fling with a bar girl or a resort guest back in Cabo, but that was just sex. Being in love was something that was now totally alien to him.

For two years, Stan continued to ply the waters off Baja. With his skipper's salary plus tips, and the modest interest he earned on his secret nest egg, he lived reasonably well. But he was bored. There was no mental challenge to his work. The weather hardly ever changed and his clients were all the same: fat, rich and arrogant. And more and more of them were lawyers! That really bugged him. But all of that changed when he met Nikolai.

Nikolai Mironovich Bessolov was a Russian businessman who hit it big in the import-export business. Based in Vladivostok, the thirty-eight-year-old Bessolov was a millionaire many times over.

Stan met Nikolai when he showed up at the marina one January morning. After concluding a business transaction in Long Beach, the Russian had flown down to Cabo for a mini-vacation. Stan's yacht was available and Bessolov had chartered it for a week.

Stan Reams was never the same. He and the bear-size Russian hit it off exceedingly well. The fishing was good, the waves were mild and the vodka supply seemed endless. By the time the yacht returned to its berth, Stan and Nikolai had established a solid friendship.

The contrast between the two men couldn't have been greater. Stan had been born rich and had had everything to live for. However, through changes in government policy and his own carelessness, he had lost his wealth. Nikolai, on the other hand, had been reared in abject poverty and had had nothing but misery to look forward to. But with the breakup of the Soviet Union came opportunity, and Nikolai had seized it with a death grip.

During the voyage, Nikolai continually probed into Stan's background. Stan never told him the complete story—only bits and pieces—but it was enough for the Russian. Two weeks after returning to Russia, Nikolai faxed Stan a letter, offering him a job and new chance to start over. It was an offer he couldn't refuse.

It was late February when Stan finally visited Vladivostok. The weather reminded him of Seattle—drizzly and gray. The giant seaport, located on Russia's Pacific coast, was thriving with activity. The harbor was full of ships and barges.

Nikolai was the consummate host. He set Stan up in a luxury suite in the city's best hotel, all expenses prepaid. He then personally took Stan on a day-long tour of the port and surrounding region.

Stan was amazed at how run-down the city looked. The streets were full of potholes, most of the buildings were old and drab and there was trash strewn everywhere. There had been little effort to maintain the city for years. It was literally falling apart day by day.

As pitiful as Vladivostok's infrastructure appeared, what really shocked Stan was the abandoned military equipment: it was everywhere. Tanks, rocket launchers, artillery pieces, armored personnel carriers and legions of heavy-duty trucks were parked haphazardly throughout the city. Most of the equipment was new. There were even scores of high-performance jets and heavy-lift aircraft parked in a massive storage yard near the airport. Most impressive of all were the rows of abandoned nuclear-powered submarines in the harbor. The majority were floating but he counted half a dozen grounded hulks on the mud flats. They looked like beached whales.

Nikolai's tour had the desired impact. On the way back to the hotel, Stan couldn't contain his curiosity any longer. ''What the hell is all this stuff doing here?'' he finally asked.

"I hardly see any military supervision at all—anyone could walk right in and take it."

Nikolai smiled. "That's right. Anybody can, and that's why I brought you here. I wanted you to see it firsthand."

"But why?"

"Because of your technical background, you know far more about missiles and aircraft than I will ever know."

"I don't understand."

"Stan, I want you to help me sell it."

"Sell what?"

"Everything you saw. I have the exclusive rights to sell it all."

"What?"

Nikolai smiled again. He expected the confusion. "You see, Stan, Moscow has all but abandoned the Far East. We're more or less on our own out here. Consequently, we have to take care of ourselves. And that means . . ."

For the next half hour Nikolai told an amazing story, one that was hardly ever reported in the Western press. Russia was an economic misfit and would be for decades to come. There was no money available to help the outlying territories. Every extra ruble was being spent in the major population centers in the European half of the country. Food was again scarce and the only hope of preventing civil war was to take care of the masses. And that meant that the remote areas of Russia suffered—badly.

With only token support from the central government, Vladivostok had evolved into a frontier city. Gangs of thugs roamed the streets, drug addicts were everywhere, pilferage of cargo in the harbor was rampant and prostitution was a growth industry. Yes, there was a police and military presence, and most of them were honest. But it wasn't nearly enough and there were more than a few bad apples in the lot. At best, the authorities helped control the traffic and occasionally picked the drunks off the streets.

The real power in Vladivostok rested with men like Nikolai Bessolov. There were just a handful of them. Several years earlier, they had formed a loose confederation, merging their independent operations into a single organization. They called it Red Port One.

Red Port One controlled nearly every illegal activity in the city, continually expanding operations into the outlying areas. Besides the routine of petty theft, gambling, extortion and prostitution, it specialized in two high-profit ventures: drug trafficking and the illegal export of weapons. Nikolai Bessolov headed up the weapons division.

Nikolai went on to explain that Red Port One had cut a deal with several local military commanders to sell off the excess hardware. The corrupt officers were paid hundreds of times their annual salaries in order to turn a blind eye when a brand new T-72 tank disappeared or when a MiG-29 was gutted for its parts. One Naval officer had even officially reported to Moscow that an older attack submarine had been towed to sea and sunk because its nuclear reactor was leaking radiation. In reality, however, the perfectly intact hull had been sold to Pakistan for five million dollars.

"You want me to help you sell all of these weapons?" Stan asked, still overwhelmed at the enormity of Nikolai's proposal.

"Yes, you understand how all of this hardware works. All you'll need to do is . . ."

Nikolai went on to explain the arrangement. Stan would serve as a roaming technical sales agent for Red Port One, putting deals together. He'd receive a 1.5 percent cut on the gross sales price of every transaction he put together. It was a sweet deal indeed. The year before, Bessolov's division had grossed $100 million. He was expecting to double that volume for the current year.

Stan didn't have to think it over. He accepted on the spot.

Stan spent the next week inventorying Red Port One's assets. Nikolai supplied him with a new Mercedes, complete with a driver and a bodyguard. Stan used his laptop Apple computer to record the equipment supplies. He thought it strange that not one person challenged his authority to examine the weaponry. It wasn't until later that he learned that the tiny red flag on the car antenna identified the vehicle as belonging to Red Port One. It was a key that could open any and all doors in Vladivostok.

After completing his inventory, Stan planned to return to Mexico. He would be traveling through South America, Europe and Asia for the next three to four months and wanted to make sure his Cabo property was taken care of. A few days before he left, however, Nikolai invited him to visit his *dacha*. That's where he met Irina.

Nikolai's country home was about twenty miles north of Vladivostok. The *dacha* fronted on a beautiful lake that was still ice-covered. The purpose of the visit was to introduce Stan to the other leaders of Red Port One. The five men were all scheduled to arrive by seven that night. Besides Stan, two dozen guests were also invited.

The party was lavish, even by Western standards. The tables were full of fresh fruits, vegetables and meats of all kinds. There were also lavish cuts of smoked salmon and trays full of the finest caviar. And the vodka flowed freely.

There was even a photographer. The middle-aged woman roamed through the crowds, randomly triggering her flash.

By 9:00 P.M. most of the hosts were smashed, including Bessolov. Stan, however, was stone sober. He drank nothing but ice water. He had no idea what to expect from the other *capos* and wanted to maintain all of his faculties, just in case.

While Bessolov and his comrades jabbered away in Russian, Stan turned away, heading back to the table to fill up on more salmon. And then he saw her. There were a dozen women in the smoke-filled room and most were attractive, but none matched the beauty he was looking at.

She was young—mid to late twenties—blond, and very slim. The sleek dress she wore highlighted her figure. Her bustline was on the small side, but her slender legs and rounded hips diffused raw sex.

They made eye contact. And then she walked toward him.

"So you must be the American." she said. Her English was exceptional; there was only a trace of accent.

Stan smiled. "Yes, and whom do I have the privilege of meeting?"

She held out her hand. Her nails were chopped back to the quick. "I'm Irina. You must be Mr. Williams," she said.

"Stan," he said, shaking her delicate hand.

"Tell me, Stan," she said, "what is America really like?"

"Well, I don't live there anymore—by choice—so I'm probably not the best person to ask."

Irina nodded. "I understand all of that. Nikolai told me. But please, tell me anyway. I'm very curious—I've never been to the United States."

"Okay."

They moved to a quiet corner and Stan began to speak. He was surprised at how easy it was to talk with the woman. Her interest was genuine.

While Stan and Irina chatted, the hired photographer walked up and said something in Russian to Irina. Irina smiled and slipped her arm around Stan's waist, pulling herself close to him. She then pointed toward the far end of the room. Nikolai was standing there, looking back.

"Smile for the camera, please," Irina said. "Nikolai wants a picture."

Stan wrapped his arm around her waist and grinned. He now understood. Irina was his date for the evening, a present from Nikolai.

Stan and Irina left the party early, retiring to Stan's bedroom on the second floor. Stan hadn't felt the need for months but it hit him like an avalanche. He wanted the petite Russian in the worst way. And she seemed to express equal passion. Whether it was real or not, he didn't care.

By midnight Stan's desire had been sated. He and Irina were lying side by side in the huge bed. She was sleeping; he was wide awake.

The room was hot. Their lovemaking had been intense but it was the faulty thermostat that made it so warm. The covers were lying on the floor and there was just enough light from the flickering candle to see by. That's when Stan spotted the marks. They were just tiny pinpricks, but they covered Irina's left underarm and there were more around her ankle. *What the hell's wrong with her?* he wondered.

Stan was about to take a closer look when the shooting started. It sounded like World War III.

Nikolai Bessolov and his partners had still been going full-bore downstairs when the special police unit attacked. Dispatched from Moscow, the Federal Security Service commandos had been ordered to capture the leaders of Red Port One. Their activities were becoming a real threat to the government.

Irina woke instantly. "We must leave now," she shouted. She stood up and began to throw her clothing on.

"What's all that shooting about?" Stan asked as he followed her lead.

"I don't know. It could be the police or the Army. Maybe

even one of Nikolai's competitors. Anyway, we've got to leave now. This could turn into a real slaughter.'' She was almost dressed; she hadn't bothered with her underwear.

''But where do we go?'' Stan was struggling with his trousers.

''I know a way out.'' Irina opened the door and looked down the hall. It was clear. The noise from the automatic gunfire, however, resonated down the corridor. She turned back to Stan. Stan's eyes focused on her purse. She was fumbling with the latch. A moment later she pulled out the pistol. It was a nine-millimeter automatic.

''Jesus, where'd that come from?''

''It's mine.'' She paused for a second. Her eyes were cold and alert, like a cat ready for the kill. ''Now here's what we're going to do. I want you to . . .''

Irina had thought through the escape plan well in advance of the police raid. The threat was always there, following her wherever she went.

She and Stan made it out of the *dacha* undetected and ten minutes later they found the shed. The tiny log cabin was hidden in the trees a few hundred yards away. Inside were half a dozen sets of down parkas, boots, wool caps and gloves as well as skis and snowshoes.

Stan was shivering as he pulled on the garments. Irina, almost half naked in her evening gown, didn't appear to be suffering from the near-freezing temperature.

''What the hell do we do now?'' asked Stan. He could still hear the gunfire. The battle continued.

''We walk to the other side.'' She pointed to the lake, off to her left. There was just enough moonlight reflecting off the ice-covered surface to see it.

''But isn't that ice starting to break up?''

''Yes. We'll have to be careful. Come now, we must go. There's no time to talk.''

Irina turned and headed toward the lake. Stan followed, too confused and too scared to do anything on his own.

Stan and Irina were the only ones to escape. Nikolai and three of his partners were killed in the firefight. The two surviving Red Port One principals and the rest of the support staff were arrested. The Special Forces unit had choreographed the assault with pinpoint precision. The attack had been designed to decapitate the crime syndicate—and it did.

It was a textbook raid, except for one problem: the principal quarry, the prime target, the one they really wanted—Irina Sverdlova—escaped.

For three days, Stan and Irina hid out in a tiny shanty in Vladivostok. The one-bedroom shack was located on the harbor's edge, near the port docks. It was one of Bessolov's safe houses. Only he and Irina knew about it.

On the second day, after a long session of lovemaking, Irina told Stan about the special cargo. It was sitting in a wood crate inside a warehouse in South Korea.

At first he didn't believe her story. But when she began to recite technical specifications and highly complex design details, he changed his mind. To his utter amazement, Irina Sverdlova was a highly educated engineer. She knew what she was talking about.

Stan refused to help. The risk was too high, and besides it was immoral. He had to draw the line somewhere.

Irina persisted, and in the end, she pleaded for his help. She couldn't do it herself; she needed to lie low for at least a few weeks. The police were looking for her everywhere, and she would have to arrange for a new passport before she could attempt to leave.

Stan, on the other hand, was an outsider, not yet tainted by his association with Red Port One. As far as anyone else in Vladivostok knew, he was just another of the many potential arms buyers that shopped in Red Port One's citywide store.

Stan finally agreed. Irina gave him the location of the crate and its identification number. It was to be shipped by ocean transport to a holding company in Italy. From there, it would pass through several more hands before it ended up at its ultimate destination.

The regime in Tripoli had already made all the arrangements and paid Red Port One the twenty-million-dollar down payment. The remaining twenty million dollars would be deposited in Bessolov's personal numbered Swiss account upon the cargo's arrival in Palermo. Irina planned to be there when the ship arrived. She had the code to Nikolai's account. She desperately needed access to the money.

Stan left the safe house early on the fourth day. He needed to change airline tickets and make reservations for a flight that would eventually get him to Korea. When he finally returned, around noon, he found Irina lying across the bed on her back. Her dilated eyes were wide open, staring at the peeling paint on the ceiling. Her lips were turquoise. She didn't move a muscle.

She was dead.

Stan stared at her body, unbelieving. And then he saw the syringe. It had a small plastic cartridge. The needle was inserted into a vein on the top of her left foot. *My God, what happened?*

He had asked her about the needle marks before. She had explained that she was a diabetic and that she rotated between different parts of her body for her daily insulin injections. Stan had believed her lies.

Stan remained in the tiny shack until nightfall, unsure of what to do. He was torn by the woman's death but there was nothing he could do for her now. When he finally left, he placed a sheet over her corpse.

Stan left Vladivostok that night. He took the first flight out he could get. The Alaska Airlines jet landed in Anchorage early the next morning.

FOURTEEN
NIGHT WORK

DAVE SIMPSON WALKED OUT OF THE RESORT AT A QUARTER to seven. Pete Chambers was waiting for him in a Chevy van. It was double-parked along the asphalt driveway that fronted the main lobby. The van took off as soon as Dave climbed inside.

Tom Parker wasn't around to observe the rendezvous, but two of Arnaldo Rodriguez's men were. They had been waiting all afternoon in the hotel's parking lot, sitting inside a beat-up Ford sedan. Both men recognized Simpson the second he stepped out of the lobby. His size alerted them and then Ernesto Diaz's Polaroid photo confirmed the sighting.

Dispatched from Guadalajara earlier in the day, the sentries were under strict orders to locate the *norteamericano*. He wasn't to be touched, only discreetly followed.

Twenty minutes later, the van pulled into the harbor parking lot just as the sun was in its final descent. The ocean horizon was alive with brilliant vermilion and jasmine tones. It would be black in minutes.

Dave Simpson opened the passenger door and stepped onto the asphalt. Pete Chambers followed a second later. "You remember to take your seasick pills?" asked Simpson as he headed down a concrete pier. The *Pacific Salvor* was moored at the end of the 300-foot-long structure.

Chambers caught up with his partner. "Yeah, I took two of them this time."

"Good. That should do the job."

"I guess so—if they don't put me to sleep first."

"Well, the sea's been a lot calmer today so maybe we'll get this sucker put to bed tonight."

Chambers just nodded. He didn't say what he was really thinking. *Dear God, please let me get that money back tonight.* The attorney was running out of time. He had to replace the missing funds from the trust account or the automatic audit would reveal his theft.

Just ten minutes after Simpson and Chambers boarded the *Pacific Salvor,* the salvage vessel slipped its moorings and headed for the harbor entrance. The ocean was a millpond.

Rodriguez's men tracked the ship's running lights as it headed northeastward into Banderas Bay. Both men were at a loss to explain what they had just witnessed. When the vessel was no longer visible, they tried to find a pay phone—a sometimes difficult task in Mexico. Ten minutes later they phoned in their observations.

The message finally reached Arnaldo Rodriguez at half past eight. He was in a tiny restaurant on the outskirts of Guadalajara, entertaining his favorite mistress. He ordered the spies to remain at the pier. They were to report directly to him when the ship returned.

*　　*　　*

Tom Parker knocked on the door. There was no response. He knocked again, this time louder.

"Just a minute," called out a voice. He could barely hear it.

A few seconds later, Tom heard the *click-clack* of sandals on tile. "Who is it?" asked the voice.

"It's Tom. I need to talk with you."

The dead bolt was pulled back and the door swung open. Tom's eyes almost burst from his head as he stared at Linda Nordland. She was only partially dressed. She wore a terry-cloth bathrobe that came halfway down to her knees and her obviously damp hair was wrapped up in a white towel. But what really received his attention was the partially open front of her bathrobe. It was secured only by a belt around her waist and there wasn't much of an overlapping collar. Consequently, the cleavage of her breasts was exposed.

"Come on in, Tom. I just got out of the shower." Linda turned around and walked back into her suite. She was completely oblivious to Tom's astonishment.

Tom walked into the living room. Linda headed into the adjoining bedroom.

"Make yourself a drink. I'll just be a minute," she called out.

"You want anything?" he asked as he moved to the bar.

"Sure—a little Bombay and tonic. On the rocks."

"You got it."

Tom found the gin bottle and had just begun to mix Linda's drink when he happened to look up at the wall mirror next to the bar. He could see the double reflection of his client through another mirror in the bedroom. She was standing by her bed, well away from the partly open doorway. But because of the angles of the two mirrors, he could see her. She had dropped the bathrobe and was now completely nude. She had her slim back to him and was leaning over a suitcase on the bed. She was searching for something inside. A moment later she reached down and started to slip on a pair of black lace panties.

Stop it, you damn fool, Tom told himself. But he couldn't turn his eyes away. *God, she's beautiful.*

When Linda started to hook a brassiere, Tom finally regained control. He stepped away from the mirror, breaking his line of sight.

A minute later Linda entered the living room. She wore a loose-fitting white cotton blouse and a tan skirt.

Tom handed Linda the drink. She sat down on the couch and crossed her legs. "Cheers," she said as she momentarily held out her glass.

"To your health," Tom replied.

They both took a sip and then Linda met Parker's eyes. "Well, Tom, what's up?"

He smiled. "He's still around."

"He's still here?" Her voice was filled with hope. "Then maybe we can do it tonight."

Tom raised his hand up. "Hang on a sec. All I know is that he hasn't left town. After striking out by the pool this afternoon I did a little checking at the lobby desk. I told the clerk I was buying a unit from him and was trying to find out when he'd return. He bought my line. It turns out that Simpson left a message saying he wouldn't be back until some time tomorrow."

"Where'd he go?"

"The clerk had no idea, but based on what I've observed so far I'd say he's probably up to something shady." He paused for a moment. "But then I don't have a clue as to what it could be."

"Hmm, that sounds just like the jerk. Anything else?"

"No, but it does appear that we'd be wasting our time tonight so I don't think you need to get all dolled up."

Linda laughed. "You mean I don't have to wear my sleazy-lady outfit tonight."

Oh, God, no. I want to see you like that again! is what he wanted say. Instead, he replied: "Yeah, that won't be necessary." He carefully chose his next words. "I was thinking that since we have a free night, maybe we could go out together— have dinner and see the sights."

"You mean like a date?" she asked with a friendly smile.

"Well, yeah, kind of." And then he added, "This would be strictly off the clock and my treat."

Linda smiled again. She didn't think of Tom as a paid hand. He was more than that now. "I'd like that very much, Tom. Now, what do you suggest that I wear?"

Parker's heart beat a little faster. He hadn't felt like this in a very long time. "Gee, what you've got on now is perfect."

"Great," she said as she stood up. "Let's go."

Okay, old boy, Parker said to himself as he escorted Linda out of the room, *what have you done now?*

The mooring was complete by half past eleven. Compared to the previous evening, anchoring over the wreck of the *Korean Star* was strictly routine. All four of the *Pacific Salvor's* anchors bit hard into the sandy bottom and the two-foot swells that rolled in from the west hardly strained the steel mooring cables.

Captain Osterback didn't waste any time deploying the ROV. It was immediately launched and four hours later the salvage mission was complete. The ROV was reeled back aboard the *Pacific Salvor,* along with Pete Chambers' Samsonite suitcase and the mysterious timber crate, both recovered from Captain Yook's secret compartment.

Simpson and Chambers were now in the ship's main salon, busy examining the booty.

Pete Chambers had commandeered the dining table, emptying the suitcase's contents onto it. He already had hundreds of soggy twenty, fifty and hundred-dollar bills neatly laid out on the tabletop. He was humming a catchy tune while using a portable hair drier to dry out the money.

Dave stood off to the side watching his partner. *This ought to make him happy,* he thought.

Pete Chambers was indeed happy. His spirits skyrocketed when the suitcase was opened and the waterlogged bundles of cash spilled out.

Dave Simpson hated to think that the million-plus dollars would be on its way back to San Diego within twenty-four hours, but he was resolved to that fact. Several times he had tried to convince Pete to keep the money for another deal, but Chambers would have nothing to do with that plan. Every dime was going back into the trust account, including what would be left over from the emergency funds he had borrowed to finance the salvage operation.

Dave Simpson stepped forward and picked up a hundred-dollar bill. It was still a little damp. He held the bill next to his nose. It smelled like seaweed. Dave grinned as he turned to face his friend. "Pete, is this what they call laundered money?"

Chambers laughed. "I don't know about laundered, but at least it's had a good salt bath."

"How are you going to return it?"

"I'll deposit it in the bank and then have Lorca wire the funds back to San Diego."

"How much is that pirate going to charge for that service?"

"I don't know for sure, but it'll probably be a couple of points."

"Jesus, that's outrageous!"

"Yeah, I know, but I've got no choice. There's no way I can get that much cash back into the States without setting off major alarms. This way it's all cleaned up, neat and proper."

Simpson shook his head. *Twenty-five grand for his just handling the cash for half a day. Bankers—they're the real bandits,* he thought.

Dave moved toward the aft end of the compartment to where Captain Osterback was sitting in a chair. He was sipping a cup of coffee.

"Lots of green, eh, Skip?" asked Simpson.

"You two are very lucky to get your money back."

"Boy, you're telling me." Simpson sat down beside the vessel owner. "You know, Einar, that other box I spotted in the freezer compartment might just be chock-full of heroin. It's just waiting there for us to get it."

Osterback took another sip before responding. "Yeah, but do you think it'll be any good?"

"What do you mean?"

"Well, that stuff ain't like cash. If it gets wet, it'll turn to shit for sure."

"Don't worry about that. I saw how they had it wrapped up. That stuff'll be just fine if we get to it soon. The only reason we lost our load was that the cardboard box and the bags inside were shredded by bullets."

Osterback nodded. "Okay, then I suggest that we head back out tonight and do a recon dive."

"Great. Same time?"

"Yep."

"Okay, I'll be there." Dave was delighted. He was still going to pull off this deal after all. He stood up and was just heading to the galley when Captain Osterback called out to him.

"I'm going to check out that crate," he said. "You want to see what's inside?"

Dave had forgotten about the mysterious crate that was now sitting on the fantail. "You bet."

A few minutes later Simpson and Osterback were at the stern of the ship. A ribbon of white water trailed off into the distance as the ship charged forward. The timber crate was sitting on the steel deck, next to a hydraulic davit. A ten-foot-diameter puddle of water surrounded the box.

Dave Simpson was wondering how they'd open the container when Captain Osterback stepped into a nearby passageway. When he returned he was carrying a crowbar in one hand and a large claw hammer in the other. He handed Simpson the hammer and then both men set about disassembling the crate. It took them about a minute to remove the top panel.

Both men peered into the open box. It was stuffed solid with some type of packing material that was now completely saturated. Dave reached inside and removed a handful of gooey material. It looked like papier-mâché.

"What the hell is this stuff?" he asked.

Captain Osterback grabbed a thin scrap of the material. Holding the object up to the light, he could see lettering. "It's newsprint, I think."

Simpson retrieved a small fragment and examined it. "Yeah, you're right." He stared at the funny-looking lettering a few seconds before continuing. "But what the hell language is it? None of the words make any sense and a lot of the letters are backwards."

Backwards? thought Captain Osterback. He again looked at his own piece. And then it hit him. "I'll be damned. I think this is Russian newsprint."

"Russian?"

"Yeah, this is Russian newspaper. I'm sure of it now."

"Jesus, you mean whatever's in this box came from Russia?"

"Yeah, I guess so."

Both men's interest suddenly surged as the mystery deepened. A couple of minutes later, after jointly bailing out the pulp, they found the steel case. It was about three and a half feet long, two feet wide and two feet tall. It had settled to the bottom of the crate.

Dave Simpson was now standing inside the crate. His jeans were soaked up to his ankles as he waded in the muck that surrounded the box. He was leaning over, trying to lift the box. "This son of a bitch is slipperier than snot," he said. He finally managed to get a grip on one side, but he could barely move it.

Simpson looked up at Captain Osterback. "Give me a hand, will ya? This thing feels like a million pounds."

What could be inside? wondered Osterback as he leaned forward to help. And for just a few seconds he let his imagination run wild. *Gold bullion! It's got to be gold bullion.*

Both men were now kneeling on the deck next to the timber crate. The mysterious steel case was sitting on the metal decking. Captain Osterback was shaking his head while Simpson cursed. "Shit, how the hell do you open this sucker? It's sealed up tighter than Fort Knox."

The steel case had been welded shut along every edge. There were no openings nor any makings to indicate how to open it. The mystery continued.

"I guess we'll have to burn it open," answered Osterback.

"Burn it?"

"Yeah, with a torch. It won't take long."

"Well, let's do it, then." Simpson's curiosity was really getting to him now.

"Can't. We'll have to wait until we get back to port."

"Why?

"I don't have any acetylene. Ran out a couple of days ago and haven't replaced it yet."

"Can you get that stuff in Puerto Vallarta?"

"Sure. I was supposed to pick up a couple of bottles yesterday but I forgot. Don't worry about it, though. Once we're in port I'll have one of the boys pick up a bottle and then we'll crack this baby open."

"Okay."

Neither man said anything, but they both had the same thought. *It's got to be gold!*

FIFTEEN
A NEW BEGINNING

TOM PARKER ROLLED FROM HIS RIGHT SIDE ONTO HIS BACK. The four-bladed fan above the bed was still whirling away at a frantic rate. The bedroom had already warmed to eighty degrees and the air descending onto his naked body helped cool him.

Tom turned his head to the left, spotting the clock radio on the nightstand. It was a few minutes past 6:00 A.M. He had slept only a few hours but he still felt wonderful; it was as if his body had been recharged with unlimited energy.

Tom again rotated his head, this time turning to the right. The mat of blond hair on the pillow next to his own was still there. *God, she's wonderful,* he thought as he stared at her.

Linda Nordland purred softly as she slept. She was on her left side, facing Tom and curled up under a single white sheet. Her right hand clutched the sheet's end under her chin. There was just a trace of rouge remaining on her cheeks and her blue-tinted mascara was slightly blurred. Otherwise, she looked perfect. He wanted to kiss her but didn't. Unlike Tom, Linda was exhausted and had fallen into a deep sleep.

Parker needed a cigarette but didn't feel like getting out of bed just yet. Instead, he closed his eyes and thought back to the previous evening. It was a whirlwind, a time he would never forget.

Linda and Tom had started the evening with a fabulous dinner in the Marina Vallarta district. The restaurant was built on the peak of a lighthouse-shaped tower that looked out over the harbor. The fresh swordfish was excellent and the wine smooth.

After taking a long walk around the marina basin they ended

up at a nightclub at one of the megaresorts that fronted on the ocean. The smoke-filled lounge was packed with tourists, but they were able to find a tiny table just off the dance floor. It was a perfect spot and they had a marvelous time.

At first, Tom was reluctant to let his guard down. Although he was with a beautiful woman and they were on a date, she was still his employer. Linda Nordland was paying him eight hundred dollars a day plus all of his expenses.

For years Parker had adhered to a simple canon of his profession: don't get emotionally involved with a client. With Linda, Tom recognized the obvious conflict of interest and did his best to remain aloof. But he failed. Miserably. It was the band that did it.

The group was from L.A. and throughout the evening it played a medley of '60s and '70s rock-and-roll hits. Many of them were his favorites and, as it turned out, Linda's favorites too. The high-voltage tunes were fun to fast-dance to but it was the slow love songs that really got to both of them. When the last song, a classic by the Righteous Brothers, played out at 2:00 A.M. Tom's defenses had completely broken down. He was putty in Linda's hands.

They hurried back to the resort. Linda almost dragged Tom into her suite and before they ever made it to the bedroom, all of their clothing was stripped off.

For over an hour, the lovemaking was nonstop. Tom was thankful that he had stopped drinking at midnight; otherwise he would never have been able to keep up with Linda. She was like a caged tiger that had escaped from her pen. All she wanted was to run and run and run. . . .

The sex was satisfying. It had been three years since he'd been with a woman—his wife. But more important, it was the intimacy of the encounter that he cherished the most. He had forgotten how wonderful it was just to hold a woman in his arms, taste her lips, smell her scent, feel her skin, caress her hair.

Tom had not allowed himself to get close to another woman after losing Lori. He just couldn't handle it. Besides, he had to remain focused and that meant he couldn't afford to get close to anyone—except for Keely and his mother. The bastards were still out there someplace and he was going to find them.

The antidepressant hadn't helped matters, either. One of its side effects was loss of sex drive.

Tom slid his legs over the side of the bed and carefully stood up. He didn't want to disturb Linda. He found a towel hanging over the back of a chair and wrapped it around his waist. He then walked over to the dresser and discovered a pack of Linda's Merits. He extracted one of the cigarettes and grabbed a matchbook.

Tom walked out onto the bedroom balcony. The heavy sliding glass door was already open; Linda favored natural ventilation over air-conditioning. Parker didn't mind, though. He was acclimating well to the tropical heat.

While staring at the ocean, he lit up. Tom felt the familiar rush after the first couple of drags. For just a fleeting moment he wondered if he'd ever quit smoking.

The Pacific was quiet this morning. The beat of the surf was barely audible and there was just a faint band of white water at the sand/sea interface. The beach in front of the resort was deserted, except for an elderly Mexican woman who walked along the crest of the beach berm. She was scavenging through the sand with a stick, looking for anything of value that might have been left by the hordes of tourists who camped out there every day.

Tom again inhaled deeply. He was thinking about taking a shower when he felt the moist kiss on the back of his neck. He turned around. Linda stood next to him. Like Tom, she had wrapped a towel around herself. Her breasts were barely contained by the garment; her long tan legs were exposed from midthigh down. And she had combed her golden hair so that it cascaded onto her shoulders. She looked stunning in the early morning light.

"Well, good morning, darling," Tom said.

Linda didn't reply. Instead, she just smiled as she reached for his right hand. He guided the cigarette to her mouth and she inhaled deeply.

"Thanks," she said as she let go of his hand.

"Did I wake you up?" he asked.

"No. The sunlight woke me up." That was true enough but what she didn't add, however, was that her full bladder had really awakened her.

"I guess we should have drawn the blinds last night."

"No, that's okay. I like the sunrise. It's the best time of the day for me."

Tom nodded and raised his hand with the nearly spent cigarette. Linda leaned forward and took the final drag. Tom crushed the butt in an ashtray on the balcony table.

Tom's energy level was increasing as the sun continued to rise. He felt like jogging. "You want to go for a run, along the beach? The temperature's just right."

Linda smiled as she stepped closer. "Maybe later, lover. But I had a different kind of exercise in mind right now."

"You did!" Tom said with a wide grin on his face.

"Yeah, I feel like running another marathon." She then gestured to the nearby bed. "Are you up for it?"

Tom pulled her close and gave her a long, wet kiss.

He was up to it all right. Linda found that out when she reached under his towel.

The lookouts in the Ford sedan spotted the *Pacific Salvor* when she turned down the main navigation channel and headed toward the pier. Ten minutes later the ship was moored at the T-head end of the pier.

"Where do you think they went?" asked the driver in Spanish.

"I don't know," answered the other man who sat in a bucket seat next to the driver. "Maybe they were fishing."

The driver shook his head. "Fishing—that doesn't look like any fishing boat to me."

"Well, what else could they be doing? It was gone all night."

"Who knows? Anyway, it's not our concern. All we're supposed to do is watch."

"Should we report in that the ship has returned?"

The driver hesitated for a moment. "Yeah, might as well. You make the call this time. I'll keep a watch out from here. No telling when those Yankees will leave."

"Okay."

The two Mexican lookouts didn't have long to wait. About twenty minutes after the ship docked, they spotted the Americans. Pete Chambers and Dave Simpson were walking along the pier, heading toward shore. Pete carried the suitcase in his right hand. It was heavy.

Simpson was talking. "Say, Pete, I don't think it's such a great idea to be carrying all this cash around right now."

"Yeah, well, I'm sure as hell not going to leave it with Captain Osterback. I don't trust that pirate a bit."

"Oh, I think he's okay."

"Yeah, well, that's fine for you, but just the same I'm not taking any more chances. My butt's been hanging out in the wind for too long as it is."

Simpson couldn't really blame his partner. Pete wasn't cut out for the business. "Well, what the heck are you going to do with the money? That damn bank won't open until ten A.M." He looked at his watch. "That's three hours from now."

"Don't worry about that. No one's going to take this from me. I'll cut their balls off first." Pete then reached into his jeans pocket and removed the switchblade knife. Then, with a flip of his wrist the six-inch-long blade snapped into position.

"Damn! Where'd you get that thing?" asked Simpson.

"I bought it from Carlos, at the resort. It's my security."

"Yeah, I guess so."

Wow! Pete's really wired up for this one, thought Simpson as he silently walked alongside Chambers. All thoughts of trying once again to convince Pete to hang onto the cash evaporated.

The lookouts watched the two men as they climbed into the van. When the vehicle pulled out of the parking lot, they followed. Rodriguez's new orders had been explicit: don't lose sight of the *gringos* under any circumstances.

At the opposite end of the harbor, about a mile away, a man dressed in tan shorts, white T-shirt, and a wide-brim Panama hat was starting his rounds. The cab had just dropped him off.

Stan Reams had no idea where to look or who to talk with. But his intuition told him that the answer to the mystery was somewhere along the waterfront. He was possessed with his mission. He would not stop until he discovered the fate of the *Korean Star.*

*   *   *

The mysterious FIREWATCH intercept was finally routed to someone who could make sense of it. The Russian cipher remained an enigma to the Fort Meade analysts.

It took the DIA specialist at the Pentagon just a minute to figure it out. Her Ph.D. was in East Asian history. She was now on a secure phone to her counterpart at the National Security Agency.

"Operation Choson," she said. "That's simple. It's got to stand for the Choson Dynasty."

"The what?"

"The Choson Dynasty, in Korea. Lasted from the late fourteenth century to the beginning of the twentieth."

Shit! thought the man on the other end of the line. Instinctively, he knew that the Defense Intelligence Agency operative was right. Until just a moment ago, he had convinced himself that there had been a screwup in the decoding/translation process. Operation "Chosen" was what he had predicted, not "Choson."

"Well, Korea," he finally said. "That's got to be it. I feel like an idiot for not seeing that earlier."

"Hey, don't let that bug you. That's not your area of expertise. Ask me something about Ukraine or Azerbaijan and I wouldn't have a clue."

The NSA operative thought for a moment before responding. "This Operation Choson—which Korea does it mean, North or South?"

"Could be either one. Back then the country was unified."

Son of a bitch, thought the man. *So that's what is going on in Pusan!* "Well, I do appreciate your help, Doctor. It's all starting to make sense now."

"So, you folks think the material may have been smuggled out?"

"It's beginning to look that way."

"That doesn't sound too good. Are we going to try and find it?"

"I don't know. Right now it's the Russians' problem."

"Hmm. You know, if the North has it, it's going to become *our* problem."

"Yeah. We're going to have to really study this one now."

"Okay, let me know if you need any more assistance."

"I will. Thanks for your help."

"You're welcome."

SIXTEEN

THE BOARDING PARTY

THE MOLTEN SUN WAS HALF SUBMERGED IN THE PACIFIC. What little breeze there had been during the long afternoon had died out an hour earlier. It was now so hot that sweat poured out of his body as if he were sitting inside a sauna. And his feet ached too.

Stan Reams had been walking most of the day, scouring the industrial waterfront of Puerto Vallarta. He was currently standing next to a steel bulkhead, looking out toward the harbor basin. The harbor waters smelled like a sewer. *What a fucking waste of time,* he thought. Stan had come up empty-handed. Not one person he talked with had ever heard of the *Korean Star.*

Stan spent all day at the harbor. He visited numerous marinas and boat repair yards, climbed aboard dozens of smelly fishing boats to quiz crew members and interviewed the master of every large vessel he could find. He even managed to meet with the Port Captain at the local Mexican Naval base. But it was all for nothing.

For each visit he posed as an American insurance investigator. His story line was simple: the *Korean Star* was missing and one of its last known port calls was to have been Puerto Vallarta. He explained that his company had insured the vessel and that he was trying to determine its fate.

No one questioned his story. Stan's fake business card, one of the many different types he carried, looked impressive and very official. The company name was real—it was one of the largest in the States—and the New York City telephone number listed on the card was also valid. The only problem with the card was that the individual's name was completely made up. No such person existed at the company. Despite this flaw, Stan's deception was nearly perfect. If someone had tried to verify his identity it would have required a very expensive phone call and taken hours to complete. The insurance company had over 15,000 employees. Trying to track down just one person would be a nightmare.

At first, most persons had no interest in talking with Reams. It seemed that no one wanted anything to do with an insurance company, especially one from the United States. However, when Stan mentioned the reward, everyone perked up, especially the Port Captain. The possibility of obtaining a $20,000 payment for information leading to the discovery of the *Korean Star* was more than enough inducement to rekindle interest. Every person he talked with agreed to keep their cars open. If they heard anything, they were to call his hotel and leave a message.

Stan guessed that he was on the proverbial wild goose chase. The chances of finding the missing vessel and his precious cargo were dismal but he had no easy alternatives. Other than returning to Pusan, his only lead was in P.V.

Stan turned toward the south half of the harbor. There were dozens of large yachts and oceangoing vessels moored along the commercial piers and wharves that jut out from the shoreline. He would check them all tomorrow. But for now it was time to retire. He wanted nothing more than to take a shower and sip a few cold beers.

He turned away from the bulkhead and headed north. The main thoroughfare through town was a quarter of a mile away. He would hail a cab there to take him back to the hotel.

Had Stan Reams decided not to postpone his investigation, he would have discovered an important clue. About two hundred yards to the south, a Ford van turned off the perimeter road and drove onto a concrete pier. Simpson and Chambers were about to pay another visit to the *Pacific Salvor*.

"Good evening, Captain," called out Dave Simpson as he stepped into the *Pacific Salvor's* main salon. Pete Chambers was right behind him.

"Good evening to you," replied Captain Osterback as he looked up from the dining table. He was sipping a can of beer.

Dave pulled up a chair next to the table and sat down. Chambers remained standing.

"Well, Captain," Simpson said, "are you ready to head back out? I've got a feeling that we're going to get real lucky tonight."

The Captain grinned. "Of course. Anytime you're ready we'll shove off."

Pete Chambers stepped forward, now entering the conversation. "Captain, do you really think you can swim that robot of yours into that cargo hold? I think it's going to be a lot more difficult than getting into the cabin. From what Dave's told me, you'll have to navigate through half a dozen hatchways before getting to the right compartment."

Osterback nodded his head. "Yeah, you're probably right. That's why I've decided to torch our way in."

"Torch?" asked Pete.

"Yeah, we've hooked up an electric arc torch to the ROV and will . . ."

While the captain explained the salvage procedure to Pete, Dave Simpson smiled to himself. He was impressed with Osterback. The man was clearly motivated by the potential value of the sunken ship's contraband. Simpson just hoped that the cardboard box buried under the tons of once frozen and now rotting fish really did contain heroin. Otherwise, the whole effort would have been for naught.

"Captain," asked Chambers, "how long do you think all this will take?"

"Well, if we get a move on right now, we'll be done tonight."

"Let's do it, then."

"You going to come along, Pete?" asked Simpson, surprised at his partner's sudden interest in the salvage effort. "I thought you didn't want to go out again."

Chambers looked his partner straight in the eyes. "Damn right I'm coming along. I wouldn't miss this for the world."

Pete Chambers' negative attitude had changed drastically earlier in the day. After depositing the rescued money into the bank, his worries disappeared. He, too, was now caught up in the heroin recovery operation. Greed was once again clouding his judgment.

"Well, gentlemen," Captain Osterback said as he stood up, "I think we should head out."

"Great. Let's go," replied Pete, now eager to proceed.

Dave Simpson was just about to agree when a new thought emerged. "Hey, wait a minute," he said. He turned to look aft. The mysterious steel box that had been recovered during the previous evening was still sitting in the corner of the compartment. He pointed to it. "What about the box—you've got the acetylene now so why don't why open it before leaving?"

"Yeah, I guess we could," the captain said. "It'll only take a couple of minutes to cut it, but we'll have to move it outside. It'll be too messy to work in here."

Simpson turned to face his partner. "That okay with you, Pete?"

"Yeah, sure." Pete was feeling lucky tonight. For all he knew the steel box was full of rocks, but there was also a chance that it might be loaded with gold or silver.

Simpson grinned. "All right, then, let's move this fucker and then crack 'er open."

Half a minute later, the three men were huddled around the steel case. They had just struggled to lift it from the deck when the forward cabin door opened and a stranger walked in.

The Mexican was of average size. He was young, no more than thirty. His only distinguishing feature was his long black hair. It was pulled back along his head into a ponytail.

Captain Osterback spotted the intruder first. "Who the hell are you?" he said.

The man pulled his right hand up. It had been hidden behind his leg. He pointed the nine-millimeter pistol at Osterback. With his other hand he gestured for the men to lower the box.

Without saying anything, the three men simultaneously set the steel box down. It made a dull thud when it hit the deck.

Captain Osterback locked onto the gunman's eyes. "What do you want?" he asked.

The intruder waved the pistol at the dining table. "Sit over there and shut up." His English was good.

Pete and Dave sat on one side while the captain moved to the other. The gunman remained standing at the head of the table. No one spoke.

Osterback stared across the table, wondering what Simpson had gotten him into. He was just about to ask permission to light up a cigarette when he spotted the headlights through a cabin porthole. A vehicle was driving down the concrete pier. It was heading for the *Pacific Salvor's* berth.

The Mercedes was out of Osterback's view when it finally pulled up alongside Simpson's van. He never saw the three passengers climb out.

Dave Simpson was growing impatient by the minute. Once again he smelled a setup. *Son of a bitch,* he thought, *someone's ratted on us again.* He wished that he had brought his pistol. He would have shot the man without the slightest hesitation.

Pete Chamber's stomach felt like a volcano about to erupt. His euphoria of just a few minutes earlier had been jolted away. He was on the verge of panic. No one had ever pointed a gun at him before.

Captain Osterback couldn't wait any longer. *"Amigo,"* he said, his voice friendly, "may I smoke?" He gestured to the pack of Marlboros and the lighter on the table.

The man nodded.

Just as Osterback finished his smoke, the cabin door opened and two of the men from the Mercedes filed in. The first man was in his late thirties. He was short and stocky. His once-black hair was graying and it was cut short. His dark brown eyes looked like marbles as he stared at the captives.

The second man was at least ten years younger and half a foot taller. His hair was longer, hanging down to his shoulders. A heavy gold chain was draped around his neck.

The two men took up position on either side of the doorway. Each was armed with an Uzi submachine gun; they held the deadly Israeli-made weapons diagonally across their chests.

A moment later, Arnaldo Rodriguez walked through the door between his two bodyguards. He was dressed in a light blue summer suit with an open-neck white silk shirt. His patent leather shoes were a high-gloss white. He wore a gold watch on his right wrist and assorted diamond-studded gold rings on both hands.

"Good evening, gentlemen," he said as he surveyed his captives.

"What's going on here?" demanded Osterback. "How dare you board my ship with guns?"

"Ah, you must be Captain Osterback," Rodriguez said.

"Yes, and who the hell are you?"

Rodriguez ignored the question. Instead, he turned to face Chambers and Simpson. "So, you must be the ones who are stealing from me."

"Stealing?" protested Simpson. "What the hell are you talking about?" He started to stand but was shoved back into his seat by one of the thugs.

Rodriguez focused on Simpson. "Listen to me, *gringo*. No one, and I mean no one, operates in my territory without my permission."

"What are you talking about? We're not doing anything wrong."

Rodriguez laughed. And for the next two minutes he proceeded to recite young Juan Diaz's vivid description of the aborted drug transfer operation that led to the sinking of the *Korean Star*.

Fuck! thought Dave Simpson as Rodriguez completed the story. *He knows everything!*

"What do you want from us?" Dave finally asked.

"Just give me the heroin and we'll be finished with this unpleasantness."

"There isn't any heroin. It's gone—dissolved by the sea."

"And how do you know that?"

Simpson shifted position on his chair. He was more than anxious. "Because we've been looking for it, with this ship. We've been diving on it with a robot—ROV. We found where the dope had been stored, but the bags had been damaged. There was nothing left to recover."

Rodriguez walked to the far end of the dining table and sat down. He removed a cigarette from a gold case and lit up. Everyone remained silent, all eyes focused on him. "You know, gringo, your story seems reasonable to me, except for one fact."

"What's that?" asked Simpson.

"We just chatted with one of the crewmen on the dock." He gestured with his head toward one of the portholes. "Now he told me a slightly different story. It seems that you're planning to head out again tonight. Something about searching inside a freezer compartment."

Shit, thought Simpson. He decided it was useless to continue his deception. "Yeah, well there's a chance that a second load of heroin was aboard. We don't know for sure. We were going back out to see if it's really there."

A second load—how convenient, thought Rodriguez. He was convinced that the American was lying. "This so-called second load—it was not intended for you?"

"No. And I don't know for sure if it's heroin or what. I just spotted a similar box in the hold next to the one that had my stuff."

Rodriguez was tired of the cat-and-mouse game. It was time for closure. "Tell me, then, where is the merchandise that you recovered last night?"

"What merchandise?" asked Simpson.

Rodriguez ignored Simpson. Instead, he turned to face Osterback. "Your crewman reported that you recovered a suitcase and some kind of steel box. I wish to examine them. Now!"

Pete stirred in his chair. Fear gripped him like the jaws of a steel vise. His mind was running at a furious rate, searching for a way out. *They're going to kill us, right here, right now, unless we give something—something to appease them. But what?* The money from the suitcase was already gone and there was little to bargain with. And then a new thought flashed into focus.

"Sir," Pete said, "we haven't been completely honest with you. We did recover a kilo of heroin. It was in the suitcase. It's back in our hotel, in a safety deposit box."

Dave Simpson turned to face his partner. His face telegraphed his astonishment. *What the hell are you doing?* he wondered.

Rodriguez smiled at Chambers. Sweat beaded up on the American's brow. His hands trembled slightly. *Good. This man's too scared to lie.* "One kilo, eh? Now we're making some progress. Tell me, what really happened to the rest of your shipment?"

"It's gone—dissolved like Dave said. The other bags were ripped open when the ship sank."

"So all you got was the one bag?"

"Yes, sir. But it's worth a lot. We'll give it to you—just let . . ."

Dave Simpson continued to listen to the talk between his

partner and the drug lord. He remained stunned at Pete's fantasy. *What's he up to?*

"So you offer me a kilo of heroin for your lives," Rodriguez said as he continued to grill Pete Chambers. "Somehow, I don't think that's quite enough."

Shit, thought Pete, *now what?* His plan was to get Dave and himself off the ship alive. If he couldn't entice Rodriguez with the phony dope story, then they would be shot on the spot. Pete had to come up with something else and quick. He turned away from the Mexican leader and glanced to his right. His mind was racing as he tried to find a way out. And then he saw it. *Of course—that'll work!*

He pointed aft toward the far corner of the compartment. "That box. We found it on the ship yesterday. It's real heavy and we think there might be gold inside it."

Rodriguez stood up and walked aft. He kneeled down beside the sewing-machine-sized steel box. He ran his fingers over the welded steel seams. "This is completely welded up. How do you know what's inside?"

Dave Simpson decided to reenter the conversation before Pete or the captain could respond. He too understood the need to buy time. "We don't know because we can't get it open."

"Why not?"

"It has to be cut open and we don't have the right gear."

Rodriguez turned around. "You expect me to buy that? This is a salvage ship. You could burn a hole in it in just a few minutes."

"Of course we can," Simpson said. "But what if there's no gold in there? What if it's loaded with cash or, for that matter, more drugs? The cutting torch will destroy it for sure." Dave Simpson's serpentine story line sounded plausible to him even though he had just invented it.

Rodriguez nodded. "Yes, I see what you mean. So how were you planning to open it?"

Simpson was just about to reply when Captain Osterback took over, now on track with his partners. "We need some kind of heavy-duty grinder to grind off the welds. We don't have anything like that on the ship. I was planning on renting one tomorrow."

Rodriguez didn't respond. He had already made up his mind. He walked forward, stopping next to the bodyguard with the ponytail. After whispering into the man's right ear for a few seconds, he walked through the doorway and disappeared.

Rodriguez's confidant turned to the two remaining guards and issued a short command in Spanish. The men moved forward, their guns pointed at their captives.

Oh shit, thought Simpson. *Now what?*

Dear God, thought Captain Osterback. He started to cross himself.

Pete Chambers threw up.

SEVENTEEN
THE INTERROGATION

EVEN THOUGH IT WAS HALF PAST MIDNIGHT, THE WAREHOUSE was broiling. Its tin roof, sheet-metal walls, and concrete floor retained the heat from the long hot day. The building wasn't very big, only seventy-five feet wide by a hundred feet long. About half of the floor space was filled with chest-high piles of fifty-kilogram bags of salt. Assorted wood crates and cardboard boxes were also stacked along one wall of the building.

In the back of the warehouse, off to one corner, was a walled-off room. The office was about twenty feet square. It was empty except for one file cabinet and a single chair. The one window in the back had been boarded over from the outside. A single dim lightbulb hung from the center of the ceiling.

Dave Simpson and Captain Osterback were sitting on the dirty concrete slab next to the file cabinet. Their hands remained tied behind their backs, making it hard to lean against the wall for support. Their blindfolds had been removed, but there was nothing to see. They were alone. Their captors had left them in the office about an hour earlier.

The makeshift prison wouldn't have been so bad if it hadn't been for the screaming. It had been going on for about forty minutes. The thin wood walls of the office transmitted the sound from the opposite end of the warehouse as if there were no walls at all.

"What do you think they're doing to him?" asked Osterback.

"Sweet Jesus, I don't know," Simpson said. He then turned toward Osterback, his face now contorted by an amalgam of dread and revulsion. "After what they did to your crew . . ." Dave hesitated for a moment. "Those fucking sadistic bastards are capable of just about anything."

"Yeah, I know what you mean," Osterback said. "They must be beating the crap out of him."

Dave Simpson just shook his head, refusing to acknowledge reality. He did not want to know what Rodriguez's men were doing to Pete Chambers. *This is all a dream—it can't be happening,* he continually repeated to himself. However, each time Pete let out a bloodcurdling scream, Dave was jolted back to the real world. *Stop it, you bastards! You're killing him.*

The pain was excruciating, but that wasn't the worst part of the ordeal. It was the way his captors reacted to his torture. They relished his misery, smiling and grinning among themselves as each stage of the carefully orchestrated campaign of terror was carried out.

Pete Chambers was naked. He was sitting in a chair, and his legs and arms were bound to the chair's wood frame with layers of duct tape. The chair had been placed in a shallow steel tub filled with water.

There were half a dozen of them, standing around the chair. The fat one was the worst of the bunch. His name was Pepe. He was maybe five and a half feet tall but weighed almost 300 pounds. The grubby stubble from his day-old beard and the thick mat of long filthy hair matched his body image. And he reeked of sweat and tequila.

"Hey, pretty boy. You gonna like this one!" he would call out each time he did his duty. His English was barely passable.

Pete Chambers gritted his teeth, his entire body tensed up for the inevitable. And then it hit. It felt like his guts were being torn out. The electric current surged through his lower extremities at near the speed of light, passing through his feet before grounding out in the water. The copper wire taped to his penis was the worst, though. The thin wire strands that were wrapped around the soft skin heated up to several hundred degrees during each cycle. If the fat man hadn't doused his crotch with a can of water after every charge, it would have burned up.

The thirty-volt, twenty-amp current had been applied a dozen times now. Pepe Ramos was surprised at the American's resistance. They usually talked by now. He dialed up the voltage to fifty volts and hit the switch.

Once again the current raced through Pete's body. But this time something different happened. Unknown to Pepe, the voltage regulator had a defect. The output voltage increased linearly from zero to thirty-five volts, but above thirty-five volts, both the voltage and amperage increased exponentially. At the fifty-volt reading, the device actually delivered one hundred ten volts and eighty amps.

Pepe watched the American react. Instead of screaming, the man uttered a deep, guttural grunt. His back arched. His facial muscles contracted. The veins in his neck bulged. His hands gripped the metal chair like a vise grip. It was as if his entire body was locked in one enormous convulsion.

Fifteen seconds later, Pepe flipped the switch off. *That should make him talk,* he thought.

Pete Chambers slumped to his right side, his head hanging loosely over his chest. A tiny wisp of smoke rose from his groin.

The Mexican torturer used a pail of water to douse Pete's smoldering penis. No response. He then dumped the rest of the water onto Pete's head. Again no reaction.

Pepe moved closer, grabbing Pete's head and shaking it. "Hey, *gringo,* time to wake up."

But Pete didn't wake up. He never would. He had just been electrocuted. His heart had stopped cold—dead cold.

"Shit," muttered Pepe.

"What's wrong with him?" asked a new voice.

Pepe turned to his right as Arnaldo Rodriguez stepped out of the shadows. He moved to his brother-in-law's side.

"I don't know what happened. He's so still."

Rodriguez leaned forward and checked one of Chambers' pupils. It was fully dilated and nonreactive.

"This man is dead."

"What?"

"He's dead. You killed him."

"It was an accident. I only turned it up to fifty volts—that shouldn't have killed him."

Arnaldo shook his head. "We can't do anything about it now. What's done is done."

"But I don't know what . . ."

"Don't worry about it," interrupted Rodriguez. "The man probably had a bad heart. He seemed so weak to begin with."

Pepe breathed a sign of relief. "What should we do now?" he asked.

Rodriguez removed a cigarette from his shirt pocket and lit up. After inhaling he looked back at his brother-in-law. "Actually, Pepe, this may work out better. Now, here's what I . . ."

A few minutes before 1:00 A.M., Pepe and an assistant dragged Pete Chambers' corpse into the warehouse office where they deposited it on the concrete slab next to Simpson and Osterback. They left without saying a word.

"God damn, what did they do to him?" asked Captain Osterback as he stared at the black scorch marks on Chambers' genitals.

For once in his life, Dave Simpson was speechless. He couldn't believe that his friend was gone. *Come on, Pete,* he thought, *wake up. I know you can do it.*

While the two Americans were left to contemplate their future, Arnaldo Rodriguez remained at the opposite end of the warehouse. He was standing near the entryway. Sweat dripped down his face. His underarms were soaked. The door was open but it didn't help much, with no wind to help ventilate the sizzling building.

Rodriguez ignored the heat as he watched Pepe Ramos. The fat man was kneeling on the concrete floor about ten feet away. He was examining the mysterious steel box that had been taken from the *Pacific Salvor.*

"Can you open it?" asked Rodriguez.

"Not without cutting tools. It's sealed up tight. All of the seams are welded." He paused a few seconds as he rocked the steel case. It was incredibly heavy for its size. "With a cutting torch I should be able to open it in just a few minutes.''

''No, we can't use that. The *gringos* said the flames might damage whatever is hidden inside.''

''*Si*, that's a possibility.''

''But how do we open it, then?''

Pepe leaned closer to the box, examining one of the welds. ''The steel plates don't look too thick. With a power hacksaw I should be able to open it by cutting open one of the sides.''

''That will not damage the contents?''

''*Si.*''

''Excellent. Get one and open it.'' Rodriguez was more than a little curious as to what might be hidden inside the steel box. Chambers' rambling about gold had really sparked his interest.

''Of course, Arnaldo, but I will have to wait until later this morning to get the tool. We have nothing like this in our inventory. I will have to get one from one of the construction sites in town. I'm sure one of them has what we need.''

''Very well; see that it is done. I want that box opened by nine this morning.''

''It will be done.''

Rodriguez nodded and then turned around, walking out of the building. His driver and bodyguard were both standing next to the Mercedes. A minute later they were gone.

Two thousand five hundred miles northeast of Puerto Vallarta, it was now half past eight in the morning. The two general officers—a one-star in the Air Force and a two-star in the Army—were alone in the conference room. It was buried deep inside the Pentagon.

''How much of that stuff do you suppose they lost?'' asked the senior officer.

''Sir, we have no way of knowing at this time. But based on the amount of manpower they're putting into the recovery effort, we've got to assume there's more than enough to make up one unit.''

''Shit. This is not good.''

''I know.''

''Do you think it's in the North?''

''Not anymore. We now know for certain that they've been concentrating their search efforts in the South, mainly in the Pusan area. We've been tailing them for several weeks, trying to figure out what they were up to." The officer paused. "When NSA intercepted that FIREWATCH message, the DIA finally made the connection."

The Army general picked up his coffee mug and took a sip. "Do you think the Russians know that we know about their Operation Choson?"

"There's no indication of that."

"Good. Now, what about our ROK counterparts—how are they reacting to all of this?"

"They don't know anything about it—yet."

"Good. Let's keep it that way. It'll just complicate things if we have to bring them in."

"Yes, sir. We agree."

The Army general drained his mug and then looked back at the U.S. Air Force officer. "Has the State Department been apprised of the situation yet?"

"No, sir. We wanted to update you first."

"Okay. I think it's time that we give 'em a formal briefing. They need to be made aware of the threat—even as thin as it is at this point."

"Yes, sir. I'll take care of it immediately."

The two men stood up. The meeting was nearly over. As they headed for the door, the Air Force officer made a parting comment. "You know, sir, there's a chance that the material may have already been smuggled out of Korea by now. The CIA thinks the stuff might have been stolen some time ago."

"I know. And that just scares the crap out of me."

EIGHTEEN
TICKLING THE DRAGON'S TAIL

"WHAT DO YOU THINK WE SHOULD DO?" ASKED LINDA Nordland. She was speaking into a telephone handset from her eighth-floor hotel suite.

"We wait. We have no other choice," answered Tom Parker. He was four floors below, inside Dave Simpson's apartment.

"What if he doesn't show up again?"

"I don't know." Tom paused, looking around the living room. It had a view of the ocean. The sun had risen a few hours earlier. "It sure doesn't look like he's taken off to me. Everything looks normal. If he were on the run, I'd expect to see things messed up a little as he grabbed last-minute items. But everything appears to be in its place."

"Then you think we should continue to wait for him?"

"Yeah. I'll hang around here till noon. If he doesn't show by then we'll pick it up tonight."

"Okay." Linda hesitated for a moment. "Tom, do you need anything? I can bring down some breakfast from room service."

"No, I'm fine. There's plenty to eat in the kitchen. I'll get something later."

"Well, okay. But if you need anything, just call."

"I will."

"Be careful, honey."

"Always."

Tom stood up, stretching his back. He was tired. It had been a long night. He had been staked out inside Simpson's fourth-floor apartment since ten o'clock of the previous evening. He hadn't had much trouble picking the lock. Long ago he had learned that trade. But the waiting was utterly boring. To break the monotony, he found a deck of cards and played dozens of hands of solitaire. And every hour, on the hour, he would call Linda. They would chat for five minutes or so. He liked that part of the waiting game.

Because Dave Simpson had failed to follow his normal bar-hopping routine in the late evenings, Tom and Linda were forced to take a more direct approach toward capturing him. But it was all for naught. Once again, Simpson was a no-show.

Where in the hell is that son of a bitch? thought Tom as he paced across the living room carpet.

Tom Parker was tired of the whole affair and he was mad at himself. He was losing his patience and that was one discipline he could not afford to shortchange. *That's just the time that things go wrong!* he reminded himself repeatedly.

And then there was Linda. That was far more of a problem than his impatience. Tom was too personally involved in the case. Linda was no longer a client; she was much more than that. His feelings for her were driving his actions, overriding his normal rock-solid objectivity. He now wanted Simpson just as much as Linda—maybe more.

Pepe Ramos drove his ten-year-old Toyota pickup into the gravel parking lot and hit the brakes. The truck skidded a few inches on the loose pebbles before stopping. A few seconds later he stepped out of the cab. The truck had a permanent list on the left side from his bulk. He was already sweating and the front of his wrinkled white shirt was unbuttoned to the navel. A hairy mound of bulging fat poured from the opening. It giggled like Jell-O with the slightest movement. A metallic medallion hung from his thick neck on a gold chain.

Pepe stepped to the rear where he leaned over the side panel and removed the power hacksaw from the partially rusted-out truck bed. He then lumbered toward the warehouse, gripping the thirty-five-pound tool with just one hand.

The guard detailed to watch over the Americans heard the truck drive up. Although not grossly obese like Pepe, José nevertheless had a fleshy frame. He looked like a walking fire hydrant.

José was ready when Ramos pounded on the locked steel door. He opened it. "Ah, Pepe," he said, spotting the cutting tool, "you finally got one."

"Yeah, it took a lot longer than I thought. I had to go clear to the airport to get it." What Pepe didn't add, however, was that he had had to threaten to beat the construction foreman over the head with a tire iron in order to "borrow" the tool.

Pepe stepped into the building. It was five degrees warmer than outside. "How are the *gringos*?" he asked.

"Quiet. I haven't heard anything from them."

"Good." He paused as he set down the heavy tool. "And Don Arnaldo—has he returned yet?"

"No, not since you left."

Pepe Ramos nodded. *That's good,* he thought. *Now I have time.*

Pepe still smarted from the verbal lashing he had taken earlier in the morning. His brother-in-law's anger had boiled over like a steaming kettle when he learned that Pepe had not found the right cutting tool. Rodriguez had arrived early so that he could witness the opening of the mysterious steel box. But Pepe's assistant, sent hours earlier to locate a power hacksaw, had not yet shown up. As a consequence, Pepe had been forced to acquire the tool on his own.

The guard closed the warehouse door and walked up to Pepe's side. Both men were now staring at the steel box. It was parked on the concrete slab near a stack of bags filled with salt.

"Do you think that saw will cut the steel?" asked the guard.

Pepe Ramos squatted down to examine the machine. It had a five-horsepower electric motor and the heavy-duty blade was lined with hundreds of tiny industrial-grade diamonds. "Yes, José, it will chew that steel up as if it wasn't there."

"Then Don Arnaldo will be pleased when he returns."

Ramos ignored the man's statement. Instead, he issued a new order. "Go fetch the power cord from the back of my truck."

"Are you going to test the saw?"

"Yeah, you could say that." Ramos had no intention of failing his leader again. He had to be 100 percent certain that the tool would do the job. And there was only one way to do that.

The saw blade sliced though the steel plate, spewing sparks and metal fragments like a blowtorch. Ramos ignored the high-pitched scream of steel against steel as he worked his way around the perimeter of the lid.

He momentarily pulled the saw back. Three of the four sides had been severed. *Just one more pass and it'll be open. Then there won't be any reason for Arnaldo to be mad at me.*

Dave Simpson and Captain Osterback listened intently to the muffled screeching of the saw. They could also feel a slight vibration in their buttocks as the cutting action was transmitted through the interlinked steel reinforcing bars embedded in the concrete floor.

"What the hell do you suppose they're doing now?" asked Osterback.

Simpson just shook his head. He didn't know what to think.

*   *   *

Pepe Ramos sliced though the last inch of steel. The wall plate fell inward about an inch. He set the power tool on the floor. The blade was still smoking. The air stank of scorched metal.

Pepe used a screwdriver to pry up the loose steel plate. After removing it, he tossed it to the floor. It clanged loudly when it collided with the concrete.

The guard watching Ramos leaned forward to look into the box. "Looks like there's some kind of container in there."

"Yeah," agreed Ramos. "Like a box in a box."

"Can you get it out?"

"I think so, if I can just remove some of this padding material." Pepe leaned over the box and began to pull out the foam packing.

It took about a minute to remove the inner container. It was now sitting on the concrete floor, next to its spent steel casing. The box was three feet long, about a foot wide and a foot high. It was painted black and was very, very heavy. José had to help Ramos lift it out of the steel shell.

"What is that thing?" asked the guard.

"I don't know," Pepe said as he ran his hand across the dark surface. It was metallic, but it wasn't steel. He reached into his pants pocket and removed a pocket knife. He open a blade and jammed its tip against the top of the box. The blade penetrated a few millimeters, trenching a tiny furrow into the metal. The outer walls of the container were composed of a soft metal.

Pepe leaned closer, carefully examining the top of the box. He then lowered his head and looked at its side. That's when he spotted hard steel tabs set inside the soft metallic lining. There were four, one near each corner. Set in the center of each tab was a screw head. The tabs were fastened to a structural steel plate fused to the thicker soft metal. "Get me the screwdriver," he ordered.

José complied, walking a few steps to a nearby workbench. "Here," he said as he handed the tool to Ramos.

The screws were difficult to remove but Pepe finally backed all four away from their threaded bases. Each screw was about two inches long. He then used the screwdriver as a pry bar, inserting its tip between the edge of a steel tab and the liner. He twisted the handle and the lid separated from the side walls.

"You opened it!" shouted José.

Pepe stood up and, using his fingers, grabbed two sides of the lid. He pulled off the top of the box. It was incredibly heavy for such a small object. As he set the plate on the floor he noticed for the first time that it was about half an inch thick. There were three separate layers of material bonded together: two soft metallic sheets, each about an eighth of an inch thick, one on the inside, the other on the exterior—and sandwiched between the two was a quarter-inch-thick steel plate.

Pepe turned back to the open top of the box. It was covered by a greenish hard-foam packing. He dropped to his knees and then carefully pulled the covering out of the way.

José reacted before Pepe. "Sweet Jesus, look at that!"

The top of the box was divided into three separate compartments, each one isolated from the other by the same composite wall construction as the lid. The left compartment, the one closest to Pepe, contained a purple-black metallic ball about the size of a bowling ball. It was housed in polyurethane foam that was perfectly shaped to fit the bottom and top halves of the sphere.

The central compartment was filled with solid foam packing; the spacer was designed to maintain an eighteen-inch separation between the left and right compartments. Encased in the center of the foam spacer was a half-inch-thick plate of a stainless steel alloy.

The compartment on the right contained a solid metallic cylinder about two and half inches in diameter and just over eight inches long. The cylinder was resting on one end; it was also held firmly in place by foam padding.

"Are they gold?" asked the guard, his voice excited.

Pepe stroked the exposed surface of the cylinder. "I don't know—maybe," he replied. He then he touched the top of the sphere. "They feel a little hot, like they've been cooking."

"Must be the warehouse. It's boiling in here today."

"Yeah, I guess you're right," Pepe answered. He again ran his hand over the sphere, feeling the sides next to the foam padding. A couple of seconds later he found the hole. He inserted a finger in the opening and pulled. The sphere rotated within its foam padding. "Hey," he called out, "this thing's got a hole in it."

"What?" asked José.

"Yeah, this ball's got a hole through it." Pepe next grabbed the globe, using both ends of the penetration for hand grips. Despite his obesity, Pepe remained a powerful man, capable of lifting heavy loads. But he struggled to remove the seven-inch-diameter sphere from the case. It weighed an incredible forty-eight kilos—over a hundred pounds. Its mass reminded Pepe of the much larger lead weights he had once used when deep-sea fishing.

Pepe eventually removed the ball from the case and stood, holding it at waist level for the guard to see.

"Why would they put a hole in it like that?" asked José.

"I don't know. That doesn't make any sense to me."

"Can I see it?"

"Just a second," Pepe said as he squatted down, setting the metallic ball on the concrete floor.

The guard kneeled down and cupped the metallic ball with both hands. He tried to lift it but gave up. "Damn, but this thing's heavy!" he commented.

"I know." Pepe then reached down and carefully pried out the matching cylinder from its foam padding. It looked like a large can of beer. But like the sphere, it was far too heavy for its size, weighing in at almost thirty pounds.

Pepe held the cylinder up to his eyes, examining the outer surface. The dark metal had been polished. He could just see the distorted reflection of his eyes on its surface.

"What do you think these things are for?" asked the guard as he continued to examine the sphere, slowly spinning it on the floor like a top.

"I have no idea," Pepe said as he turned the plug over, examining the bottom end. Unlike the rest of the dark cylinder and the sphere, its exposed surfaced was shiny, like polished silver.

Pepe had just started to reinsert the metallic slug into its preformed foam padding when he finally made the connection. *Of course*, he thought. *They must fit together.* He looked back at the guard, holding the cylinder up. "José, I think this thing is some kind of plug that fits into the ball."

The guard looked down at the hole in the sphere and then back at the cylinder in Pepe's hands. "Yeah, you're right. They look like they match. See if it fits."

While José steadied the sphere on the floor, Pepe leaned

over and lined up the end of the cylinder with the exposed hole. The medallion suspended from Pepe's neck was now hanging out of his open shirt, just a few inches above the sphere. It was not quite in the way so he ignored it.

"Okay," Pepe said as he slid the slug forward, "here we go." It slowly penetrated the slot in the side of the ball. A moment later all hell broke loose.

The slug had barely entered the opening when the sphere underwent an enormous transformation. In less than a heartbeat, its temperature skyrocketed. And then it began to fluoresce. A brilliant bluish-purple light radiated from the globe, filling the entire warehouse with an eerie unnatural glow. It looked like something from hell.

"*¡Chingar!*" screamed José as the sudden burst of light startled him. Something was terribly wrong. His eyes instinctively snapped shut and he thrust the ball away from his body.

Pepe, also startled, released his grip on the plug just as José shoved the sphere away. Still partially connected, the sphere-plug rolled across the concrete floor, continuing to glow like a miniature sun. A moment later it crashed into the bottom of a stack of bags filled with salt. The collision ejected the plug from the sphere. The blinding light stopped the instant the two objects separated.

Both men collapsed to the floor, temporarily incapacitated by the horrible light. They lay prostrate on the concrete for about fifteen minutes, too stunned to talk. Finally, Pepe Ramos began to regain his faculties. "José, are you all right?" he asked while rubbing his eyes with his hands. He was still seeing double.

José repeatedly shook his head and blinked his eyes. He was not all right. Something was very wrong. "I don't know, Pepe. I feel . . . I feel kind of weird, like I'm numb all over."

Pepe moved closer to his friend while continuing to rub his eyes. He could see a little better now. A moment later he saw it.

"Sweet Mary, Mother of Jesus," he muttered.

"What's wrong?" asked José.

"Your hands and arms. Something's wrong with them."

José looked down. He wanted to vomit. His exposed forearms and hands had been broiled lobster-red. "What's wrong with me?" he screamed.

* * *

Simpson and Osterback both saw the transient glow of bluish-purple light when it diffracted around the loose door frame. They then heard the metallic clang of the plug when it crashed onto the concrete floor. And then, about a quarter of an hour later, someone started to scream.

"What the hell are they doing now?" asked Captain Osterback.

Dave just shrugged his shoulders.

Pepe Ramos continued to stare at his friend. He could not believe what he was witnessing. The discoloration in José's arms and hands had turned an even deeper shade of red. And now his neck and face were reacting—massive skin boils were erupting everywhere.

Poor José looked as if he had been slow-roasted over a fire pit.

"You wait here," Pcpc said, "and I'll get help."

"Don't leave me," pleaded José. His voice was only a whisper now.

"Just stay put. I'll be right back."

Pepe ran outside. He returned a few minutes later, this time holding a pistol in his right hand. He kept the .22-caliber automatic hidden under the driver's seat of his pickup. It had a black suppressor screwed to the barrel. "You okay, José?" he asked as he ran to his friend's side.

José had now collapsed to the floor. He was on his back, his useless arms folded into his chest. His eyes were glazed over and spittle drooled out of his mouth. He did not—could not—respond to Pepe.

Pepe kneeled down next to José, grabbing one of the man's shoulders and shaking him. "Come on, José, stay awake now. I'm going to bring those *gringos* out here—they'll know what to do for you."

The office door burst open and Pepe stormed in. There was fire in his eyes. "*¡Levantanse, chinga tu madres!*" he yelled, ordering the prisoners to stand in a most insulting way.

Dave Simpson didn't make the complete translation but the way the man was waving the pistol around he understood. He struggled to his feet. Captain Osterback followed his lead.

"¡Vamos!" Ramos shouted while gesturing with the pistol toward the open doorway.

Within a minute, Simpson and Osterback were at the opposite end of the warehouse, standing next to their jailer.

Only twenty minutes earlier, José Gomez had been in normal health for a thirty-two-year-old male. But now he was literally disintegrating in front of their eyes. It was like some terrible sixteenth-century plague had been ravaging his body for weeks.

"What's wrong with him?" asked Simpson in Spanish.

Ramos pointed to the globe at the base of a stack of salt bags. "Your devil machine did it."

"What are you talking about?"

"The thing—it made a terrible light and now it's killing José."

Dave Simpson was baffled. He hadn't the faintest idea what the Mexican was babbling about. He was about to ask another question when he spotted the mysterious steel box that had been removed from the Korean ship. It was off to one side and its lid had been removed. And sitting on the concrete next to the box was some kind of an internal container that had been stored inside of it. *What the hell is that?* he wondered.

"The steel ball?" Dave asked, pointing to the floor. "It came from the box?"

"*Sí*, now what is it for?"

"I don't know—we never knew what was inside." Dave took a step toward the sphere, wanting to examine it.

Pepe Ramos lunged forward, slamming the side of the pistol barrel across Simpson's right cheek. The impact drove Dave to the floor.

"You lying *gringo* dog," Pepe yelled. He then started to point the gun at Dave's head.

Captain Osterback, knowing he only had a second to make a decision, reacted in a flash. He lowered his head and took a giant leap. He hit Ramos on his right side just as the man pulled the trigger. The bullet smashed into the concrete floor, an inch from Dave's right shoulder.

Osterback's momentum was more than sufficient to knock the fat Mexican to the floor. Pepe flopped onto the dusty concrete like a sack of flour. The impact ejected the pistol from

his hand and at the same time knocked the wind out of his
lungs.

Dave Simpson's head was still ringing from the pistol-
whipping when he spotted the fat one lying on the floor. Captain Osterback was also down, partially dazed from the
collision. Ignoring the pain, Dave struggled to stand up. He
then walked up to the wheezing Mexican.

"You son of a bitch," he shouted, "eat this." Simpson
reared his right foot back and then let loose. His shoe landed
just below Pepe's fat-covered rib cage, catching him at kidney
level.

Pepe bellowed out obscenities and tried to turn away.

"And this one's for Pete," yelled Dave as he let loose with
another vicious kick.

Dave Simpson continued his attack, trying to keep the fat
Mexican down. His hands were still tied behind his back and
he had to keep the monster away from the pistol.

Something happened on the sixth kick. It was a little lower
than the others and Pepe was again turning. Dave's shoe hit
the man near the center of his gut. He buried his foot in the
soft flesh.

Pepe was instantly paralyzed by a blinding pain. It was as
if his belly had just been ripped open. Part of his lower intestinal tract, already severely burned by the same light that had
devastated José, had ruptured from the blow. Blood and feces
poured into his abdominal cavity.

Pepe lay rigid as the pain multiplied. A few seconds later
he vomited. Unable to turn his head to the side, he aspirated
much of what he threw up. His windpipe and part of his lungs
filled with partially digested *chilaquiles*. He was suffocating
and internally bleeding to death at the same time.

Dave Simpson stood over the motionless slab of fat. The
man's eyes were open and a gurgling, choking sound broadcast from his mouth. And then it stopped.

Dave nudged the man with his shoe again. There was no
response. He turned to the other captor. José was now nothing
more than a huddled mass of flesh on the floor. Blood, vomit
and body wastes poured from his various orifices. He was no
threat.

Dave walked over to Captain Osterback, who was now

standing. Like Simpson's, the captain's hands were still tied behind his back. "You okay?" asked Dave.

"Yeah, and you?"

"I'm all right."

Osterback stepped toward Simpson. "What the hell happened here anyway?"

"Damned if I know."

The ship captain looked at the innocuous metallic sphere lying on the concrete floor a few feet away from his shoes. He had already inspected the nearby cylinder. "What about these things? Are they gold or not? And what's this light he was jabbering about?"

"I don't know and I don't care. All I want to do is get the hell out of here, like right now."

"No shit—let's do it."

It took several minutes for Simpson and Osterback to free themselves. They managed to cut the cable ties from their wrists by rubbing the plastic bindings against a file on a workbench.

Captain Osterback grabbed Pepe's pistol off the floor while Simpson removed a two-foot section of steel pipe from the bench. It was a perfect club. Both men were ready to head out of the warehouse when Osterback once again eyed the contents from the steel box. "Wait a sec," he said. "Maybe we ought to take this stuff with us. We might need it to trade with if this Rodriguez turkey comes after us."

Dave glanced down at the metallic ball. He had been in such a hurry to leave that he hadn't thought about keeping the booty. "Well, it don't look like gold, but maybe it's got some value. It could be platinum or something like that." He paused. "You're right that we should take it with us—maybe we can sell it."

"All right, but let's do it quick. We don't have a minute to spare."

Osterback picked up the soup-can-size cylinder while Simpson retrieved the sphere. They carefully inserted both metallic items into the carrying case. Neither man bothered to examine the objects. Their combined thoughts were focused on a single goal: escape.

A couple of minutes later, Pepe Ramos' four-wheel-drive pickup truck pulled out of the parking lot and headed onto the adjacent side street. Simpson drove while Osterback sat in the passenger seat, cradling Pepe's pistol in his lap. The heavy carrying case, now wrapped in a badly weathered tarpaulin, was stowed in the Toyota's open bed, just behind the cab.

NINETEEN
THE WAITING GAME

ARNALDO RODRIGUEZ STARED AT HIS BROTHER-IN-LAW'S corpse. It looked like a beached tuna. The open shirt exposed slabs of fat. The medallion, still suspended from the neck, rested on the sternum. The normally brown skin of the chest had further darkened, especially around the waist.

Rodriguez turned toward the other victim. José was curled up, fetuslike, a few feet away from Pepe. Fluids continued to ooze from his body orifices. His arms and hands were blood-raw. His breathing was labored. He was just minutes away from death.

"What happened to them?" Rodriguez asked, directing the question to one of the men who had accompanied him. They had just returned to the warehouse, missing Simpson and Osterback's escape by fifteen minutes.

"I do not know, Don Arnaldo." The bodyguard paused. "But from the look of their skin, I'd say they were burned."

"Those *gringos*—they did this!"

"*Si*. They're not here so they must have escaped."

Rodriguez scanned the warehouse floor area. "They took that steel box from the ship, too."

"*Si*, we could not find it."

Rodriguez shook his head in silent rage. He then kneeled down by his brother-in-law's body. He leaned forward, removing the medallion from Pepe's neck. The medal was about the size of a silver dollar; it was grayish-silver. The form of a charging bull was richly embossed on its exterior.

"That is a most handsome medallion," commented the bodyguard. "The artwork is exquisite. The *toro* looks so real."

"Yes, I know. I gave it to Pepe myself," Rodriguez lied. Pepe had won the necklace at a cockfight five years earlier. Rodriguez had always admired it.

Rodriguez slipped the chain over his own neck. "I will honor Pepe's memory by wearing it for the rest of my life."

"That is very honorable, Don Arnaldo. I'm sure that Pepe would like that."

Rodriguez stood up. "Take them to Santiago," he ordered. "He'll know what to do."

"Si." The man hesitated. "And what about the *norteamericanos?"*

"Find them and bring them to me—alive. Then they will pay for what they have done!"

The pier looked new. It had a concrete deck and was founded on steel piles. The pier's trestle section stretched several hundred feet into the harbor. There was just enough room for two small trucks to pass each other without driving off.

The seaward end of the pier branched into two halves, each wing perpendicular to the long approach trestle. The T-head section was about 300 feet long and 50 feet wide.

The *Pacific Salvor* remained moored to the south half of the T-head. It was the only vessel tied to the pier.

After checking several other leads during the morning, Stan Reams finally returned to the harbor area, picking up the search where he had left off during the previous day. His first target was the 120-foot ship moored at the end of the pier.

Stan approached the *Pacific Salvor* from the stern. It looked deserted. There were no vehicles parked on the adjacent pier deck and he couldn't see anyone aboard.

He stood next to the ship, studying its deck hardware. There were several hydraulically operated winches on the fantail as well as a massive A-frame davit system that hung over the stern. Off to the starboard side and welded to the steel deck was a cylindrical object about four feet in diameter and fifteen feet long. It was painted white and had dozens of thick black hoses connected to it. *Must be a decompression chamber,* thought Reams.

Stan walked to the end of the pier and studied the ship's name and home port, both stenciled in black on the aft end of the rusting gray hull. *Hmm,* he said to himself, *she's called the* Pacific Salvor *and is out of San Francisco. This looks real interesting.*

Stan started his search at the stern. He simply stepped off the pier's bull-rail and walked onto the vessel. There was a little rust on the steel plating but in general the ship was well maintained. Stan began to pick through several storage lockers mounted to the deck near the A-frame. They contained a variety of tools, heavy clamps and assorted fittings used on anchor lines. He next spotted a dozen steel cylinders stacked up horizontally on a special steel rack. Although the wording on the four-foot-long tanks was in Spanish, Stan recognized their contents: acetylene and oxygen—standard components for any ship that specialized in salvage work.

Stan was just starting to head forward when he spotted the crate. *It can't be?* he thought.

The wood-frame container was sitting on the deck next to one of the massive deck winches. Its lid was missing but inside, scattered on the bottom, were globs of a paperlike material. His heart raced as he reached in and removed a clump of the material. The paper quality was poor and it was partially crumbled up, as if it had once been wet and then dried out. He peeled several sheets apart, studying the faint print. The wording wasn't Spanish and it certainly wasn't English, yet it was familiar.

He had seen the cyrillic print before. The Russian newspaper was published daily. He searched for a publication date. The paper was over six months old. Stan smiled. *They must have found it after all!*

When the wood crate was originally shipped from Vladivostok to Pusan, Nikolai Bessolov had used the newsprint as packing material, crumpling it up and stuffing it around his precious cargo. And before Stan resealed the shipping crate he had personally replaced the six week's supply of newspaper.

Stan had found the mystery box in a Pusan warehouse, exactly where Irina Sverdlova had described. When he had opened it for the first time, all doubts of her incredible story evaporated.

At first, Stan had thought of selling the contents—he could

have made millions. But then he had changed his mind. Money no longer motivated him. He had a better plan.

Stan had welded up the steel box himself, making it tamperproof. He had then started to search for the right connection. He had found it a week later. The Yellow Sea Shipping Company had agreed to ship his special cargo to Mexico, no questions asked. But the price the Korean merchant had demanded was outrageous: a $25,000 cash down payment and then another $25,000 on delivery in Cabo. The price was exorbitant, but Stan was willing to pay. His conservative roots told him it was too risky to smuggle it in on his own.

Stan folded up a section of the newsprint and slipped it into his pants pocket. He then started forward, heading toward a cabin doorway. It was time to explore the ship's interior.

Dave Simpson drove the Toyota up the steep grade. The dirt road was more of a trail than a roadway, but the four-wheel-drive pickup handled the terrain.

The thick mat of trees and shrubs on either side of the road partially obscured the view. However, once in a while, when the switchbacks were lined up just right, the distant ocean was visible. It was a brilliant turquoise.

Captain Osterback, sitting next to Simpson, was speaking as the truck crawled forward in first gear. "How much farther are we going?"

"Not far—maybe ten minutes or so. Then it'll be safe to stop."

"Do you think they spotted us?"

"No, I doubt it. I'm sure we got out before anyone else showed up."

"So we're just going to hang out up here, then?"

"For now. When it gets dark tonight we can head back in. But I sure as hell don't want to drive this thing in town until then. No telling who might recognize it."

Dave Simpson and Einar Osterback had fled from P.V. over an hour earlier. They were now halfway up the steep western slope of a coastal foothill. The minimountain was covered with lush vegetation—it was perfect camouflage.

After escaping from the warehouse and commandeering Pepe Ramos' truck, Simpson and Osterback had had a critical decision to make. Both men's initial reactions had been the same: get out of Puerto Vallarta ASAP. Simpson had planned to drive to the airport and take the first flight to the States he could buy. Captain Osterback, on the other hand, wanted to get back to his ship. It was his home and everything he owned was aboard. Somehow, even without his crew, he was going to head her out into the ocean and run north for San Diego. His days of working south of the border were over.

The instinct to instantly run from Mexico had been overwhelming. However, as the men drove on the back streets, working their way out of the industrial park where they had been imprisoned, reality had finally sunk in. Neither man had a dime to his name. Everything of value they had had been taken from them when they had been captured the previous night. It was all gone: their cash, their credit cards, even their watches. And worst of all for Captain Osterback, Rodriguez's men had found the safe in his cabin. He had wanted to retch when they forced him to open it and then hand over the cash. Most of the $20,000 came from the down payment that Simpson had made.

Although the two men had escaped with their lives, they were still trapped. Dave Simpson couldn't buy an airplane ticket and the *Pacific Salvor* had barely enough fuel aboard to make it to Baja, let alone all of the way to San Diego. Without money, there was no quick way out. In the end, they had decided that their only choice was to disappear.

The Toyota was now parked. Both men were standing by the hood, looking out toward the distant ocean. Dave was smoking—one of Pepe's Mexican brands. Osterback was munching on an apple he had found in the pickup.

"You know that prick's probably going to have your hotel watched," the captain said, his mouth half full.

"Yeah, I know, but I've got a way around that." Dave paused to take a drag. "But what about the boat? I'm sure Rodriguez is going to have it staked out too, just like the airport and all of the car rental places."

"Don't worry about that. I'll take care of securing the ship. You just get back to the dock with the green and then we'll be able to get out of here."

"No problem."

Dave Simpson had some cash hidden away inside his apartment. It would buy a lot of diesel.

*   *   *

Tom Parker was in his own room on the ninth floor of the resort. It was now midafternoon. After leaving Simpson's apartment, he had lunched with Linda in the garden court cafe. He had then excused himself, telling Linda that he was going to spend a few hours checking up on some leads regarding Simpson's possible whereabouts.

It was a lie.

What Tom really wanted was some privacy. He cared for Linda but it was all happening too fast. He needed some time to himself.

Tom had taken a long shower and was now lying on his bed, wearing only a pair of shorts. It was dark—the blinds were drawn—and the hum of the air conditioner was helping to lull him under. But he wasn't asleep yet.

He was thinking about Lori.

The heartache was still there; it was a terrible wound. But Tom had accepted that consequence. It was forever a part of him. His wife was dead and there was nothing he could do to change that cold, cruel fact.

It would have been so easy to end the anguish. A bullet to the brain and it would have been over with long ago. He used to think about doing it, sometimes even toying with his Smith & Wesson. In the end, fortunately, he talked himself out of it. Keely needed a father and that need became his existence.

There was also something else that had driven him and, for a time, possessed him.

Tom had tracked them for almost two years. It was a never-ending pursuit. The police had helped, and so had the FBI, but there had been little evidence to work from. Nevertheless, he had persisted.

During the hunt he had neglected his clients, concentrating on his own account. And he had spent nearly every spare dollar he had. In the end, he had failed.

Lori's killers had vanished.

Tom had kept pounding away, driven by an unholy alliance of vengeance and grief. He would find them, come hell or high water, and then they would pay, that he had been certain of. But what then? The pain would still be there, the hole in his heart might never mend. And he had feared that more than anything.

Tom would never have stopped the search if it hadn't been for his mother's intervention. She had watched her son steadily deteriorate. It was slowly tearing her apart too.

Alice Parker had saved her son by using Keely. It was the only bargaining chip she had. Tom would never have visited the psychiatrist on his own.

Keely had never really understood her mother's death. She had been only four years old at that time. But as she aged she clearly perceived that something important was missing. Her grandmother helped fill the void, but it wasn't quite enough. What she really needed was more time with her father. Tom, however, had hardly ever been home.

Keely's emotional problems really hadn't been all that bad. She'd been a little more withdrawn and shy than normal. And she had seemed to be uncommonly fearful of strangers. But when Alice explained the warning signs to her son, Tom had immediately agreed to help. He would do anything for his daughter.

Keely's counseling sessions had gone well. Tom and Alice had attended most of them. And after about a month the child therapist had finally convinced Tom to seek help for himself, recommending a specialist.

The psychiatrist was an expert in grief mitigation. Tom Parker had been a walking textbook example of a grief-driven victim. Almost anything could have happened if he had continued without help.

For the better part of the first year of therapy, Tom had visited the psychiatrist weekly, and then monthly thereafter. The hour-long sessions, in combination with the drugs, had saved him.

Tom had never quite accepted Lori's death but he had finally learned to live with it.

As to the two men who had taken her life, he had given up that useless chase after nearly two years of pursuit. But he had never forgotten them. Someday, somehow, he would find them. And then he would kill them.

TWENTY

THE TRAP IS SPRUNG

It was 10:30 P.M. The sun had set hours earlier and the sky was pewter-black. Thick clouds blanketed Banderas Bay, extending from Cabo Corrientes beyond Nuevo Vallarta. Lightning strikes, miles offshore, lit up the distant horizon like a gigantic fireworks display. The muffled thunder, however, was nothing more than a meek whisper by the time it reached the shore. Although the sea storm wouldn't reach Puerto Vallarta for a few more hours, the air already had an earthy odor to it, hinting at the deluge that was to come.

Captain Osterback rowed the boat with the rigor of a robot. His strokes were even, full and powerful. The twelve-foot skiff ghosted across the water. Every tenth stroke he would turn his head for just a second. He didn't have any trouble spotting his target. The pole-mounted pier lights illuminated the *Pacific Salvor*. The salvage ship was still tied up at the end of the long pier.

Osterback would have preferred walking along the pier to board his ship, but that wasn't possible. The two men sitting in the Ford sedan had an unobstructed view of the pier's shore connection. From several blocks away, he and Simpson had watched the car in the parking lot, hoping it would drive off. But it didn't. That meant only one thing: the men inside were sentries, sent by Rodriguez to find them.

After heading down from their mountainside hideout, Osterback and Simpson had driven to the harbor. Instead of heading straight to the *Pacific Salvor*, they had stopped at a small marina located near where the salvage ship was berthed. They had scaled the chain-link fence that guarded the marina's access pier and then walked out onto the floating docks. Osterback had commandeered the rowboat a few minutes later. It had been tied up to the end of one of the vacant slips.

Before Captain Osterback had shoved off, he had agreed to return to the marina at midnight to pick up Simpson. In the interim, each would have completed his individual task. Once reunited, they would jointly maneuver the ship away from the pier and head out to the open sea. The captain even welcomed the approaching storm; it would make their escape easier.

Captain Osterback shipped his oars, being careful not to make any noise. The skiff's oak gunwale kissed the steel hull of the *Pacific Salvor*. Half a minute later he was on the fantail of his ship, using a huge winch as cover. He looked down the length of the approach pier. The Ford was in the same spot. *Good. Those two are still in the parking lot.* He wasn't sure, however, what might be waiting for him aboard the ship.

Osterback stealthily moved along the deck, staying in the shadows and hiding behind more equipment. By the time he reached the entry to the main cabin, his heart was pounding. *Calm down; everything's going to be okay*, he told himself. He then pulled the pistol from his waistband. It was the silenced .22 he had liberated from Pepe Ramos.

He took a deep breath and slowly exhaled. *Time to check inside.* He then pulled open the watertight door and disappeared into the dark companionway.

Stan Reams never heard the rowboat or spotted Captain Osterback crawling on the decks. Instead, he sat in the darkened bridge house and looked down the long approach pier. The car was still in the parking lot. He was beginning to wonder if he had been wasting his time.

Around midafternoon, the car had driven onto the pier and stopped next to the ship. Two men had climbed out, each one armed with a small pistol-size submachine gun. While Reams watched from a porthole in one of the aft cabins, the men had proceeded to search the ship. They had started at the stern and worked their way forward.

Stan had been able to evade their search by staying several compartments ahead of the gunmen. It had been easy. The sentries knew little about ship construction and had missed several areas that could have hidden a dozen men. He eventually had been able to slip past the Mexicans, finding temporary refuge in a storage compartment aft of the galley.

About half an hour later, the two searchers had climbed back into their car and driven to shore, parking in the lot by the gate. Reams had returned to the bridge house. He had decided to wait and see what developed.

Stan looked at his watch. It was a quarter to eleven. *I'll hang around till midnight; then I'm going to head ashore.* He already had one of the ship's inflatables checked out. All he had to do was toss it over the side and jump in. It might take him a half hour to paddle to shore, but the dumb sentries would never see him.

Stan stepped off the elevated captain's chair and walked aft. He was headed to the galley, hoping to find a beer or something else to drink. He was bone dry.

Captain Osterback slowly made his way along the aft companionway. It was strictly a touch-and-feel affair. There was no light. The ship's generating plant was switched off and the shore power feed hadn't matched the vessel's electrical system. Until he reached the forward section of the ship, where portholes would allow the exterior dock lighting to penetrate, he was blind.

After running into an open hatchway and bruising his knee, Osterback changed tactics. *Enough of this shit,* he said to himself. He slipped the pistol back into his waistband and then ran his hands along the steel bulkhead, searching for a wall locker that he knew was there. He found it a few seconds later. The emergency fire station was mounted three feet above the deck. It contained a fire extinguisher, a hundred feet of fire hose, and a full-face fire mask with companion air tank. And attached to the top of the mask was a battery-powered light.

Osterback opened the hinged door and fumbled around until he located the light. He found the switch. It worked. He removed the light from its housing and carried it in his right hand. The bulb was tiny, but it illuminated the companionway like a floodlight.

Osterback continued forward, shining the light onto the tile deck. The pistol was back in his right hand. The galley was around the next corner.

Stan Reams spotted the diffracted light just as he was about to flip the pull tab on the Coke can. Like a cat, he pulled himself back into the shadows, pressing his body against a locker. He then reached down and removed the knife that had been strapped to his ankle.

Captain Osterback walked past the galley. He wasn't hungry. He was heading to the bridge.

Reams watched the light trail as it diffused through the open doorway. He stepped up to the opening and ducked his head out, just for an instant. It was all he needed. *Only one,* he thought.

Reams scanned the interior of the dark galley, looking for another weapon. The knife wouldn't do the job he had in mind. He found it a moment later. *There! That'll work!*

Captain Osterback never heard a thing. He was just about to step into the pilothouse when a blinding light flashed across his eyes. He crumpled to the deck, landing on his back. The pistol and the flashlight spilled onto the deck near him.

Reams straddled the unconscious man, cast-iron frying pan in his right hand. He picked up the flashlight and pistol. He then shined the light on the man's face. *I'll be damned—he's not Mexican!*

Dave Simpson parked the Toyota pickup in the resort's long-term parking lot. It was separated from the lobby's main entry driveway and guest parking area by a grove of palm trees. The lot was set aside for hotel staff and permanent residents.

Dave had just climbed out of the truck and was deciding on how best to make his way back to his apartment when a new thought occurred to him. He turned around and looked into the bed of the truck. The black carrying case, still covered with the tarpaulin, occupied one corner of the bed. *What the hell am I going to do with that?* he wondered.

Leaving it in the truck was absolutely out; he knew Puerto Vallarta too well. Anything not secure was fair game for the bands of vagrants that roamed the area. He thought about locking it up in the cab, but eliminated that idea when he discovered that the driver's door lock was broken. *Shit, I'll have to take it with me!*

Dave pulled the tarp away and grabbed one of the box's handles. "Jesus!" he said as he started to lift the container. It was like a block of concrete. Finally, after a struggle he deposited the box on the asphalt. *I can't carry this sucker and I sure as hell can't leave it here. Now what?*

Dave scanned the parking lot. It was half full and there were no overhead lights. No one could see him. He grabbed the carrying case and dragged it to the edge of the lot. There was a drainage ditch next to the asphalt. He dropped into the depression, pulling the box with him. He then dragged the container about twenty-five yards to the west, finally stopping in a deeper section of the ditch beyond a bend in the channel. No one would see the case unless they walked right to the same spot. *This'll work fine*, he said to himself.

When Captain Osterback finally came to, his first conscious thoughts were of pain. The back of his head throbbed as though a jackhammer were pounding away on his skull.

Osterback's next problem was the darkness. He couldn't see anything as he blinked his eyes. *Am I really awake?* he wondered.

Finally, he tried to move his arms, wanting to touch the back of his head. But he couldn't budge them. They were solidly lashed behind the seat back of the chair he was sitting in. "Dammit," he shouted in frustration, "what the hell's going on?"

A couple of seconds later, a light flashed in his face.

"Who's there?" Osterback called out, staring into the blinding glare.

"Who are you?" asked an unseen voice.

American! was Osterback's first reaction. The voice didn't have the slightest hint of an accent. "I'm Einar Osterback, Captain Osterback. I own this vessel."

Stan Reams smiled. *Finally! Now I can get to the bottom of all this.* "Tell me, Captain, just what have you been searching for down here?"

Osterback struggled to see the man behind the light. "Take that damn thing out of my eyes."

Reams lowered the light to chest level. "I'm waiting," he said.

"Just what is it you want to know?" asked the captain.

"What are you doing down here?"

Once again Osterback worked his wrists. There was no escape. "All right," he said, "it started about a week ago, when this guy showed up on my ship in Manzanillo. His name's

Simpson. Dave Simpson. He told me that he wanted to charter my ship to . . ."

Dave Simpson made his way to the rear of the resort, walking along the beach. Rodriguez's men, if they were watching, wouldn't have had any trouble spotting him if he had tried to enter from the main entrance. The lobby and driveway were lit up like a Broadway marquee.

Simpson entered the building from an emergency fire door that opened up onto the pool area. The door was locked to the outside, but he had found the key. It was hidden in a tiny hole in the mortar between two bricks of a nearby garden planter. He and several other salesmen used the stolen key to get back into their rooms when they wanted to avoid the lobby. The front-desk crew kept a running tab on the philanderings of the time-share hustlers so it paid to be discreet, especially when they were screwing the resort's guests.

Dave was now standing in the doorway of the stairwell, scanning the long hallway that led to his room. It was deserted. As he started to walk toward his door he reached into his pants' pocket, automatically searching for something. And then it hit him. *Shit, I don't have a key to my apartment. Those bastards took it. Now what do I do?*

Simpson retreated to the stairway, seeking cover, when another thought popped up. *Of course—that'll work!*

A minute later Dave was standing beside the doorway of an apartment adjacent to his own. He had to knock only twice before the door opened.

"Well, hello there," the man said as he eyed Simpson.

"Hiya, Billy," Dave replied, greeting his neighbor. The thirty-something salesman had been working at the resort for almost a year. He and Simpson were drinking buddies.

"We all wondered where you were this morning."

"Yeah, well, we didn't make it back from fishing until late this evening."

"Catch anything?"

"A couple marlin," Simpson lied. "Nothing big, though. Just little guys."

The salesman nodded and was about to ask another question when Simpson continued. "Say, Billy, I'm sorry to bother you, but I'm locked out and I was wondering if—"

"Come on in," interrupted Billy. "I'll call the desk for you. One of the bellhops will bring your key up."

"Thanks, but there's no need for that. If you'll just let me out on your lanai, I'll hop right over. I never lock my sliding door.

"Sure, but wouldn't it be a lot easier to just get a spare key from the desk?"

Dave smiled. "Yeah, sure—but, you see, I think Maria is on duty tonight and I don't want her to know I'm back." He winked. "I'm just going to grab a few things and bug out."

"You screwing two gals at the same time again?" Billy asked, smirking.

Dave shrugged his shoulders as if to say, "What am I supposed to do?"

Billy nodded his understanding. Dave and the night clerk had once been a couple, but Billy hadn't known they were seeing each other again. He wondered who the other woman was.

Simpson and the salesman were now standing on the balcony. It overlooked the beach area.

"Jesus, Dave," Billy said, "you'd better be careful. If Maria ever finds out you're double-timing her, you're going to be in the shit for sure."

"I know."

Dave picked up a deck chair and placed it beside a six-foot-high wall at the far end of the balcony. The wood barrier separated the salesman's balcony from his own. He stepped onto the chair and then, just before slipping over the wall, he turned to face his friend. "Thanks, Billy. You're a lifesaver."

"*No problemo!* I hope you have a good time with your lady."

"I will."

"Tell me more about this crate you found," asked Stan Reams. He was standing next to the still-seated and bound Captain Osterback. They remained in the blacked-out galley of the *Pacific Salvor*. The only illumination came from the pier lights that beamed through the portholes.

"Well, it was about four feet square and it was heavier than hell. After we opened the crate we found a steel case packed inside. It was all welded up. We were going to open it with a blowtorch, but that's when the pirates showed up.''

"Pirates?''

"Yeah, well, actually they're a bunch of local cocaine cowboys. Drug dealers, smugglers—you know. Anyway, they came aboard the boat, killed my crew, took me and Simpson and another guy named Chambers.''

"What about the steel case?'' Reams asked. His pulse accelerated.

"Oh, yeah. They took that along too.''

Christ! It's gone for sure now, Reams thought. "What happened next?'' he asked.

Captain Osterback described how he and the other two Americans had been locked up in a warehouse somewhere in Puerto Vallarta. He then explained how Chambers had been killed.

Reams was about to inquire about the missing case when Osterback brought the subject up.

"They had us both locked up in this stinking back room— me and Dave. It was hotter than hell and sometime during the next morning something weird happened. I'm not sure what but I think it had something to do with that funny steel box we found.''

"I thought you said they took the box.''

"They did. But they brought it to the warehouse. Anyway, apparently they opened it up and. . . .''

Tom Parker was tired of waiting. This was his second night in Simpson's apartment. He had slipped back inside just after nine o'clock. If the con man didn't show tonight, he'd have to come up with a new plan.

Tom craved a cigarette, but he had run out an hour earlier. He was tempted to return to his room for a fresh pack but didn't dare leave. *That's just when the SOB will come back!* He settled on a fresh stick of gum instead.

Tom considered calling Linda, but decided to wait another fifteen minutes, until the scheduled hourly check-in.

He settled back in his chair and shut his eyes. He wasn't trying to sleep. Instead, his thoughts focused on the woman who had so dramatically changed his life. *I think I love her!*

Tom had never believed it would be possible again.

*   *   *

Like Tom, Linda Nordland was bored and tired of waiting. Unable to leave her hotel room, she had camped out by the TV. A movie was playing but she wasn't watching it. Instead, she was thinking about Tom. The physical attraction was always there. She had recognized that fact the first time she had met him. But there was far more to it than sex. *He's such a good man,* she thought. *So kind and tender. A real gentleman!*

There was also something else. It was nothing overt—more of a radiated sense that her internal radar had somehow managed to register. *Something's troubling him, deep, deep down. I can feel it. But what?* She wanted to help but was powerless to act. There was an impenetrable wall in the way.

Linda turned away from the TV, distracted by a brilliant flash of lightning. She glanced out the windows. The offshore storm was getting closer. She then started to reach for the nearby phone. She wanted to call Tom, telling him to give it up for the night. She desperately wanted him back. But she stopped herself. *No, you damn fool!* she thought. *Keep focused on why you're here.* She created a mental image of Dave Simpson. That instantly brought her back to reality.

"What did these burns look like?" asked Stan Reams, now puzzled.

"I don't know—red, beet color. And their skin was all boiled up in blisters—big ones."

"Both of them were like this?"

"Yeah, but the one lying on the floor was the worse. His neck and face were all burned up."

"And what did the other one say?"

"It was hard to understand—he was jabbering away in Spanish so fast I couldn't get it all. It was something about what they found in the box."

"They opened it?"

"Yeah, I guess so because when he brought us out there, the top was off."

"What was in it?"

"Just some foam padding and metal spacers."

"Nothing else."

"Well, there was this metal globe, about the size of a bowling ball. It was lying on the floor." Captain Osterback paused for a few seconds. "It was kind of weird, though—it had this hole in the middle of it and off to the side we spotted this other piece of metal, like the globe but shaped into a tube.''

"What kind of metal?" asked Reams. He already knew the answer but wanted to hear Osterback's explanation.

"The Mex called it *el dorado*—gold. But I don't know what it was.''

"Did you say these pieces of 'gold' were out of the carrying case?''

"Yeah, both pieces were lying on the floor. And that's why the Mex brought us back there, to look at them. He kept jabbering away about how the gold had burned them. But Dave and I couldn't figure out what he was talking about. The man was acting nuts.''

Good God, thought Reams. *They must have combined them. No wonder they were burned!* "What happened next?" he asked.

Captain Osterback shifted position in the chair, trying to get comfortable. "Well, the Mex, the one who brought us out happened to turn away and . . .''

Tom Parker's eyes snapped open the second the master-bedroom sliding door opened. He didn't actually hear the heavy slider as it moved on its tracks. It was the sound of the ocean that startled him. The condominium unit was well insulated and the beat of the ocean was muffled when the doors and windows were sealed up. But the unmistakable roar was there for just a few seconds—long enough for someone to have entered the unit. *Dammit!* he thought. *Someone's breaking in.*

Tom stood up and moved to a wall next to the hallway. It led to the master suite. *You dummy! Why didn't you check that door?* Tom had been waiting for Simpson to come in through the front door. He hadn't counted on a burglar.

Tom heard footsteps and then a light clicked on. He could hear someone searching through a dresser drawer.

Dave Simpson grabbed a small nylon bag from the drawer and began to stuff in clean underwear and socks. He then opened another drawer and removed a pair of cotton trousers. Next, he walked to the closet and began to remove a couple of shirts.

What the hell's that prick doing in there, anyway? Tom

wondered as he cocked his ear toward the bedroom. A moment later the phone started to ring. Tom's heart skipped a beat. *Not now, Linda!*. He had forgotten to call in for the hourly check. He pressed his back against the wall. He was sweating again.

For just a second, Dave Simpson thought about picking up the telephone handset next to his water bed. But he resisted. *Who knows who might be calling?* he thought. *Maybe one of Rodriguez's goons is checking.*

Linda let the phone ring nearly a dozen times before finally hanging up. *Something's wrong!*

Tom hadn't called at the scheduled time. He had never been late. She waited a few more seconds and then jumped to her feet. *He's in trouble!*

She ran toward the door.

Tom wasn't sure what to do. Someone was in the bedroom, that much he was certain of. For just a moment he considered slipping out the front door, waiting for the thief to finish his work. But that wouldn't work. The intruder might hear him open the door. *Shit, what do I do now?*

Dave Simpson had just about everything he needed from the bedroom. His bag was stuffed. He looked around, checking for anything else he might need. *That's it; I'm done here,* he thought. He then headed for the hallway. He had one last stop—in the kitchen. The floor safe was cleverly hidden under a false bottom below the refrigerator. It held about five thousand dollars in cash plus assorted jewelry—mostly loose diamonds—a handful of stolen MasterCard and Visa credit-card blanks and half a dozen fake passports. He would need them all to start over.

Tom caught a glimpse of the figure as it passed by him. He couldn't see the man's face but he was big—much bigger than he had been expecting. Most second-story burglars are small and lithe. The man he had just seen was a hulk.

Dave had flipped on the kitchen light and was just standing next to the Frigidaire. He was about to maneuver the six-foot-tall refrigerator out of its built-in alcove when the knocking started. It wasn't loud—just enough to get his attention. *Someone's at the door.* He looked toward the adjacent entryway.

He could see the doorway. For just an instant, he thought about flipping off the lights but decided against it. Whoever was outside might notice the change in light that escaped under the door frame.

Tom Parker's heart was racing. The man was still in the kitchen and he was certain that Linda was outside, knocking on the door. *Linda, get out of here!* he wanted to scream.

Dave Simpson wondered who was at his door. *Maybe it's Billy,* he thought. *That's it; it must be Billy.* Then, without thinking any further, he stepped into the hallway and opened the door, expecting to see his next-door neighbor.

Linda Nordland almost fainted when Dave Simpson swung open the door. *You, you!* is all she managed to think as she backed up into the hallway.

Simpson eyed the attractive woman. There was something familiar about her face. "What do you want?" he asked.

"You killed my mother." Her voice cracked under the strain.

Simpson wished he had never opened the door. Something was wrong with the woman. "Sorry, lady, you've got me mixed up with someone else." He started to close the door but Linda rushed forward, jamming her foot in the doorway.

"Where's Tom? What have you done with him?" she demanded.

Dave Simpson had just started to shove her shoe out of the doorway when his left shoulder erupted into a torrent of searing agony. "Jesus!" he cried out. And then, out of sheer instinct, he reached backward over his shoulder with his right hand, searching for the source of the pain. A second later he found it. He yanked on the foreign object.

"What the hell?" Simpson asked as he held the four-inch dart in front of his eyes.

And then he collapsed.

Tom Parker rushed forward, the CO_2 dart pistol now tucked into his waistband. "Quick, Linda," he said, "get in here and help me move him inside so I can shut the door."

Half a minute later the job was done.

While standing next to the unconscious Simpson, Tom and Linda embraced. They were both pumped up with what seemed like gallons of adrenaline.

"See, honey," Tom said as he held Linda, "I told you we'd eventually get the sucker."

It was raining now. The tropical storm blew into Puerto Vallarta just after midnight. It was brutal. Vicious gusts of wind picked up anything not nailed down. Lightning burned the night sky with the brilliance of a thousand suns. Thunder boomed like an artillery barrage. But most dramatic of all was the rain. Buckets descended from the heavens.

The *Pacific Salvor* strained at her mooring lines as the wind and harbor waves relentlessly attacked the exposed hull. The ship, still moored at the seaward end of the concrete pier, groaned and creaked as the intensity of the battle increased. It seemed that Mother Nature was bound and determined to drive the vessel onto the shore.

As bad as the storm was, it wasn't enough. The lines were new and strong; they would hold. And the thick rubber fenders that hung over the side would cushion the ship, preventing the rock-hard face of the pier from tearing into her steel hull plates.

Reams and Osterback were still in the galley. They were conscious of the war taking place outside but showed little concern.

The questioning had been nonstop for forty minutes. Stan Reams had the whole story now. Captain Osterback told him everything—at least as he knew it. He had described how they had found the *Korean Star,* how they had been captured by the Mexican drug lord, and how they had escaped. But most important of all, the man had confirmed that they were still in possession of the steel box and its precious contents.

"Tell me again," Reams said as he paraded in front of Osterback, "you're certain your friend still has the case."

The captain shuffled in his seat. His arms, still bound behind his back, were cramping. "Yes, it's in the truck. Dave wanted to return to his condo to get some money. Then he's supposed to bring it back here."

"He's going to drive out here?" Reams asked as he gestured to a nearby porthole. The pier's rain-soaked concrete deck was just visible in the background.

"No. Not here. Rodriguez's goons are still in the parking lot. I'm supposed to row ashore and pick him up."

"When?"

"Around midnight"

Stan looked at his watch. It was 12:14 A.M. *There's no way that's going to happen tonight—not with this weather.* "Where does this Simpson live?"

"He's got a condo in town. I can't remember the name of the place, but he said it was right next to that new downtown plaza that's under construction."

Reams nodded. He recalled seeing the construction site during an earlier reconnaissance.

"Tell me more," he said.

TWENTY-ONE
RECONNAISSANCE

THE STORM BLEW OUT AN HOUR AFTER SUNRISE AND THE transformation was striking. The dark, forbidding thunderheads were replaced with crystal skies. The gale-force winds had vanished, leaving just a ghost of a breeze in their wake. And the once-broiling surf had simmered down to a steady, dull beat.

The cobblestone streets of old Puerto Vallarta were still flowing. The runoff temporarily halted traffic, but the rush scoured the dirty streets with an efficiency that surpassed any human effort. Elsewhere in the city, the asphalt overlays and macadam roadways were similarly washed. Even the air was cleansed. The stale, stagnant collection of man-generated smells, cooked day after day by the tropical heat, had been replaced with the fresh fragrance of the sea. The summer storm had renewed the city, giving it new energy and new life.

"Looks like it's going to be a nice day," Tom Parker said as he scanned the beach from the balcony. A half-spent cigarette hung from the corner of his mouth. He was wearing a pair of white boxer shorts and nothing else.

"Do you think it'll rain anymore?" asked Linda Nordland. She was standing by his side, leaning on the railing. She wore a T-shirt, one of Tom's. It didn't quite cover her naked rear.

"I don't think so. I don't see anything threatening out there."

"Then maybe we can leave today?"

"Yeah, if I can get the plane, we should be able to do it."

"When will you know?"

Tom looked down at his wrist. His watch was missing. *Where'd I leave it?* And then he remembered. Linda had complained that it was scratching her so he had taken it off. It was on the nightstand next to her bed. Tom looked back up. "I'll call the charter company around eight. Someone should be there by then."

"It's Saturday. Do they work on the weekend?"

"Oh, shit! I forgot about that." Tom's faced paled.

Linda frowned. "Oh, no. What if we can't get the plane until Monday?"

Tom shook his head in disgust. He had forgotten an important detail. "We'll have to wait."

"Can we do that? I mean, will the drug last that long?"

Tom raised his hands in frustration. "Honey, I don't know. The stuff's supposed to work for a minimum of twenty hours. After that, there are no guarantees."

"Maybe you'll have to inject him again?"

"Yeah, I guess I might just have to do that. I've got an extra cartridge."

"Will it hurt him?"

"What?"

"The second dosage. Will it harm him? I don't want you to do that if it does."

"I don't know, Linda. The doc never said anything about what would happen if we had to keep him on ice for more than a day."

"Then maybe we'd better pull out all the stops and really try to get out of here today."

"Yeah, you're right. I'll get right on it." Tom flipped the cigarette butt away. It landed in the sand eighty feet below. He then disappeared through the open sliding glass door.

Linda wasn't ready to go back in just yet. Instead, she sat down on a lanai chair, first placing a towel on the damp seat.

She removed one of Tom's cigarettes from the pack he had left on the table. She lit up. It took half a dozen lungfuls before the nicotine finally kicked in.

Linda hated her addiction but was powerless to stop. Despite all of her achievements, all of the wealth she had accumulated, she still failed at self-discipline. *I've got to stop or these damn things are going to kill me*, she repeatedly told herself. Yet she persisted. The pleasure was illusory.

Linda refocused on the task at hand. Dave Simpson was flat on his back, on top of the bed in the second bedroom, right next to her own room. He was out cold, drugged into a sleep state that would be impossible to reverse until the barbiturate finally wore off. Until then, he was no threat—just a heap of flesh and bone, a sorry excuse for a human being. Nevertheless, Tom had insisted on making certain that he was secured, should he awaken prematurely. His hands and ankles were shackled to the bed frame. Tom had also wanted to tape Simpson's mouth shut, but Linda had vetoed that plan. If he were to throw up—a real possibility because of the drug—he might aspirate the contents of his stomach into his lungs. It was a surefire way to die and a horrible way to check out—drowning in one's own vomit.

As much as Linda hated Simpson, she didn't want his death on her hands. A morally weaker person might have acted differently, especially if their mother had been victimized by such a despicable man. But Linda's resolve remained steadfast: it was her duty to return him for justice. She wanted him to waste the next ten years of his life doing hard time in Walla Walla.

Linda crushed the remains of her cigarette in the ashtray. She stood up, took one last look at the deserted beach, and then stepped back into her bedroom. She needed a shower.

Stan Reams walked into the hotel at precisely half past eleven. He was wearing a fresh change of clothing: tan cotton trousers, a blue pullover shirt and a pair of white deck shoes. He carried a softcover suitcase in his right hand and a leather briefcase in the other.

Reams walked up to the marble countertop and set his suitcase and briefcase on the floor. "Excuse me, miss," he said, directing his attention to the clerk who was standing on the other side of the counter. She had her slim back to him, filing something in a built-in cabinet.

The woman spun around. American brunette, forty-something and starting to look it, tall and well-built. Her smile was automatic as she faced Reams, "Good afternoon, sir. How can I help you?"

"I don't have a reservation and I was wondering if you might have a room available, preferably a suite, high up on the water side. I'll need it for a couple of days."

Are you kidding? thought the assistant hotel manager. It was the height of the off-season. The resort was fifty percent vacant. "Certainly, sir. We have an excellent ocean-view suite available on the tenth floor. It has a large living room with bar and minikitchen. The bedroom opens onto a deck. It's two fifty per day."

"Great—I'll take it." He tossed a credit card onto the counter.

She smiled again as she handed him a guest registration form. "Please fill this out, sir, while I enter your card into the computer."

Reams nodded as he pulled out a pen.

She picked up the bankcard and headed toward the card reader.

Stan had the guest form filled out by the time the clerk finished running the computer check. The card was valid and his credit line more than adequate. She reserved five days of credit.

"Here you go, Mr. Martin," she said, referring to his new alias as she handed him a key and the resort's passport ID. The new identification number had just been assigned to Stan's room by the hotel. "If you want to charge anything here, just show this card and sign the charge ticket."

"Okay, got it." He started to walk away from the counter when he suddenly turned back. The move was deliberate and calculated. "Oh, one other thing," he said. His eyes momentarily dropped to read the name tag on her blouse. "Marle, I was wondering if you might help me locate an old friend of mine. We used to work together in Florida, and I understand he now works here. I'd like to surprise him."

"If I can. What's his name?"

"Simpson, Dave Simpson," he said, broadcasting as friendly a smile as he could manage.

"Ah, yes, Mr. Simpson is employed at the resort, but I believe he's out of town today." She paused momentarily to consult a computer terminal built into the countertop. "He was signed out through yesterday . . ." She paused, still studying the screen. ". . . and he's supposed to be back today but I don't think he's here yet."

"Hmm," Stan said, his face now neutral, deliberately exhibiting disappointment. "Do you have any idea when he might return? I'd sure like to know when he'll be back."

"Let me check something else." Marle turned and walked into an alcove behind the desk.

As soon as the woman disappeared, Stan reacted. He leaned forward, pulling his upper body onto the countertop with his outstretched arms. He could see the computer screen. The lettering was upside down.

An instant later, Stan dropped back to the tile floor. He didn't try to read the main body of the text. He was only interested in one item: the suite number. Simpson resided in unit 403.

Marle was back to the reception desk now. "I'm sorry, Mr. Martin, but none of our office staff has seen Mr. Simpson this morning and I rang his room. There's no answer so he must have been delayed. When he does come in, I'll be happy to let him know you're here."

"No, no. Please don't do that—I want it to be a surprise."

Stan expected Simpson to be long gone from Puerto Vallarta and probably never to return. If he had been able to get to the hotel earlier he might have had a chance of intercepting him. But the storm had torpedoed that plan.

For hours he had been temporarily marooned on the *Pacific Salvor*. Rodriguez's lookouts remained camped out at the base of the pier, preventing him from walking to shore. And there was no way he would have made it in the rowboat or swimming. The harbor was a whirlwind.

He had finally rowed to shore at 8:30 A.M., leaving Captain Osterback tied up in the galley. If the seaman worked at it long enough, he'd eventually free himself. After coming ashore Stan had flagged down a cab and returned to his own hotel.

"Well, okay. I won't tell him you're here," Marle said, "but you know that he might not come back until after you've checked out."

"That's all right; I'll leave him a note if that happens."

It was over a hundred degrees outside, but the air-conditioned room was a chilly sixty degrees. There was just a hint of rubbing alcohol in the air, but it was masked by a rank odor that invaded everything. The lighting in the room had been deliberately suppressed, but it was more than enough to illuminate the awful contents.

Arnaldo Rodriguez stared at the corpse. His brother-in-law's body was laid out on the stainless steel table in the mortuary basement. The body was nude, except for a small white cloth that covered the groin. The rolls of once-soft fat on the dead man's abdomen and upper thighs had congealed into a semirigid bloated mass. The mortician had cleaned up where Pepe Ramos had soiled himself, but the foul stench of rotting death still permeated the air.

"How did he die?" Rodriguez asked.

"I do not know, Don Arnaldo," answered the mortician. The elderly man wore a rubber smock that covered his front from chest to knees. His hands were encased by a pair of surgical gloves. He leaned forward, pulling back one of the dead man's sealed eyelids. "Other than some bruises and the discoloration on his chest, there are no signs of lethal trauma." He hesitated. "It might have been his heart. He was grossly overweight."

Rodriguez shook his head. "No, Pepe may have been fat, but he was strong, like a bull. Something else happened to him; I know that."

"Well, without an autopsy, I'm afraid there is no way to know for sure."

For a fleeting moment Arnaldo thought about ordering the postmortem examination but then dismissed it. *Anna would never approve.* He had not yet told his sister that her husband was dead. He would have to do that later in the day.

Rodriguez turned away from the body, now looking at the mortician. "I want you to make him look good, Santiago. He must be presentable to the family."

"*Si*, Don Arnaldo. I will see to it personally."

Rodriguez started to walk toward the stairway. The stench

was overpowering. He stopped after a few paces and turned around. "What about the other one? How was he killed?"

"That is a great mystery to me." The mortician walked a few steps toward the rear of the room, stopping beside another table. A white sheet covered its contents. "I've never seen burns quite like these before," he said as he pulled back the sheet.

Rodriguez viewed the second corpse. Even from twenty feet away he could see the tortured skin. It was worse than he had remembered from the warehouse visit. The man's entire body looked as if it had been lowered into a vat of boiling water. *What did those* gringos *do to him?*

"Can you examine him to find out what happened?"

"These kinds of burns are beyond my knowledge. I would have to have an expert at the hospital examine him. Do you wish me to do that?"

"No. That will not be necessary. Just prepare him as best you can and put him in a good coffin." Rodriguez paused. "He's from Colima. Can you make the arrangements to ship him home?"

"*Si.* I will take care of it."

Rodriguez nodded and then headed up the stairway. He could hardly wait to get back into the sunlight.

"Everything's set for tomorrow morning," Tom Parker said as he flopped into a living room chair. It was almost three in the afternoon. He had just returned from the airport.

"That's great!" Linda replied. She was sitting cross-legged on the couch. She held a paperback novel in her right hand. "What time do we leave?"

"We're scheduled to take off at 6:30 A.M." Tom paused. "There was one hitch, though."

Linda frowned. "What's the matter?"

"I couldn't get the same plane we had lined up before. It's already been chartered. All they had available was a twin-turboprop Beachcraft."

"So we're not going in a jet?"

"No, I'm afraid not. There aren't any available until early next week. I figured you didn't want to wait that long."

"How long will it take us, then?"

"We'll be able to get to San Diego in about five hours. We can then hook up with a charter jet that'll get us back to Seattle by early evening." Tom hunched his shoulders up in apology. "I'm sorry, but that's the best I could do."

Linda smiled. "That's okay. As long as we get Simpson back to Seattle, that's what counts."

"Good—then we're all set."

Tom and Linda's plan to smuggle Dave Simpson out of Mexico was surprisingly simple. Linda would pose as the wife of a man who had suffered a stroke while vacationing in Puerto Vallarta. Using the alias of Mrs. David Sommerville and relying on fake IDs procured by Tom, Linda would escort her ailing husband back to Seattle. Tom's job was to function as a male nurse. With his military background and extensive first-aid training, that task would be routine for him.

Parker stood up and headed to the refrigerator. He wanted a beer. "By the way, how is our boy?" he asked as he opened the door and reached inside.

"Sleeping like a baby."

"Good. Hopefully, we won't have to drug him again until tomorrow morning." Tom removed the cap and took a long pull on the bottle of *Dos Equis*. The ice-cold fluid was smooth as silk. A moment later he turned back toward Linda. "You want one of these?"

"Yeah, sure."

"In the bottle or a glass?"

"Bottle's fine."

"Coming right up."

While Tom and Linda enjoyed a couple of "cool ones," the two men assigned to monitor the resort hotel remained hot and dry. They weren't allowed to drink while on duty.

The sentries did their job, but just barely. Sitting in the Chevy sedan, hour after hour, with nothing more to do than to watch the entry to the hotel lobby was utterly boring. They had been ordered to P.V. the previous afternoon, joining the others who had arrived earlier from the ranch. The two newcomers longed for their regular jobs.

Back in Guadalajara, each man had his own air-conditioned pickup truck. They were part of Arnaldo Rodriguez's personal security force. They constantly patrolled the sprawling grounds of his ranch, looking for intruders. Even though Rodriguez was the region's reigning drug czar, he could not let his guard down. Given the slightest chance, his competitors, especially the nasty crowd from Chihuahua, wouldn't hesitate to remove him. With Rodriguez gone, his empire would be ripe for the taking.

At least one of the guards always kept his eyes glued on the resort's entryway. Despite the hordes of guests and visitors that streamed through the lobby area each hour, no one could pass their parked car without being observed.

The guards were looking for two *gringos*. They were aided by a color Xerox blow-up of a Polaroid photo of the big one and a hand-drawn sketch of the other man. An artist had drawn the crude portrait of the ship captain, based on a verbal description provided by Rodriguez himself.

So far, no one matching the photo or sketch had passed the guards' vantage point. Both men figured they were wasting time.

Had the Guadalajara *nacos* been more aggressive, they could have done a lot more than just sit in the car. One man could have staked out the beach area fronting the resort while the other monitored the lobby. A maid could have been bribed to gain access to Simpson's suite. And finally, if just one of the men had gotten out of the car and walked around, he might have discovered Pepe Ramos' abandoned pickup. It was still parked in the resort's staff parking lot, only a couple of hundred feet away from the Chevrolet.

As it was, the guards did exactly what they were told and nothing more. It was the easy way out and that was their nature.

TWENTY-TWO
WOUNDED IN ACTION

THE RESTAURANT WAS NOISY AND STANK OF CIGARETTES BUT no one cared. The oppressive heat had finally let up just after sunset when an ocean breeze swept across the city. The cool sea air had a calming effect on everyone in Puerto Vallarta.

The mood of the early evening was festive.

Stan Reams sat at a small table off to the side of the main dining floor. He had a view of the harbor. The background lighting in the restaurant was subdued, enhancing the illumination from the tiny candles on the tables. The yellowish-white flames danced about, casting just enough light to illuminate the faces of the patrons. There were dozens of gregarious diners surrounding his table. The restaurant sounded like Grand Central Station—it roared with chatter.

Stan ignored the din. Instead he stared out the window, occasionally sipping his martini. He looked calm and relaxed, maybe even a little drunk. But it was a facade. He was busy working, his mind running at *mach* velocity.

Long ago, during his chaotic university days, Stan had learned to tune out the extraneous. He could work almost anywhere, from a bar stool in a tavern stuffed full of beer-guzzling undergrads to the turbine room of the wind tunnel running a supersonic test. That extraordinary ability enabled him to concentrate on the most challenging problems: quantum mechanics, advanced thermodynamics and orbital escape velocities, to name a few.

Stan's ability to focus his intellect had served him well during his twenty-five-year career as an engineer, catapulting him to the pinnacle of his profession. Where others had thrown up their hands in frustration at an impossible technical dilemma, he'd quietly worked out a series of options and alternatives, all logical, orderly and neat: just like a computer. Only after thoroughly analyzing the problem in his head had he then committed the final solution to paper.

And tonight Stan just about had it all figured out. After a few more minutes of refinement, the plan to trap the elusive David Simpson would be complete. He would then eat his dinner, walk back to his hotel room and turn in early. He was worn out from the previous evening's excursions and desperately needed a good night's sleep.

While Stan Reams sat in the stuffy dining room, Tom Parker and Linda Nordland were seated at a table on the balcony of Linda's suite. Endless trains of rollers crashed onto the sandy beach eight stories below. A room-service waiter had just delivered their meals.

"Umm, this looks good," Linda said as she eyed her plate of red snapper. The tender fish fillet was garnished with tiny red potatoes and other assorted vegetables. She picked up her knife and fork.

Tom had already sliced into his steak and taken his first bite. The slab of Mexican beef was tender and well done, just as he had ordered. "Yeah, this is wonderful." He looked toward Linda. "You sure you don't want to try a little?"

She shook her head as she swallowed her first mouthful of the fish. "No, thanks, Tom. I don't care for red meat."

"When did you quit eating beef?"

"Oh, I don't know. I guess when I was in college. I was never fond of it to begin with and then when my dad died of a heart attack, that was enough to stop."

"What do you mean?"

"Dad loved greasy foods. He ate beef all the time—hamburgers, steaks. He had high cholesterol—that's what killed him: plugged up arteries."

Tom nodded. He too liked beef and ate a lot of it. For just a fleeting moment he considered pushing the thick steak aside. But then he popped another chunk of meat into his mouth. It tasted wonderful.

After chewing he took a sip of water. He would have preferred a beer or a glass of wine, but he elected not to have any more liquor. The next day would be a busy one and he didn't want anything to interfere with his work.

Tom looked back at Linda. "Fish okay?" he asked.

"Perfect. I'm amazed that the room service is so good here."

"Yeah, I know what you mean. Even though most of the units here are time-shares, they do run the hotel section pretty well."

Tom and Linda finished their meal about fifteen minutes later. Tom then poured two cups of coffee from a steaming pot. She took a little cream. He liked his black.

"Maybe we should have ordered decaf," Linda said as she sipped her cup.

"You think this'll keep you awake?"

"Oh, probably not. But I don't think I'll sleep anyway."

"Worried?"

"A little, I guess. A lot could go wrong."

For just an instant Linda Nordland considered calling the whole thing off. All she and Tom had to do was walk out of the hotel and take a late flight back to the States. One of the maids would find Dave Simpson the next morning. He'd wake up with a terrific headache but wouldn't have the faintest idea what had happened to him. *No way!* Linda said to herself as she dismissed her thoughts of capitulation. *That son of a bitch is going to jail!*

Tom smiled. "It's going to be fine, honey. All we have to do is follow the script and it'll go like clockwork."

"Yeah, you're right, Tom. It'll be fine."

Tom Parker's scheme to smuggle Dave Simpson out of Mexico was set. They would rise at 5:00 A.M. While Linda finished packing, Tom would inject Simpson with another syringe of the knockout drug. After wrapping Simpson's head in gauze bandages to hide his face from the resort staff, Tom would strap the unconscious man into the wheelchair he had rented. Then, while Tom carried their luggage, Linda would wheel Simpson through the hotel lobby to the parking lot. After loading Simpson into the backseat of the Jeep, they would drive to the airport.

The twin-engine Bonanza would be waiting on the tarmac next to the private charter company's office. It was scheduled for a 6:30 departure. That part of the airport would be deserted in the early morning hours, especially on a Sunday.

Even if they were to be questioned by the police or a curious airport employee, Tom was prepared. The fake report from the local hospital explained the need for the medical emergency: the American patient had suffered a stroke and was returning to the United States for treatment.

Tom and Linda's goal was to get Simpson back to Seattle. They planned to drop him off, still heavily drugged, in a cheap hotel room near the airport. An anonymous call would then be made to the local police, reporting that a dangerous fugitive was hiding out in their city. Tom would stay near the hotel until Simpson was arrested, just to make sure the drug didn't wear off before the cops arrived.

*   *   *

Stan Reams woke early. He wanted to sleep—needed to sleep—but the pain was too much. His head was throbbing. The ache was in the same place—over his right forehead— and it was deep inside. It came in minispasms, cycling with the cadence of his heartbeat.

Reams had been plagued by the migraine attacks for months now. Aspirin used to work, but no longer provided relief. The Mexican doctor who treated him back in the La Paz clinic had prescribed a powerful painkiller. The narcotic helped but it left him feeling listless and drained, usually for several days. Stan couldn't afford to let his guard down for now, so he dismissed any thoughts of taking the medication. Instead he decided to get up and take a walk. Sometimes fresh air and a little exercise mitigated the pain.

At half past four he walked out of his suite, heading for the beach. The piledriver inside his skull was working overtime.

Two floors below Stan Reams' room, Dave Simpson tossed about on his bed. The restraints on his hands and legs kept him from rolling off, allowing his nightmare to play out.

Dave was back aboard the *Pacific Salvor*. It was dark on the ship's fantail as he watched the two crewmen kneel on the steel deck. Their hands were tied behind their backs. He could see the fear that paralyzed them—it also gripped his own body. The Mexican with the ponytail stood behind the victims, an automatic pistol equipped with a fat suppressor in his right hand. The gunman turned to face another man who stood behind. Rodriguez nodded and the gunman turned back. He shot the one on the left first. The man's head flipped forward, carrying the rest of his body into the open hold.

And then, to torment the remaining victim, the killer waited. He waited almost a minute before finally pulling the trigger. During that interval of terror, Dave Simpson lost it. And now, as he relived that terrible time, he again lost control.

The pungent odor of urine soon permeated the tiny bedroom.

The night sky was just beginning to lighten as the sun peeked over the coastal mountain range. Tom Parker and Linda Nordland, however, were too busy to notice the change. They had been awake for twenty minutes. He was dressed in blue jeans and a light cotton T-shirt. She wore a pair of shorts and a loose-fitting blouse. They both had sandals on their bare feet.

"You all packed?" Tom asked.

"Yep. I'm set. How about you?"

"Yeah, I'm pretty well set here, but don't let me forget that I've still got my briefcase and a duffel bag up in my room."

"You want me to go get it?" she asked.

"No, that's okay. I'll take care of it, but first let's get our patient ready."

"You going to inject him now?"

"Maybe," Tom said. "It depends on how he's doing. If he's still out cold, I'll wait. I don't like the idea of giving him any more of that stuff unless it's absolutely necessary."

Linda nodded her agreement.

Tom opened the door to the spare bedroom and walked in. Dave Simpson was spread-eagled on the bed. His arm and leg restraints were secure, but something was wrong. And then the smell hit home. "Oh, shit," Tom said.

"What's wrong?" Linda asked as she followed Tom into the room.

"Something I didn't think about."

"What?"

Tom shook his head. "I'm afraid old Dave here has pissed in his pants."

Linda gasped. "Good Lord, I never gave any thought to that. He's been out for over a day now."

"That's right. And his bladder must have filled up and then automatically vented."

"We can't take him out like that." Linda pointed to Simpson's crotch. The tan trousers he wore were soaked. "What'll we do now?"

"We'll have to clean him up and get him into some clean clothes."

"Have you got anything that we can use?"

Tom studied Simpson for a few seconds. The man was at least forty pounds heavier and a couple of inches taller. "No, nothing I've got will fit."

"Maybe I can clean his pants in the sink and then dry them with my hair dryer."

Tom checked his watch. "We don't have the time." He

paused while turning to face Linda. "Besides, he could do this again. We need some of his clothing."

"You want me to run back to his room and get some?"

"Yeah. Check the bedroom. He was packing some stuff in a bag—it's in there someplace."

"Where's the key you made up for his room?"

"It's on the coffee table."

"Okay, I'll be back in a few minutes."

After Linda walked out of the bedroom, Tom untied Simpson's legs. He then began to remove the soiled trousers and underwear. *God, I hope his bowels aren't full too.*

Stan Reams walked along the beach for over an hour. The fresh air helped. His migraine had subsided to a dull ache by the time he started back to the resort. He was now standing in front of the main building, looking upward. The concrete monolith towered over the shore.

Most of the rooms were blacked out, the inhabitants sound asleep or the units vacant. But in a few he could see lights. His unit was the only one illuminated on the tenth floor; he had left the lights on when he went out. There was another unit on the eighth and a few more on the lower floors.

Stan was just about to head for the lobby when he spotted it. A new light had just switched on. *Another early riser,* he thought. *Can't these people sleep-in around here?* He turned away, looking for the brick pathway that led to the lobby.

By the time he had taken half a dozen steps, it hit him with hurricane force. He stopped cold in his tracks. *Jesus, the fourth floor! Could it really be . . .*

He tilted his head back for another look.

As soon as Linda had walked into Dave Simpson's apartment, she had flipped on the master light switch in the entryway. It lit up the nearby living room. She then headed for the bedroom, turning more lights on.

She found the duffel bag. It was on the floor next to the bed, just where Tom-had told her he had seen it. She then emptied its contents on the bed. It didn't have everything she needed so she began to rummage through the nearby dresser.

*   *   *

Reams sprinted up the stairwell to the fourth floor. He was half-running down the hallway when the door to suite 403 opened. A woman walked out, carrying a canvas bag. She closed the door and then headed his way.

He slowed up, his heart pounding away in chest.

She smiled as she walked by. Mid-thirties. Pretty face. Nice figure. *Who the hell is she?* he wondered as he turned about.

His carefully thought-out plan had never considered this scenario, yet it made all the sense in the world to him now. *He sent you!*

Tom had Simpson cleaned up. He had just fashioned a make-shift diaper out of a pair of towels from the bathroom. Simpson looked like a giant version of the Baby Hughey cartoon character.

That ought to hold you, Tom thought as he stood by the bed. *Now, when we get you some fresh trousers we'll be ready to shove off.*

Tom debated as to whether he should inject Simpson again with the knockout drug or wait until he was on the plane. The man was still unconscious, but he seemed to be moving around more than ever. *Shit, what'll I do?*

He glanced at his wristwatch. It was a quarter past six. *Dammit! There's no way we'll make it to the airport by six thirty. Well, I'd better let 'em know we're going to be late.*

Tom headed into the living room to make the telephone call.

"Don't move or I'll cut your fucking head off," he said, his voice low and menacing.

Linda blinked her eyes shut, desperately trying to block out the terror. *Oh, God, he's going to rape me!*

It had happened in a heartbeat. One moment she was walking along the hallway, the next she was totally incapacitated.

He had clamped one hand over her mouth, effectively muffling any attempt to scream. His other arm was wrapped around her chest, gripping her diaphragm with viselike pressure. She could hardly breathe.

He then half-carried, half-dragged her down the deserted corridor. Her arms and legs flailed about, but to no effect. He had completely overpowered her. The shock was total.

Half a minute later they were inside the tiny alcove near the elevator landing. It contained a refrigerator-size Coke vending machine and an ice-maker.

Reams had Linda pushed up against the Coke dispenser and an adjacent wall, using the bulk of his body to pin her in place. His left hand was still cupped over her mouth, ready to instantly clamp down if she tried to scream. The knife was in his other hand. It wasn't very big—it fit into the palm of his hand—but the three-inch-long blade was stiletto-sharp.

"Where's your boyfriend?" he asked, his voice a whisper.

Her eyes were as round as saucers. She couldn't help but focus on his face. His head was just inches away. The stale odor flowing from his mouth was overpowering.

"My boyfriend?" Linda asked, now panting from fear and a lack of breath. The pressure of his body, rammed tight against her own, continued to inhibit her breathing. "What are you talking about?"

Stan guided the knife closer. The steel tip was just an inch from her right eye.

"Where's he hiding out?"

"I don't know what you're talking about."

Reams pushed harder, further jamming Linda's back against the cold metal of the vending machine. She let out a groan as a spike of pain erupted in her lower back.

"Come on now, missy. If you don't cooperate, I'll just have to cut you. Now where's old Dave hiding out?"

"Dave? You mean Dave Simpson?"

Reams backed off—just a little. Linda felt immediate relief.

"Of course I mean Simpson. Now where's he hiding out?"

What does this man want? Linda thought. She didn't know what to do. "Ah, I don't know where he is," she lied. "He just left word for me to get some of his clothes. That's all I know."

Reams didn't believe the woman. She was a lousy liar. He pushed back harder and moved the knife until it was a quarter of an inch from her cheek.

"No more lies, lady, or I'll cut your eye out."

Linda's resistance wilted.

Tom Parker had just finished his telephone call to the local charter company. The pilot had answered; he was the only one in the office. Their departure was delayed an hour.

Tom stood up and looked out of the windows. The sky was clear. It would be another hot day. Once again he checked his watch. It was now 6:27 A.M. *Where the heck is Linda?*

He sat down on the couch and again picked up the phone. He dialed Simpson's apartment number and waited. It rang twenty times before he finally gave up. *She must be on the way now.*

Linda was now heading to her eighth-floor suite but she wasn't alone. Stan Reams' right hand was clamped to her arm. She was so scared that her legs barely held her up.

After leaving the fourth floor, they had taken a detour. Instead of stopping the elevator at her floor, they had gone up two more stories. Half a minute later she was inside another hotel suite. The man said nothing to her as he maintained his armlock. Linda almost fainted when he removed the pistol from his suitcase. She had seen ones like it in the movies. It was black and had an ugly-looking extension on the barrel. She had never seen a sound suppressor before.

Tom Parker was hovering over Dave Simpson. The man was still comatose but he continued to stir. His legs, no longer restrained, flopped around. *Oh, no! I think he's starting to wake up*, Tom said to himself. He then headed into the bathroom.

Tom was preparing the injection when he heard the suite's front door open. *It's about time*, he thought. "I'm in here, Linda," he called out. "Come and help me with this turkey."

Tom was leaning over the bed, using an alcohol wipe to cleanse Simpson's upper arm. He had just released a wrist binding so he could move the man's right arm into the proper position. After disinfecting the skin he held the needle up to the light and gently pushed the plunger. A tiny squirt of fluid erupted from the needle tip. *Good—no bubbles.* Tom lowered the syringe. He was about to penetrate the skin when Linda walked in. He pulled the needle away as he turned to look.

Linda's face was ashen. All of the color was drained away. "What's wrong, hon . . . ," he started to say. And then the man stepped out from the hallway. He stood behind her. The barrel of the automatic was aimed right at Linda's temple.

"Now, just relax, Mr. Parker," the gunman said, "and no

one's going to get hurt.'' The man gestured with the pistol. ''Get your hands up. I know who you are, so no funny business.''

Tom dropped the syringe and raised his hands.

''That's a good boy. Now just lace your fingers on top of your head and follow us.''

Half a minute later all three were seated in the living room. Tom sat in the center of the couch, his hands still resting on his head. Linda sat in a chair next to Reams.

''So you're a bounty hunter?'' Reams asked, locking onto Parker's eyes.

''No. I'm just a private investigator.''

Reams continued his stare. ''What kind of weapons have you got around here?''

''Nothing. I don't need anything.''

''Oh, then you're some kind of martial-arts expert?''

''My specialty is finding people. I don't need any weapons for that kind of work.''

Reams didn't believe the man for a second. Parker was fit and probably could put up a hell of a fight. He wouldn't let that happen, though.

''Tell me, Parker, what did Simpson tell you about the core? Your lady friend doesn't seem to know anything about it.''

''Core? What the hell are you talking about?''

Reams frowned. ''The merchandise he liberated from the *Korean Star*—my merchandise. Now where is it? I know Simpson had it. Captain Osterback told me.''

Korean Star? Captain Osterback? thought Parker. *What the hell's this guy up to?* ''Like I said, mister, I don't what you're talking about?''

Reams let out a deep sigh. He then lowered Pepe Ramos' .22 pistol, aiming at Parker's left leg. He squeezed the trigger.

Tom Parker watched in horror as the pistol spat out a silent sheet of flame. The bullet pierced the left side of his calf, boring a clean hole through skin and muscle. It missed the shinbone by half an inch.

Tom doubled over, grabbing his wounded leg with both hands. Blood spurted through both ends of the wound. The pain was awful. It like someone had jammed a red-hot poker through his leg.

Linda started to scream when she saw the blood. Reams

turned and with his free arm grabbed her by the neck. "Shut up, bitch," he ordered, "or I'll shoot him again."

Linda complied.

Reams turned back to face Parker. "Okay, my friend, now that I've got your attention, let's start over. Now, tell me about . . ."

Linda Nordland's piercing scream was short-lived, but it was long enough to wake David Simpson. For the past half hour he had been hovering on the fine line behind the dreamworld and consciousness. The drug had finally worn off.

Dave's eyes slowly reacted to the light. It took him half a minute to focus. He tried to sit up but found that his left arm was tied to something. He rolled onto his side and looked up toward the head of the bed. *What in the hell?* he thought as he studied the binding on his left wrist.

Dave pulled himself forward. The rope went slack. A minute later he was free.

Still groggy, Dave Simpson swung his bare legs over the side of the bed. He still hadn't noticed the towels wrapped around his crotch. He stood up but only managed to remain upright for a second or two before sitting back down. His head felt like it would explode. *Motherfucker!* he thought, *I must have really tied one on to feel this shitty.*

"All right, Parker, I'm getting tired of the runaround. Now what the hell did Simpson do with my property?"

Tom was at a loss for words as he bent over at the waist, both hands still grasping his wounded leg. The free-flow of blood through the entry wound had stopped but the ugly exit wound was still leaking.

Tom realized that if continued to tell the truth—that he knew nothing about whatever it was the madman wanted—he'd get shot again. And then the nut might start working on Linda. *Lord, I can't let that happen,* he told himself. Tom finally decided he had no choice but to appease the bastard.

Tom looked up. "Okay, okay," he said. "I'll tell you what you want to know. Just put that thing away, will ya?"

Stan Reams smiled. *Well, it's about time. This guy's pretty tough but I knew he'd eventually talk.* Reams placed the pistol in his lap. "Very good, Mr. Parker. Now, where's my merchandise?"

"It's at the airport," Tom lied. "With a charter company. We're going to fly it back to San Diego today. The plane leaves at seven thirty this morning."

"What kind of precautions are you taking?"

"Precautions? I don't understand."

"Is the shielding still in place?"

Shielding? thought Tom. *What is this turkey talking about?* "Oh, yeah, it's still there. We didn't change anything."

"Good, that's very good." While holding the pistol in his right hand, Reams reached into his shirt pocket and removed a soft pack of Winstons. He tapped out one of the few remaining cigarettes and inserted it into his mouth. He returned the pack and then reached into his pants pocket, retrieving a silver Zippo. He was just about to light up when he noticed a change in Parker's eyes. He was staring at something behind Reams' back. Stan turned out of instinct.

"Hey, who the fuck are you people?" called out a new voice.

Dave Simpson was standing in the hallway, leaning against the wall. The makeshift diaper was still fastened around his waist. His appearance would have been comical if the situation hadn't been so intense.

Parker waited until Reams turned. And then, ignoring his leg wound, he reacted, launching himself off the couch like a missile.

Reams caught the movement out of the corner of his eye and turned just before Parker plowed into him. Both men rolled over the chair, carried by the momentum of Parker's vicious body thrust. Reams' lighter went flying and the cigarette was ejected from his mouth. The .22 spilled onto the tile floor, landing a couple of feet away from Reams' head.

Tom frantically grabbed for the pistol but wasn't fast enough. Reams gripped the handle and slammed the butt against Parker's skull. Tom collapsed. Reams hit him again and again.

When the weapon struck bone for the fourth time, Reams' index finger slipped off the guard, accidentally hitting the trigger. The bullet blasted out of the barrel. In a microsecond it traveled across the room. It hit Linda Nordland in the right side of her head, just forward of her ear. She collapsed. Blood spurted onto the tile.

Stan Reams pulled himself up. The man who had attacked him lay at his feet. He was no longer a threat. He looked at the woman. *She's a goner,* he thought. And then he turned toward the hallway.

Dave Simpson, still suffering from the effects of the knock-out drug, stood steadfast. He couldn't believe what he had just seen. He shook his head and turned around. *What a fucking nightmare. I've gotta quit drinking,* he mumbled as he shuffled back to the bedroom.

Reams followed. He would now get the answers to all of his questions.

TWENTY-THREE
NO BODIES, NO QUESTIONS

IT WAS A FEW MINUTES BEFORE 9:00 A.M. AND THE TEMPER-ature had already skyrocketed into the high eighties. It would reach a hundred by noon. The sentry sitting inside the Chevy was thankful for the shade from the towering palm trees. Otherwise, the automobile would have been unbearable.

The twenty-six-year-old Mexican was temporarily alone. His partner had just walked across the busy frontage road to eat breakfast at a cafe. Rodriguez's orders had been explicit: one man had to remain on duty at all times. Under no circumstances was the surveillance of the hotel lobby to be suspended. That meant the two men had to eat, sleep and relieve themselves in shifts.

Pedro had already eaten. His belly was filled with *huevos revueltos con frijoles.* He felt like dozing, even though he had slept through most of the night. His partner was used to night duty and had volunteered for the long shift from 2:00 to 8:00 A.M. Later in the morning, after he returned from his meal,

Pedro's companion would crawl into the backseat and take an early siesta.

Pedro stretched his arms out and yawned. He sank deeper into the seat. It would be another long, boring day. He looked up at the resort lobby. There was a little more activity now; some of the guests were up and moving about. He liked to look at the *gringo* women. Many were young and almost all of those wore skimpy clothing. He especially favored the ones in short shorts—the kind that displayed the roundness of the buttocks. Pedro would never allow his sisters to dress like that but it was okay for the *norteamericanos*. They were all a bunch of heathens anyway!

Pedro had just lit a match and was ready to light up a cigarette when he spotted the target. The tall man walked right through the main lobby door and stepped onto the brick plaza that fronted the hotel. A second later another man walked through and took up position by the target.

Pedro flipped the match out the window and sat up straight in the seat. He then reached for the photo and sketch lying in the center of the bench seat. He scanned them both. The first man—the big one—was a dead ringer for the one in the Polaroid copy. "That must be him," he said to himself. The second man didn't match the sketch—the image with a beard. Simpson's companion was clean-shaven and smaller. But he looked American. *I wonder who that is.*

Dave Simpson squinted under the overhead sun. He needed sunglasses but there hadn't been time for that.

"All right, Simpson, let's go."

Simpson didn't bother to look at the man. Instead he just pointed toward his left. "It's someplace over there, in the other parking lot."

"Lead on, mister," Stan Reams said. "We haven't got all day."

Pedro watched the two Americans as they strolled across the guest parking lot. They were heading north toward the more distant long-term parking lot—the one used by the hotel staff.

Shit, what do I do now? His orders were to phone in immediately if the *gringos* showed up. No one had anticipated that they would leave so soon after being spotted. *If I go to a phone, they might drive away!*

He waited a few seconds before making up his mind. That's when he decided to follow the two men.

Dave Simpson and Stan Reams were standing near the front of a Toyota pickup. Dave was talking. "I left it right down there, in that ditch, about twenty-five paces to the west."

Reams leaned over the bank for a better look. "Well, I sure as hell don't see anything now."

"It was there, right in the center of ditch, just around the bend in the . . ." Simpson stopped when he realized what had happened. "Shit, the damn thing's full of mud now. It must have rained and flushed the ditch clean."

"You mean it washed away?"

"I don't know. The ditch looks all different—it's deeper than before." Simpson paused for a moment. "But that damn box was heavy. I don't think it could have gone too far."

Reams scanned the parking lot. It was deserted. He pulled the pistol from his waistband. "All right, you dickhead. Quit screwing around and get my stuff or I'll shoot you dead, right here and now."

"I swear to you it was there. Let me go look—I'm sure it'll be there."

"Do it," ordered Reams.

Dave dropped into the ditch. Reams followed.

Pedro crouched by the fender of a Ford Taurus. He could see the two men. They were looking at something next to the parking lot. And then he saw the pistol.

They're armed! He had left his own sawed-off shotgun in the trunk of the car. *Now what should I do?*

He had two choices: phone in his observation and wait for help or fetch his weapon and take them down himself. When both men descended into the drainage ditch, disappearing from sight, his decision was easy.

Dave Simpson plowed through the soft muck that lined the drainage ditch. It would take a couple more days of the sun's heat to transform the silty mud into its usual brick-hard consistency.

Stan Reams followed a few paces behind. He held the pistol tight against his right leg, barrel pointed down. The ditch was now about six feet deeper than the surrounding terrain.

Simpson had walked about seventy-five feet down the eroded channel when he abruptly stopped. He dropped to his knees. The lid of the carrying case projected above the bed of the ditch. "Here it is," he yelled.

The torrential storm from the previous night had eroded the channel, causing the heavy box to sink into the mud.

Reams pulled up beside his captive. He instantly recognized the top of the case. He had repacked the container himself, back in Pusan. "So you were telling the truth, after all," he said.

Simpson smiled when he turned to face Reams. "You want me to dig it out?" he volunteered.

"Yep."

Dave dropped back onto all fours and began to claw at the earth. The moist earth was soft. It was easy digging.

Pedro stuffed the thirty-inch-long Remington pump into a duffel bag he carried in the trunk of the car. There were too many guests moving about to freely display the weapon. He couldn't risk someone alerting *la julia*.

He carefully worked his way along a row of vehicles until he had a clear view of the field. He looked down at the ditch. He could see the footsteps in the mud. They led off toward the west.

Pedro removed the shotgun from its carrying case and racked the chamber. He then dropped down into the ditch.

Dave Simpson struggled with the heavy steel case, dragging it with his right hand. It was tough going in the mushy soil. Stan Reams walked behind. His pistol was tucked inside his waistband. Neither man spoke as they approached a bend in the channel.

When Dave rounded the bend, he almost ran into Pedro. The Mexican sentry was only a few paces away. Pedro stopped, instantly raising his shotgun in defense.

Dave, staring at the business end of the ugly twelve-gauge, dropped the elevated end of the steel box. It hit the soft ground with a terrific wallop. A slug of mud blasted outward.

The blob smacked Pedro in the ankles, startling him. He pulled the trigger by reflex.

The shotgun roared. The cluster of double-ought pellets tore into Dave Simpson's chest, ripping open a fist-size hole. He fell backwards, flopping into the muck.

Before Pedro could pump another round into the chamber, he saw the other man, just for an instant. That was his last vision. And then there was nothing but blackness.

Stan Reams stood between the bodies of the dead men. Simpson's heart was blown out. The Mexican had a tiny hole just below his right eye. The .22 slug had had sufficient energy to penetrate the cheekbone, but not enough to exit on the opposite side of the skull. Instead, it had ricocheted off the interior bone, churning the man's brains into oatmeal.

Reams grabbed the heavy container by one end and began to drag it toward the parking lot. He didn't think anyone had heard the shotgun blast. The steep walls of the ditch muffled most of the noise. Anyway, he wasn't about to take any more chances. He finally had his merchandise.

Reams pulled out of the parking lot at a quarter to ten. Pedro's partner had finally returned by that time and was standing by the Chevy. He never gave the *gringo* a second look as Reams drove by in Dave Simpson's Ford Explorer. The sentry was too busy scouring the lobby, looking for Pedro.

Arnaldo Rodriguez's Mercedes roared into the resort parking lot almost two hours after Reams had left, finally summoned by the remaining sentry. The Mexican gangster and carload of bodyguards had just come from the pier where the *Pacific Salvor* had been moored. An hour earlier, the salvage ship had silently slipped away from her moorings, piloted by Captain Osterback. The lookouts on shore did not notice that the ship was gone until it had cleared the harbor channel and entered Banderas Bay. They had been too busy listening to a soccer game on the car radio.

It took Rodriguez and his men another half hour before they discovered the bodies in the drainage ditch. After studying the killing ground, Rodriguez concluded that Simpson's partner, Captain Osterback, had shot the sentry and that Simpson had been gunned down in the process. For a moment, the drug baron thought of pursuing the American seaman, but then rejected the idea. The man was not worth the trouble.

In the end, Rodriguez ordered his men to bury Simpson and Pedro where they lay. It was easier that way. No bodies, no questions.

TWENTY-FOUR
CRITICAL CARE

PARKER'S HEAD WAS ABOUT TO BURST. TOM HAD BEEN knocked around before, but he'd never had a concussion. He was sitting up in the hospital bed, his back propped up by a couple of pillows. The room was air-conditioned and he thanked God for that comfort. He looked out the nearby window. It was black outside.

Tom reached up and touched the bandages on his head. It hurt like hell. The torn skin on his forehead and right cheek had been stitched up several hours earlier. The surgeon's skill was exceptional. Once healed, the scars would be nearly invisible.

Tom's left leg was elevated by another pillow. The thick bandage wrapped around his calf covered the bullet wounds. The doctor had told him that he was very lucky. The .22 had punched a clean hole through the skin and muscles. The bones had been spared. He would have a limp for several months but would eventually walk normally.

His body wanted sleep—the painkillers circulating through his bloodstream made him drowsy. Yet he fought to remain conscious. He was desperate to know what had happened to Linda.

Although the bed next to Tom was vacant, he was not alone in the two-patient suite. A man about forty-five years old was sitting in a chair next to Tom. He was slightly built, maybe 140 pounds and at best five foot six inches tall.

Ricardo Vergara may have been small in stature, but he had

a lot of clout. As the senior detective for Jalisco State, the federal policeman reported directly to the Chief of the Judicial Federal in Mexico City. He had been assigned to the case only a few hours earlier. An Army helicopter had flown him directly to the hospital from his home in Guadalajara. The Mexican government was treating the attack on Linda Nordland as a matter of national concern. Tourism was the nation's lifeblood and whenever a foreign visitor, especially a VIP like the president of Nordsoft, is attacked, the negative publicity could produce devastating financial repercussions.

"Now, Mr. Parker," the detective said, "tell me again: what kind of business was Señorita Nordland conducting here?"

Tom pushed his head back in frustration. He was tired of the incessant questions. "Look, Vergara, I'm not going to answer any more of your questions until you tell me how she is"

The *federale* sighed. The American was obviously emotionally attached to the woman. Parker had told him that he was Nordland's bodyguard. Vergara could tell, however, that the man's devotion went far beyond that duty.

"I spoke to Dr. Perez about half an hour ago. He told me than Señorita Nordland is in a coma. The bullet grazed her skull but did not penetrate. The impact, however, caused a severe concussion, like your own but much worse. She also lost so much blood that she was near death by the time the maid checked on your room."

"Is she going to live?" Tom asked, not sure if he wanted to hear the truth.

Detective Vergara looked Tom right in the eyes. "They do not know. The next twenty-four hours will be critical."

Tom turned away. He felt horrible. He blamed himself for the mess they were in. He should have called it off long ago.

"Mr. Parker, I know you're not well, but I do need to ask you a few more questions before I leave."

"What do you want?" Tom asked. He didn't turn his head, though.

"Now, you're certain this man acted alone?"

"Yes, no one else was involved."

"And you're certain he was there to kidnap Señorita Nordland?"

"Of course," Tom said as he continued his lie. "What else would the bastard want?"

"I see. Now, can you tell me what kind of business Señorita Nordland was working on—who her contacts were, where the meetings were held, that kind of thing."

Tom turned to face the policeman. "Look, I don't know much. I never attended any . . ."

For the next few minutes Tom continued his story, mixing truth with fabrication. His purpose was to shield Linda from possible criminal charges. The fact that Dave Simpson was a fugitive and was wanted back in the U.S. held little weight south of the border. However, if the Mexican government learned that he and Linda had drugged Simpson and were attempting to smuggle him out of the country, they both would be thrown into prison. Kidnapping in Mexico, regardless of the reason, is a very serious crime.

Tom Parker had no idea what had happened to Dave Simpson. Not one question had been asked about the American con man. Tom didn't know if the intruder had killed him, taken him hostage or turned him free. All Tom knew was that Simpson was long gone.

Detective Vergara scribbled notes on a pad as Tom continued his story. Parker's tale seemed plausible, yet Vergara still had a feeling that the American wasn't telling everything. *He's holding back something—I'm sure of it!*

Tom was released from the hospital in the evening of the day after the attack. His facial lacerations were healing and the pain from the concussion had subsided to tolerable levels. But walking was still a problem. The doctor had told him he would need crutches for a couple of weeks and then maybe a cane. His leg would be tender for months.

Although Tom was free to leave the hospital, he didn't. Instead, he camped out in Linda's room. He remained at her bedside throughout that night and most of the next day. She finally woke up a few minutes before noon. She had been comatose for over forty-eight hours.

At first, Linda was confused and scared. The drugs flowing through her system clouded her memory and judgment. But when she finally recognized Tom's voice, she calmed down. It was his soothing words that did it. He repeatedly called out to her, telling her that he loved her and that she would be okay.

Over the next few hours, the doctors and nurses ran a battery of tests on Linda. The brain swelling had subsided and her scalp was healing. But there was another problem: her vision was off. Her right eye was blurred. Even when she slipped on a pair of glasses, retrieved from her hotel suite by a policeman, she still couldn't see clearly. The hospital's resident ophthalmologist speculated that the optic nerve had somehow become swollen as a result of the trauma caused by the bullet. He prescribed powerful anti-inflammatory drugs, hoping to relieve pressure on the nerve.

Late in the day, after all of the tests had been run and the doctors had gone home, Tom and Linda talked. Detective Vergara had been kept at bay by the hospital staff, but that would soon end. He would be allowed to question Linda the next day and Tom had to tell her what to say.

"Honey," Tom said, "I know you're still feeling lousy, but we've got to talk for just a few minutes about what happened. The police will be questioning you tomorrow."

Linda turned to face Tom. Her head was encased in a thick white bandage. She looked like a mummy. Linda didn't know it yet, but over a third of her beautiful blond hair had been shaved away in preparation for the forty-five stitches that had been required to repair her ripped scalp. "What do they know?" she asked, trying to smile.

"Only that some madman tried to kidnap you. I told 'em that I was your bodyguard and that you were down here for some business and then a little rest."

"What about Simpson—what happened to him?"

Tom shook his head. "I don't know. They haven't said a word about him. I think he either took off or that nutcase took care of him."

"Took care of him?"

"Yeah, you know what I mean."

Linda turned away. Her stomach flip-flopped. Everything had gone wrong.

"You okay, honey?" Tom asked.

Linda turned back. A solitary tear cascaded down her right cheek. "Do the police know what we were doing?"

"No, and we've got to keep it that way. You must not say anything about Simpson."

Linda nodded her head, as best as she could manage. "I understand, Tom." She paused for a moment. "I'm so sorry to have gotten you involved in this mess. It's all my fault."

Tom stroked her forearm. "No, Linda, it's not your fault. You were just trying to do the right thing. Simpson belongs in jail. He's the one responsible for all of this, not you."

Linda tried to smile. Despite her blurry vision she could see enough of Tom's face to again notice his wounds. "That man—he really hurt you. I'm so . . ."

"Shhhh!" whispered Tom. "Don't worry about me. I'm fine." He touched the bandages on his cheek. "These little things will heal up in no time. Now you need to rest up so you can go home."

"Home?"

"Yes, tomorrow. You should be strong enough by then."

"Good, I want us to leave this place as soon as possible."

"We will, sweetie. You just rest now."

Tom waited until Linda drifted off to sleep. He then leaned over and kissed her. "Sleep well," he whispered softly.

As Tom walked out of the room, his thoughts were focused on the medevac plane that would be arriving the next day: *God, I hope Bill's got it set up. We've got to get her out of here.*

When Tom had first phoned Nordsoft, from his hospital bed the day after the attack, no one back in the Seattle area knew that Linda had been injured. The American press had not yet gotten wind of the story. Luckily, Marisa was on the switchboard. Tom's friendship with the receptionist paid off. Making an outgoing call from the hospital was tough enough, but trying to receive an international call in his room would have been a nightmare.

While Tom was on hold, Marisa immediately tracked down Bill Sullivan; Nordsoft's senior vice president was in a meeting in downtown Seattle. And then, through a sophisticated call transfer procedure, Marisa linked Tom directly to the conference room where Sullivan was working.

After Tom informed Sullivan of Linda's injury, the Nordsoft executive was ready to catch the first commercial flight south. But Tom convinced him to wait. There was nothing he could do until Linda was well enough to travel. Besides, as the acting CEO he would be inundated by the press when the story of the attempted kidnapping finally broke. Although Linda Nordland wasn't in the same class as the senior Microsoft executives, she was nevertheless quite famous locally. It would be a big deal in the Northwest.

During subsequent telephone conversations, Tom and Sullivan jointly decided to send a medically-equipped aircraft from California rather than chartering a plane from Puerto Vallarta. Bill Sullivan would meet the medevac jet in L.A. and then accompany it on its flight to P.V. The jet was scheduled to land in P.V. the next day.

Tom really didn't want to return to the hotel. Right now he hated the place. But he had no alternative. Although he had more or less moved in with Linda during the last few days of the surveillance operation, he had still kept his own room on the floor above Linda's suite. And locked away in a briefcase in his room were the files on Dave Simpson. He had to destroy the incriminating evidence before Detective Vergara discovered it. The state policeman was a pro; he would eventually find out about the extra room.

Tom had registered under one of the aliases he often used during stakeout work: Tim Parkinson. He had reserved the unit for two weeks in advance, paying in cash.

The cab ride to the hotel was miserable. The ancient Chrysler's shocks were broken and every time the car hit a bump in the road, a new torrent of pain erupted in his leg.

Tom struggled on the crutches, eventually making it up the elevator to his room. But then he discovered that he didn't have his key. It was still in Linda's bedroom, on the dresser, along with the other keys to Linda's suite. *Shit,* Tom thought as he stood by the door. *Now what?*

He didn't have anything to pick the lock with. The tools were in his briefcase.

Five minutes later, Tom hobbled up to the reception desk. A man was standing behind the counter—Mexican, late twenties. "Excuse me," Tom said, "could you help me?"

"Certainly, sir," replied the clerk. His English was perfect.

"I seemed to have locked myself out of my room. Name's Parkinson, suite nine-oh-six."

The clerk nodded and then pulled out a printed form and laid it on the counter. "Please sign here, sir, and then I'll get you a replacement key.

Tom signed the form. A moment later the clerk disappeared behind a partition.

He reappeared within a minute. Tom's signature had matched the one on the registration card. "Here's your key, sir. Is there anything else I can do for you?"

"No, thanks."

As Tom hobbled away, he wondered if the night clerk recognized him. He hoped not. But then he really didn't care at the moment.

The clerk didn't make the connection. It was his first night back on the job after a week's vacation. He had missed out on all of the hullabaloo.

The shootings and attempted kidnapping were the biggest thing to hit Puerto Vallarta since Richard Burton and Liz Taylor had had their fling back in the early 1960s. The local police were everywhere. Earlier in the day, the reporters and TV people, U.S. and Mexican, had inundated the resort hotel. But tonight all was quiet. No one had expected that either of the victims would return.

Tom spent the first twenty minutes in his suite taking care of business. First, he pulled out the briefcase that had been stored in the closet. It had not been tampered with; the innocuous thread, purposely glued across the seal between the two halves, was still in place.

He unlocked the briefcase, removing all of the incriminating documents and the dart gun used to drug Simpson. He tore the papers into tiny little strips, eventually flushing them down the toilet. He next dismantled the dart gun. It didn't look like a gun, though. It consisted of a ten-inch-long aluminum tube connected to a tiny CO_2 cartridge and simple trigger mechanism. Tom had made it back in Seattle. When broken into its components, it was inconspicuous. That had been vital for getting it past a spot luggage check by border agents when entering Mexico.

Tom then dumped the disassembled dart gun into three different trash bins located near the elevator. Before discarding it, however, he carefully washed all of the parts, removing his fingerprints.

Tom next planned to change his clothes, wanting to strip down to a pair of clean undershorts and a T-shirt. He was hot and sticky, having been forced to wear the same clothing he had been brought to the hospital in. But that's when he remembered that all of his clothes were packed in a suitcase— back in Linda's room. *Ah, shit!*

The door to Linda's suite wasn't sealed up with police tape as Tom had expected. Instead, it looked like all of the others along the long hallway. He picked the lock and swung the door open.

He was rocky on the crutches as he headed through the entryway.

Housekeeping hadn't touched the room. The blood on the rug by the couch—his blood—was still there. And in the far corner, on the tile, was a larger carmine-black stain—Linda's.

Tom found his suitcase in a corner of the master bedroom. It had been obviously opened and then hastily fastened back up. *Must've been the cops,* he speculated.

Tom struggled with the suitcase and his crutches. He barely made it to the living room without falling. "Damn, this sucks!" he said as he dropped the case on the floor. Although he was beat, his thirst was more pressing. He'd get something here first and then head back to his own room. *No frigging way am I going to stay in this place!*

He hobbled into the kitchen and opened the refrigerator door. He grabbed a *Dos Equis* but, in the process of leaning forward, lost his balance. He crashed to the floor. The bottle went spinning across the tile. "Shit," he yelled. His left leg burned like hellfire.

Tom was now sitting on his buttocks. The pain had finally subsided. He ignored the crutches for the time being. He was too winded to try standing.

Still parched, he searched for the bottle of beer. "There you are," he finally said. It had rolled across the tile until it came to rest under the overhang of a storage cabinet.

Tom pulled himself forward and reached for the bottle. That's when he first spotted it—just a tiny flash of silver next to the bottle. You would never see it standing, but down low, like Tom now was, it was visible. *What the hell is that?* he thought as he reached outward. He stopped himself an instant before touching the metal. His investigative training told him not to touch it.

Tom pulled himself forward until his face was just six inches away from the object. It was a cigarette lighter—a silver Zippo. Tom used a Bic and Linda had something else. *Who does this belong to?* he wondered. And then he remembered. Just before he had attacked the intruder, the man had been lighting up. The impact of Tom's body-crash had knocked the man's hand loose; he was certain of that. *Could the lighter have sailed over the counter and landed in here, too?*

Tom eyed the kitchen counter and its relationship to the adjacent living room. The conclusion was simple: *yes, by God, that's what happened. This must be his!*

Tom scrounged around in the kitchen until he found a plastic bag in one of the drawers. He then deposited the lighter in the bag, being careful not to touch the metal with his fingers. If he was lucky, the intruder's fingerprints would still be on it.

Tom considered turning the evidence over to Detective Vergara. The federal policeman and the local *preventivos* had obviously missed it during their initial search of the apartment. After a few seconds of thought, however, Tom elected to say nothing. He had a much better idea.

TWENTY-FIVE
THE HAUNTING

HE WAS BACK INSIDE THE HOUSE, THE REVOLVER GLUED TO his right hand.

He had walked right in—the front door had been unlocked. That had been the first warning.

He couldn't see anything as he entered the living room. The darkness shouldn't have been a problem; he had resided in the house for over a year now. But then he tripped over something, some unseen object that shouldn't have been there. That was the second warning.

He picked himself up, his heart now thundering in his chest like a racing locomotive. He found a wall switch and flipped it. The ceiling light illuminated the room. It was a war zone: furniture overturned, paintings and photographs ripped from the walls, bookshelves tipped over.

"Jesus," he muttered, "what's happened?"

He ran down the long hallway and pulled open the door to the first bedroom. He looked inward, not knowing what to expect. A moment later he stepped inside. There was a tiny night-light in one of the electrical wall sockets. He leaned over the crib. Thank God! *he thought.*

He quietly backed out of the room, gently closing the door. He then walked to the end of the hallway and stopped opposite another doorway. He took a deep breath before turning the knob.

Unlike the first bedroom, the master suite was blacked out. He could see nothing. He felt for the lamp switch on the dresser by the doorway. He found it.

At first he was relieved. His bedroom had not been trashed like the other sections of the house.

He stepped to the side of the bed. She was buried under the thick down comforter, just a mat of blond locks projecting outward.

"Honey," he said, "what happened?"

There was no response.

"Honey, wake up!"

Nothing.

He leaned forward and pulled the comforter away.

Parker woke from his nightmare screaming. It was a violent waking, as bad as it had ever been. His naked body was sweat drenched, as if he were suffering from malaria. His breathing was rapid, like after running wind sprints, and his heart pounded away with an unnatural cadence.

But worse, far worse, was the new mental image that had just been fused into his brain. This time, when he pulled the comforter back, displaying the hidden face, the real horror hit Tom.

It wasn't Lori. It was Linda.

As Tom slipped his legs over the side of the bed, the first wave of nausea hit. His stomach was about to explode. He just made it to the bathroom, hobbling all the way, when he lost control. For the next fifteen minutes he hugged the porcelain bowl, venting the vile contents that churned deep inside.

It had taken him almost an hour to recover. Tom had desperately wanted to take a shower but had settled for a sponge bath. The doctor had warned him to keep his leg dressing dry. And then, while balancing on the crutches, he had shaved himself, somehow managing to avoid the bandages and stitches that covered his face. He had then struggled to dress himself.

Tom was now sitting on the bed. It was half past eight in the morning. His damaged leg was propped up by a pillow. He had a pad of yellow paper and a pencil; he was busy making notes. His description of Stan Reams was remarkably accurate: *Male, Caucasian. Looked to be in his mid-forties, but might be older. 5' 10" to 5' 11" Slight build, around 160 pounds. Brownish-blond hair, cut short. Part on left side. Very tan face. No freckles, moles or obvious scars. Spoke without any trace of accent. Probably American. Face kind of looked like Robert Redford—maybe a little rougher. Good taste in clothing. Silver watchband. No rings or other jewelry. Smoker—Winstons. No glasses. Contacts? Used a lot of profanity. Cool under pressure. Knows how to use a pistol. Strong hands and arms—once an athlete?*

Tom closed his eyes and again pictured the man. His remarkable memory for faces hadn't failed him. He would never forget the man who had almost killed Linda.

The hotel lobby was crowded with guests. Many had finished breakfast and were waiting to head back up to their rooms. Others were milling around, waiting for friends and relatives to make their descent. Almost everyone was upset with the delay.

Another one of the hotel's elevator units had broken down during the early morning hours. That meant that two of the four cars were now down for repairs. The first car had gone out a day earlier. The repairman wasn't due until two in the afternoon; he was flying in from San Diego.

The assistant hotel manager checked her wristwatch. It was a few minutes past nine. Already she was tired. She had been summoned by the desk clerk three hours earlier. With two elevators out of commission, the hotel would be in a state of chaos in no time.

While reviewing the day's reservation list on a computer terminal, Marle Boyer kept a constant watch on the elevators. She had a perfect vantage point as she stood behind the check-in desk. *So far, so good,* she thought. *No big complaints yet.*

The number three elevator chime went off again and Marle looked up. About a dozen people piled out; most were dressed for the beach. She had just started to look back at the computer screen when she spotted him. Tom Parker hobbled out of the elevator. A bellhop trailed, carrying Tom's suitcase and brief-case.

Tom walked up to the desk, still awkward with his crutches. "Good morning," he said.

"Good morning, sir," Marle replied, an automatic smile breaking out.

"I'm Tom Parker . . ." He didn't bother with an alias any longer. The incriminating evidence on Simpson had been destroyed. ". . . I was with Miss Nordland when she was attacked and—"

"Oh, my gosh," interrupted Marle, now recognizing the guest. "I'm so sorry about what happened. How's Miss Nordland doing?"

"Better—I'm hoping to take her home tonight."

"Wonderful. Is there anything I can do?"

"Yes, could you arrange to have her luggage delivered to the hospital?"

"No problem, sir. I'll have it sent over later this morning."

"Good. Thanks." Tom turned around and headed toward the entryway. The bellhop with his luggage had a cab waiting. He only managed to take a few steps before stopping. While resting the crutches under his armpits he reached into his shirt pocket and removed a folded sheet of yellow paper. He turned around and hobbled back, holding out the sheet. "Oh, miss, I almost forgot. This is a description of the man who attacked us. I'd appreciate it if you'd ask your staff if they recognize him and then give me a call at the hospital. I'm trying to help the police.''

"Certainly, Mr. Parker," Marle said as she took the paper. She unfolded it and began to scan the contents.

Tom was starting to turn toward the lobby door when Marle let out a sudden gasp. He looked back. She had her left hand in front of her open mouth. Her eyes were glued to the paper. The tan skin of her face was noticeably paler.

"What's wrong?" he asked.

"This man—I think I know him."

Marle and Tom were now sitting inside a tiny office located behind the resort's lobby. They were alone. Marle had just finished her story about checking in a guest named Stan Martin.

"You said this guy was an old friend of someone named Dave Simpson," Tom said. He was stunned at what he had just learned.

"Yeah, that's what he said. Something about knowing him in Florida."

"Did he say why he wanted to meet him?"

"No, only that he wanted to surprise him."

He sure as hell did that, Tom thought. "Anything else about him you can remember?"

Marle shook her head. "I'm sorry, Mr. Parker, but I don't think so. Your description's right on and I've haven't seen him for several days now. I'm sure he's long gone." Marle paused as a new thought gelled. "Wait a minute. I may have something else."

She turned to a computer terminal at the side of her desk. She typed in half a dozen commands. Twenty seconds later she turned back to face Tom. "He paid with a credit card— issued by a bank in Los Angeles."

"Ten to one it's stolen."

"It was okay when he checked in—I verified that. But I'll find out for sure right now."

Marle picked up her phone and dialed a long series of numbers. They were typed on a card in her Rolodex. Just after dialing she glanced at Tom. "I'm calling the credit card division right now. I'm going to check on that account."

It took a minute and a half to complete the call. The results were a shock. The card had *not* been reported stolen.

"It's a good card?" Tom asked.

"That's right. They wouldn't give out any more info other than to say that it had a standard limit."

Tom shook his head. "I can't believe this Stan Martin character would be dumb enough to use his own personal credit card."

"You're probably right—at least it's a start. If you get the police to call the bank, they may be able to get more information for you. You might need a court order, though."

"Yeah, that's a good idea. I'll look into it when I get back to Seattle." Tom would check it, all right, but he wouldn't involve the police or a judge. He had a much better source.

Before Tom left, Marle gave him a photocopy of the bankcard imprint. All of the account numbers were clearly visible. The receipt wasn't signed so there was no sample of the man's signature; he had checked out by phone. But it didn't matter because he had filled out the hotel's registration card. The San Jose address he had listed was bogus, but his signature as Stan Martin was remarkably similar to the way he used to sign when he was known as Stan Reams.

The chartered jet from Los Angeles touched down at Puerto Vallarta International at 4:35 P.M. Besides the flight crew and the medical support team, Bill Sullivan was the only passenger aboard. The Nordsoft executive had no idea what to expect.

The cryptic telephone call Monday morning had hit like a twister. He had never met, or for that matter, heard of Tom Parker until the man had called him. Parker's story of how Linda had been assaulted was especially troublesome to Bill. He had worried for months that the CEO of Nordsoft might be a prime kidnapping target.

At Parker's request, Bill had arranged for the medevac flight for Linda. He had then called an emergency meeting of key Nordsoft management staff members to inform them of the crisis. The press would soon be hounding the firm for information on Linda and the attempted kidnapping. The firm's public relations officer was assigned to handle all press inquiries.

With the immediate situation under control, Bill had set about a new task. He wanted to know just who Tom Parker was and what he was doing with Linda in Mexico. Nordsoft's attorneys had worked all night, digging through records and making dozens of phone calls. Bill had been relieved to learn that Parker was a reputable private investigator. His concerns were further alleviated when he found a copy of Parker's letter in Linda's desk. The letter was brief. It discussed Parker's retainer for investigative services related to locating an individual named Dave Simpson.

Bill had been confused. He thought he knew Linda well enough that she would confide in him if she was having personal problems. But he was totally in the dark about what had happened in Mexico. His head was filled with mixed thoughts when he finally left Seattle: *There's no doubt about it, Linda hired Parker to work for her. But just what was he doing down there? And who the hell is this Dave Simpson character?*

Parker was waiting at the terminal when the executive jet landed. As soon as Sullivan cleared customs, he and Tom headed back to the hospital. They were now inside a cab, heading south. Traffic was bad. The Ford crept forward.

"How's she doing today?" asked Bill Sullivan.

Tom studied the man. Sullivan wasn't much to look at; he had the build of a scrawny teenage girl. He wore horn-rimmed glasses with thick lenses—the kind that looked like the bottom of a Coke bottle. Although he was still in his thirties, his bushy hair was almost entirely gray. The goofy look didn't fool Tom; Linda had filled him in earlier. Sullivan had a brilliant mind. He excelled in everything he did. Tom would exhibit extreme caution around him.

"Well, Bill, I'm happy to say that she's feeling much better today. The wounds are healing okay now and her headaches have subsided a little."

"That's great. How about her eye—that clear up?"

Tom shook his head. "No, that's the only bad news. She still can't see straight out of that eye. There's something else going on that the doctors here can't figure out."

"Then we've got to get her to a specialist ASAP."

"Yep, that's right. You still got that guy lined up in San Francisco?"

"Yes, they're all set to see her tomorrow morning at eight thirty."

"We should make it fine, assuming they'll let us go."

"What do you mean?"

"The federal police are still investigating the whole thing. Linda and I can't leave until we get approval from the chief inspector."

"That's bullshit. We've got a medical emergency here. As soon as we get to the hospital I'll have our people call the State Department. I can get our embassy in—"

"Wow, Bill! Slow down. I know how much you care about Linda's welfare, but let me give it a try first. The inspector should be waiting at the hospital when we get there. If it goes okay, we may be outta there in an hour."

Sullivan settled back into his seat. His blood pressure returned to normal. "Okay, Tom, we'll give your method a try. But come hell or high water, Linda's going to be in San Francisco tomorrow morning."

Tom just nodded. *Linda was right,* he thought. *This guy may look like a nerd but he's tough as nails.*

While Bill Sullivan visited with Linda, Tom Parker and Ricardo Vergara met in a vacant office. The Mexican detective sat behind the desk with Tom in front. Tom's injured leg was stretched out across a second chair. He had been walking too much. His calf throbbed.

"I understand that you returned to the apartment," Vergara said. He took a deep drag on his nearly spent cigarette.

Tom had already finished his smoke. The tiny room stank of cigarettes. "Yeah, I needed to get my things and arrange for Linda's luggage."

"So you're planning to leave?"

"Of course. Linda needs immediate attention for her eye and I'm going with her."

Vergara blew another cloud of smoke. "You know that you will not be allowed to leave until our investigation is completed."

Tom was ready for the bombshell. He had rehearsed his answer long ago. "I understand and that's one of the reasons I went back. I found out a few things you need to know about."

Vergara was caught off guard by Parker's comments. He was expecting the man to blow up, threatening to call the

American embassy—better yet, calling in the U.S. Marines to rescue the innocent hostages that were being held by the fascist *federales.*

Vergara snuffed out his cigarette. "What kind of information?"

Tom reached into his rear pants pocket. He removed several folded-up sheets of paper and handed them to the policeman. "I wrote my notes on what this guy looked like—there's a photocopy in there. I then talked with some of the hotel staff. The assistant manager, Marle Boyer, recognized the man from my description. He was a guest at the hotel."

Vergara's interest was building by the second. "Yes, go on."

"Turns out this guy is an American—at least that's what he told Miss Boyer when he checked in. And I think she's right. He looked American, but sometimes it's hard to tell."

Vergara nodded.

"Now this guy was calling himself Martin, Stan Martin. He used a credit card to pay for his room. A copy of the card and registration are in there too."

The detective scanned through the documents. "Stolen card?" he asked.

"Apparently not. The hotel checked with the credit card company. So far it hasn't been reported stolen."

"That's odd. Surely he wouldn't use his own card."

"Right. He must have stolen it off someone who doesn't know that it's being used."

"You are going to report this back in the States?"

"Yes. I've already started the trace," Tom lied.

"Good. Now what else do you have to report?"

The next part of Tom's plan was a real long shot. But he had to try. "Ah, when I was talking with Miss Boyer at the resort, she indicated that this Martin character was interested in one of the other hotel guests. No, actually he wasn't a guest. He works there—one of the time-share sales staff. His name's Simpson. Dave Simpson."

Vergara had never heard of the man. "What about him?"

"That's just it—I don't know. Miss Boyer told me that this Martin said something about knowing him twenty years ago and wanting to meet him."

"Did they?"

"What?"

"Did Martin and this other one—Simpson—did they meet?"

Oh, brother, did they ever, thought Tom. "No, I don't think so—at least according to the hotel. Apparently this Simpson fellow has been gone for several days. He hasn't returned to his apartment at the hotel and no one knows where he's at."

"Do you think he might be involved in the kidnapping?"

"I don't know. I was hoping that maybe you can track him and find out."

Vergara nodded. "We'll look into it. What else do you have?"

"Nothing—that's it," Parker lied again. He carefully omitted any discussion about the lighter he had found in Linda's suite or the fact that he had maintained a separate room. He was prepared to defend the room if necessary. It wasn't.

Vergara leaned back in his chair. Parker's cooperation was commendable. His own men had gone back to the hotel earlier in the day and once again scoured the apartment for clues. They had found nothing new. Everything Parker had told him made sense. But there was still doubt. All the pieces were not yet in place.

"Well, Mr. Parker, it seems that you have done some of our detective work. So I guess you really are a private detective as well as a bodyguard." *And her lover!* The forensic lab tests confirmed that Parker had been sleeping in the same bed with the woman victim.

Where's this guy going? Tom wondered. He had never said anything about being a PI. "Yes, I'm trained in both professions."

Vergara reached down by his feet and pulled up a leather attaché case. He opened it and pulled out a four-page document. Tom couldn't quite make out the writing, but it appeared to be in English.

"Your State Department faxed this to us today. It is most interesting."

"What is it?"

"It's about you. Your education. Your military service—quite impressive, I must say. And it has a history of your business activities." Vergara paused as he scanned the document. "I'm sorry about what happened to your wife."

"Who in the hell sent you that?" Tom barked, now really pissed.

"Calm down, Parker. Actually its source was your own FBI. We asked for a complete history on you. We had no idea they'd report that."

It was all making sense to Tom now. Detective Vergara suspected that he was somehow involved in the kidnapping. "Well, what's all of that stuff tell you?"

"It appears to support everything you've been telling me."

"Good—then let us go home."

"In a moment. First, I have one last question." Vergara again reached into the case. This time he retrieved a clear plastic bag. There was something inside.

Fuck! Tom thought as he recognized the syringe. He had been going to use it to inject Simpson with the second dose of the knockout drug.

Detective Vergara studied Tom's reaction. The man had a poker face. "This look familiar to you?" he finally asked.

He knows something. Be careful now. Tom's mind shifted into overdrive. The first dose had been fired by the dart gun. The gun was now history and he had thrown the spent needle and its cartridge into the toilet after drugging Simpson. But this other syringe, the one in the bag, had his fingerprints all over it. *What should I do now?*

Tom reached forward. "May I look at it?"

Vergara handed him the bag.

Tom pretended to study the injection needle for a few seconds while he searched for a way out of the trap. He then met the policeman's eyes. "Yeah, this thing looks familiar. That bastard was going to make me inject Linda with it."

"Do you know what was inside?"

Tom raised his hands, signaling his frustration. "He said it was some kind of knockout drug, but I don't really know."

Vergara nodded his head again. Parker's fingerprints covered the device and the state lab had confirmed that it was filled with a powerful barbiturate. "Why would he want you to inject her?" he asked.

Tom was ready now. "I think that prick was trying to set me up—Make it look like I kidnapped her. As soon as he had the ransom, he'd kill Linda and leave enough evidence to implicate me. Then everyone would be searching for me while he escaped. But I'd already be dead, rotting away in some unmarked grave.''

Detective Vergara had come to the same conclusion only moments earlier. He genuinely liked the American but would never let him know.

The two men talked for a few more minutes and then Vergara pulled out a set of papers and signed them. They were official travel documents from the federal government of Mexico. Tom Parker and Linda Nordland were free to return to the United States.

The Gulfstream lifted off from Puerto Vallarta International at precisely 9:30 P.M. Linda Nordland rested comfortably on a well-padded stretcher while a female physician and a male nurse monitored her vital signs. Tom Parker and Bill Sullivan sat in the two lounge chairs located just aft of the flight deck. Both men sipped ice-cold cans of Pepsi.

Neither man talked; it was too noisy inside the cabin as the engines roared at full throttle. The jet was in a steep climb over Banderas Bay.

Tom set his can into a special slot on the armrest next to his chair. He then looked out his porthole. The aircraft was just starting to turn toward the right, preparing for the long northward track. He could still see the lights of Puerto Vallarta to the south. It was a spectacular view, but he didn't care. His mind was focused on a single thought. *You son of a bitch. You almost killed that sweet woman back there. God only knows what's wrong with her eye.* Tom gritted his teeth and gripped the armrests of his chair. His fingers dug deep into the leather. *If it's the last thing I do, I'm going to find you and rip your heart out!*

PART TWO

CRITICAL MASS

TWENTY-SIX
THE SPECIALIST

HE HAD BEEN WAITING ALMOST AN HOUR NOW. HE WASN'T used to it. *Dammit*, he said to himself, *who the hell does he think he is, making me sit out here with the* muerto.

He looked around the room again. Every seat was filled and several people were forced to stand. The majority were elderly, several decades older than he was. But there were also a few children, even one baby. They came from every part of the country. Most were poor but a handful, like himself, were rich. He would pay dearly for the visit.

"Señor Rodriguez," called out a female voice.

It's about time, thought Arnaldo Rodriguez as he stood up. He walked to the receptionist.

"Señor Rodriguez?" asked the woman behind the counter.

"*Si.*"

"Please go into room C." The young woman pointed toward an adjacent hallway. "The doctor will be with you in a moment."

Rodriguez nodded. *Finally!*

The shoe-box-sized room was cool—too cool for his liking. The chilled air blasted out of a ceiling vent above his head. The paper-thin gown covering his naked body provided little warmth. He was sitting on a stainless-steel stool near the foot of the examination table. It looked like the kind used for pregnant women. Twenty minutes had already passed by and he still hadn't seen the doctor. *This is ridiculous! I should never have let Hernandez talk me into this.*

It had all started several weeks earlier—just after the problem with the *gringos*. At first, Rodriguez thought he was coming down with the flu: headache, fever and vomiting. It lasted for a couple of days. And then the diarrhea hit. It was the worst he had ever had. Nothing would stay inside his bowels; everything passed through, including a lot of blood. So far he had lost fourteen pounds—almost ten percent of his body weight. He was beginning to look like a scarecrow.

His physician in Guadalajara was baffled at the symptoms. He thought that Rodriguez might have contracted malaria, but the tests were all negative. He was then certain that his patient had been exposed to some other exotic tropical disease and had been planning to send blood samples to the CDC in Atlanta for analysis. But that all had changed.

When Rodriguez had started to lose his hair—not just the occasional strand but wholesale chunks—the internist knew he was out of his league. That's when he had referred Arnaldo Rodriguez to Dr. Louis Aragon.

Aragon was a cancer specialist. His practice was based in Mexico City, but he traveled throughout North America and Europe, lecturing on his specialty: colon cancer.

Rodriguez was not yet aware of what his physician suspected. He was told only that he needed more tests and that Dr. Aragon was an expert in intestinal disorders. Rodriguez had flown into Mexico City the previous day. Today was his first visit with Aragon.

The door opened and a short, heavy-set man entered. Dr. Aragon was about sixty. He was bald and wore wire-rim glasses—trifocals. His uniform was the standard white lab coat with a pair of tan cotton trousers. He looked like a grandfather, which he was.

"Señor Rodriguez, it is a pleasure to meet you."

Rodriguez shook the man's outstretched hand. "Hello, Doctor," he said. All thoughts of the long wait vanished in a flash. His impatience had been a smoke screen, a personal facade. He wouldn't admit it to anyone—his wife, his doctor, his priest—but he was terrified. Something was very wrong with his body.

"And how are you feeling today?"

"About the same."

"Still can't keep anything inside?"

"That's right."

"You've been taking the medication that Dr. Hernandez prescribed?"

"Of course, but nothing seems to work." Rodriguez was

weak from his condition. He was slowly starving to death.

Aragon spent a couple of minutes rereading the patient's records. One of the reasons he had been late was that he had spent fifteen minutes on the telephone with Hernandez. This case was an enigma. Rodriguez was far too young to be having these types of problems. The diarrhea, the loss of blood, the inability to gain weight were all symptomatic of a massive shutdown of the intestinal tract. The hair loss, however, didn't fit anything.

Aragon had seen it before—in cancer patients. But only after the treatment had been rendered—not before. Most patients can stand the radiation therapy without severe side effects. However, some can't. Their bodies adversely respond to the high-energy waves that kill cancer cells. In some cases, the X-ray treatment literally cooks the internal tissues that surround the target area. It happens more often in men when the prostate is involved. The radiation will neutralize the cancer in the gland, but its residual effect destroys the bowel. The patient is cured of cancer but he dies anyway.

Dr. Aragon checked the last blood test on the chart. *This just doesn't make sense,* he thought. Everything indicated that Rodriguez's bowel had been subject to excessive radiation therapy. But the man hadn't even had a chest X-ray until a week ago.

Aragon closed the notebook and faced Rodriguez. "Well, you've certainly had a thorough set of tests back in Guadalajara."

"Yeah, I'll say. I'm sick of giving blood and having all of those other things done."

Aragon nodded. "Yes, I know the probes are uncomfortable. But I'm afraid I'm going to have to take another look, just to be sure."

Rodriguez stomach flipped. *Oh, no! Not again,* he thought. He absolutely hated the sigmoidoscope. "How far are you going to go this time?"

"Well, Dr. Hernandez examined the lower colon thoroughly. I reviewed his video record. But I'd like to go farther—all the way to the small intestine. I'll use a smaller endoscope than what Dr. Hernandez used and we'll sedate you so you'll be comfortable."

Rodriguez nodded.

"Did you follow our instructions?" asked the physician.

"Yes, I'm ready."

"Good, then I suggest we start. You can sit up here." He patted the tabletop.

The exam took over an hour. The probe was inserted almost the full length of Rodriguez's large intestine. The results were not a surprise to Aragon. The upper half of the colon was in an advanced stage of deterioration. The normally pink and flexible tissue was ulcerated and thin. He suspected Crohn's disease. *No wonder he can't keep anything,* he thought. *The man's very sick.*

Dr. Aragon was writing notes at the desk as Rodriguez began to dress. Aragon happened to look up just as his patient was slipping his shirt on. That's when he spotted the rash. It was a slight skin discoloration in the center of his chest, right below the breastbone.

Aragon was about to ask about the rash when Rodriguez leaned his head forward and slipped a chain over his neck. A silver-dollar-sized medallion hung from the chain. When he pulled his head up, the medallion covered the rash.

Dr. Aragon stood up and walked over to Rodriguez just as he started to button his shirt. "I couldn't help but notice this discoloration of your skin." He pointed to the man's chest.

"Where?"

"Under your medallion."

Rodriguez pulled the chain out of the way and then looked down. "I don't see anything."

Aragon moved closer. The brown skin was definitely inflamed. It was subtle but nevertheless it was there. "How long have you had that?" he asked.

"I don't know—I just noticed it."

"No, I mean your medallion."

"Oh, that." Rodriguez thought for a few seconds. He had removed it from his dead brother-in-law. "I guess about three weeks or so."

"Three weeks?"

"Yeah, something like that. It was just about when I started having these . . ." Rodriguez voice trailed off as he too made the connection. "Come on, Doctor, this little thing couldn't be causing me all of this trouble, could it?"

"I don't know. What is it?"

"It's just made out of steel. It was a gift from one of my relatives."

"A gift?"

"Yeah, kind of."

"Well, it's just possible that it might be contaminated with a chemical or something. Where was it made?"

"You mean I could have something like lead poisoning?"

"Well, probably not that. But I'd like to get it tested anyway, just to make sure. Do you mind if I send it out to a lab? I'll make sure you get it back."

"No, I guess not." Rodriguez removed the neck chain. He deposited it into a plastic bag held open by Aragon. The doctor was careful not to touch the medallion.

"Well, now," Dr. Aragon said, "I'd like to see you tomorrow afternoon for a few more tests. Then I think I'll have enough to recommend a course of action."

Rodriguez didn't want to ask but couldn't help it. "Doc, you going to have to put one of those bags on me?"

"You mean a colostomy bag?"

"Yeah, the thing you crap into."

Aragon really didn't want to discuss that option right now. He feared that the man might be in much worse shape than he suspected. "That is an option, but there are several others. I want to confer with another one of my colleagues here and with your physician first. Then we'll make a recommendation."

Rodriguez nodded, knowing he was going to be condemned to the appliance for the rest of his life. "Okay, I'll see you tomorrow."

After Rodriguez left the clinic, one of Aragon's technicians transported the medallion to a government testing laboratory. The neck chain, still enclosed in the plastic bag, was sealed tight in an airtight stainless-steel container.

TWENTY-SEVEN

A NEW PLAYER

IT WAS ALMOST NINE IN THE EVENING AND STAN REAMS WAS
still going strong. He had been at it all day, starting at sunrise.
His project was coming together with the precision of a fine
Swiss clock, just as he had planned.

He was inside a huge garage—it had three full-size stalls
plus a long workbench along one wall and a dozen overhead
storage cabinets. A bank of fluorescent fixtures hung from the
ceiling, bathing the concrete floor with more than enough
light.

He had rented the contemporary-styled home primarily because of its work space and remote location. He could work
at all hours and no one would bother him. The house was
located at the very end of a dead-end gravel road, high up in
the Oakland Hills. A massive stand of eucalyptus trees surrounded the ten-year-old home. It was the perfect hideaway.

Stan had been in the U.S. for nearly a month now. After
finally recovering the missing cargo, he had left Puerto Vallarta in a rush. He traveled north in Simpson's Ford Explorer,
reaching Mazatlán the following day. He had then boarded the
ferry to La Paz, eventually returning to his condominium at
Cabo San Lucas. He had stayed just long enough to secure his
unit and ditch the Explorer. He had then headed north, now
in his own Toyota Land Cruiser. He drove for a thousand
miles, the length of the Baja peninsula, finally arriving at the
San Ysidro.

The U.S. border crossing was a zoo at that time. Hundreds
of cars were backed up for what seemed like miles. American
Border Patrol officers and U. S. customs agents were out in
force. Another campaign to intercept illicit drugs had been
underway.

As Stan had waited for his turn to cross into the U.S, one of the cars in a nearby lane was searched by several agents, assisted by a drug interdiction canine team. The Chevy's trunk had been the center of the attention.

Stan had made it through the border checkpoint without incident. But the teenagers in the Chevy had not. They were caught trying to smuggle in twenty-five kilos of marijuana. The dog had found it, attracted to the pungent odor emanating from the spare tire.

Like the hapless teenagers, Stan had also hidden his special merchandise inside the Toyota's spare tire. However, his illicit cargo emitted no organic odor at all. The dope-sniffing black Lab hadn't given the Toyota a second look when Stan drove by. He wasn't trained to sniff out uranium.

The garage floor was covered with sections of aluminum and high-density plastic. A set of blueprints was strung across one end of the workbench. Stan was studying the drawings, trying to figure out how he'd attach the next portion of the plastic siding to the fuselage.

Behind Stan, in the middle of the floor, was a peculiar object. It was cylindrical, about eighteen inches in diameter and roughly a dozen feet long. Its internal structural frame was aluminum, but the exterior coverings were made of a special high-strength, low-weight carbon based plastic composite.

Stan grabbed a section of plastic sheeting from the workbench. It was about a quarter of an inch thick and was pre-curved to match the roundness of the cylinder. He fixed one end of the plastic in a vise on the bench. He then used a red marking pen and ruler to scribe a line on the sheet. He next took a power saw and cut away the excess material. When he kneeled down next to the cylinder and placed the plastic sheeting over the opening, the fit was faultless.

Stan stood up and walked back to the bench. *I'll put one more of these in; then I'll call it a day*. He was again studying the drawings when it hit. There was no warning other than the dull ache above his right eye. The precursor usually lasted only a few minutes and he hardly ever noticed it, especially when he was busy. But then the migraine would break loose with its full fury. It was as if someone had slammed a hammer into his head. The pain was savage. "Oh, God, not again!" he said as he dropped to his knees.

Stan cupped his head with his hands and shook his head. It would be useless to continue working. He'd never be able to concentrate. *The hell with it,* he thought. *I'm going to bed.*

Stan was ahead of schedule; he could afford to take a few days off. He'd been working almost nonstop since leaving Mexico.

Stan switched off the garage lights and headed up a stairway to the main floor of the house. He'd take a hot shower before climbing into bed. Sometimes the heat and steam gave him relief. He'd then down a couple of painkillers. He still had a bag full of codeine tablets he had bought in Mexico. The powerful narcotic would numb the ache but it would also knock him out. He'd sleep until at least noon of the following day.

The headaches had started a year earlier. Back then the attacks were mild and occurred only once a month or so. Stan had ignored them at first, but when their severity and frequency increased he had sought help. The Mexican physician's diagnosis was chronic migraine. He had recommended a few dietary changes and prescribed a painkiller.

This was Stan's third attack in as many weeks. The migraines were getting worse, yet he didn't want to admit it.

The mammoth building appeared to be filled to the brim. There were wooden crates of all sizes stacked everywhere. Mixed in with the crates were dozens of twenty-foot-long shipping containers—the kind that are loaded onto truck trailers and hauled away.

Forklifts scurried across the concrete floor, spewing noxious fumes from their propane-powered engines. The machines moved crates about, stacking them in one location, removing them from another. They worked with robot precision, automatically carrying out their monotonous work tasks twenty-four hours a day.

Thick plumes of frosty breath spewed from the man as he walked along one of the open aisles. It was late September and the early morning air had a chill to it. The warehouse wasn't heated.

The man worked his way along the edge of the building, following the white arrows stenciled on the floor. He carried a leather briefcase in his right hand. A thick parka kept him warm.

He was about forty, tall and well-built. His thick brown hair hung over his ears, clear to his collar. He wore glasses, the black plastic-frame type. His face was slightly leathery and beginning to wrinkle, the result of his two-pack-a-day habit.

Major Yuri Alekseyevich Kirov figured he was on another lost cause. He had visited a dozen similar warehouse complexes. It was like looking for the proverbial needle in a haystack.

Kirov had arrived in Pusan a week earlier. He had flown in from Vancouver, masquerading as a Canadian businessman. His English was flawless; he had spent several years in western Europe and Canada as a KGB operative for the former USSR. But now he had a new job, one that was not like anything he had ever undertaken before.

Others had been sent in earlier, always in two-man teams. But he was working alone for this assignment. The CIA remained strong in South Korea and there were suspicions that the Americans might have discovered some of the others. But there was no way he would let himself be compromised. He was too experienced for that to happen.

The earplug in Kirov's right ear continued to issue a steady tone. His hair concealed it. A tiny wire linked the earphone to his briefcase. It was taped to the skin of his left shoulder and arm. There was a quick-disconnect at the wrist.

The electronic device built into his briefcase detected nothing more than background emissions. *This is just a waste of time,* he thought. *We're never going to find it.*

Kirov followed the white arrows to the far side of the warehouse. They terminated at an office area built in the corner of the building. The hand-painted sign over the doorway was printed in Korean script and in English letters. Kirov was fluent in English. The sign read YELLOW SEA SHIPPING COMPANY.

Kirov reached down with his right hand and disconnected the wire from his left wrist. He then pressed a hidden button on his briefcase and the exposed wire was reeled inside. Kirov walked up to the door and opened it.

Kim Hyun-Jae never heard the door open. He was talking on the phone and the computer's printer was busy churning out inventory records. It spit out sheet after sheet of paper at lightning speed. It sounded like a machine gun.

Kirov stood silently in the entryway of the office. It looked just like the rest of the warehouse. File boxes were stacked everywhere with hardly any open floor space. There were a half dozen desks along the far wall. Only the one with the computer was occupied.

Kim was talking with a customer in Seoul. It was not a pleasant conversation. The crate full of auto parts from Yokohama had not yet arrived. It was supposed to have been shipped from his warehouse two days earlier.

After a minute, Kim hung up. When he turned to the side, ready to check the computer output, he spotted the stranger. "What do you want?" he asked in his native tongue.

Kirov shook his head. "English, please?" he said, purposely accenting his voice.

Kim recognized the strong Russian inflection. Many of his new customers were Russian.

"What do you want?"

"My name's Panov, Yuri Panov. I'm from Vladivostok." He reached out with his right hand.

"Kim Hyun-Jae," replied Kim as he shook the man's hand.

"Ah, Mr. Kim, I'm hoping that maybe you can help me locate some missing cargo."

Oh, no! Not again, thought the Korean merchant. He was preparing to sell his company, but for the past week he had been plagued by untold problems. It had all started with the new inventory-tracking software he had installed a month earlier. The Japanese-developed software was supposed to streamline his operations, making it easier to sell the company. Instead, there was an error in the program that was now causing havoc. The defect mislabeled every tenth bill of lading. As a result, he had shipped cargo all over the Pacific—addressed to the wrong destinations. So far, he had recovered fifty-three items but another hundred-plus were still missing.

"What's your customer ID number?" Kim asked as he rolled his chair toward the computer keyboard.

"Well, I'm not sure," replied Kirov. "All I know is that it was supposed to have been shipped out of Pusan about eight weeks ago."

Kim turned away from the keyboard. "You have no identification number?"

"No, the cargo is stolen. It's my job to recover it."

"You are with the police?"

"Yes, I'm with the Vladivostok Port Police." Kirov pulled out a black leather wallet and flipped it open, displaying an impressive-looking silver badge with an accompanying photo ID. He handed the wallet to the Korean.

Kim stiffened as he studied the document. The writing was in Cyrillic lettering. It looked authentic yet it was a complete fabrication. No such force existed. But to Kim, and all of the other Korean merchants that Kirov had met, his presence made perfect sense. The Russian Mafia owned the Vladivostok waterfront. Nearly everything that came into or out of the port city by sea or rail was subject to pilferage and, in some cases, outright thievery. The new-age gangsters had a reputation for ruthlessness that would impress the toughest Sicilian crime boss.

Kim Hyun-Jae pretended to study the Russian lettering. Instead, his mind was running at breakneck speed. *Why is he here? What does he know? Did someone tell him about me?*

Kim handed the ID wallet back. His hand trembled—not much, but just a little. "How can I help you, officer?" he asked.

Kirov noticed the shaky hand.

"The missing crate was about a meter square. It weighed around one hundred fifty kilograms. We know it was shipped out of Vladivostok in early February, sometime between the fifteenth and eighteenth." Kirov paused. Everything he had just said was the truth. The next statement, however, was a fabrication. Kirov was on a fishing expedition. He used the same line on all of the other merchants. "Our informants have told us that the crate was shipped to your warehouse."

Kim fidgeted in his chair. He had no idea what the Russian was talking about. "I'm sorry, officer, but I don't think I can help you. We receive hundreds of commercial carrier shipments each week. Without an ID number it would be impossible to track down."

"It wasn't shipped by a commercial carrier," answered Kirov. He was now telling the truth—at least as far as he understood it. "We believe the cargo was smuggled into South Korea and then prepared for shipment by a legitimate freight-forwarder—your company."

"And we then shipped it out?"

"Yes, we think it was stored for a couple of months and

then shipped out, maybe sometime in late June or early July. That's what our informant tells us," Kirov lied again. All he knew was that the illicit cargo had been sent to Pusan. It could have been shipped through any one of the legions of cargo companies that ringed the harbor.

Kim raised his arms in frustration. "It's possible that we did ship it, but there's no way I can trace it for you—not without some form of tracking number."

"Maybe this will help." Kirov removed a color photograph from his coat pocket. He handed it to Kim. "The man in this photo is the smuggler. He would have personally brought the crate in for shipment."

Kim studied the print. It was a picture of a man and a woman. *Caucasians.* They were standing arm in arm, facing the camera. Both were smiling. The woman was young, in her twenties. Blond and pretty. The man was a lot older. Slim build with brown hair. There was something familiar about his face but to Kim most non-Asians were nondescript.

"Sorry, but I do not know these people." He started to hand the photo back.

"The man is an American. We don't know his real name but he goes by Williams, Stan Williams. That's what he used when he was in Vladivostok."

Kim's face paled at the mention of the name. He then re-examined the photo. It all came back in a flash. *Of course, that's him!* Kim had met Williams only once—when he paid the $25,000 in cash. The encounter had lasted less than a half hour.

Kirov watched the Korean merchant. The man's reaction to the name was like a light being switched on. Kim would have been a lousy poker player.

Kim looked up. "No, I'm sorry. I do not recognize this man." He handed the photo back.

Kirov's face remained neutral but he was ecstatic. *You're lying, Mr. Kim. I caught you!*

Kirov turned to face Kim's computer terminal. "Perhaps you could check your computer records to see if you shipped anything on behalf of this Williams person."

"Certainly," replied Kim. He turned to begin working the keyboard.

It was an easy request to comply with. None of Kim's illicit

transactions were ever entered into the company's official electronic records. Those had all been kept on a separate disk with
a supposedly unbreakable security code. It didn't matter now,
though. Kim had destroyed the disk several weeks earlier. After Captain Yook and the *Korean Star* disappeared, he had
shut down the entire smuggling operation. It was time to retire.

The inquiry took a minute to process. Kim turned to face
the Russian. "I show no record of shipping anything for an
individual named Stan Williams. However, this year we have
made three shipments to a firm in Los Angeles named Williams and Hamilton. The manifest lists the cargo as VCRs. A
total of two thousand units were shipped."

Kirov was already familiar with Williams and Hamilton.
The American distributor purchased thousands of TVs, VCRs,
radios and camcorders from Korean manufacturers every year.
It owned a chain of discount stores in southern California. The
company was legitimate.

"No other Williams listed?"

"No."

"Well, I appreciate your cooperation and thank you for your
help."

Kirov reached forward to shake hands.

Kim squeezed the man's hand. "Sorry I couldn't help
more."

"I'll keep looking—we'll find him, eventually." Kirov
turned and started for the door.

Kim couldn't contain his curiosity any longer. "Officer,"
he called out, "just what is it that this man was smuggling?"

The Russian turned around. He was ready for the question;
it had been asked numerous times before. "Stolen icons."

"Icons?"

"Yes, a series of silver engravings and assorted jewels from
St. Isaac's Cathedral in St. Petersburg."

"They must be quite valuable."

"They're priceless and we want them back. They are part
of our nation's history."

"I'm sorry they were stolen. I hope you get them back."

"Thank you."

After the Russian left, Kim leaned back in his chair. His
stomach was in turmoil. *Icons! So that's what that bastard had.
I was certain it was loaded with gold or silver. No wonder he*

was so anxious to get them. They must be worth millions.

Kim stood up. He was mortified. If Williams was somehow tied in with the Russian mob and he never recovered the artifacts, they'd almost certainly come looking for him.

Kim was charged with new energy. It was time to implement his emergency plan. By the following night he would be out of Korea. *The hell with the company!* He'd let the broker handle the sale. He could wait. He already had plenty stashed away in Tokyo and Switzerland.

Yuri Kirov had returned to his hotel lobby. It was now 10:15 A.M. He was talking from a pay phone near the reception desk. He spoke in whispers. His counterpart in the Russian trade mission office in Seoul was encouraged by the report.

"So you really think he was involved?" asked the security expert.

"Yes, sir," replied Yuri. "Of all the ones I've talked with, he fits the profile. He was nervous and reacted strongly to the photo of Williams."

"But you detected nothing in the warehouse."

"Correct. If it was there, it's now gone."

"So what do you recommend?"

"Send the team down. My gut tells me he's our man."

There was silence for a few seconds. "All right, Major. They'll be there by six this evening. Get everything ready."

"Yes, sir."

TWENTY-EIGHT
AN OLD FRIEND

THE VIEW FROM THE LIVING ROOM WAS PHENOMENAL. THE emerald lake, only a stone's throw away, sparkled in the late afternoon sun. The distant mountain range, its towering peaks painted with a fresh coating of snow, set the backdrop. And mixed in with the elegance of the natural setting were the buildings. The peaks of the downtown high-rises jutted above the low hillside on the opposite shore of the lake. Somehow, the mountains of steel and glass complemented the picture. The result was a view of unparalleled diversity: nature at its best and man trying to be his best.

Tom Parker had heard about Lake Washington's gold coast but had never visited it before. He hardly ever ventured across the floating bridges. There was no need to; most of his local clients were in Seattle. But that had all changed when he returned from Puerto Vallarta. He now spent most of his time on the eastern shore of the lake. Linda insisted on it.

Linda Nordland's home . . . no, that wasn't right . . . Linda Nordland's megahouse was perched at the edge of a steep bank that overlooked the lake. The water was about a hundred feet below. The home fronted due west, right into the afternoon sun.

The 12,000-square-foot residence was only eight months old. Linda had purchased the two-acre Medina lot a few years earlier. She had paid two million dollars. The recently renovated 4,000-square-foot rambler that had come with the property was torn down to make way for the four-story contemporary. The home had everything: six bedrooms, eight bathrooms, a commercial-size kitchen, a dining room that could seat fifty and decks and balconies that projected from every level. Outside there was a garden court, swimming pool and adjoining spa, a tennis court and a connected six-car garage.

Tom Parker had been completely blown away the first time he drove onto the brick-lined turnaround that fronted the house. He had known that Linda was rich but he'd had no idea just how rich she was.

Tom turned away from the window wall and took a few steps to his right. He walked with a limp. He had discarded the crutches a week earlier and there was no way he was going to use a cane. He'd tough it out somehow.

Linda was lying on a sofa, just waking up from a nap. She was dressed in a pair of casual slacks and a beige cotton blouse.

Linda looked normal except for the bandanna that covered

the top of her head. Over a month had passed since her injury. Most of her hair had been trimmed away to de-emphasize the butch look that dominated the right side of her scalp. Her stitches were healing and the shaved hair was growing back. However, she still refused to let anyone look at her without a head cover—especially Tom.

Tom sat on the edge of the couch next to Linda. "How are you feeling, sweetie?" he asked.

Linda stretched her arms out. She was still groggy. "Good. How long was I out?"

"About three hours. It's almost six now."

Linda dropped her right hand over the edge of the couch and swept it across the thick carpet. She found her glasses a few seconds later. She slipped the metal frames on and looked out the window. "It's not raining anymore."

"Yep, cleared up an hour ago. We should have a nice sunset tonight."

She turned back to face Tom. Her right eye squinted as she tried to focus on Tom's face. Her vision still wasn't normal. "You're not leaving, are you?"

"I'm sorry, but I've got to be in Seattle by seven. I'm meeting with that guy I told you about before."

"The FBI agent?"

"Yeah, Charlie Larson. He's going to meet me at the Palisades. We're going to have dinner."

"Do you think he'll be able to help?"

"Maybe. He owes me a couple of favors."

Linda sat up. She was slightly dizzy. It was from the drugs. She still suffered terrible headaches. "You're coming back, aren't you?"

"Yes, honey. I'll be back around eleven, no later than midnight. After dinner, I'm going to stop by my place to check on Keely and Mom."

"Okay, I'll be waiting."

Tom leaned forward and gave her a kiss.

He was out the front door a minute later.

Tom climbed into his vintage Corvette—his one cherished luxury. He turned the starter and the V-8 burst to life. He loved the Vette but the clutch pedal was murder on his bad leg. He slipped it into gear and headed down the driveway. Five minutes later he was heading west on 520. The traffic was miserable, as usual. It would be stop-and-go across the bridge; he was used to it now.

As he slowly rolled along the concrete, his mind wandered back to Linda. He was worried about her; something was terribly wrong. She was like a little girl who had lost her way. She was scared all the time and appeared to be coming more dependent on him each day—not that he minded that. But it was her acquiescence toward her business that really concerned Tom. The fierce drive that had catapulted her to the top of her profession was gone. She seemed docile and meek. Bill Sullivan had also commented on the change.

The physicians treating Linda were not able to offer any explanations. Head trauma, they explained, sometimes alters an individual's personality. Often the changes will be temporary, but sometimes the metamorphosis is permanent.

Tom slammed his hands against the steering wheel out of frustration. He desperately wanted to help heal the woman he loved but felt utterly useless. "Dammit to hell," he shouted. "What am I supposed to do?"

Tom was across the bridge now, heading past the University of Washington. The lights at Husky Stadium had just switched on. The sun was dropping fast.

Tom's rage was under control. He had refocused on a single task: *I'm going to nail the bastard if it's the last thing I ever do!*

Five thousand miles west of Seattle, it was early afternoon. The skies over South Kyongsang province, however, were dark and forbidding. A storm in the Sea of Japan, 200 kilometers to the northeast, churned away, constantly gaining energy. The baby typhoon was heading for the southern Korean Peninsula. The winds hadn't started up yet but the rains had. It poured torrentially.

The dime-size raindrops splattered on the corrugated metal roof. It sounded as if a train was roaring by. The three inhabitants inside the shack ignored the racket. They were used to it by now.

Yuri Kirov was standing adjacent to the bed, the only piece of furniture in the fifteen-foot-square room. His companion was half-sitting on the mattress, tending to the patient. Twenty minutes earlier, the Russian physician had injected several cc's of a derivative of sodium pentothal into the man. The powerful drug was designed to temporarily interfere with the processing of conscious thoughts. The result was a passive state of mind that diluted a patient's ability to lie.

"Is it time?" asked Kirov. He was speaking in his native tongue.

The doctor turned around. "You may start now," she said. "He's fully alert."

Kirov flipped on a portable tape recorder and set it on the mattress next to Kim Hyun-Jae's head. The Korean businessman was resting peacefully on the bed. The drug had taken all of the fight out of him.

Almost seven hours earlier, just before 5:00 A.M., Kim was abducted from his hillside home overlooking the Korea Strait. The intruders came in through the second story, right into his bedroom. Fortunately for his family, he was alone in the house. His wife and three children, along with his own mother, were in Changwon, visiting with relatives for the last time. By the end of the week, the Kim family was supposed to be in their new home in Los Angeles.

The black-hooded men had gagged, blindfolded and then bound Kim before he was fully awake. No words were spoken to him as he was carried out of the house and loaded into a van. The van had traveled for several hours, finally stopping in a tiny village near the base of Chiri Mountain.

Kim was convinced that he had been kidnapped by the Russian mob. He was so terrified that he would have given away his children to save his life.

"Now, Mr. Kim," Kirov said in English, "you need to tell us about your transaction with the American." Kirov held the snapshot of the subject in front of Kim's eyes. "This is the man. You remember him now, don't you?"

"Yes. That's Stan Williams. He came into my warehouse back in June and requested a special shipment to . . ."

The interrogation took only half an hour. Kirov was satisfied that Kim Hyun-Jae had told him everything. The doctor then injected him with a sedative. Kim would sleep for twelve hours before waking up inside the shack. He would remember little about the interrogation and would not report the abduction to the police. He would be thankful just to be alive.

*   *   *

The huge restaurant was surprisingly busy for the middle of the week; almost every table was filled. The food was wonderful and the service was the best. But it was the view that brought in the crowds. The vista of Elliott Bay and downtown Seattle was breathtaking. The glittery background lighting of the high-rise towers, coupled with the subdued illumination of the adjacent yacht basin, had become a landmark in Seattle.

Tom was sitting at a small table near a window. Facing him across the table was a man of about Tom's age. The African American had a husky build but he wasn't fat. His shoulders and forearms were solid muscle, the result of a religious devotion to weight training. A former lineman with Ohio State, he could still run a decent hundred yard sprint.

Tom had met Charlie Larson years earlier, when he was in Europe. He and Larson served together in Germany at the same time but were assigned to different service branches. Tom was in CID; Charlie was an MP. Although Charlie left the Army after his mandatory tour of duty, he and Tom had kept in contact over the years.

After the Army, Charlie had obtained a law degree from NYU and then joined the FBI. He had served in Chicago, Atlanta and Houston before being assigned to the Seattle Field Office. He was now the special agent in charge of counterterrorism for the Pacific Northwest. His jurisdiction covered Oregon, Washington, Idaho and Alaska. Charlie was on a fast track with the bureau; his next duty assignment would be a faculty position at the FBI's academy in Quantico, Virginia.

Tom raised his glass of Chablis. "It's sure good to see you again, Charlie."

Agent Larson clinked his glass against Tom's. "It's been a while, hasn't it?"

"Yeah, must be six months or so."

"Yep, it's really amazing how fast time goes by. Just seems like the other day when we moved here, but it's been over a year now."

"Well, how do you like the Northwest so far?" asked Tom.

"Huh, you kidding? This place is a treasure."

"How's Jeanette like it?"

"You know she's from Chicago—need I say more?" He laughed. "Hell, she loves it here. So do the boys."

"How old are they now?"

"Scott just turned seventeen and Mark's fifteen."

"Scott got a car yet?"

"No way—not until he's out of high school."

Tom grinned. "You really think you can last that long? I can sure remember what it was like when I was that age. All I could think about was cars, football and girls—in that order."

"I don't know—I hope so. Anyway, I also remember what it was like—like how easy it is to get into trouble when you have your own car."

Tom nodded.

Charlie took another sip of wine. "How's Keely doing?"

"Real good. She just started second grade."

"Wow, time really flies. I didn't realize she was in school yet."

"Yeah, it's pretty amazing." Tom sipped from his glass.

"How do you manage that . . . you have a nanny?"

"No, I can't afford that. Besides, I have someone much better than that."

"Must be your mom."

"Yep, she's moved into my place—temporarily. With all the traveling and everything I'm doing, it's the only way I could swing it."

"You're lucky, Tom. There's nothing better than a grandmother." Charlie spoke from experience. He had been raised by his maternal grandmother.

"I know."

Charlie drained his glass and then settled back in his chair. "Well," he said, "what's been going on with you? You still chasing cheating husbands and bond jumpers?" He was smiling.

"Yeah, I still do a little bit of that—you know, I gotta pay the bills." Tom emptied his wine glass. "But lately I've been doing a little corporate security work. In fact, that's one of the reasons I wanted to get together tonight. I need your advice, and maybe a little help."

Charlie Larson leaned forward. He knew Tom well enough to know that he wouldn't be asking for help unless there was a real problem. "Yeah, sure, Tom, fire away."

"You ever hear of a software development firm called Nordsoft? It's based here, in Redmond?"

"Yeah, sure. That's the one that was started by some gal . . . I don't remember her name, but she's done real well. Kind of like another Microsoft."

"Yep, that's it. I've been doing some private work for the owner—Linda Nordland." Tom took a sip of water. "Boy, I'll tell you, Charlie, I had no idea what I was getting myself into. It all started in August when she sent me down to Puerto Vallarta to locate . . ."

Tom spent the next half hour going over everything that had happened in Mexico. Charlie Larson listened professionally, frequently asking questions. And out of habit he removed a notepad from his coat pocket and took notes.

"You mean to tell me the Mexican police think this guy was trying to kidnap Linda?"

"Yeah, it was the only way I could think of to get her out without dragging her into the problem with Simpson."

Charlie leaned back in his chair. "Geez, Tom, what the hell were you going to do with this Simpson guy when you got him back here?"

"Linda was going to insist that he be prosecuted and that he serve time. She took that thing with her mom real hard."

"Yeah, I can see that. Well, since he was indicted, you guys would probably be okay here. Especially if you played up the bond-jumping part. But you were right: if the Mexican authorities discovered what you were doing, they would have thrown both of you in jail."

Tom shifted in his seat. "Yep, but all that's immaterial now. I don't give a hoot about Simpson, even if he is alive. What I want is the son of a bitch that shot Linda."

Charlie stiffened in his seat. Alarms went off. *Jesus,* he thought, *Tom's starting to do the same thing again . . . like after Lori was killed.*

Charlie raised his hands, signaling frustration. "Tom, there's nothing I can do about this. It all took place in Mexico. I haven't got any jurisdiction down there."

"I know that. I'm not asking you to start an international investigation. But I sure could use a little help from that fancy computer of yours back in D.C." Tom reached into his right coat pocket and pulled out a plastic bag. Inside was a cigarette lighter—the one he had found on the kitchen floor in Linda's suite. "Do you think you could have your forensic people check the prints on this for me?"

Charlie took the bag from Tom. He held the silver Zippo up to his eyes. "Where'd you find it?"

"It belongs to the guy that shot us. I knocked it out of his hand when I rushed him."

Charlie remained silent for a few moments. He had helped Tom in the past but always in connection with legitimate cases—cases that were administered by local authorities—like the murder investigation of Lori Parker.

It was strictly against bureau policy to conduct any investigative work without first opening a formal case file. Under normal circumstances he would have refused the request from a private investigator. But Tom was his friend and he owed Tom—big-time. If Tom Parker hadn't loaned him $3,000 during that second year of law school, he'd never have made it.

"Tell you what, Tom, I'm going to consider your request as coming from Nordsoft. If you can get Linda Nordland or one of her officers to send me a letter requesting that we open a file on the attempted abduction, I'll run the lighter through our system. If the guy that made those prints has a record or was ever in the military, we'll have his fingerprints on file."

"Great. I'll have Nordsoft fax you an authorization tomorrow morning."

"Sounds good. Then I guess I'll keep this?" He held up the plastic bag.

"You bet. I really appreciate your help with this."

"No problem."

Tom reached for the wine bottle. He could now enjoy the rest of the meal.

At twenty after nine, Tom walked through the entryway to his Queen Ann condominium. He was instantly greeted by a tan-and-white Shetland sheepdog. The sheltie barked with joy.

Tom kneeled down, stroking the dog's long, soft hair. "Hiya, Barney, how you doing, boy?" The dog continued to bark up a storm, its tail wagging back and forth like a metronome.

Just as Tom stood up, a woman in her late sixties walked into the foyer. She was dressed in a housecoat and slippers.

"Hi, Mom," Tom said as he leaned over, giving the gray-haired woman a kiss on the cheek.

"Hello, son." She hugged him back.

The sheltie continued to bark. Alice Parker looked down, raising her right finger to her lips. "Sheeee, Barney! You'll wake Keely."

The dog obeyed instantly but its tail continued to stir the air. Mother and son started to walk down the hallway. Barney followed at Tom's side.

They were now in the living room. Tom's unit had a peek-aboo view of Lake Union. The mantel over the fireplace was filled with photographs of family and friends. In the center was an eight-by-ten color print of a beautiful young woman—long blond hair, blue eyes and a captivating smile. Lori Parker had been the center of Tom's life.

Tom was sitting in a rocking chair—the one Lori had used to nurse Keely. Barney was now sitting in his lap, content. Tom stroked that special area behind his ears.

Alice was on the sofa facing Tom. She couldn't help but comment about her dog. "I think Barney loves you just as much as Keely."

Tom just smiled. He had always liked dogs.

"How's Linda?" Alice asked. She had yet to meet Linda Nordland and Tom had only told her pieces of the story. But she figured out the rest for herself. Her son had a new love and she was happy for him.

"About the same."

"Hmm. The doctors still talking about exploratory surgery?"

"Yeah, but they want to give the drugs a little more time."

"Well, I hope they work. Surgery doesn't sound too good to me."

"I know."

Tom and Alice visited for nearly an hour. Most of the discussion was about Keely and how school was going. Tom promised that the next evening he would arrive a couple of hours before Keely went to bed. She needed to see her dad in person. Phones calls only went so far.

And then it was time to head back across the lake. Before leaving, however, Tom walked into Keely's room and kneeled down by her bedside. His daughter was sound asleep. He leaned over and kissed her forehead. A tear rolled down his cheek. She looked just like her mother.

TWENTY-NINE

UNNATURAL DEATH

DR. LOUIS ARAGON HAD BEEN IN SURGERY ALL AFTERNOON. The three-hour bowel resection should have been routine but it had turned into a nightmare. The cancer had spread much farther than the preliminary tests had indicated. Instead of finishing at 7:00 P.M., the operation had dragged on until almost 10:00 P.M. The woman would live. Aragon had removed the tumors just in time.

After cleaning up and then briefing the patient's family, Dr. Aragon returned to his clinic. When he stepped into his office, he immediately spotted the manila envelope on his desk. The word "Confidential" was stamped in large red letters on the front.

What's this? he thought as he sat down at his desk. He used a letter opener to break the official government seal on the envelope. He removed the contents. There was a cover letter from the Ministry of Health, signed by the minister himself. Attached to the letter was a five-page technical memorandum from a professor of nuclear chemistry at the National Autonomous University of Mexico.

Aragon read the letter and memo—twice. He then sank back into his chair, slowly shaking his head in disbelief. He was numb. *That's impossible! How could that be?*

The medallion he had sent to the government lab for testing was radioactive.

It had taken several days for the laboratory to start the analysis. A battery of conventional chemical tests was conducted before the real contamination was discovered. The chemists could find nothing out of the ordinary until one of the technicians decided to scan it with a Geiger counter. The medallion was then sent to the university specialist for further testing.

Almost three weeks later the results were finally sent to the Ministry of Health.

By the time the specialist completed his tests, the medallion was barely radioactive. The gamma rays it emitted were of extremely low energy. But more important was the actual source of the emission.

Metallurgic analysis of the medallion determined that it was a steel alloy. The alloy, in turn, was found to contain a high percentage of manganese. The specialist concluded that the likely source of the gamma rays was neutron capture. Somehow, the medallion had been subjected to an enormous release of neutrons, which had created the radioisotope manganese-56.

The half-life of the isotope was short, resulting in its rapid decay. But by back-calculating the decay rate to when Dr. Aragon reported that Rodriguez had first begun to wear the medallion, the specialist had estimated that it would have emitted gamma rays and beta particles at a prodigious rate.

The Minister of Health's letter further informed Dr. Aragon that he was confiscating the neck chain. The minister also ordered Dr. Aragon to report to his office the following morning. He wanted a complete briefing on the patient who had worn the medallion.

Aragon reached for the phone on his desk. He punched one of its memory buttons. A minute later he was connected to the Rodriguez residence in Guadalajara.

For the past few days, Arnaldo Rodriguez had hovered near death. Dr. Hernandez, his personal physician, stayed with him constantly, his fee paid in advance.

"Rene, this is Louis Aragon."

"Good evening, Doctor," replied Hernandez. He was speaking from the den. It was next to Rodriguez's bedroom.

"How's our patient?"

"Not good at all. He may expire this evening. If not, then almost certainly by tomorrow." The physician paused. "The priest has administered his last rites and the family is now gathering."

"Well, I'm sorry to hear that." Aragon hesitated for a moment. "Rene, we've finally discovered what's wrong with him."

"What did you find out?"

"I think he's been exposed to a massive amount of radiation."

"Radiation?"

"Yes, the medallion he was wearing—remember, I sent that off to have it tested because of the rash on his chest?"

"Yes, I remember that now."

"Well, the lab tests finally came back. It was radioactive."

"Radioactive? How could that be?"

"I don't know, but I was hoping that you might try to find out from Señor Rodriguez. He told me that it belonged to his brother-in-law—who by the way expired about six weeks ago. If he was also wearing the medallion, that might explain his death."

"Louis, there's no way I'll get anything from him. He's in a coma."

"How about his wife—can you talk to her?"

"Of course, at the right time. But that might be a while. I've got her sedated right now, along with his mother. They're all here."

Aragon leaned back in his chair. He had a tough decision to make. "Rene, I have to meet with the minister tomorrow. When he finds out about Rodriguez, all hell's going to break loose."

"What do you mean?"

"You know his background—drugs and smuggling."

"You think he's somehow mixed up with nuclear materials?"

"It sure looks that way."

"What should I do?"

"Don't let the undertaker bury the body. It'll have to be shipped to a government lab for analysis and then proper disposal."

"His family will never allow that."

"They'll have no choice. There's going to be a full investigation."

"It's that bad?"

"Yes."

Three hours later, Arnaldo Rodriguez died. He never regained consciousness. His emaciated body was a mere shell of its former self.

*   *   *

The funeral service was a high incident for Guadalajara. It seemed that everyone—friend and foe—came to pay their last respects to Don Arnaldo Rodriguez. The church was packed. The eulogy lasted almost an hour and then the crowds filed out.

The burial, however, was strictly a private affair, close friends and family only.

The hearse carrying the coffin was fifteen minutes late. It was starting to rain so the priest promptly completed the ceremony. The coffin was then lowered into the grave and covered with earth.

Unbeknown to the family, however, the coffin was filled with bricks. A special military team had removed the body at the mortuary. Later that day it would be flown to Mexico City for forensic testing and then disposal. The mortician had been sworn to secrecy on the threat of being thrown into jail for ten years.

The entire clandestine operation went well except for one matter: the assistant undertaker had been napping in the adjacent prep room. No one knew that he was snoozing on a table. The walls separating the various basement rooms were all tissue-thin.

The assistant had awakened just in time to hear the Army officer spell out the reasons for confiscating the corpse. He had cringed when he heard the word radioactive. *Thank God I didn't have to work on him,* thought the man. The owner of the mortuary had personally prepared Rodriguez.

The assistant had once read a book about radiation poisoning and wanted nothing to do with a potential glow-in-the-dark stiff. He quickly realized, however, that there was money to be made from his special knowledge.

After the Army truck left and his boss began to work on a new client, the assistant sneaked out of the basement. He found a phone in one of the upstairs offices. "Hey, Ronaldo, this is your brother."

"Hi, Chepito, what's up?"

The undertaker paused for a moment. "You remember that *chovoa* we met a couple of weeks ago in the *cantina*—the reporter."

"*Si*, the one with the big tits."

"Yeah, that's the one. Do you remember what her name was?"

"Ah, it was Maria. Maria something."

"Yeah, that's it. Do you remember which newspaper she worked for?"

"What for?"

"Never mind that for now! What paper was it?"

Ronaldo told him.

"*¡Si!* That's the one. Thanks, Ronaldo."

"But what's all this about?"

"I'll tell you later. *¡Adios!*"

The assistant undertaker set the handset back onto the cradle. He picked up the thick phone book. *I wonder how much they'll pay*, he thought as he searched for the phone number of the newspaper. The Mexican version of America's shock tabloids specialized in sex, violence and grotesque death.

Yuri Alekseyevich Kirov spent three hours searching Stan Reams' apartment. He found nothing of value. Other than some clothing, there was nothing personal—no photographs, no wall paintings and no written records whatsoever. It was a huge disappointment and another dead end. The man called Stan Williams—and probably a host of other aliases—was an enigma to Kirov and the Russian intelligence forces. He existed, that they were certain of, but he was more elusive than a Siberian tiger.

After the clandestine interrogation of Kim Hyun-Jae in South Korea, Major Kirov had returned to Moscow to confer with his superiors. Two weeks later he flew to Mexico City. Based on the information obtained from Kim, locating the target had proved to be relatively easy. Agents from the Russian embassy had long ago tapped into the computer system of Mexico's national telephone company. A few simple changes to an already existing program allowed the spies to screen all billing records of phone calls that had been placed from Cabo San Lucas to South Korea during the dates in question. From there it was downhill. There was only one address that consistently called Pusan. Stan Reams had never dreamed that someone might back-trace his telephone calls to the Yellow

Sea Shipping Company. He had always called Kim, never once giving out his own phone number.

Kirov walked back into the living room and sat down on one of the chairs. The view of the white sandy beach and the turquoise ocean was fantastic. The weather in Cabo was perfect. But he hardly noticed. Instead, he was reminiscing, thinking back to when he began tracking the American.

It had all started months earlier. Kirov was stationed in Vladivostok at that time, serving as an undercover agent with the Federal Security Service. The successor to the KGB was now almost exclusively engaged in fighting organized crime. Kirov held the rank of major and was heading the unit that was responsible for trying to curtail the rampant drug trafficking in the port city. It was a hopeless task. With too few men and insufficient funding, it was hardly worth the effort. Nevertheless, Kirov and his men persisted.

Kirov's unit made their share of busts, locked up a couple of the local kingpins, and even received special citations for their efforts from Moscow. But everything had changed the previous winter. That's when the Russian government's worst fear materialized.

The nuclear core from a missile warhead had been stolen from Chelyabinsk-70, a weapons laboratory located east of the Urals, near Kasli. The highly enriched uranium (HEU) inside the obsolete weapon was to be reprocessed for use in a nuclear reactor. There had been close calls before; the warheads had always been retrieved. But not this time.

Kirov became involved when military security agents tracked the thieves to Vladivostok. The woman who had stolen the core had been spotted in the train station by an agent. But before she could be apprehended, she had disappeared. The car and its driver had been waiting just outside the station. The license number was fake, making it untraceable.

Damn her! thought Kirov. Irina Sverdlova continued to elude them. They searched everywhere. Moscow spared no expense in trying to recover the HEU. Helicopters outfitted with neutron and gamma ray detectors scoured the city, looking for telltale traces of radioactivity. An army of truck-mounted units drove endlessly down every street and alleyway, sniffing for the presence of nuclear materials. They found nothing—absolutely no trace of the sixty kilograms of ninety-five percent pure U-235.

Russia was desperate to recover the missing warhead components. Unlike the more modern weapons that required sophisticated, shaped explosive charges and complex timing devices to detonate them, the stolen materials could be exploded with the simplest of hardware.

At first, Moscow feared that the weapon would be used at home. There was growing unrest in several of the republic's central-Asian states, and acts of terror against the central government were growing. But when the bomb was tracked to Vladivostok, the purpose of the theft was clear. It was for export.

Kirov centered his investigation on the woman. Irina Sverdlova had originally been trained as an electrical engineer. She had then received an advanced degree in nuclear engineering. That's how she had gotten the job at Chelyabinsk-70. Since the bomb material was to be converted to reactor fuel, it made perfect sense that she become involved in the recovery process. As a consequence, she assisted in the disassembly of several nuclear warheads.

Kirov could never understand why Sverdlova would choose to commit murder—she had killed four men while stealing the bomb material—when she had such a promising future. She was young and smart and attractive. With her background in reactor engineering she would have had a secure future. She might even have ended up running a nuclear power station.

Irina Sverdlova's treachery remained unfathomable to Kirov until he discovered her addiction. Incredibly, Irina was a heroin user. She had been hooked a year earlier, while still in graduate school. Her lover was responsible.

Irina and Mikhail lived in a tiny apartment in Nizhni Novgorod, formerly known as Gorkiy. Mikhail had been a small-time drug user for years, mostly a hash smoker with an occasional sniff of cocaine. Irina, on the other hand, never took anything stronger than vodka. She put up with his habit because she thought he had it under control. Calamity struck, however, when Mikhail began to experiment. It was an innocent act at first; he mainlined once, to experience the rush. It was the most incredible sensation of his young life. He tried it a few more times, once every few weeks or so. And then once a week. And then once a day. And then it had him.

Mikhail had hidden his addiction. He secretly shot up with the other hopheads who hung out in his apartment building. The dependency on the drug was bad enough. But when he contracted the AIDS virus from sharing needles, his world disintegrated. And worst of all, he feared that he had passed the virus on to Irina.

Mikhail lasted a little over two years before he withered away. There was no incubation period, no dormancy, no remission, nothing. He just came down with full-blown AIDS and died.

To help ease his misery during the final days, Irina had injected the heroin for him. The drug was still cheap back then.

After Mikhail died, Irina remained healthy. But worry was her constant companion. She had tested positive and would probably die before reaching thirty. It was an awful secret to conceal.

Finally, her depression had become so burdensome that she could no longer cope. She had witnessed firsthand how the hideous disease ravaged the human body, and she would not let that happen to herself. If Mikhail's pistol had had any bullets on that dreary, drizzly fall day, she would have used it.

Instead of pursing a swift death by other means, Irina embraced a surrogate specter on that landmark day. She injected herself with the remnants of Mikhail's stash. She was an expert at it, having administered the narcotic to Mikhail dozens of times during his last weeks of life.

The euphoria was astounding. It started with a warm tingling in her vein. And then, as the drug poured into her brain, the transformation was truly miraculous. The pleasure started at the back of her neck and surged upward until her mind was completely consumed by pure gratification. Good sex, even exemplary sex, was a mild diversion compared to the heroin fix. And best of all, the veil of depression that had engulfed her whole being for so long magically lifted. She was alive again.

It took just that one time for Irina to give up her former life. From then on the narcotic would consume her.

She hid her addiction skillfully, completing her master's degree with honors. She then went to work for Minatom, the

Russian nuclear regulatory agency. At that time, Minatom barely had sufficient funds to pay its employees, let alone institute a drug-testing program. Her first assignment was to Chelyabinsk-70.

Major Kirov and his team never found Irina alive. Her body was discovered in a cheap one-bedroom shanty located near the docks in Vladivostok. Kirov's team had also found, hidden behind a false wall, assorted correspondence addressed to Irina including an expensive four-color brochure from a private mountaintop medical facility located in Switzerland. The clinic specialized in the treatment of HIV-infected patients. It was one of the few places in the world that actually succeeded at keeping the deadly virus at bay. The one-year treatment program was designed to build up the immune system through a rigorous protocol of drug treatment, diet and exercise. The hope that the clinic offered didn't come cheap, though. The cost for one person for one year was one million dollars U.S. The correspondence indicated that Irina was scheduled for enrollment two months after the time of her death.

The autopsy was conducted at a nearby Army base. It revealed that Irina had died from an accidental overdose of heroin. And, ironically, there was no trace of the HIV virus in her blood. She had not been infected. The state-run clinic in Nizhni Novgorod that had originally tested her had a pathetic record for false positives. Irina had never bothered to be retested.

Major Kirov reached into his shirt pocket and pulled out the color snapshot. Irina had been happy when the picture was taken. She was smiling and her blond hair had a golden, radiant sheen. The photo had been taken just hours before Kirov and his commandos raided Nikolai Bessolov's *dacha*. The leaders of Red Port One were all captured or killed, but she had escaped—with the American.

The man standing next to Irina in the photo was his quarry; Kim Hyun-Jae had verified that much. *But who is he, anyway?* Kirov asked himself. *Stan Williams had to be an alias. Where is he now and what has he done with the uranium?*

THIRTY

TOM PARKER WAS IN THE FEDERAL BUILDING IN DOWNTOWN Seattle. He was sitting in the reception area of the FBI's field office. He had been waiting nearly twenty minutes. The meeting was supposed to have started at 10:30 A.M.

Tom was thumbing through a month-old issue of *Time* magazine when a bear-sized black man appeared in front of him. Special Agent Charlie Larson thrust out his hand. "Geez, Tom, I'm awfully sorry to keep you waiting."

Parker stood up and shook his friend's hand. "That's okay, Charlie. I know you're busy."

"I was on a conference call with headquarters and just couldn't break away."

"No problem."

"How's Linda doing?"

"A little better. Her depression seems to be lifting some but her eye's still bothering her."

"Are they going to have to operate?"

"Don't know yet. They're going to try another antiinflammatory drug this week. It might relieve the pressure."

"I sure hope that works."

"Yep, so do I."

"Well, let's head back to my office. I've got some fresh coffee brewing."

"Great."

Tom and Charlie were now sitting at a small circular conference table. Larson's office was positioned on the northeast corner of the building. It had a commanding view of downtown Seattle.

Tom sipped at his coffee mug while Charlie thumbed through a stack of files piled on top of the table. "Ah, here it is,'' he said. He set the remaining files on the floor by his feet. ''This came in last week. I was out of town then or I would have called you earlier.''

Tom nodded and said, ''No problem.'' It had been several weeks since he had asked Larson for help. He hadn't been expecting anything for a month, anyway.

Charlie opened the file folder. It was about an inch thick. He removed a four by five color photo and handed it to Tom. ''We got a match on the lighter's prints. Does this guy look familiar?''

Tom studied the photo. It took only a second to register. ''That's the guy!''

''You're certain?''

''Absolutely.''

As Tom studied the familiar face his mind filled with thoughts from that terrible day. For just an instance he relived the bullet's sting. He unconsciously reached down with his hand to rub his left calf. The puncture had healed but he was still limping. And then he remembered Linda's horrific head wound. That made his blood boil. *I want the bastard!*

Larson took another sip of coffee before making eye contact. ''His name's Reams, R-E-A-M-S. Stanley Steven Reams. Born right in this area, up in Anacortes. Age fifty-one. Divorced. Three kids, all girls—eighteen, twenty, twenty-three. His ex lives in Malibu. She's remarried. The youngest daughter, Terry, still lives with the mother. The others are married. Megan lives in L.A.; she's the oldest. Christine lives in Portland. No grandchildren yet.''

Tom soaked up the information. But it wasn't what he wanted. ''What else have you got?''

''Our Mr. Reams is a very special character. That's why we have this file.'' He held up the thick folder. ''He used to own a high-tech company in Kent. Some kind of aerospace manufacturing facility. It specialized in manufacturing lightweight airframe components. It did a lot of work for the Pentagon. That's how we got involved.''

''I don't understand. The Pentagon?''

''It was about five to six years ago. Reams was heavily involved with the development of the B-two. You probably remember that one—the Stealth Bomber?''

Tom nodded. The image of the all-black, bat-shaped aircraft flashed in his memory.

"Turns out Reams needed a Top Secret clearance for himself and his company to work on the project. That's where we came in."

"You mean this guy has a security clearance to work on military projects?"

"Yeah, well, he did. But it's not valid anymore."

Tom was confused. At best, he had expected the man to have some kind of criminal record—likely drug-related. But what he was now hearing from Charlie sounded more like the man was an upstanding businessman. "What happened?" he finally asked.

"Well, after the Soviet Union broke up, Congress slashed the defense budget and the original B-two program was gutted. They were supposed to build a hundred or so of those billion-dollar babies. In the end, though, they only built twenty or so. Reams ended up losing his shirt."

"You mean he went broke because the B-two program was cut?"

"Yeah. Big-time. Turns out he had borrowed heavily to tool up for the project, gambling that the entire fleet of B-twos would be built."

"What the heck was he making?"

"I don't have all the details, but it had something to do with the wings. He had a contract with the Air Force to supply Boeing and Northrop. Reams' company was heavy into exotic materials. Carbon-based composites, high-strength plastics and epoxy materials. Stronger than aluminum but much lighter."

"Is he some kind of chemist?"

"I don't know—just a sec." Charlie thumbed through the file again. "Let's see. No, not a chemist but he has a BS in aeronautical engineering. Went to school right here at the UW. Smart guy, graduated magna cum laude. Then OCS and four years with the Air Force in R and D." Charlie paused as he continued to scan the file. "He then went to work for an aerospace firm down in the L.A. area, ended up as the assistant manager of the missile division before going out on his own."

"You said his company went under—what happened?"

"He was way overextended. Borrowed heavily to enlarge

his plant. When his workload was slashed he apparently tried to make up for the lost business by going after civilian work. His timing was bad, though. He got caught up in the recession back then—there wasn't any work out there. He lost almost everything.''

''Bankrupt?''

''Yep. The company went into Chapter Eleven but never recovered. The trustee sold off the assets. Reams got nothing.''

Tom was actually beginning to feel sympathy for the man.

''But that wasn't all of it. Turns out that before he got into trouble with the B-two, his wife divorced him. She got the waterfront house on Mercer Island, the condo in Hawaii and most of the cash and bonds. He kept the company and his inheritance.''

''Inheritance—what was that?''

''Turns out his family owned a yacht-building yard in Anacortes plus a huge waterfront estate on Guemes Channel. His grandfather and his younger brother ran the business. Did real well until the late eighties—made custom yachts up to a hundred feet or so. Then it went bust too.''

''What happened?''

''You remember the luxury tax Congress enacted back then?''

''Something about a surcharge on high-end boats and planes?''

''Right. For yachts, anything costing over a hundred grand was subject to a ten percent surcharge. A million-dollar one would get hit with an extra tax bill for ninety grand.''

Tom's memory cleared. The tax that Congress had enacted was supposed to soak the rich. Instead, it had backfired. ''That's the tax they repealed a couple of years ago, isn't it?''

''Yep. Congress really blew it with that one. Didn't hardly raise any revenue and ended up costing thousands of jobs. Hundreds of small yards went tits-up as a result. Turns out the rich refused to pay. They went without or bought their yachts overseas.''

''So Reams' Anacortes yard went out of business?''

''Exactly. Most of their back-orders were canceled. Reams' brother was running the family business at that time; the grandfather had passed away by then. Let's see, his name was . . . ,'' Larson paused momentarily to re-check the file. ''Oh, here it is. Tom. Tom Reams was his name. Anyway, he ended up killing himself—with a pistol. He apparently couldn't take the pressure of running a failing business." Larson again paused as he made eye contact with Tom. "Our man Stan ended up inheriting the whole mess—just about the time things were turning south for him on the B-two project."

Damn! Tom said to himself. *This guy really got screwed.*

Larson continued. "Reams closed the Anacortes yard and laid the staff off. The yard and his grandfather's mansion didn't have any debt so Reams used them for additional collateral for his aerospace company. That turned out to be a big mistake."

"What do you mean?"

"When his manufacturing company went into Chapter Eleven, the Anacortes property was attached. He lost it along with his Kent plant. The trustee sold the boatyard and the home to pay back the bank." Charlie pulled out another color photograph; it showed a massive three-story Victorian-style building sitting on a rock promontory. The sparkling waters of Puget Sound framed the beautiful structure. "This was his grandfather's house—Reams Landing was what it was called." Charlie shook his head. "That must have been awfully hard to lose."

Tom shook his head in disbelief. He had learned far more about the assailant than he ever dreamed. "Charlie, how the hell do you know all of this stuff? Have you guys been tracking him or something?"

"You're right. It turns out that we were asked to investigate Reams several years ago. One of Reams' former employees was caught peddling Top Secret info from the B-two project to a Japanese company. All I'm allowed to tell you is that the design data was related to the composite wing materials."

"Was Reams involved?"

"No, not at all. But the records indicate that he was put through the grinding mill. Apparently the former employee tried to implicate him but it didn't work."

Tom was confused. He raised his hands in frustration. "Charlie, what the heck is going on with this man? He sounds like an okay guy that somehow got screwed by the system. But why would he turn into a killer?"

Larson shook his head. "Sorry, Tom, but I just don't know."

"So where'd he go?"

"Don't know. Our last file entry is over three years old. We have no records on the man now. We checked with other defense contractors where he might have found employment. Nothing. We even asked the IRS and Social Security to run a trace on him. Zip. No tax returns have been filed for the past couple of years and there's no record of any FICA payments to his account." Larson paused. "Tom, paper-wise, the man is invisible. We have no idea where he is."

Tom again shook his head. "None of this makes any sense, Charlie. The only thing I can think of is that he was living in Mexico and somehow got mixed up with drug smuggling."

"Yeah, that's certainly a possibility. That might tie him in with this Simpson character you were telling me about."

Tom pushed his chair a few inches away from the table. "Well, Charlie, you've certainly given me a lot to think about. Quite frankly, though, I'm more confused than ever. This guy's profile doesn't fit with what I observed. Somehow, he's changed—because when I ran into him, he came across as a stone-cold killer. He shot me without the slightest remorse and then he damned near killed Linda."

"People change, Tom. A guy that got screwed over like he did could easily turn into a renegade. I've seen it before." He paused for a moment. "Remember, now—he lost his family, his business and his inheritance. Everything he had worked for was taken away. Believe me, that can really warp your mind."

"Yeah, I guess you're right."

Larson leaned forward, handing the photo of Reams to Tom. "This is an extra. You can have it. But I can't release anything else from the file."

"Thanks. I understand."

"So what are you going to do now?" asked Charlie.

"I don't know. I've got one other lead I'm working on. Turns out he used a credit card to pay for his hotel bill while in Puerto Vallarta. It was probably a fake but I've been running some traces on it anyway. You never know."

"Sorry, but I can't help you with that. Credit-card fraud's out of my jurisdiction. You'll have to talk with the Secret Service."

"That's okay. I've got a bank contact helping me."

Tom was now standing. The meeting was over. As he

headed for the door, Charlie walked along. The FBI agent had one last question for his friend.

"Say, Tom," Charlie said, "how are you doing with all of this?" He hesitated. "You know, after Lori and all of that other business."

"I'm just fine, Charlie. Everything's just fine."

"Good—I'm real glad to hear that." But Charlie didn't believe a word of it.

Tom shook his friend's hand and walked out of the room.

By the time Tom reached the elevator, his head was spinning. Charlie's question had hit home with deadly precision. Tom had had the dream again the previous night. And once again, Linda had replaced Lori. *God, am I going crazy?* he wondered. *I can't go through that again.*

After spending over two years searching for Lori's killers, he had nothing to show for it . And now it was déjà vu. He was headed down the same path.

Yuri Kirov was now in Puerto Vallarta. The early November weather had finally turned for the better. It was partially cloudy and a comfortable seventy-five degrees. Humidity was low and there was a pleasant onshore breeze.

Kirov had no idea where to look. All he had to go on was Kim Hyun-Jae's confession. The *Korean Star* was supposed to have dropped off a shipment of heroin in Banderas Bay and then head to Cabo. But as far as Kim knew, the ship never made it to Mexico. The Korean smuggler repeatedly stated that he feared the fish processor had sunk somewhere in the Pacific.

Kirov didn't know what to believe. If the ship went down, as Kim speculated, then his job was over. The stolen warhead was no longer a threat. But if the enriched uranium had been removed before the ship disappeared, then he had a huge problem to solve.

Kirov wasn't one to leave a stone unturned. If he was the American named Stan Williams, he would have traveled to Puerto Vallarta to search for the missing vessel. Kirov would now scour the waterfront until he was convinced that the ship had never made it to port. Only then would he give up.

Yuri was operating out of a tiny hotel on the outskirts of town. He was lucky to have found a room; P.V. was a madhouse. It was chock-full of tourists—it seemed that everyone from the eastern United States and Canada wanted to escape the Arctic express that was now inundating their homelands.

A week earlier, the city had been even more crowded. Thousands of Mexican nationals had returned home for a very special celebration: the Days of the Dead. On the first and second days of November, *fiestas* are held throughout Mexico to honor the *difuntos*. The parties take place at local cemeteries and family altars.

Each family member leaves an offering at the family altar or crypt. The dead children are honored with miniature sugar skulls, sometimes with their names written on them. Special breads, sweet *tamales* and small bottles of tequila are left for the older deceased. The souls of the lost children are honored on the first of November. Older *difuntos* are remembered on the second.

The family *fiestas* that are held during the Days of the Dead are strictly private affairs. It is a time of quiet that is used to recall fond memories of loved ones. None of the offerings are consumed until the departed souls have had first helpings.

Although each family celebrates the Days of the Dead independently, there is one common custom that reaches most everyone. Some newspapers and magazines use the occasion to spoof local political leaders and anyone else in the public eye. The editors show little mercy with their satirical stories, bawdy poems and off-color jokes. Called *calaveras*—skeletons—the stories strive to bring out old "skeletons" from the closet. Cartoon characters, usually portrayed as skeletons, often accompany the *calaveras*. The editors particularly enjoy skewering the local politicians, digging up any dirt they can unearth. And a new target that was finding favor lately were the local crime bosses. Characterizations of drug lords were particularly popular. This was where Kirov found his first lead.

The Russian intelligence officer was sitting in his room, scanning through a stack of Mexican newspapers and magazines he had purchased, when he spotted it. It was in a week-old issue of a raunchy tabloid. The cartoon was mixed in with the dozens of others, but his eyes were instantly drawn to it. The skeleton was walking a tightrope across a deep canyon. In one arm it carried a package labeled *mota* (marijuana). The package in the other arm didn't have a written label. Instead, a logo consisting of three triangles centered around on a small circle was displayed. Kirov recognized the universal warning symbol for radioactive material. And written under the cartoon was the caption: *Ode to Don Arnaldo Rodriguez: may his tormented soul burn bright like the sun.*

The *calaveras* fascinated Kirov. It meant something—something important, that he was sure of. He would not rest until he had the whole story.

THIRTY-ONE
FIRST FLIGHT

STAN REAMS DROVE ALL NIGHT. THE TRAFFIC HAD BEEN heavy at first. Highway 80 was a zoo all the way to Sacramento. Tens of thousands were bailing out of the Bay Area for the Thanksgiving holiday. Most of the travelers were planning to spend the four-day break with their families. Some were heading up into the Sierras for a skiing break. A few, like Reams, were working.

He reached Reno a couple of minutes before five in the morning. He pulled his four-wheel-drive Ford pickup and its fifth-wheel trailer into the parking lot of a twenty-four-hour truck stop. Two weeks earlier he had traded in his Toyota Land Cruiser for the F-250 Supercab. He needed the truck's powerful V-8 to pull the forty-foot Fleetwood.

Stan parked in a tractor-trailer slot near the restaurant's front door. There were a dozen other patrons inside. Most were drinking coffee, a few were eating breakfast and one die-hard gambler was feeding a slot machine. Stan ordered steak and eggs. He took his time eating and then leafed through a copy of *USA Today.* Finally, just as the sun was rising, he left. He drove for half an hour, eventually pulling off the highway onto a gravel road. He headed east into the sagebrush.

He found the perfect spot an hour later. The flat valley floor was sandwiched between two sets of rolling hills. The ground was covered with a light dusting of snow. The cold desert air held the bittersweet scent of sagebrush. The tough little plants, only a foot or so high, covered the rock-hard soil for miles in all directions. There was no one around, except for the occasional jackrabbit.

Stan turned his rig off the gravel road and slowly drove north for about half a mile. He then parked his rig. From the distant roadway, Stan's truck and trailer looked like a campsite.

It would take him all morning to assemble the "special project." He could have used some help in moving the larger sections from the trailer, but he managed. He had purposely designed it so that he could put it together by himself.

Stan finished at a quarter after noon. He was proud of his accomplishment. Everything fit and the electronic package was 100 percent operational. It was time for the test.

Stan moved the truck and trailer about 100 yards to the west. He then returned to the trailer. The Fleetwood had been partially rebuilt inside. The bedroom at the forward end had been converted into a storage compartment. The rear two-thirds of the trailer remained intact.

Stan sat down at the kitchen table. The window in front of the table provided a clear view back to the original site. He could see his property sitting on the aluminum frame.

It was solid black, about a dozen feet long. The fuselage was only eighteen inches in diameter. Delta-shaped wings projected from each side of the cylinder's rear half. A rounded nose cap covered the forward end. The tail assembly consisted of a flared conical housing about three feet in diameter. It was topped with a short vertical rudder.

The engine was mounted at the tail end of the cylinder. The forty-five-horsepower gas-driven motor was completely enclosed within the black fuselage. Only the four-foot-diameter propeller, partially concealed by the flared conical housing, revealed its presence.

Stan pulled up a briefcase-size aluminum case and set it on the Formica table. He opened the lid and snapped it upright. It was filled with electronic switches and gauges. He plugged a set of black and red wires into receptacles on the side of the case. The trailer's built-in generator was already purring away, supplying plenty of electricity.

Stan flipped a switch inside the case and looked out the window. Almost instantaneously the propeller turned over. He then reached forward and turned on a small Sony TV set that was mounted on the wall next to the table. The screen was filled with static. After flipping another switch, the static disappeared. He could see gray sky. *Perfect*, he thought. The television camera was mounted inside the forward end of the cylinder. Its lens penetrated the nose cap.

The image on the screen vibrated as the engine warmed up. He let it run for two minutes at low speed before increasing power. The airframe strained at its moorings. Two stainless steel clamps secured it to the inclined support frame.

Well, everything checks out so far, Stan told himself. *It's now or never*. With that thought he reached forward and flipped another toggle switch.

A microsecond later, the transceiver antenna mounted on top of the trailer broadcast a high-frequency radio signal. A six-inch-long wire antenna on the cylinder intercepted the signal. Almost instantly, a small solid-fuel rocket motor mounted on the bottom of the fuselage ignited. It took just a half second to reach maximum thrust. The restraining clamps released and the black winged cylinder blasted upward at a thirty-degree angle.

"Go, baby, go!" shouted Stan as he watched the launch through the trailer window. The rocket expended its energy in just fifteen seconds and then automatically jettisoned itself, falling back to earth. The aircraft continued to climb into the cold sky. The gas engine now had plenty of power to keep it in the air.

Stan turned to face the TV screen. The airborne camera was working as designed. The microprocessor inside the fuselage was converting the camera's black-and-white images into an encrypted digital signal and then transmitting it back to an antenna on top of the trailer. The screen's clarity was remarkable. He could see the snow-capped peaks of the Humboldt range in the distance.

Stan reached for the tiny control stick built into the briefcase. It was similar to a video game joystick. The device functioned like the control column in a real plane. Push forward and it will dive; pull back and it will climb. Push to either side and it will bank in the same direction.

Stan spent several minutes testing the control surfaces. Everything worked as he expected. He had run countless bench tests on the equipment back in Oakland.

The aircraft was now in a slow half-mile orbit west of the trailer. It was about a thousand feet high. Its air-cooled engine was so quiet that it was barely noticeable at ground level. Stan was studying the television monitor, trying to accustom himself to its limited field of vision. He was trained as a pilot but trying to remotely fly the tiny craft was alien to anything he had done before. There was no peripheral vision nor any physical sense of up or down. Despite the cool weather, beads of sweat broke out on his brow as he struggled to learn a new way of flying.

It took Stan about twenty minutes to adjust to the camera's eye. He then decided to test his skill. He leveled the craft and pushed the joystick forward. The robot raced for the ground. The sudden change in attitude startled him. He pulled back on the stick, leveling it out. "Son of a bitch, this sucker's really sensitive. I've got to be real careful."

Stan continued testing his skill for another twenty minutes. He was getting good at controlling it. The craft was much more agile than anything he had flown before.

Stan made another low-level pass over the launch site; it passed just fifty feet overhead. Its speed was ninety miles an hour. He was thinking of making another pass when a built-in timer in the briefcase began to beep.

Darn, he thought. *I was just starting to have fun.* The warning was designed to alert Stan that the plane was running low on fuel. He had calculated that the engine would consume around ninety-five percent of its gasoline supply after forty-five minutes of flight.

Stan gently pulled back on the joystick, sending the craft into a shallow climb. When it reached five hundred feet he turned it around so that it was heading back to the trailer. About 300 yards out he switched the engine off. A second later he hit the parachute release.

The craft landed with a gentle thump 200 feet away from the trailer. The thick covering of sagebrush helped to cushion the landing.

Stan Reams was euphoric. His home-built drone worked

better than he had imagined. It was a day to be truly thankful. All of his hard work had paid off.

While Stan Reams experimented in Nevada, Tom Parker and Linda Nordland, accompanied by Keely and Tom's mother, celebrated Thanksgiving Day with Bill Sullivan and his family.

The Sullivans lived in Woodinville, another affluent community east of Seattle. Their residence was built on a ten-acre parcel that overlooked the Bear Creek Valley. The main floor of the 6,000-square-foot home had an extraordinary view of the Cascade mountain range. And surrounding the house were five acres of grass pasture. Bill and Sally Sullivan were avid equestrians. They had a stable of six horses—one for every member of the family.

The turkey dinner was a knockout. Tom stuffed himself. Even Linda had a good appetite. She was slowly returning to her old self. But she was by no means healed. The doctors were still talking about exploratory surgery to correct the eye problem.

The women were all outside now, bundled up in parkas, gloves and wool ski hats. Sally and Linda, along with Keely and Alice Parker, were standing next to a wooden fence, watching the Sullivans' four daughters gallop their horses across the pasture. Although it was freezing, the bright sun made for a pleasant afternoon.

Tom and Bill were in the den. Tom was sipping from a long-neck Bud. Bill was drinking wine—a Chardonnay from the nearby Ste. Michelle Winery. They were watching the girls through the picture window.

"Your kids ride pretty well," Tom commented.

"Yeah, Sally had 'em all on horseback early. They took to it like ducks to water."

Tom nodded as he stared at the window. He wasn't a horse fan. The one time he had tried riding, twenty years earlier, the mare had dumped him. "Has Linda ever been riding?"

"Yeah. A couple of summers ago Sally invited Linda and several other gals from the office to go riding. They took an all-day trip along the Tolt Pipeline Trail. Sally said they had a ball."

"Hmm. Maybe you could get Sally to take Linda out again,

assuming her doctor approves. She needs to get out of the house more.''

''Sure, I'll mention it to her.''

Tom turned away from the window, now facing Sullivan. ''Bill, you wouldn't believe what a hassle it was to get her to come today. I think she's really having a good time now, but she just doesn't want to go anywhere. She spends too damn much time in that mansion of hers.''

''I know. I'm worried too. I can't get her into the office for anything. She'll talk on the phone or meet with me at the house, but that's it.''

Tom plopped in a soft leather chair next to an oak desk. Bill sat on the couch by the window.

Tom took another sip of beer. ''Bill, I know it's none of my business, but are things going all right with Nordsoft?''

''Yeah, we're doing great.'' Bill's guard was suddenly up.

Tom could see the puzzled look on Sullivan's face. ''That's good. Then you could continue to get by for some time without Linda's presence?''

''Yes, but what are you getting at?''

''If she doesn't have to have surgery, I'm thinking of taking her on a trip. She needs to get out and see the world again.''

''That's a hell of a good idea. Where are you planning to go?''

''I was thinking of Europe—maybe do some skiing in Austria and Switzerland, then stop in the Caribbean on the way back.''

''Great. When do you think you'll leave?''

''Sometime after the first of the year. We'll spend the holidays here.''

''That's wonderful. I'm sure Linda will enjoy the trip.''

Tom nodded and then turned to watch the Sullivan equestriennes. They were racing each other across the grass. The horses kicked up thick divots of frozen turf while expelling huge plumes of frosty breath.

Bill Sullivan studied Parker. He believed that Tom was sincere in his affection for Linda. He knew Linda was. He took a final sip and placed his empty wine glass on a nearby table. He then looked back at Tom. ''Have you had any more luck in tracking that guy down?''

''Reams?''

"Yeah, the one the FBI identified for you."

"No, I'm afraid not. I've tried everything but it's like the bastard disappeared into thin air."

"No records about the guy at all?"

"That's right. He dropped out of sight several years ago and hasn't resurfaced."

"Except in Puerto Vallarta?"

"Right."

"How about that credit card angle you were working—anything turn up there?"

"No. It looks like another dead end. I had a banker friend of mine up here do some checking with its parent company in California."

"What did he find out?"

"The card's legit. The account was taken out about six months ago."

"Damn, then you can trace the bastard!"

"Yeah, that's what I thought. My friend got me a copy of the account application. It's a fake."

"Then the card's no good."

"No. That's the weird thing. This Stan Martin character, a.k.a. Stan Reams, doesn't exist. But as far as the bank's concerned he's alive and well."

Bill raised his hands, signaling confusion. "I don't understand."

"It's a clever sham. This guy opened up an account through the mail. Filled out one of those applications you see everywhere. Somehow, he got a copy of the credit report of a real Stan Martin—there's got to be a zillion of them in California. He used the guy's Social Security number, listed his employer, referenced the man's other credit cards. But he changed one thing: instead of listing the man's home address, he gave a P.O. box in Oakland. One of those private-mail-services places."

"So the guy used a fake application. The bank should have figured it out after the bills weren't getting paid."

"That's the beauty of it. They were paid, every month."

Bill shook his head. He was still confused. "This guy wasn't trying to cheat the bank?"

"No. Just the opposite. He started out with a standard five-thousand-dollar credit line. But then he deposited another thirty thousand dollars in cash over a two-month period.''

Sullivan had it now. "Damn, he could use the card without raising any alarms.''

"Yep. And the bank was as happy as a clam. They had his cash to work against. Whenever he made a purchase, it would be automatically deducted.''

"Sounds just like a debit card, then.''

"Exactly. As long as he kept the balance up, no one at the bank would raise an eyebrow.''

"So this guy could use the card as he needed and remain anonymous.''

"Right.''

Bill stood up, stretching his arms. "So what's this guy been using the card for?''

"He's been busy. My buddy showed me copies of some of the charges. His hotel bills in Puerto Vallarta showed up. There were also a bunch of hardware and electronic store purchases in September—almost thirty grand worth.''

"Wow, where were those made?''

"Most were in the Bay Area. But some were made in L.A. and Santa Barbara. All at high volume retail and discount stores: Price-Costco, Sears, Radio Shack—places like that.''

"Well, that's something—he's living in California. Are you going to check down there?''

"Maybe. I haven't decided for sure. Those stores have thousands of customers every day. Asking a clerk to ID someone who made a purchase a couple months ago isn't going to pan out. It'll be like looking for the proverbial needle in the haystack.''

"What's he buying lately?''

"Nothing. The account's been dormant for the past month. No purchases at all. And the balance is right at the original credit limit—five grand.''

"He's used up the cash, then.''

"That's right. He's probably finished with the card.''

"So what are you going to do?''

"My friend at the bank is going to have his counterpart in L.A. electronically monitor the account. If this guy uses the card again, it'll get flagged and I'll be notified.''

"What good will that do?''

"If he buys just about anything with the card, the seller will request verification of the account by telephone check.''

"You mean with one of those card readers you see every-where.''

"Yep. If he stays below the credit limit, the purchase will be approved but I'll know about it.''

"And?''

"And I'll hop the first flight south to wherever he used it. If I get there soon enough, I might get a lead on where the bastard lives. You never know, he might screw up and use it to buy something where someone knows him—the local gro-cery store, a gas station, a favorite restaurant. It's a real long shot but that's all I've got.''

Bill Sullivan nodded his head in sympathy. His thoughts, however, were elsewhere. *He's grasping at vapors. Anyone who's set up such a sophisticated screen isn't going to screw up like Tom's hoping. Tom's never going to find the bastard!*

He was wrong.

THIRTY-TWO
THE BRIEFING

IT WAS LATE NOVEMBER. MAJOR KIROV HAD SPENT OVER A week in Puerto Vallarta, researching the story behind the mys-terious death of Arnaldo Rodriguez. He had then moved on to Guadalajara, continuing the investigation. He was now at the Russian embassy in Mexico City. He was sitting inside the ambassador's plush office, attending a meeting with the am-bassador himself and another Russian operative.

"Major Kirov, you're certain this man died of radiation poi-soning?'' asked the ambassador.

"Yes, sir. There is no question about it. I read the autopsy report. His body was exposed to an incredible amount of ra-diation—at least five hundred rem. That's like having several thousand chest X-rays.''

The Russian diplomat turned away from the conference table to scan a wall-mounted map of Mexico. The sixty-one-year-old man looked like the consummate emissary: handsome, tall and lean. He was dressed in an immaculate dark blue suit. His gray hair was professionally trimmed each week. He was fluent in Spanish and English.

"This thug, Rodriguez," the ambassador said as he continued to study the map, "he operated out of Guadalajara but was irradiated in Puerto Vallarta?"

"Yes, sir. That's what it looks like."

"Was he tied in with those bandits in Vladivostok?"

"No, we don't think so. He may have functioned as an intermediary for the transshipment of drugs into the U.S. He was well connected with the Cali cartel in Columbia. But other than that, we have no hard intelligence that he's linked to any Russian groups."

"Well, Major, what's your opinion? Was Rodriguez involved in the theft or not?"

"It's possible, sir. Let me explain what I've pieced together so far." Kirov made new eye contact. "First, I got wind of this man Rodriguez through a newspaper article while I was in Puerto Vallarta. Actually, it was some kind of cartoon that . . ."

For the next ten minutes Yuri Kirov described how he had tracked the story of Rodriguez's mysterious death. After stumbling onto the *calaveras* of Rodriguez in the tabloid newspaper, he had discovered the origin of the cartoon. An article in another paper, issued several days earlier, told the story. A rumor had swept through Western Mexico that the infamous drug kingpin had been targeted for death by a rival leader based in Chihuahua. It all stemmed from an old dispute between Rodriguez's older brother and the Chihuahua gang he had once worked for. Arnaldo's brother broke away from the gang and started trafficking in drugs on his own. He was subsequently murdered and that's when Arnaldo took over. Arnaldo's meteoric success had infuriated the Chihuahua gang leader and over the years he had become sick with jealousy. He eventually issued a standing reward of a million dollars for the head of Arnaldo Rodriguez.

The newspaper story reported that after dozens of failed attempts at assassination, the Chihuahua gangster finally infiltrated Rodriguez's staff. The woman was a cook. However, instead of ordering Rodriguez shot, the Chihuahuan had targeted Rodriguez for a much worse fate. The rumor was that the cook had poisoned him with radioactive material. There was no explanation as to where the radioactive material came from other than that it was probably mixed in with his food. The nuclear poison destroyed his internal organs, causing him to die a horrible death.

Kirov explained that the newspaper story was pure speculation, designed to sell a lot of newspapers. He then stated what had really happened, starting with how he had tracked down Dr. Aragon. He had posed as a German journalist, one of his many aliases. Hardly anyone ever challenged this approach. Most of his sources would never speak to him if they knew he was a policeman, but to a reporter they frequently opened up.

After interviewing a family member, he had met with Rodriguez's family physician. Dr. Hernandez would say nothing, other than to refer him to Dr. Aragon in Mexico City. Like Hernandez, Aragon refused to discuss his former patient. That's when Kirov had asked for help.

The black operations team had had no difficulty breaking into Aragon's clinic. They made a complete copy of Rodriguez's file. Nearly everything was included in the thick folder: Hernandez's prediagnosis observations, laboratory test results, lengthy transcripts of Aragon's dictation notes and, most importantly, the federal Ministry of Health's official autopsy report. It had been marked "Confidential—Not for Public Release."

"All right, Major," the ambassador said, "let's assume all of what you discovered is correct. Rodriguez did, in fact, die from radiation poisoning. How does this tie into our missing warhead?"

"Sir, there is no direct linkage—at least not that I have been able to make out yet. But consider these events. First, we know for certain that the American lived in Cabo San Lucas. Kim verified that and I actually searched his residence. Second, the American most likely visited Puerto Vallarta about the same time Rodriguez was exposed to the radioactive materials. Third, there is no sign of the missing Korean ship—none. It's like it disappeared off the face of the earth. As a consequence, there are really only two alternatives as to the fate of the war-head components. The material went down with the ship and it's sitting somewhere on the bottom of the Pacific or—''

"Or Rodriguez intercepted the shipment," interrupted the ambassador.

"Exactly, sir. And the fact that he just happens to become contaminated during this whole mess leads me to believe that he had the uranium."

The ambassador was impressed by Kirov. The man was thorough but there was still one fact that bothered him. "Major, what you have just described makes sense, except for one element. The U-two thirty-five—I think that's what you called it?"

"Yes, sir."

"Well, from what I understand, that stuff's not all that ra-dioactive. In fact, you can pick it up with your bare hands."

"You're right, sir. That's what stumped me until the colonel reminded me what happens if a critical mass is reached." Ki-rov turned to face the meeting's third participant. "Colonel, would you please explain the process."

The late-middle-aged man sitting beside Kirov shifted slightly in his seat. He was heavy-set and nearly bald. Alex-ander Suslov wore civilian clothing but held the rank of col-onel in the Russian Army. He was an expert in nuclear weaponry.

"Mr. Ambassador," Suslov said, "nuclear materials from the warhead were made of highly enriched uranium."

"U-two thirty-five," the ambassador said.

"Correct. The U-two thirty-five core weighs about forty-eight kilograms. It's about the size of a cabbage. Now, the other element is much smaller and is cylindrical in shape. It weighs twelve kilograms and looks like a tin of beans." The colonel paused as he took a notepad and drew a sketch of the sphere and can.

"Ah, one other thing, sir," Suslov said. "The sphere has a hole in the center of it. It penetrates all the way through the ball." The colonel drew a dashed line on the sphere.

"This type of nuclear weapon is quite obsolete compared to modern warheads. Nevertheless, we still have hundreds in our inventory." He paused, pointing back to the sketch. "The missing uranium was originally encased in a special armored missile body that was built to penetrate deep into the ground before exploding. 'Penetrators' is what they're called. These types of weapons are designed to destroy underground command bunkers and to take out sub pens and other installations that are carved out of solid rock or encased inside thick walls of concrete. They achieve supercriticality with what has been termed the 'gun system.' Now, when the two—''

"Colonel, what do you mean by 'supercriticality'?''

"Oh, sorry, sir. Let me back up a little. In order to sustain a chain reaction, like in a nuclear reactor, the mass of the uranium fuel has to be increased to a point where the energy release is self-sustaining. That's called reaching a state of critical mass.''

The ambassador nodded.

"Now, for a nuclear reactor to reach critical mass, you don't need very much highly enriched uranium. Just a small percentage of U-two thirty-five is all that's required. The rest of the mass is usually low-grade uranium.'' The colonel paused as he pointed the pencil tip at the sketch. "However, in order to create an atomic explosion, the fissile material has to be of the highest possible quality. For uranium, almost pure U-two thirty-five is needed. That isotope can be massed only through a long and enormously expensive diffusion refinement process. The other energy source is plutonium, also known as P-U-two thirty-nine. Plutonium is easier to come by these days because it's a by-product from low-grade chain reactions, like in a nuclear reactor for a power plant.''

The ambassador again nodded his head, signaling his understanding.

"Once you have accumulated enough enriched uranium or plutonium you can create a nuclear detonation by reaching a physical state known as supercriticality. It's similar to a chain reaction in a reactor but thousands of times faster.'' Colonel Suslov could see that he was still confusing the ambassador. "When a critical mass is achieved,'' he continued, "like in a power reactor, that simply means that enough nuclear fuel is present so that there are sufficient slow neutrons available to split uranium atoms. Each time an atom is split more neutrons are released, thereby reaching a state that is a self-sustaining level.''

"The splitting of atoms—that's what creates the heat?''

"Yes, sir. When the natural rate of neutron-splitting is accelerated, by providing just enough nuclear fuel to reach the critical mass, a lot of heat is released. It's the heat that turns the water into steam which, in turn, drives the turbines."

The ambassador again nodded.

"Now, for a nuclear weapon to detonate, the uranium or plutonium isotopes must be rapidly brought to a state of supercriticality. With U-two thirty-five, that can be accomplished in one of two ways: implosion or with the gun method. Like the Americans' arms, almost all of our modern weapons use the implosion method. It's much more efficient and allows a variety of yields. Simply put, it works like this: you take a subcritical mass of enriched uranium or plutonium. You then—"

"How big are we talking here, Colonel?" interrupted the ambassador.

Suslov looked at the wall-to-ceiling bookshelf to the side of the ambassador's desk. It was covered with photos, plaques and awards. The ambassador loved tennis and had placed in several amateur tournaments. One of the trophies displayed a gold-plated tennis ball. Colonel Suslov pointed to the award. "A small weapon might have a core about the size of that tennis ball."

"But that's much smaller than the missing warhead."

"I know. I'll explain that in a moment. As I said, one of the advantages of the implosion method is that the nuclear core can be very small—like the tennis ball." He drew a small circle on the notepad. "Now, to achieve supercriticality, the ball has to be compressed to a fraction of its former size, increasing its density." Suslov drew a series of arrows around the circle, all pointing inward. "The compression has to occur instantaneously and uniformly to work. That can be accomplished only with special chemical-explosive charges. I can't go into the intricacies of that process other than to say that it is highly technical and very secret. Nevertheless, the explosives compress the nuclear material and in a tiny fraction of a microsecond, supercriticality is reached."

"And the bomb explodes?"

"Yes, sir." Suslov stopped the explanation. There were other elements to the process, such as the size and composition of the containment structure and the need for an initiator to trigger the explosion, but they were not important for the moment.

"Okay, Colonel, I think I understand that. Now, what about this gun method and our missing warhead?"

"Compared to the implosion process, it's child's play. Basically, all you need are two subcritical pieces of highly enriched uranium. One piece is placed at the end of a muzzle or, if you will, a gun barrel. It's called the target and is sized below the threshold necessary to maintain critical mass. The other piece is placed in the breach of the barrel. That's the bullet. It's a lot smaller but of sufficient size that, when combined with the target, there is far more fissile material than necessary to achieve a critical mass."

The colonel again pointed to the notepad. He drew a tube around the sphere and the can symbol. It was the gun barrel. "A plastic explosive is placed at the end of the gun barrel, behind the can-shaped bullet." He pointed with his pencil tip. "When the explosive is detonated, the force of the escaping gases propels the bullet forward, just like in a rifle." He drew a line from the can symbol to the sphere. "The bullet enters the hole in the target and the two masses assemble, achieving a state of supercriticality. The bomb explodes."

"That's all there is to it?" The ambassador's face mirrored his horror.

"Basically, that's right, sir.

The ambassador shook his head in disbelief. "A damn schoolkid could build one if he had the uranium," he muttered to himself.

"That's right, sir—if the right amount of U-two thirty-five were available." He paused. "We don't use the gun system much anymore because it only works with HEU. Plutonium tears itself apart before reaching supercriticality." Suslov hesitated again. "Besides, the gun system requires a lot more U-two thirty-five than with the implosion method. It works well only in penetrator-type weapons because the detonation system can survive the enormous impact forces much better than any implosion-type warhead."

"But this stuff that's been stolen—it will still blow up if it's put into another gun-type system, won't it?"

"Absolutely."

Major Kirov watched the color drain from the ambassador's

face. He had sat quietly during Colonel Suslov's tutorial. The primer in atomic-bomb-building had had the desired impact.

"Sir," Kirov said, "if I may elaborate on Colonel Suslov's excellent briefing?"

"Yes, go ahead."

"As the Colonel stated earlier, the warhead components stolen from the Chelyabinsk-seventy laboratory consisted of two elements: a target and a bullet.

"Yes, the ball with the hole in it and the tin can."

"Correct. Now what we haven't mentioned yet is that the gun-barrel method has one inherent safety problem. There's potentially too much uranium and if—"

"What do you mean?" interrupted the ambassador. "I thought the uranium was safe to handle."

"It is, if you avoid critical mass—like, for example, in an implosion weapon. There isn't enough fissile material to reach critical mass until the actual explosion."

The ambassador's eyes lit up as if a switch had been thrown. "I see what you're getting at. The gun system has more than enough material to achieve critical mass without an explosion."

"Correct. And if someone were foolish enough to try to combine the bullet and target, there'd be massive release of radiation."

The ambassador pointed to Suslov's notepad. "But if they slipped the can into the hole in the sphere, wouldn't it explode?"

"Possibly, but nothing like a nuclear detonation. You need to bring the pieces together instantaneously at high speed to do that. Instead, what would happen is that the critical mass would turn into a miniature nuclear reactor. Tremendous heat would be released along with deadly radiation. The U-two thirty-five would either tear itself apart in the form a small explosion or possibly melt into a superheated glob."

"Do you think this is what happened in Puerto Vallarta?"

Suslov responded next. "No, sir, not exactly. If there had been a nuclear fizzle—that's the term for a misfire—we'd know about it. The radiation release would be enormous. And if it occurred in a populated area, such as Puerto Vallarta or Guadalajara, there would be hundreds of casualties."

The ambassador shook his head. The military men were

again confusing him. "What the hell are you two getting at, then? Do you think this gangster had the bomb or not?"

"Yes, sir, I do," replied Kirov. Colonel Suslov also nodded in agreement. "We think Rodriguez or one of his men somehow accidentally brought the target and bullet together, but only for an instant. Critical mass probably occurred for only a second or so, but that's all it would take."

"Radiation release?" asked the ambassador.

"Yes, sir. A monstrous spike, and if anyone was standing within a few feet of the release, they'd probably have received a fatal dose."

"Major, don't forget to mention the medallion," Suslov interjected.

"Right. The testing laboratory's analysis in Dr. Aragon's files reported that the steel medallion Rodriguez was wearing may have been highly irradiated at one time. That would be consistent with the type of accident we just described. The sudden burst of neutron radiation would ionize any metal in the medallion, contaminating it. Either this Rodriguez character witnessed the event directly or someone else wearing the medallion did, and then, for whatever reason, Rodriguez put it on shortly afterwards. Either way could have killed him."

Everything was beginning to gel for the ambassador. The two officers had made their case. He sensed that he was going to have to make a tough decision in a few minutes. "Okay, gentlemen, I get the picture. Chances are very high that our warhead components made it to Mexico and that they are now in the hands of criminals. What do you recommend?"

Kirov turned to his superior officer. "Colonel, if I may?"

"Go ahead."

Kirov faced the ambassador. "Sir, I see three possible scenarios: one, the near-fizzle scared whoever has the material so badly that they've buried and abandoned it." He hesitated for a moment. "But I doubt that happened. The U-two thirty-five is worth millions of dollars to the right entity. It could be reconfigured to make several implosion-type weapons or used as originally designed."

"That makes sense," the ambassador said.

Kirov continued. "Now, the second alternative is that Rodriguez's successors are trying to market the warhead materials. This is what I believe is currently taking place or will soon."

Colonel Suslov joined in. "And I agree with the major. We recommend that you request Moscow to order a worldwide alert for all of our foreign operatives. If any of them get a whiff about fissile material for sale, we should instantly pounce on them."

"That makes sense, Colonel. I will send the communication immediately." The ambassador turned to face Kirov. "Now, you said that there were three possibilities. You only mentioned two."

"Yes, sir. The last one's a real long shot. It's about the American I've been tracking. It's possible that he may have ended up with the warhead materials."

"Do we know anything more about this man?"

"No—only what Mr. Kim told us and the photograph we recovered of him and Irina Sverdlova when we raided Bessolov's *dacha*."

"What do you recommend we do about him?"

"He shouldn't be allowed to walk away. I wish permission to continue to track him. He almost certainly doesn't have the uranium but we must verify that."

"Do you think he's still in Mexico?"

"Possibly, but he may have returned to the United States by now."

"How will you track him?"

"I'd like permission to inform the American authorities about this entire matter. Maybe they can trace his identity from the photograph. And they may also be able to help check out the connection to the drug-smuggling ring. We know they've been monitoring some of our people in South Korea but we don't think they know anything about what we're looking for."

The ambassador stiffened. His first reaction to Kirov's suggestion was negative: *Tell the Americans we have lost one of our bombs and that the thief might be an American citizen? Moscow will never agree to that—we'll look like a bunch of bumbling idiots.*

The ambassador said nothing as he continued to mull over Kirov's suggestion. His opinion was changing. The more he thought about it, the better it sounded. Every day the bonds between the new Russia and the West were solidifying. The American FBI even had an office in Moscow. But the linkages were still weak. If a renegade nation or a terrorist group were to obtain the Russian weapon and then use it to incinerate a Western city, Russia would pay dearly for its incompetence. Without massive aid from the Free World nations, Russia could easily slip back into a state of chaos that would cripple the country for a century. *Kirov's right. We must tell the Americans. They have resources we've never dreamed of. And maybe, just maybe, if we work together we'll recover the uranium before it is used.*

"All right, Major, I agree with your suggestion. I will so communicate your request to Moscow. However, until we receive a formal directive you are not to contact the Americans about this matter. Is that clear?"

"Yes, sir. But do you have any idea how long it might take?"

"This is of the highest importance. I'm sure the president will provide immediate authorization."

"Good. That should work fine."

After the ambassador dismissed the two officers, he sat down at his word processor. The communication to Moscow was far too sensitive to allow his secretary to prepare. He'd type it himself, encrypt it and then transmit it.

The ambassador was confident that Moscow would respond immediately, especially about Kirov's request to inform the Americans. But events didn't play out as he had expected.

The Mexican ambassador's special request was duly logged in and decoded at the Foreign Minister's office in Moscow. However, it was temporarily placed on a back burner. A much more demanding situation had developed inside the Kremlin: another plot to overthrow the central government had been uncovered. Arrests were being made pell-mell. And there was fighting along the Ukraine border. The mess wouldn't be resolved for several weeks.

THIRTY-THREE
FINAL PREPARATIONS

"MR. MARTIN, HOW WOULD YOU LIKE THE CASH? HUNDREDS okay?"

"Yeah, that'll be fine."

Stan Reams watched as the bank teller began riffling out a series of hundred-dollar bills. She stopped at twenty-five.

Stan picked up the stack of bills and slipped them into his wallet.

The teller looked at him again. She flashed a smile. "Now, for the rest would you like a mixture of fifties and hundreds, say evenly split?"

"What kind are they?"

"American Express."

"Okay, fifties and hundreds will be fine."

"Good. It'll take just a moment while I get them ready." The teller turned away from her counter and walked back into a hallway, disappearing from view.

He was familiar with the routine; this was the third bank he had visited this morning. Stan was running low on funds and was in the process of replenishing his cash reserves.

For the past six months he had kept a savings account in four different banks, all located in the East Bay area. He started out with five hundred dollars in each one. He had never drawn on the accounts until today. A week earlier, $10,000 had been wired to each one. Stan's bank in the Cayman's had initiated the electronic transfer.

Stan was now in the process of withdrawing $7,500 from each of the four accounts. He was preparing for a trip and wanted plenty of cash in reserve. He could have requested the total amount, but that would have triggered additional regulatory review. Any cash disbursements of $10,000 or more required the bank to report the transaction to the IRS. The rule was designed to encumber drug dealers. In reality, it was a burden to anyone who liked to use cash. If reported to the IRS, you were automatically suspect.

Stan thought about recharging his credit card account with some of the cash. It would have been easy. All he would have needed to do was go to a post office and convert the cash into money orders. He could then mail them to the bank. In the end, however, he decided against it.

Stan didn't need the convenience of the credit card any longer. It had served his purpose during the acquisition period. Using the card to purchase the expensive equipment had presented fewer hassles than trying to use a check or even pay with cash. The economy of the nation was geared to plastic. The card had also become invaluable in Mexico. His unexpected trip to Puerto Vallarta had proved that. Trying to reserve a hotel room or rent a car without a credit card can be a major hassle.

Although the bankcard had been convenient to use, Stan recognized the risk. Every transaction was permanently recorded. If someone wanted to trace him, it was possible. That's why he went to such an elaborate scheme to hide his identity. The fraudulent but accurate credit application was his first line of defense. It would frustrate the authorities should they ever decide to investigate. Second, everything was done remotely. He had never once gone into the bank that had issued the card. He mailed his deposits in, always using postal money orders. And to monitor the checking account he used the telephone— always a different public telephone, never where the number could be traced back to him. Finally, he had used the prepaid private mailbox only once—to pick up the new credit card. He had never gone back to collect the bank statements that were piling up inside.

Stan actually thought about destroying the card. He had used up the cash surplus a couple of months ago and all that remained was the standard $5,000 line of credit. In the end, however, he decided to keep it. The card was still clean and it might come in handy in an emergency.

"Ah, Mr. Martin, I've got your traveler's checks." The teller was back in her booth, filling out a sheet that listed the serial numbers of a stack of American Express checks. She scribbled her initials on the bottom of the sheet and slipped it across the counter to Stan. "Would you please sign this copy of the receipt?"

Stan complied and then she handed him a thick plastic folder. She counted out each one of the checks inside. The total came to $5,000.

"Well, I sure hope you enjoy your trip to Africa. I'd like to visit there someday too."

Stan smiled. "Thanks. I've been looking forward to this trip for years."

He had used the same line on the other bank tellers. He told them he was going on a monthlong photo safari of Kenya. It was a perfect explanation as to why he was withdrawing so much cash.

Stan slipped the AmEx checks into his coat pocket. He had one more bank to visit and then he'd be set.

What a frigging waste of time. I've gotta quit this crap or I'm going to go broke for sure!

Tom Parker sat alone in his tiny Seattle office. It was half past ten in the morning. He had just arrived. After dropping Keely off at her school and then taking his mother to a late breakfast, he had finally made it to his office. Although he had slept in until 8:00 A.M., he was still weary. His flight hadn't landed at Sea-Tac until a quarter past midnight.

Four damn days and nothing to show for it.

Tom had been in the Bay Area, hunting. He had traced the Reams' credit-card purchases as best he could. Some of the store managers cooperated, opening up their computerized records to search for old sales receipts. Others, however, refused to help, citing a lack of time and inadequate backup records.

What the hell is he buying all that stuff for?

He had been able to identify several of the purchases: a $3,500 low-light television camera, a box full of Craftsman tools, something called a Differential GPS Magellan NAV 6000, assorted electrical components and dozens of smoke detectors. Unfortunately, the sales receipts listed nothing more than Reams' alias: Stan Martin. There were no addresses, phone numbers or shipping instructions. Reams had taken everything with him when he made his purchases.

At least I got to spend some time with Bob and his family.

Tom's younger sibling, Robert, lived in Piedmont, an up-scale community near Berkeley. He was a name partner in an Oakland-based midsize law firm. Married with five kids and living in a huge modern home with swimming pool and tennis court, Bob was doing very well for himself.

Tom had never once hinted as to the true purpose of his visit. He told Bob only that he was working on a Seattle client's case, conducting a background investigation.

Reams is slipperier than an eel and there's no way I'm going to track him down with what I've got so far.

On the flight back from Oakland, Tom had finally made up his mind. He would call off his vendetta—at least for the immediate future. He wasn't going to give up completely, but he would no longer actively search for the man. Instead, he'd keep his eyes and ears open, and if Reams popped up again, he'd be ready.

I'll just back off for a while—until I get back on my feet.

Tom had no choice but to stop. He was running out of money. He had used up most of his cash reserves to finance his excursions and the only way he made any money was when he worked on his clients' accounts, not his own. And there was absolutely no way he'd take money from Linda. She would have gladly given him anything he needed, but Tom kept closemouthed about his dwindling resources. It was a matter of pride.

At least Linda's getting better—thank God for that!

Her headaches were infrequent and she seemed to be regaining a little more of her vision. She was still taking powerful anti-inflammatory drugs but the physicians were no longer talking about surgery.

It'll be good to get back to the old routine.

It was time for Tom to concentrate on his practice. In spite of his current cash-flow problems, he would be back on his financial feet after just a couple of months of hard work. He had plenty of bread-and-butter projects to keep himself busy: two missing children cases, both where one of the ex-spouses had taken off with the kids; an insurance fraud case; and the search for a bank officer who had stolen a million dollars in securities.

Well, let's get going.

Tom removed the first folder from the stack of case files on his desk and opened it.

Stan had completed his banking and was now back at the rental house, high up in the Oakland Hills. Everything was on schedule. He would finally be ready in about a week. The drone was working perfectly. The unique design was a testament to Stan's technical skills. Despite his business failures he was still a consummate engineer.

After the shakedown flight in Nevada, Stan made a few minor refinements to the robot's flight controls and repositioned the television camera by a few inches. He then installed a tiny handheld GPS receiver, linking it directly to the drone's computer. The aircraft was now capable of computing its own earth coordinates by interrogating the network of global positioning satellites that ringed the earth. The system was accurate to around five meters.

Once the navigation system was upgraded, Stan removed the parachute and its launching mechanism from the payload compartment. The safety chute would no longer be needed. Instead, a simple device of pure terror would take its place.

Stan had designed the drone so that it could accommodate up to 400 pounds of cargo. He was now working on the payload module that would eventually be housed in the carbon composite fuselage, just forward of the engine compartment. It was sitting on his garage workbench, supported by a wooden cradle.

The payload module was constructed of anodized aluminum. Its overall shape was cylindrical with a diameter of fourteen inches and a length of forty inches. The top half of the aluminum housing was hinged longitudinally so that its interior was completely accessible. The interior was separated into two main sections: the tamper and the gun barrel.

The tamper consisted of a thick-walled steel sphere that was positioned at one end of the compartment. The nine-and-a-half-inch-diameter sphere was constructed of stainless steel. It was split vertically down the middle so that its hollow interior could be accessed from the side. Two-inch-wide flanges on each side of the half-domes allowed the chamber to be fastened together with high-strength bolts. There were a dozen one-inch-thick stainless steel bolts.

Fused to the inside of each half-dome of the tamper was a lining of depleted uranium. The DU layer would reflect neutrons from the assembly of U-235, fortifying the chain reaction. The tamper's heavy outer casing was designed to "contain" the chain reaction for the infinitesimal time it took to reach supercriticality.

Connected to the side of the tamper was another section of high-strength steel. The walls of the thirty-inch-long gun barrel were an inch and a quarter thick. The threaded end of the barrel was screwed into the exposed side of the sphere. Its opposite end was capped with another flanged access fitting.

The entire assembly—tamper and gun barrel—was supported inside the aluminum housing on shock-absorbing rubber pads. Polyethylene foam spacers were located at either end.

Everything inside the warhead compartment fit together with the precision of a fine Swiss clock. It really hadn't been that hard to construct. Stan had hired a small machinist shop in San Leandro to mill the split sphere from a solid block of stainless steel he had purchased from a supplier in Houston, Texas. He had explained that the sphere was to be used as a pressure-resistant housing for a deep-ocean probe.

The depleted uranium had come from a salvage yard in New Mexico. The uranium ore had been originally mined in a mountainous area near Albuquerque. The carnotite was then processed to remove the tiny amount of U-235 it contained. The fissile material was eventually incorporated into fuel rods for nuclear reactors. Because huge amounts of uranium ore were required to extract U-235, there were tons of the dense, heavy U-238 residual left over. Stan had paid a pittance for it.

Stan had assembled the gun barrel mechanism himself, purchasing the steel tube from a Navy surplus store in Alameda. It had been salvaged from an obsolete naval cannon. The aluminum enclosure came from a boat-building yard in Richmond.

The warhead was not yet armed. There was no need to do that yet. But Stan had checked all of the components. The U-235 target core fit perfectly inside the tamper. Four screws held it in place so that its hole lined up with the gun barrel. The bullet of enriched uranium fit equally well in the opposite end of the tube. Half a dozen set screws penetrating the barrel's side walls anchored the beer-can-sized slug, preventing it from sliding prematurely down the barrel. The bullet would move only when the plastic explosive ignited. The C-4 would be molded into the firing chamber at the far end of the tube, just behind the bullet. When detonated, the explosion would sever the bullet's set screws and drive it straight into the target core.

The office was huge and elegantly decorated. The dark mahogany paneling on the walls diffused a warm, rich feeling. The thick multicolored rug fronting the antique desk depicted a battle scene from the Civil War. The window backdrop of snow-covered trees completed the setting.

Four people sat at the conference table in the far corner of the room—the secretary of state and his deputy on one side; the Russian ambassador to the United States and a military officer on the opposite side.

Major Kirov sat next to the ambassador. He had finally received his orders in late December. The attempted coup in Moscow had crippled the Russian leadership. It had taken almost three weeks for the government to crush the rebellion. Only then did some form of order return to the Kremlin.

Kirov had arrived in Washington at eight the previous evening. During the long flight from Mexico City he had speculated as to how the Americans would react to the warning. If he was in their place, he would have been petrified.

The fifty-four-year-old secretary of state was speaking. He had just ushered the Russians to the table. "Do you gentlemen care for coffee or tea?"

"No, thank you," replied the ambassador.

"How about you, Major?"

Kirov shook his head. "No, thanks, sir." Kirov had been drinking tea all morning back at the embassy.

The secretary took a sip from his cup and turned to face his guest. "Well, Mr. Ambassador, what is this urgent information you have for us?"

The Russian diplomat shifted on his chair, pulling himself a little closer to the table. "Mr. Secretary, I have been directed by our president to brief you on what we now believe to be a very ominous situation for both of our governments."

The secretary stiffened. *What the hell is going on?*

The Russian continued. "As you are aware, we have been following our treaty obligations regarding the dismantling of certain elements of our nuclear weapons arsenal. Like your own Department of Energy, our people have been removing the warheads from outdated weapons. The nuclear cores are then reprocessed for reactor fuel or other, more modern weapons." The ambassador paused for a moment. "All went well until early this year. That's when one of our weapons was stolen." He turned to face Kirov. "Major Kirov will explain what happened."

Kirov cleared his voice. "It all started back in February at our Chelyabinsk-seventy nuclear weapons plant; it's now called the town Snezhinsk. One of our engineers, a woman, killed her supervisor and then . . ."

It took Kirov forty-five minutes to cover the entire story. He left nothing out, including the abduction and drugging of Kim Hyun-Jae and the death of Arnaldo Rodriguez. The instructions from the Kremlin had been explicit: tell the American authorities everything. The Russian leaders did not want to be accused of holding back vital facts should the worst ever happen.

The secretary of state was now standing next to the table. His lower back was killing him. It always started acting up whenever his stress level rose above the normal day-to-day routine. Right now it was pegged out to the max. He was looking directly at Kirov, "Good Lord, Major, you mean to tell me that you think those nuclear components are now in the United States?"

"I'm afraid so. It makes the most sense."

The secretary turned to face his assistant. "Susan, have there been any threats lately?" He was referring to nuclear bomb scares; each year, dozens of threats are made—all hoaxes, so far.

"No, sir," replied the thirty-six-year-old director of DOS's Bureau of Intelligence and Research. "Not that I'm aware of. But I'll have to check with Energy and the FBI to be sure."

She was lying. She was forced to by her boss's direct question. *This must be what all that talk about FIREWATCH was about,* she guessed. The NSA alert had been called off weeks earlier when nothing more materialized from the CIA's surveillance operation in Pusan. If she said anything about it in front of the Russians, then they would know that the United States had been following their operatives in South Korea. That would open a huge can of worms.

The secretary turned back to face his guests. "Mr. Ambassador, I can't tell you how shocked I am about what you have just told us." He shook his head in disbelief. "It sounds like anyone with a rudimentary science background can assemble these uranium units into a functional bomb."

Kirov responded, "Yes, sir. That's why we're here, warning you."

The ambassador spoke next. "Mr. Secretary, I've been instructed to make Major Kirov available to your military and police officials. He has more firsthand knowledge about this grave situation than anyone else."

"Good—I'm sure we can use him." He again turned toward his assistant. "Susan, I want you to get hold of NEST right away and brief them on this situation. I suggest that you have the major here coordinate directly with them."

"Yes, sir. I'll start setting up right now." She stood up and quickly exited the room. The frown on her face mirrored the grim feeling that permeated the office.

The American diplomat walked to his desk and picked up a phone. He waited about ten seconds for his secretary to respond. "Nancy, please put in a call to the White House for me. Tell Matt Barrett I'll be arriving within a half hour and that I'll need to see the president immediately. Oh, and be sure to tell him that I'll be bringing the Russian Ambassador with me."

Kirov watched the Americans swing into action. He was impressed. His warning had galvanized the American secretary of state. The diplomat was clearly agitated—and he should be. There was a loose nuke. It could go off just about anywhere.

THE CONFERENCE ROOM WAS PACKED. EVERYONE WAS there: an army of representatives from all service branches, senior officers from the CIA and DIA, the Federal Bureau of Investigation with the director himself sitting in, the attorney general, the president's national security advisor, the secretary of defense and a host of other governmental representatives. It didn't matter that Christmas was just a few days away. There was no talk of winter skiing trips or family visits to Grandma's house. All vacations and leaves for the assembled had been canceled by a secret White House directive.

The person presiding over the collection of armchair warriors and high-powered bureaucrats was the youngest of them all. Dr. Cathryn Schalka was a month shy of her thirty-fifth birthday. She worked for the Department of Energy in a tiny subagency that almost no one outside the government had ever heard of. Schalka was the program director for NEST, an acronym for the federal government's Nuclear Emergency Search Team. It was her job to ferret out nuclear bomb threats.

Cathy was highly educated, having received a BS from Stanford and then a master's and a Ph.D. from Caltech. Her specialty was nuclear physics. Before being transferred to DOE headquarters in Washington, Cathy had spent seven years at the Lawrence National Laboratory in Livermore, California.

Cathy had been heading NEST for almost a year now. She managed a core staff of thirty. Most were located near the capital, working out of the Department of Energy's offices and Andrews Air Force Base. A handful, however, were stationed at Nellis Air Force Base in Nevada. This remote group had the responsibility of coordinating the deployment of NEST's vast supplies of communication and nuclear-detecting equipment. With just a few hours' notice the Nellis team could have a fully loaded jet aircraft ready to fly anywhere in the world.

Besides the full-time employees, Cathy had an army of volunteers to call upon, if needed. Over 600 employees of the massive Department of Energy were NEST-qualified. This group of dedicated employees clearly understood the risks of nuclear terrorism; many worked directly on the nation's own nuclear weapons research programs.

NEST had been mobilized countless times before. The covert search teams had scoured metropolitan areas on both coasts. The public never knew about the threats. The NEST investigators blended right into the background. They looked just like average citizens—no uniforms, no guns. The portable neutron and gamma ray detecting equipment they carried in their briefcases or operated in the vans, automobiles and helicopters was invisible to the public's eyes.

The American government didn't kid around when it came to nuclear threats. Just the act of phoning in a nuclear bomb scare was punishable by ten years in jail and a huge fine. So far, every threat had turned out to be a hoax. Not once had NEST uncovered any hard evidence concerning a real bomb threat. Until now.

Cathy Schalka was standing behind the podium, pointing a light pen at the slide screen to her right. The room's lighting had been dimmed so that the color slide was visible. It was a map of Mexico.

For the past fifty minutes, Cathy had provided an overview on the latest threat. She had even invited Major Kirov to address the group. The fact that a Russian military officer briefed the officials for almost twenty minutes underscored the seriousness of the threat. Everyone was concerned.

Cathy was now outlining her program of action. Senior NEST officials, with consultation from Kirov and the State Department, had worked on the plan all night.

Cathy rotated the light pen, highlighting an area of the map. "Our first search group will be arriving in Puerto Vallarta tomorrow morning. We plan to deploy six walking teams and two vans. The search should—"

"Excuse me, Dr. Schalka," said the assistant secretary of state. He was sitting a few chairs away from the podium.

"How are you coordinating your activities with the Mexican government?"

"We're not, sir. There isn't enough time to go through normal diplomatic channels. There's a slight chance that the U-two thirty-five is still in Mexico, most likely somewhere around Puerto Vallarta or Guadalajara. If we notify the Mexican government, requesting permission to conduct a search, they're going to drag their feet. It's only natural. Besides, there are no assurances that our interests will remain confidential."

"What do you mean by that?"

"The Mexican government is somewhat porous when it comes to state secrets." Cathy's polite comment brought a round of laughter from the room, especially the military section. Mexican bureaucrats liked to talk and keeping a huge story like this under wraps would be nearly impossible. The Washington crowd, however, was just as bad at keeping secrets.

"But the Mexicans will go ballistic when they find out."

"Sir, I assure you that they will not find out. Our people are very careful and highly trained."

Another man spoke up. He was the undersecretary of the Department of Energy. "Just what are you going to do if you find the material in Mexico? Do we have the authority to take it?"

Cathy turned in the direction of the attorney general. "Sir, would you mind responding?"

The AG sat up in his seat. "As you're all aware we have no legal authority to operate in Mexico. But, under our own national security laws we have a duty to neutralize such a threat when it is demonstrated that it is a clear and present danger to the safety of our nation. If the missing uranium is discovered in Mexico, I will declare that it is a national threat. The president will then authorize our forces to capture it."

"How will that happen, especially if those gangsters have it?" asked the man from State.

Before Cathy could respond, the chairman of the Joint Chiefs of Staff spoke. "Harry, we've got two fast-response units ready to go. Seal Team One from Coronado will deploy to Puerto Vallarta. The Delta Force will hit Guadalajara. If that stuff's in either place, we'll recover it."

The DOE official nodded, satisfied.

Cathy turned back to the screen and clicked the selector button. A new slide appeared. It was another map, this time of the continental United States. The final part of her presentation would be the most difficult. She was going to describe how NEST planned to search the U.S. for the missing uranium. It would be like scouring the Caribbean for sunken Spanish treasure, but a hundred times more arduous.

"Now, assuming that we find nothing in Mexico, we plan to launch a full-scale search in every major metropolitan center along the U.S.–Mexican border. We'll also set up two sub-command posts, one in L.A. and the other one here. We've already initiated a full recall of all DOE/NEST-qualified employees as well as special units from the Army, Navy and Air Force. By this time tomorrow we should have over a thousand persons in the field. We plan to start . . ."

As Cathy Schalka outlined the enormously complicated and expensive search operation, Major Yuri Kirov sat in the lobby outside of the DOE conference room. Russia and the United States were no longer at each other's throats, but there was no way the NSA security officer would allow Kirov to listen in on the details of the rest of the ultrasecret NEST briefing. Kirov had been discreetly whisked out of the room after completing his presentation.

The Russian officer didn't mind. He understood the need for security. What amazed him, however, was the American government's practice of assigning high-profile positions to women. Back home, women were hardly ever placed in positions of power and authority, regardless of their education or experience. Males continued to dominate almost everything.

Kirov wasn't so sure that Dr. Schalka had the experience to run such an important undertaking. But then he really couldn't complain. She had personally asked him to brief the assembly on his experience, and so far he couldn't find one fault with her response efforts.

The trailer was packed. All of his special equipment and hardware was securely stored inside. The truck had been serviced the day before and he had filled both tanks later that same evening. Stan was finally ready. He locked the front door to his rental house and then took one last walk around the grounds. It was a cool, foggy morning in the Oakland Hills.

A couple of neighborhood kids were riding their mountain bikes on the trail behind Stan's house. They were on their Christmas break from school. He waved to them and then walked back to the driveway. The Ford F-250 and its fifth wheel stretched over fifty feet along the edge of the gravel roadway.

Stan climbed into the pickup cab. It was toasty-warm. The V-8 had been idling for ten minutes. He flipped the radio on. The talk show had just started. Rush was just beginning his daily diatribe against the liberals. Stan liked the radio host. He was a great performer.

Stan reached over and popped open the glove compartment. His container of painkillers was right where it was supposed to be. The migraine attacks had subsided lately, but he was ready if they came back.

Stan removed one of the half dozen maps stored inside the glove compartment and closed the lid. He unfolded the highway map on the bench seat. He would try for 400 miles today, or until he felt tired. There was no hurry. He had plenty of time.

The afternoon breeze was mild. It blew from the north, further chilling the Puget Sound region.

Tom Parker and Linda Nordland didn't mind the cold. They were dressed in down parkas and wool caps. They even wore sunglasses. There wasn't a cloud in the sky.

The thirty-two-foot sailboat glided silently through the blue waters of Lake Washington. The yacht was in the middle of the lake, offshore of downtown Kirkland. There were a few other boats out on this midweek afternoon, but Tom and Linda had this section of the lake to themselves.

Tom should have been working but he couldn't let the opportunity slip by. For the first time since Linda had been injured, she had asked if they could go on an outing: "Something fun," she had requested. *Hallelujah!* Tom had thought. *She's finally coming around.*

He rented the sailboat from the Carillon Point Marina. They had been out since noon and it was half past three. The boat was due back at its berth by five.

"Honey, would you hand me another beer?" Tom asked.

Linda reached into the cooler by her legs and pulled out a

Heineken. "How can you drink this when it's so cold outside?" she asked as she handed him the bottle.

"I like it cold. It's the only way."

Linda just shook her head.

Tom twisted the cap off. He was going to throw it overboard but Linda gave him a sharp look. He tossed it into a trash bag by the cooler.

Tom took a long pull. The German brew hit the spot. He checked the waters in front of the boat and then turned back to look at Linda. She had her back to the cabin bulkhead, with her knees pulled up to her chest. She was reading again. The J. A. Jance mystery was hard to put down.

Dear God, she looks wonderful, Parker thought as he scanned Linda's face. She was happy, almost content. Her eyesight was nearly normal and the headaches were infrequent. Her scalp wounds had finally healed and the new hair growth covered up the scars. She no longer wore the bandanna that had been her trademark for weeks. Tom even liked her short hair. The pageboy cut reminded him of a college coed.

Linda felt Tom's stare and looked up.

He smiled. "Your book any good?" he asked.

"Yeah, it's great. I love these Beaumont mysteries—they're all set in the Northwest."

Tom nodded. He wasn't much of a fiction reader. He liked military history and sports chronicles.

Linda slipped the paperback into her coat pocket and then looked over the bow. The boat was riding with the light breeze, ghosting along at four knots. It was a perfect way to sail.

Tom felt his stomach flip. It didn't have anything to do with the boat. He was nervous. *Well,* he said to himself, *now's as good a time as any.* "Honey, I checked with the travel agent yesterday. Everything's all set for our trip."

Linda turned back to face Tom. She smiled again. "Wonderful. We still going to that ski resort in Austria?"

"Yep. We'll spend a week there. But I was also able to find us another spot in Switzerland. It's a private chateau overlooking Lake Lucerne. The owner rents it out during the winter. We've got it for a week."

"That sounds perfect."

"On the way back we'll stop off in the British Virgins.

We've got a beach condo reserved for ten days.''

"I can't wait!''

The trip was going to cost Tom an arm and a leg. But he had it covered. His vintage Corvette was worth at least $30,000 and he had five collectors bidding on it.

Linda slid across the cockpit and nestled against Tom. "You're such a good man; I don't know what I'd do without you." She kissed him on the cheek and then turned toward the bow.

Tom's heart was pounding. His mind was racing: *Should I do it? Of course you should. But maybe she's not ready. Yes, she is, you damn fool. Do it. Now! What if she says no? Then you'll know, won't you!*

"Honey," Tom said as he slipped his arm around her shoulders, "what do you say . . ."

He never finished. The flashback was there for just an instant, maybe a heartbeat long. But it was more than enough time to resurrect the horrible image, once again burning it into his consciousness: *He pulled the comforter away, exposing the back of her head and naked shoulders. Her rich golden hair was fanned out across her back, as if displayed in a magazine advertisement. Her arms were extended outward across the mattress, each wrist bound to the corner of the bed frame by a necktie—his ties. And her life fluid had invaded everything. By now it had congealed into a gooey carmine ooze that corrupted the once-milky-white bedding.*

The tidal wave of nausea inundated him. He couldn't stop himself—no one can.

Tom just managed to pull himself over the rail when the first eruption hit. Everything came up: the beer, the ham-and-cheese sandwich, the potato chips, the chocolate chip cookies. The retching continued for two more minutes. And then, finally, it was over.

Tom pulled himself back into the cockpit. His face was pallid and a thick band of sweat glistened on his forehead.

Linda leaned forward, grabbing his right arm, trying to help him back in. "Are you okay, honey?" she asked, clearly startled at what she had just witnessed.

"Yeah, I think so." He paused to catch his breath. His mouth tasted horrible; his nostrils burned. "Boy, I don't know what happened—it just hit like a ton of bricks."

Linda handed him a napkin. He thanked her and then began to wipe the remnants of his lunch from his chin.

"You must be coming down with something." Linda was being polite. She suspected that he was suffering from a combination of sea sickness and exhaustion.

"Yeah, you're probably right. I feel okay now, but maybe we better head back in anyway."

"Yes, I think that's a very good idea. You need to get some rest."

In a way, Linda was right. Tom was worn-out. He had been running nonstop lately, juggling his life between work, Linda, and Keely and his mother. But that kind of fatigue had nothing to do with what had just happened. He almost always vomited after one of his hauntings; it was how his body helped purge the ugly memories.

Ten minutes later, as Tom piloted the vessel toward the marina, he silently cursed. He was disgusted with himself. *Damn it! You had the perfect opportunity to ask her and now you've blown it. You screwed up good, buddy!*

THIRTY-FIVE
A FRIENDLY INVASION

THE THREE LEAR JETS DESCENDED ON PUERTO VALLARTA IN the early morning. They came from California, Arizona and Texas. The Mexican air traffic controllers thought nothing unusual about the executive aircraft. Dozens of similar planes had already arrived in the resort communities that made up the Mexican Riviera. It was the peak of the high season and the rich *gringos* were gathering, just like every year.

The Mexican customs officials didn't even bother to examine the aircraft. The unofficial proclamation from Mexico City had preceded the Americans' arrival. They were not to be bothered. The millionaires would be spending a lot of money in Mexico during their visit and the government did not want any problems. The bribes paid to the right bureaucrats insured noninterference.

The twenty-four men and women who deplaned from the Lears fit the image the Mexican officials were expecting. Most were young, in their thirties and forties. They were all dressed in fashionable apparel. And they played the part well—a mixture of arrogance and self-consciousness. What the Mexican officials did not know, however, was that not one of the Americans was wealthy. They were all government employees with modest incomes.

The assignment would have been fun if the consequences weren't so dire. Each NEST member treated their work as if their family's lives were at stake.

The six walking teams had spread out along the length of the city. The couples fit right in with the thousands of tourists who lined the shops, restaurants and hotels. Each NEST employee carried a portable neutron/gamma ray detector. The women hid their units inside the large canvas handbags they carried. The men used fake camcorders—the camera's guts were removed and replaced with highly sensitive radiation measuring devices. Tiny wireless radio receivers in their ears announced the presence of any suspicious materials.

Besides the walking teams, there were three mobile units in rental cars. They repeatedly crisscrossed the city, driving down narrow alleyways and over cobblestone streets.

There was even an airborne NEST unit. A Cessna 185 was rented and the two-person team flew long transects up and down the coast.

The entire operation was choreographed from a penthouse condominium near the north end of the town. The $1,000-a-day unit had been picked because of its rooftop location. The deck fronting the main living room was screened from below but provided unobstructed access to the sky. The portable satellite transceiver was in constant communication with Washington. It was of military quality. The built-in scrambler encrypted all outgoing transmissions and automatically decoded all incoming calls.

The on-scene NEST supervisor was making her hourly report back to headquarters. NEST program director Dr. Cathryn Schalka was taking the call.

''Still no sign of the material?'' asked Cathy.

''That's right. We're coming up blank here. We're going to expand our walking units toward the south end this afternoon, but I don't think we're going to find anything there. The plane didn't find anything when it flew over this morning.''

''Well, okay. Use your judgment as to where you think is best.''

''I will.'' The DOE employee paused. ''Ah, Cathy, any word on the Guadalajara unit?''

''No, looks like we're drawing a blank there too.''

''This doesn't look too good, does it?''

''No. We may be too late.''

''Then we'll be recalled soon?''

''I'll let you know tonight.''

''Okay, talk to you then.''

The line went dead as the woman switched the phone off. She looked out at *Bahía de Banderas*. The blue water was inviting. She wanted to go for a swim. She had never been to Mexico before and suddenly realized that it was unlikely that she'd get to enjoy the beach. The team would probably be redeployed in the evening.

She wondered where Cathy would send them. She hoped it would be warm, like PV. She had no desire to return to her home in Maryland. A winter storm had moved in and there were six inches of snow on the ground.

Major Yuri Kirov didn't mind the snow and ice. It was much worse back in Russia.

Kirov was in the FBI's Hoover Building in downtown Washington. He was sitting in the office of a senior FBI official. The forty-year-old man interviewing him was the embodiment of a career G-man: his dark suit was new and professional; he looked fit, with hardly an ounce of fat on his flat stomach; he even had all of his hair, although it was graying.

Paolo ''Paul'' Trasolini had been with the FBI for almost eighteen years. He loved his job with a passion and he had just been appointed by the director to head up the federal task force searching for the bomb.

Agent Trasolini listened carefully as the Russian told his tale. He had read it all before in briefing memos but wanted a personal meeting. It allowed him to ask his own questions.

Major Kirov had just finished the part where he discovered the body of Irina Sverdlova. Trasolini raised his right hand, signaling him to stop. "This woman, you're absolutely certain she stole the uranium?"

"Yes, there's no question about that. The surveillance camera at the outer door of the plant spotted her leaving. She had the core in one of our special containment boxes. We have it all on videotape."

Trasolini nodded. "And you think the American was with her when she died?"

"Probably, but we have no proof. All we know is that they were seeing each other and then he disappeared."

Paul Trasolini toyed with the color snapshot in his hands. The woman was twenty something and quite sexy in her slinky dress. The man, however, looked twice her age. "This is the only photograph of him?"

"Yes, we found it in the *dacha* we raided near Vladivostok. It was in a camera, undeveloped."

"I'd like to borrow this if I could. I want copies made so we can distribute it to all of our offices."

"Certainly. Are you going to put him on television?"

"What?"

"You know, your program—*America's Most Wanted.*"

Trasolini laughed. "Where'd you hear about that?"

"It was on TV last night. I watched it. It sounds like a great way to catch criminals." Kirov was indeed impressed with the show. He really thought it was produced by the FBI.

"Well, Yuri, I really hadn't thought about that. But I don't think we can afford to go high-profile with this one."

"Why not?"

"The American public would go crazy if they thought a nutcase was running around the country with a nuclear bomb. We just can't do that."

Kirov thought hard before responding. "I understand, but you could make up some kind of story about him—you know, a mass murderer or bank robber, something like that. All you need to do is get his face on the TV. Someone might recognize him."

Trasolini nodded his head. *Not bad,* he thought. *Not bad at all!* "That's an interesting idea, Yuri. I'll give it some thought.

If we come up dry in Mexico, this Williams character will take on more importance.'' He hesitated as he held up the snapshot. "I assume it's okay if I keep this for a few days. I'll make sure you get it back before you leave.''

"Of course.''

Stan Reams had been driving on Interstate 80 for three straight days. He was now in the Rockies, fighting his way through snowstorms and icy roads. It was a demanding way to travel.

Stan didn't mind, though. He just took it slow and easy. He would reach Cheyenne by nightfall. Near the outskirts of the city he planned to pull into an RV park. He would make himself some dinner and then settle in for the evening. It wasn't worth driving at night. Although much of the trailer was crammed full with equipment, the remaining space was quite comfortable for one person. The next morning he would pull back onto the interstate and continue heading east.

"How often have these new ones been occurring?''

"I used to have one every few months, but lately it's increased . . . maybe once a week now.''

"You're always asleep—I mean they're nightmares, not some kind of conscious flashback.''

"Mostly dreams, but I've had some flashbacks too. I used to be able to turn that off but not anymore. They can pop up just about anytime.''

"The flashbacks—can you think of anything that triggers them, like maybe a photograph, her clothing, something like that?''

Tom Parker shifted in his chair, trying to get comfortable. He desperately wanted a cigarette but his psychiatrist didn't allow smoking in his office. "I don't know, Doc, I can't pin it down to anything in particular. They just pop into my head—kind of like out of the blue.'' Tom raised his hands to massage his temples. His eyes were bloodshot, puffy, as if he hadn't slept in a week.

The psychiatrist studied his patient, now worried. Tom Parker had been making such good progress during their past year of therapy. But now, in the space of just a month or so, he had stumbled badly. *He's really hurting. I've got to find out what happened.*

He leaned forward. "Well, Tom, sometimes flashbacks like you've been having are symptomatic of repressed memory. We've talked about that before." He paused for a moment. "But before we get into that let's see if we can't look back over the past month to see if there isn't something that might be causing both the dreams and the flashbacks."

Tom was ready for the question. As much as he didn't want to talk about it, it was necessary. "Well, I think—" He stopped in midsentence. "No, I definitely *know* it's all tied in with what happened to Linda when we were in Mexico."

Who's Linda? What happened in Mexico? Now we're getting somewhere. "Go ahead, Tom."

"Back in August, I was hired by Linda Nordland to track down this . . ."

The incredible tale took twenty minutes to recite. The psychiatrist was astonished. "Your leg wound," he said, "it's healed now?"

"Yeah, I'm okay. It's still a little stiff."

"And Miss Nordland—she's recovered too?"

"She's a lot better, but she still has some vision problems." Tom continued to describe the physical trauma, but the core of Tom's problem had yet to be uncovered.

"Okay, Tom, I think I understand the contributing elements. Now, let's see if we can't pin things down a little more." He paused to jot a line on his notepad. "Why don't we start with the nightmares. Are they the same as the ones you had before the trip to Mexico?"

Tom once again shifted in his chair. It was now the part of the session he dreaded the most. "Mostly," he said.

Mostly! Interesting response! "I take that to mean it's still about when you found Lori."

"Yeah, well, not exactly."

"Not exactly?"

"No." Tom hesitated. "I'm not seeing Lori anymore . . ." His voice trailed off without finishing.

"What?"

"I'm now seeing Linda."

Good Lord, the doctor thought, *there's a transference going on here. No wonder he's struggling with this.*

Tom turned toward the psychiatrist, boring in on the man's

eyes, searching for the truth. "Doc, I feel like I'm losing it sometimes. Am I going nuts?"

The psychiatrist reached forward and patted Tom's shoulder. It was time for healing. "No, Tom," he said, his voice now soothing, reassuring, "you're going to be fine. What happened to you is the result of severe trauma. Sometimes, when a person experiences multiple . . ."

Twenty minutes later, Tom walked out of the office. He did feel better. The fifty-minute-long session had allowed him to talk the whole thing through with someone other than himself. He should have done it weeks earlier.

As always, the psychiatrist was optimistic for Tom's recovery. He prescribed a new drug that would help with the bad dreams and then he scheduled Tom for another session the following week. And as he escorted Tom out of the office, his parting comments were most comforting: "Just give it some time, Tom," he had said, "and it'll work itself out."

Tom hoped that he was right. But he wasn't convinced. *Am I really going nuts?*

THIRTY-SIX
JOURNEY'S END

IT WAS THE SECOND WEEK OF A NEW YEAR. WASHINGTON was back in full swing. The parking lots and garages were once again packed. The roads were as bad as ever during the commuting hours. And the muggers and car-jackers were well rested and ready to start the new year with a bang.

Cathy Schalka, however, hardly noticed the changes. While most of the federal government had shut down for the long holiday break, she and her staff worked around the clock. She had managed to take just half a day off at Christmas. She spent the morning with her husband and four-year-old daughter in their Arlington, Virginia, residence. She then returned to her office in the capital.

The search for the missing U-235 was not going well. The Mexican operation was scaled back after the third day. There was absolutely no sign of the nuclear materials. She kept skeleton teams in both Puerto Vallarta and Guadalajara but sent the rest back home.

Cathy now had NEST teams in five cities: San Diego, L.A., San Francisco, Phoenix and Las Vegas. All of the cities were located within easy driving distance of the western Mexico border. The present worry was that the uranium had been smuggled across the border and was now being marketed somewhere in the southwestern section of the country.

If the smugglers were careless about how they concealed the U-235, then the NEST teams had a chance of finding it. Even with light shielding, the detecting equipment was capable of registering the atomic emissions from a mile away. However, if the uranium was encased in a container with a thick neutron-resistant shield made of boron-grade stainless-steel alloy, the machines would have to be within a couple hundred feet to have a chance of detecting the escaping neutrons. Better yet, if the U-235 components were placed inside a water bed or other water container, they'd never find it. Water was the perfect shielding medium. It soaked up neutrons like a dried-out mop.

Cathy picked up her phone and called her boss. A minute later she was speaking with the man who headed the Department of Energy. "Good morning, sir. I just wanted to let you know that we've had no changes since last night."

"Everyone's still in the field?"

"Yes. I think, however, that we may want to shift our search farther east if nothing comes up by the end of the day."

"Where in the East?"

"I was thinking about Denver, Houston and Dallas."

"Okay, I agree. Go ahead and start setting it up. I'll call Trasolini."

"Yes, sir."

Cathy hung up her phone and looked out the one window in her office. It was snowing again. She didn't even notice. Instead, her mind was wandering. She invented the terrorists— it helped her focus on the abstract nature of her work. There were six of them: five men and a woman. She couldn't see their faces but imagined they were all from the Middle East. The ringleader was the woman. The dark-haired beauty was Cathy's age. She hated the United States and everything that Cathy stood for. *Where are you, bitch?* Cathy thought. *I know you're out there, somewhere. And I'm going to find you!*

After driving over 2,500 miles, Stan Reams finally pulled into the RV park just before sundown. The two hundred-unit park was only a few months old. There were plenty of vacant pads. He selected one at the far end, near the frozen pond.

Stan backed into one of the empty slots and then disconnected the trailer from the truck bed. After leveling the trailer out, he plugged in the power and hooked up the water and sewer hoses. By dark, his mobile living quarters were all set.

Stan was now sitting at his tiny kitchen table. It was twenty degrees outside, but a comfortable seventy degrees inside. His electric heater pumped out plenty of BTUs.

Stan didn't bother to go out for dinner. After his long trip he was too tired to drive. Instead, he made a toasted cheese sandwich and warmed up a can of soup. He was now eating. When he finished, he planned to retire. He needed a good night's sleep before starting his next task.

There were only a few days left to find the right site. The snow and cold weather would make that task difficult so he wanted to be well-rested before starting.

Stan would have arrived earlier if the driving conditions hadn't been so lousy. Back-to-back blizzards cost him almost a week. And then another migraine had hit as he was traveling down I-74, near Danville, Illinois. He had pulled off at a truck stop and collapsed into bed. The painkillers had knocked him out and he had stayed put for several days before finally moving on.

Stan finished the sandwich and soup. He was tired but there was nothing wrong with his appetite. Just before turning in, he flipped on the portable TV. After he adjusted the rabbit ears, the static cleared. It was a local station. The evening news was still on. The African American weatherman was making his prediction: ''Well, folks, looks like we're going to have another frosty night. Temperatures should drop down into the low twenties or high teens. Areas north of Baltimore might see a snow shower or two, but the Arlington–D.C. area should have clear skies. Driving will be treacherous tonight so please be careful out there. I'll have another update at eleven.''

Stan reached over and turned off the TV.

Tom and Linda were sitting side by side at the kitchen table in Linda's house. On the opposite side sat Keely and Tom's mother. It was almost 9:00 P.M. For the past hour they had been engaged in a grilling game of *Monopoly*. Keely was way ahead; Tom was almost broke.

''Okay, Daddy, time to pay up,'' Keely said, her voice filled with pride. Once again, Tom's throw of the dice had managed to land him on her expensive real estate.

''How much this time?'' he asked, feigning the hurt of knowing that he was almost bankrupt.

Keely turned to her grandmother for a little help. She raised three fingers. ''Three hundred dollars rent, Daddy.''

''That's highway robbery,'' he protested as he doled out the cash from his dwindling reserves.

''Look's like you've about had it, Tom,'' Linda said.

''Well, maybe you can loan me some money, then.''

''Can't do that, Daddy!''

Keely was right. He had already mortgaged his few remaining properties.

''Oh, you're turning into a real tycoon,'' he said, smiling this time.

''My turn,'' Keely responded as she picked up the dice.

Tom was thoroughly enjoying himself. It had been a long time since he had felt like a father, a real family man. He wondered if it was the new medication; he'd been on it for a couple of weeks now. Or maybe he was just learning to cope with the dreadful memories. But at the moment he didn't care. He was better and that's what counted.

Tom would cherish this special night for years to come.

of this, is on his way here right now. I'll be briefed later this evening. Maybe I'll know more then."

The national security adviser shook his...

THIRTY-SEVEN
MURPHY'S LAW

STAN REAMS HAD BEEN IN THE COMMONWEALTH OF VIRGINIA for half a week. He spent most of the daylight hours exploring the countryside. He traveled on the back roads, avoiding the freeways and turnpikes. It was slow going. There was a lot of snow and ice on the narrow two-lane roads. The Ford's four-wheel drive saved him several times when he missed turns and drove onto the mushy shoulders.

Stan concentrated his search near the east slope of the Bull Run Mountains. As far as he was concerned, though, they certainly weren't mountains. "Hills" would have been more accurate. Most rose less than a thousand feet above the flat plain of the Potomac River valley.

He was looking for a special spot: a small clearing in a wooded area, with a bit of elevation. He finally found it near a sparsely used county road northwest of Manassas National Battlefield Park, where the infamous Civil War Battle of Bull Run was fought.

The clearing in the snow-covered forest was below the crest of a ridgeline located southeast of Signal Mountain, a 1,300-foot peak. The abandoned dirt road petered out about halfway up the hillside. The view from the clearing was exceptional. The flat valley floor stretched out for miles in the background. Stan could see jet aircraft as they flew into and out of Dulles International. The airport was about twelve miles to the north-east; Arlington was another thirty miles east.

After noting the approximate location of the clearing on a map, Stan headed back down the road. The sun was about to set and more snow was predicted for the evening. He couldn't risk becoming stranded on the remote hillside at night.

After descending to the valley floor and working his way

through a series of rural roadways, Stan headed east on a highway. The four-lane road would take him home. His trailer was still parked in the new RV park located on the outskirts of Oakton, just north of the city of Fairfax.

It was almost dark now and the traffic was building by the minute. It was the prime commute time. Thousands were pouring out of the Capital Beltway, and to Stan Reams it looked like they were all heading toward him. The glare from the oncoming headlights was brutal. It's always bad right at dusk, but the reflection from the snow and ice compounded the problem. Stan was coping but the driver in front of him was in trouble.

She had no business driving. The seventy-eight-year-old great-grandmother wasn't supposed to drive at night. Her night vision had deteriorated to the point where she could no longer read road signs. Nevertheless she persisted, heading back to her home in Chevy Chase. She had been visiting with a friend in Warrenton all afternoon and had not paid attention to the time.

She was now hunched over the steering wheel of her Cadillac, staring straight ahead as if looking into a tunnel. Her hands were clamped to the wheel. She was lost. She knew that she needed to turn off the highway somewhere near Fairfax in order to connect with another highway that would take her north and then across the Potomac to her home. But she couldn't find it. The signs raced by at breakneck speed and the glare of the oncoming headlights destroyed what little night vision she had left.

Stan was about a hundred feet behind. Both vehicles moving at sixty miles per hour, both in the right-hand lane.

Another road sign flashed by but she was unable to read it. "Darn it," she said. "That's it. I've got to slow down and figure out where I am." She hit her breaks, hard. The roadway was free of ice. The heavy Caddy didn't skid, but it slowed up fast.

Stan didn't notice the brake lights for a second or so; he was trying to avoid the blazing headlights by glancing off to the side. When he finally spotted the red lights, his Ford pickup was about to climb up the trunk of the Cadillac. Instinctively, he slammed on his brakes and jerked the wheel to the right.

The heavy truck missed the sedan by inches, but it didn't miss the drainage ditch alongside the roadway. The F-250 rolled twice, finally coming to rest on the passenger's side about thirty feet from the pavement. The extra support from the columns of the Supercab assembly prevented the roof from crushing Stan, and his seat belt kept him from being ejected through the windshield. The terrible rolling impact, however, had relentlessly thrown his head from side to side. It was like going a dozen rounds with Mike Tyson.

The elderly driver never saw the accident. She had slowed up enough to read the next sign. A smile broke out across her face; her exit was coming up. She pounced on the throttle and thundered away.

"Well, Doc, how's he doing?"

The emergency-room physician glanced up from the Formica countertop of the vacant nurses' station. He had been writing notes in a patient chart. The state trooper looked like a professional football linebacker.

"He's lucky, Sarge. No broken bones and no serious internal abdominal damage. But he's still unconscious—there may be some brain swelling."

"He in a coma?"

"Yes, something like that. From the bruises on his face and forehead I'd say his head was banged around pretty bad."

The trooper inched closer, now resting his left elbow on the counter. It was half past midnight and the sergeant was officially off duty. Almost six hours earlier he had been the first of half a dozen emergency vehicles to arrive at the accident scene. Whenever he could, he liked to stop back in at the hospital to check up on *his* patients.

"Well, Doc, all I've got to say is that it's frigging amazing that he survived at all. When I found him, I thought he was a goner for sure. That pickup truck of his was smashed all to hell."

"Have you had any luck locating his next of kin?"

"No. Nothing. He's from outa state—California. Our people traced the street addresses on his driver's license and truck registration back to one of those private post-office-box companies in Oakland. But it's just a mail drop. There's no home phone number for the guy."

"So there's no one else I can check with?"

"No. I don't think so."

The doctor shook his head. *Another John Doe,* he thought. "Well, that's too bad. It would be a help if I could talk with someone who knows him. I'd like to get his background medical history, find out if he's allergic to anything, that kind of thing."

The sergeant nodded. "Well, I don't know what else we can do. Besides the driver's license, all we found in his wallet was some cash, a credit card, and a couple of business cards."

"No insurance ID card?"

"No. Nothing like that but if you wanta check some more on those business cards, I left the wallet with one of your nurses. She locked it up in the hospital vault. Everything's in there but his driver's license. I'm gonna hang onto that for a while."

"Okay. Maybe tomorrow morning we'll try making some calls. Anyway, thanks for stopping by."

"No problem. Take it easy, Doc."

"You too."

The physician watched the trooper march back down the long hallway. He liked the man. He really cared. A lot of cops wouldn't bother with taking personal time to check up on accident victims.

He turned back to the patient chart on the countertop. It was the accident victim's. The emergency physician was puzzled. The man named Stan Martin had been injured in the accident all right. But during his examination he had discovered something far more ominous than any injury from the wreck. It had showed up in the brain scan. That's why he was hoping the police would locate a family member. It was imperative that he talk with someone who was familiar with Martin's medical history.

Major Yuri Kirov was sitting in a stuffy conference room on the fourth floor in the FBI Building. Although it was almost half past one in the morning, there were a half dozen agents sitting around the table. Most of the men had finally taken off their coat jackets and loosened up their ties. Every one of them wore a long-sleeve white shirt, slightly starched. In spite of the late hour they all looked professional. More importantly, their minds remained stiletto-sharp.

The Russian officer was favorably impressed with the dedication of the American policemen. They seemed to be driven by a fierce determination to win the race. And in this case, the race was to find the missing U-235 before it was used.

Kirov desperately wanted another smoke, but they wouldn't let him light up inside the building. He would have to go down to the main lobby and then out on the sidewalk to satisfy his nicotine addiction. But he would wait a few more minutes. A new report had just come in from one of the remaining NEST teams in Mexico. The federal task force's agent-in-charge, Paul Trasolini, was talking via speakerphone with another FBI agent in Puerto Vallarta. The encrypted telephone conversation was being relayed via satellite through one of NEST's portable units.

"You're certain you found something?" asked Agent Trasolini, directing his voice to the black speaker box resting in the middle of the conference table. The third-generation Italian-American was senior to all of the other agents assembled around the table.

"That's right, Paul. Once we got a list of Rodriguez's real estate holdings we started checking. The initial trace was very weak. We picked it up in our roving rig. We then sent a covert team in about an hour ago to check. They got definite G-hits inside a warehouse. Showed up in some bags of salt stored inside. There might also be a trace in the concrete floor, probably from the steel rebar." He paused. "Paul, something definitely happened there."

The FBI agent was talking in code. G-hits stood for gamma-ray radiation. Even though the satellite transmission was coded and was supposed to be secure, NEST had a policy of never speaking directly about nuclear materials over any open-air communication circuits. The FBI agents were also honoring that policy.

"What's your next move?" asked Trasolini.

"We're going to look around for a while longer, but the consensus of the group here is that whatever it was, it's moved on."

"Okay, Tom. Thanks for the update. We'll check with you

later." Trasolini reached forward and turned off the speaker-phone. He then turned to face Kirov.

"Yuri, does that report fit in with your theory about how Rodriguez died?"

Kirov pulled himself closer to the table. "Yes. If he were foolish enough to somehow combine the two masses of uranium, even for a second or so, the radiation release would be massive."

"It wouldn't explode?" asked Trasolini.

"No, not like an atomic weapon. The two pieces of uranium have to be smashed together at a terrific speed before any type of nuclear detonation will occur. That can occur only with an explosive charge."

"What about the radiation?"

"If a transient critical mass were obtained, the escaping neutrons would easily penetrate just about anything in the immediate vicinity. The right materials will capture the neutrons and then emit gamma rays and beta particles."

"Is that what he was talking about—with the bags of salt?"

Kirov smiled. He had learned at lot from Colonel Suslov during his stay at the embassy in Mexico City. "Especially salt. Salt contains sodium and sodium is highly susceptible to neutron capture. Neutron bombardment creates the radioactive isotope sodium-twenty-four. Nasty stuff—releases beta particles and high-energy gamma rays." He paused. "Compared to other neutron-induced materials, sodium has a long half-life. That probably explains why it was still detectable."

"And that's what the NEST team measured in the warehouse?"

"Probably."

Trasolini nodded. "Would the uranium core and bullet be more radioactive if they were somehow accidentally combined?"

"Maybe, but I doubt it. If both masses had combined to reach a sustained critical mass for more than a few seconds, half of Puerto Vallarta would have been contaminated with lethal radiation. The U-two thirty-five would have turned into an instant nuclear reactor and would have melted down like our reactor core did at Chernobyl or, alternatively, it would have blown up. Either way, we would have known about that long ago."

"Blown up! I thought you said it couldn't blow up that way."

"That's right; there wouldn't be a nuclear explosion. It would be chemical, probably with a yield of just a few tons of TNT compared to thousands with a real detonation. Either way, it would have been a horrible mess." Kirov paused. "Now, back to your original question: what your man just described fits with a near-miss. The two components probably reached criticality for just an instant and then separated. As long as the U-two thirty-five elements didn't melt and combine with other metals, they should just continue to radiate alpha particles along with the occasional neutron."

"So this U-two thirty-five will still be just as difficult to locate?"

"Yes, I think you should count on that."

Trasolini settled back in his chair. His face was flushed. He was worried. "So, we've now confirmed that it really was in Mexico, but it's gone. That means they've probably shipped it out of the country, just like Dr. Schalka speculated."

"I think that's a fair assumption," Kirov replied. "It's always possible that Rodriguez's people have got it stashed away someplace, buried underground, but I doubt it. On the open market, that material's worth many, many millions of your dollars. It would be too valuable to throw away."

"I think you're right, Yuri. So, where would they have sent it?"

Before Kirov could respond, one of Trasolini's agents spoke up. "Paul, I think it might be wise to start checking the Eastern seaboard. So far, nothing's showed up in the border states with Mexico, and if it was sold to a terrorist group, they're much more likely to try doing something in a high-impact area. Remember the World Trade Center."

Trasolini remembered—how could he forget? He had been one of the army of FBI agents that had tracked down an extremist Muslim group with roots in the Middle East. The Arab dissidents had set off a bomb in the parking garage of New York City's largest building complex. It had killed six and caused millions of dollars of damage. And it had marked the start of a campaign of terror against America that continued to the present day.

The worst bombing occurred about a year later. This time it was homegrown terrorists that were responsible. The right-wing fanatics blew up the Federal Building in downtown Oklahoma City. One hundred sixty-eight people died, including fifteen children. The modern nine-story building was a complete loss and dozens of other buildings surrounding the blast zone were severely damaged.

Special Agent Trasolini had been assigned to that bombing too. He had flown into Oklahoma City within just a few hours of the blast. He was still haunted by the images of the dead, especially the children. Their tiny, crushed bodies were all covered in a surreal coating of grayish concrete dust stained crimson from the hideous wounds. It had been his job to collect forensic evidence in the blast zone. He still had nightmares.

In both incidents, the bombers used a simple concoction of ammonia nitrate—a common fertilizer—and diesel oil, the kind of fuel you buy at a service station. The slurry was packed inside drums and then loaded into rental vehicles. The explosive yield of the bombs had been equivalent to a couple of tons of TNT.

As bad as these bombings had been, they were minuscule compared to a nuclear weapon. The bomb that Trasolini and his fellow agents were now searching for had a yield of around 18,000 tons of TNT.

"Okay, Bill," Trasolini said, "just where do you think we ought to be looking?"

"I'd start in Miami and head north. Atlanta, New York City, Boston—and here, of course."

Trasolini turned to his right, scanning a large wall-mounted map located near the head of the table. The map of the continental United States had a series of red dots plastered throughout the southwestern and middle sections. Each dot represented a NEST-FBI team. *Damn, we're getting too spread out,* he thought. There were over a thousand men and women spread over half of the United States, all working around the clock, searching for the missing uranium.

Agent Trasolini turned back. "We'll have to shift some of our assets. NEST is fully taxed. They don't have any more trained personnel or equipment. Everything they've got is in the field."

Major Kirov raised his hand. A new thought had just occurred to him.

"Yes, Major," Trasolini said.

"This is just a suggestion, but I think I'd take a look in the New York area first. There's a part of Brooklyn on the south side called Brighton Beach. There are quite a few—"

"Geez, you're right," interrupted Trasolini. "That place is loaded with Russian émigrés."

"Correct, and as you are no doubt aware, some of our ex-citizens who settled there are—how should I say it—not so desirable."

Kirov was being charitable. The tiny waterfront community was rife with organized crime. America's Russian mob was headquartered in Brighton Beach. It was spreading its ugly tentacles throughout the region like a lethal malignancy.

"Major, you think those people were behind the theft to begin with?"

"It's very possible. We never did make the full connection, but I certainly wouldn't put it past that lot. If they could sell the weapon to Iran or Iraq or Libya, they'd net twenty to thirty million dollars or more. I guarantee you they'll sell it to anyone with cash, no questions asked."

"Do you think this man you've been looking for," Trasolini looked down at his notes, "Stan Williams—is he tied in with these characters?"

"He might be but he also could be a freelancer. Either way, you can be assured that the uranium will eventually fall into the hands of someone who is hostile to your country or another Western nation."

"I agree." Trasolini turned to face another agent sitting to his right. "Willie, pull the plug on half the teams in San Diego and Phoenix and reassign them to Brighton Beach. I want a hundred bodies with all their gear out there by noon today."

"You got it, boss. I'll start setting it up right now."

Trasolini checked his wristwatch. It was 1:47 A.M. He looked back at the Russian. "Major, I think you ought to call it a night and get some rest. I'd like you to fly up to New York in the morning to meet the NEST people. You might come in real handy if we hit the jackpot there."

"Okay."

Kirov had never been to New York before. He had heard a lot about the city and wasn't so sure he would like it.

*   *   *

He was in agony. Every time he lifted an arm or turned his head, bolts of pain surged through his upper body. *What the hell happened to me?* he asked himself, over and over.

Stan Reams was in a semiprivate room on the second floor of the hospital. It was half past noon. He was alone. The patient who had shared the room during the previous evening had left early in the morning. He had been scheduled for a triple bypass at 10:00 A.M.

Stan had never heard a thing. The drugs were so powerful that he slept through the noise and confusion of his roommate's pre-op care. Scores of nurses and technicians had worked on the sixty-six-year-old-man all morning, preparing him for open heart surgery.

The drugs had now worn off and Stan felt the full fury of his injuries. Nothing was broken but he had pulled muscles in both shoulders and also suffered from severe whiplash. He would mend, but it hurt like hell.

Stan was trying to pull himself up to look out the window when the door swung open. A young woman in white walked in. She was slim, just a smidgen over five feet tall. Her hair was jet-black and her skin was chocolate. Stan thought she was one of the most beautiful women he had ever seen.

"Ah, Mr. Martin, you're finally awake." The RN smiled. Her teeth were ivory-white. She had a distant southern accent.

"Where am I?" asked Stan. He leaned forward. Everything hurt when he moved.

"You're in a hospital. Right here in little old beautiful Fairfax."

"Hospital?" Stan said as he lowered his head back onto the pillow.

"That's right, honey."

The nurse moved to his side, lifting his right wrist. She waited a few seconds, verifying that his pulse was normal, and then began strapping a blood-pressure cuff on his left arm.

"What happened to me, anyway?"

"Well, they brought you in here last night, sometime around seven." She began to pump air into the cuff. "You were in an automobile accident. You've been unconscious until now."

While the nurse completed the blood-pressure test, Stan looked up at the ceiling. *Automobile accident? What is she talking about?* And then it hit him, like a brick through a plate glass window. He remembered the car slowing up. He had veered off to the right to avoid colliding with it and then hit the ditch. Before he could react, the truck had begun to roll. Halfway through the first roll his head had slammed into the side window. His memory was blank from that instant on.

The nurse released the Velcro binding on Stan's arm. His pressure was fine.

"My truck—what happened to my truck?" asked Stan. His voice was frantic.

"Gee, honey, I don't know for sure, but when I came on duty this morning, one of the night-shift nurses said you were in a real bad accident. She said your vehicle was so badly damaged that the rescue crew had to cut you out of it."

"Damn. The truck must be totaled."

"You shouldn't worry about that now. In fact, you should count your lucky stars that you weren't killed."

Despite the aches and pains, Stan was rapidly regaining his faculties. *I've got to get out of here. I'm running out of time.*

Stan pulled himself up and started to slip his legs over the side of the bed.

"Now just wait a minute, honey. What do you think you're doing?"

"I can't stay here. I've got work to do."

The nurse stepped to the side of the bed, blocking Stan from trying to stand. "Now I want you to just sit back in bed and stay put. You shouldn't be walking around until the doctor says it's okay. He'll be making his afternoon rounds in about half an hour."

Stan looked up into the woman's pretty face. She wasn't going to budge an inch. "Okay, okay. But what if I gotta go to the toilet?"

She turned to her side and reached for a shelf under the nearby sink. "Use this," she said as she handed Stan a stainless-steel bedpan.

"That's just lovely," he replied. He set the container on top of the sheets.

"You know how to use it?"

"Yes."

"Well, good. Just do your business and we'll take care of it for you." She walked to the window and adjusted the blinds, darkening the room. "Now, why don't you just sleep a little bit? Right now, what you need more than anything else is good old rest. And before you know it, you'll be on your way."

"Yeah, okay."

As the nurse had suggested, Stan Reams really was exhausted. After she left he lay back on the bed and shut his eyes, planning to nap for just a moment. He soon fell fast asleep. About an hour later he was in maximum REM. Stan was dreaming about a sandy beach in the Caymans. The water was warm and friendly, and so was the nurse.

At a quarter past two the hospital's chief of neurosurgery and the senior resident walked into Stan Reams' room. The two men stood beside the bed. They were talking in whispers, not wishing to disturb their patient. The older physician was holding a computed tomography transparency up to a light. He didn't like what he saw. "Good Lord, that thing's as big as a walnut."

"I know. Henry told me he had spotted something suspicious last night when he reviewed the normal skull series. That's why he ordered the CT scan."

"Well, he was right on the money. This man's very ill."

"Do you think he knows?" asked the resident as he looked down at Stan Reams.

The surgeon shook his head. "Hard to tell. Sometimes these things go undetected for years. But this much I'm sure of: there's no way he should have been driving—not with a time bomb like that inside."

"You think it might have caused the accident?"

"It's possible. With a mass that large, he could easily go into convulsions. At the very least, he must have been suffering with some brutal headaches."

"What do you recommend?"

"Let's schedule him for an MRI. I want to get a better handle on the surrounding tissue before doing anything else."

"Okay, I'll get him scheduled for tomorrow." The resident paused. "You want me to tell him what we suspect when he wakes up?"

The chief of neurosurgery checked the chart again. "No, let's wait until we get the MRI. No sense scaring him until we have the whole picture."

"Okay, I'll wait."
"Fine."

Stan woke up a few minutes after 6:00 P.M. The door to his room was closed, isolating him from the noisy hallway. He was still alone. His roommate was in recovery and wouldn't be returning until the following morning.

Stan had a full bladder but he refused to use the damn bedpan. Besides, he wanted to see if he could walk.

He was wobbly on his feet but he made it the bathroom. Afterward, he sat on the edge of the bed. He felt a lot stronger than he had earlier in the afternoon. His shoulders and neck still ached but the discomfort was tolerable.

Stan found the remote control and flipped on the television set. It was tuned to the nightly news on NBC. He watched it for about five minutes and then it happened. The thirty-second-long sound bite jarred his memory like an earthquake. *Judas Priest!* he thought. *What the hell am I doing here?*

Five minutes later he was dressed. His roommate's clothes fit surprisingly well. Stan's own clothing had been cut to shreds by the emergency-room staff during his initial treatment.

No one paid the slightest attention to Stan when he walked down the hallway and took the elevator to the first floor.

THIRTY-EIGHT
A NEW LEAD

"YOU MEAN HE JUST WALKED OUT OF HERE?" ASKED THE hospital administrator.

"Yes," answered the nurse. "I don't know what else to say. They discovered that he wasn't in his room around eight o'clock last night. Somehow, the floor supervisor thought he'd been transferred to another room on the first floor. It wasn't until this morning that they finally put it together. The guy just skipped out.''

The administrator shook her head in disgust. She was holding a computer summary of the charges for a patient named Stan Martin. During his twenty-four-hour stay, almost $2,900 had been charged to his account. The charges covered everything from ambulance service to the emergency room fee and a host of diagnostic and laboratory analyses.

"Didn't anyone check to see if this character had insurance or not?''

The nurse scanned the clipboard in her lap. "I guess not. The man was unconscious when they brought him in. His chart indicates that he briefly awoke around noon but then went back to sleep. Apparently, no one from billing made it in to check with him.''

"Well, this is just wonderful. How in the world am I going to cover these costs? He's from out of state and there's no local address for him.''

The nurse avoided eye contact. She continued to study the chart. A moment later she looked back up. "You know we might be able to trace this guy after all. His chart indicates that his wallet and watch were deposited in the vault when they brought him.''

The administrator's face brightened. "Well, let's just go and see what we can find.''

The wallet contained $380 in cash; several different business cards with the name Stan Martin printed on them, one in Spanish with a Mexican address; and a credit card. The state police still had his California driver's license.

"What are you going to do?'' asked the nurse as she studied the wad of tens and twenties on the desktop. They were now back in the administrator's office. "We can't really take it, can we?''

The administrator smiled. "I don't care. The SOB skipped out. As far as I'm concerned, we'll use the cash as a deposit. If he comes back and raises a stink, I'll deal with it then.''

"What about the rest?''

"I don't know—maybe he's got insurance.''

"But there's no insurance card in his wallet. Besides, he might not even be an American citizen—there's that business card with his name on it from Mexico.''

The administrator thumbed through the wallet again. She then looked back at the nurse "You might be right. Let's just hope the police can locate him for us."

The nurse shook her head. "There's no way he's going to be found. For someone hurt like that to sneak out, it's gotta mean only one thing: he's running away from something."

"Well, we'll just have to wait and see."

An hour passed and the administrator was still in her office. She was eating lunch at her desk while leafing through an Eddie Bauer catalogue. She had just spotted an attractive down parka. At the end of the month, she was going on a cross country ski trip in New Hampshire. Her three-year-old ski jacket was already out of date. *That looks just great,* she thought as she continued to study the garment. *I'm going to order it now.*

She set the catalogue down and reached for her purse. Her Visa card was out when she started dialing the 800 number. But she never finished the call. Instead, she stared at the other credit card sitting on the edge of the desk.

A few seconds later she picked up the plastic card. It was issued by a California bank and it had Stan Martin's name embossed on its surface. The validation date indicated that it was good for another year. *Hmm, I wonder,* she thought as she toyed with the card.

Five minutes later she was in the billing department. She had just run Stan Martin's bankcard through the hospital's credit-card scanner, requesting immediate authorization for payment of $2,515.33 for medical services.

She waited for about half a minute and then the machine beeped. The tiny display flashed the approval number. She smiled. She then wrote out the authorization code and finished filling out the rest of the credit-card slip. Under the signature block she wrote "Emergency Services."

The hospital administrator had no idea what would happen when the receipt was forwarded to the bank for payment. If they refused to honor it because it wasn't properly signed, she'd deal with that problem then. She suspected, however, that it would be passed right on through the system without challenge. Mail-order firms did it all the time. They just simply wrote the words "Phone Order" on the signature block.

*   *   *

tan Reams' neck was killing him. He couldn't turn it or bend without stabbing pain. The Mexican headache medicine helped but it was the heating pad that really worked. If he lay flat on his back with the pad on his pillow, he could rest in relative comfort.

Stan made it back to his trailer at half past nine the previous evening. After skipping out of the hospital, he walked a couple of dozen blocks before finally stopping at a McDonald's. He was going to order something to eat until he discovered that he was broke. All of his personal possessions were back at the hospital and there wasn't even a penny in the pockets of the clothing he had stolen.

He sat in one of the restaurant's vacant booths for half an hour, trying to figure out what to do. Not once in his life had he been totally penniless. It was a horrible feeling. For a few fleeting moments, he actually thought of robbing the fast-food store. The pain from his injuries was building and another headache was in its infancy. Both affected his judgment. He was desperate.

When a yellow cab pulled into the parking lot, he regained his senses. He waited until the driver finished his Big Mac and then hired him.

It took ten minutes to drive to the RV park in nearby Oakton. The cabby waited while Stan accessed his secret hiding spot in the trailer. He had over $30,000 in cash and traveler's checks hidden inside. He paid the fare, tipping five bucks.

After downing four codeine tablets, Stan climbed into bed. He felt at home inside the trailer. It was his haven. No one would find him there.

He didn't sleep much during that long night. He couldn't get comfortable. His neck ached and the migraine felt like someone was trying to drill a hole in his skull. *You damn fool,* he repeated to himself during the early morning hours, *you should have stayed in the hospital.*

Finally, around ten in the morning, he discovered the electric heating pad in one of the bathroom cabinets while searching for a bottle of Advil. He had forgotten that he had packed it.

He switched the pad to its highest setting and lay back on the bed. Within an hour the dry heat brought results. His neck

wasn't quite so sore and the migraine that had plagued hi
for so long had magically disappeared. His mind was cle
and his thoughts were focused: *I'll just rest today and the
tomorrow I'll get back on track. There's still plenty of time*

The Boeing 757 purred along at 40,000 feet. The United Ai
lines twin-jet was an hour out of Seattle, heading east. It wa
on a nonstop flight to Dulles International. It would land
7:15 A.M. local time.

The red-eye special was only half full. Nevertheless, To
Parker had had to pay full coach fare—almost a thousand do
lars for a round-trip ticket.

The call had come in to his Seattle office late in the afte
noon. He had been just five minutes away from leaving fo
the day.

"Hello, Tom, this is John," the caller had said.

Parker recognized the voice. It was his banker friend "O
hi, John. What's up?"

"Well, we finally had some more activity on that accou
you asked about."

Tom sat up in his chair. He had forgotten about the credi
card trace. It had seemed like a lost cause. "The bankcar
from California?"

"Yep. I just got a call from one of our compliance peopl
in L.A. Turns out the card was used today."

"In California?"

"Well, that's the strange part about it. It wasn't in Califo
nia. It was used in Virginia. In some town called Fairfax."

"Virginia, on the East Coast?"

"Yeah. All we know at this time was that the comput
authorized a twenty-five-hundred-dollar expense item at som
hospital back there."

"Hospital. What the heck would he be buying from a hos
pital?"

"I have no idea. All I can give you is the name of the place
You'll have to check it yourself."

"Okay. What is it?"

The banker had recited the name and address of the hospita
Tom thanked his friend and asked that he continue to monito
the account.

Tom had immediately placed a call to the hospital. Unfor

tunately, it was nine in the evening in Fairfax and the administration department was closed. After two additional calls to the emergency department, Tom had managed to discover that a patient named Stan Martin had been admitted to the emergency room two days earlier but that he had discharged himself a day later.

That was all Tom needed. *The bastard was there—just a day ago!*

Tom had reserved a seat on the United flight and then called Linda. He explained that a last-minute problem had developed with one of his Washington, D.C., corporate clients and that he had to fly out immediately for a series of meetings. Tom hated lying but he didn't want Linda worrying about him, either. He would take care of Stan Reams, a.k.a. Stan Martin, first and then tell her about it—at the right time.

After talking with Linda, Tom had driven to his own home. He'd had dinner with Keely and his mother. *Thank God for Mom*, he had thought. Alice Parker was his personal lifesaver. Trying to raise a seven-year-old child as a single parent was an enormous task. And the fact that he often had to work strange hours and travel out of town just complicated everything.

Alice Parker had accepted her son's sudden change of plans with grace. She truly loved caring for them both. It was now her prime role in life.

After reading a few stories to Keely and then putting her to bed, Tom had prepared his suitcase. Besides several changes of clothing and his toilet kit, he packed his Smith & Wesson Detective Special. He had slipped the .38-caliber pistol into a modified lead-shielded bag that was originally designed to protect photographic film from X-rays. He had then inserted it between his folded-up shirts. He would check the suitcase rather than carry it aboard.

If Tom's suitcase were randomly scanned as it passed through the baggage handling system, the telltale profile of a revolver and two speed loaders would not show up. Instead, a nondistinct black blotch would be displayed on the X-ray screen. Consequently, if an inspector were really interested in the anomaly, he'd have to open the suitcase and conduct a visual inspection. So far, no one had ever bothered.

Tom hadn't bothered with the ammunition. He left the hollow-point cartridges in Seattle. Sea-Tac, as well as most major U.S. airports, were now equipped with chemical-explosive detectors. The gunpowder inside the cartridges could be sniffed out.

The empty .38 wasn't a problem, though. Years earlier, when he had been in the U.S. Army, Tom was assigned to the Criminal Investigation Division's headquarters in Falls Church, Virginia. He sent six months there, renting an apartment in Arlington. Buying more ammo would not be a problem.

Tom was sitting by a window. The two seats next to him were vacant. He reached up and flipped off the overhead reading light. The rest of the cabin was already darkened. A movie was showing but he wasn't interested. He pushed the "recline" button and settled back in his seat. His eyes were shut but he was too keyed up to sleep. Instead, he was deliberately reliving the nightmare. He pictured Reams' face just as he pulled the trigger. *The bastard actually smiled when he shot me!*

Although the bullet punctures in his leg had healed, the searing pain from the wound remained fresh in his memory. But that was nothing compared to what had happened to Linda.

Once again, Tom pictured the gunman's face. *You son of a bitch! I'm coming for you. You're mine now!*

THIRTY-NINE
THE HUNT CONTINUES

SPECIAL AGENT IN CHARGE PAUL TRASOLINI AND HIS TEAM of nuclear detectives spent two days searching south Brooklyn. There were over two hundred FBI agents and NEST employees in all. They were divided into van and car patrols, walking toams and helicopter surveillance. There were even six speed-boats cruising the waters of Jamaica Bay, Rockaway Inlet and New York Bay. The Brighton Beach area, near Coney Island, was especially hard hit. Brighton Beach's huge population of Russian émigrés was the principal attraction. But its dominance by ex-Soviet gangsters was the target.

The search was relentless. Every building, occupied or abandoned, was scanned. Warehouses along the waterfront were checked. Ships moored in the harbor areas were boarded. Nothing was found. Not one unaccounted-for stray neutron, gamma ray, or alpha particle was detected.

Sure, they got hits. But every one of them turned out to be a dead end. A woman walking down a sidewalk was stopped when a mobile detector went off. She had just received a treatment of radioactive iodine to help control her overactive thyroid gland. An apartment on the third floor of a sixty-year-old building was broken into and searched. It turned out that the vacationing owner collected rare clocks. The numerals had been coated with radium-laced paint so they would glow in the dark. The owner of a civil-engineering company was interrogated when an airborne sensor detected a suspicious emission from his office. The source of concern was a specialized earth-density measuring instrument that used a radioactive calibration device.

Trasolini finally called off the search when the bureau's Miami office went on full alert. An informant reported that a Cali-based cocaine cartel was planning another terrorist attack, this time in Palm Beach. There was no mention of a nuclear weapon but the director of the FBI decided not to ignore the potential. The Colombian drug lords were once again seeking vengeance for the extradition and jailing of several of their brethren. The surviving cartel members were capable of almost anything.

After concluding the New York City operation, Trasolini's entire team was airlifted to Miami International. As in Brooklyn, they would find nothing.

Tom Parker's morning had flown by. After touching down at Dulles International, he rented a Jeep Cherokee and drove to Fairfax. He walked into the hospital a few minutes after nine. By ten o'clock he had more information that he had ever hoped for. The hospital's chief administrator had been most helpful.

"You mean this Martin guy is a crook?" the administrator had said.

"Yes," Tom had replied. "He somehow managed to get his hands on some of the bank's valid cards. We've been after him for months." Tom paused, continuing to invent his fable. "When you ran his card through the system yesterday, it was flagged. I took the first flight out here I could get."

She shook her head. "Then the card's no good?"

Right, it's bogus. But I'm sure the bank will help out on this matter—because of your excellent cooperation."

"They'll still honor the charges?

"I think so."

She bought Tom's fabrication without question. Tom's photograph of Reams (provided earlier by Charlie Larson) helped to solidify her cooperation. Her enthusiasm to trap the criminal, however, was partly inspired by her own self-protection. She worried that her quasi-unauthorized use of the bankcard would get her into trouble. After all, she had never really had the patient's consent to charge the balance of the hospital's billing.

After visiting the hospital, Tom headed to the local state-police station. This time he posed as an insurance adjuster. By noon he had a copy of the official accident report and was headed to a wrecking yard on the outskirts of Fairfax where the wrecked pickup had been towed.

The yard was locked up when Parker arrived. Inside the chain-link fence, a mean Doberman stood guard.

Tom didn't have any trouble locating the truck. The California license plate stood out in the sea of Virginia plates. The Ford F-250 had been dumped near the entry gate. It looked like it had been picked up by a tornado and thrown a couple hundred yards.

Other than the obvious damage, Tom didn't notice anything particularly unusual about the pickup when he viewed it from the gate. However, after walking to a nearby fence corner and then looking back toward the wreck, he spotted it. The universal coupling for the trailer was clearly visible in the truck bed. *I'll be damned,* he had thought. *This thing's set up to tow a fifth-wheel trailer.*

Tom next pulled out the accident report from his coat pocket and scanned it once again. There was no mention of a trailer anywhere in the report

Later that afternoon he returned to the state-police station. He had to wait until almost four o'clock before he got his answer. The highway patrol officer who had filled out the accident report had just reported in for duty.

"You're certain that truck wasn't towing a trailer?" Tom had asked.

"Of course," the trooper had replied. "There was just the pickup—a Ford F-250, Supercab."

"Did the driver say anything about it?"

"About what?"

"Towing a trailer. You know, where he might have left it?"

The officer shook his head. "Hell no. He was unconscious. He didn't say jack."

"Are there any trailer or RV parks around here?"

"Sure, lots of them." The state bull hesitated. "You think that's where he went after skipping out on the hospital?"

"Maybe, just maybe."

After leaving the police station, Tom checked into a motel. It was dark now and he would have to wait until morning to resume his search. He wasn't disappointed, though. If anything he was pumped. The fifth-wheel trailer hitch was a major find. *That son of a bitch is out there somewhere, sitting in a damn trailer*, he repeatedly told himself. I just know it!

Stan Reams was worn-out. He collapsed onto his bed, kicking his shoes off. He left his heavy down parka on. The trailer was frigid. The electrical power to the park had been shut down for hours in the afternoon, the result of a collision between a truck and a power pole.

His trailer was equipped with two separate heating systems: electric and propane. While staying in a park that supplied power, he always used the electric system. He used the gas heater only when a power hookup wasn't available.

As soon as Stan had arrived he had fired up the portable propane burner, but it had petered out within just twenty minutes. The tank was empty. About half an hour later, utility crews finally finished restoring the electricity and the main heating system switched on. However, it would take another hour before his trailer finally warmed back up. In the interim, he would have to tough it out.

Stan lay flat on his back, staring at the ceiling. Frosty plumes diffused from his nose and mouth as he breathed. He was lucky. If the power had remained shut down for much longer, then the trailer's plumbing would have frozen up. That would have been bad enough, but it would have presented him with a far more serious problem.

The enriched uranium was hidden inside the trailer in two well-concealed containers located over the trailer's main axle. The bowling-ball-size U-235 sphere was on the left side; the soup-can-size projectile was on the right. Each container was completely lead-lined and they were also filled to their brims with water. The combination of lead and water shielding rendered the uranium virtually undetectable, except at extremely close range.

As in everything else Stan did, he had again been meticulous in his research. He was aware of NEST and its highly sensitive detection equipment, especially the sensors that were permanently installed in and around the District of Columbia.

But as clever and careful as Stan was, there was a problem with his design. It was the water. He had forgotten to add antifreeze to the containers. Consequently, if the water-filled steel tanks froze, they would probably burst their welded seams. When water freezes, it expands. And like a can of Coke that's left inside a freezer, the containers would be torn apart by the resulting forces. If the seams opened up, the tanks would no longer hold water when the trailer returned to its normal temperature. It would simply leak out. Without the water shielding, and with holes in the tank seams, neutrons and alpha particles could escape into the atmosphere.

While Stan lay on the bed, he tried to relax. But the ache was still there. It was deep and extended down both sides of his head. The heating pad helped but it wouldn't cure the injury. Tomorrow he planned to find a walk-in medical clinic and get help. He cursed himself for not doing that earlier in the day. But he had been too preoccupied. Finding the replacement truck had been an all-day job.

After scouring a dozen used-car lots, Stan had finally found the pickup near Reston. He had paid $8,500 cash for the rig. He didn't like using up so much of his reserve but he really didn't have any choice. If he didn't replace the wrecked truck, everything he had planned would be flushed down the drain.

The four-year-old Ford was sitting in the parking stall next to the trailer. It had a lot of miles on it, almost 100,000, but it would work out just fine. It was similar to his wrecked pickup: an F-250 Supercab with four-wheel drive. Other than being several years older, the only difference was that it wasn't set up to haul a fifth-wheel trailer. But he had that covered too. A local auto shop was scheduled to install a new bed-mounted trailer coupling at eight the following morning.

Stan closed his eyes. His stomach growled but he was too tired to cook. And he didn't feel well enough to go out to eat. *Screw it!* he said to himself. *I'll eat something later. Right now, I don't want to move an inch.*

Before Stan fell asleep, he pictured himself back in Cabo. He was lying on the sandy beach that fronted his condominium. The surf was pounding in the background. He was no longer cold. His last conscious thoughts were of contentment: *it won't be long and then I'll be back home.*

"Hello."

"Hi, honey. How are you feeling?"

"Oh, Tom, I'm glad you called. I've been worried about you."

"What's wrong?" asked Tom Parker, sensing the nervous undertone in Linda Nordland's voice. It was half past seven in the evening. Linda was three hours behind.

"Nothing's wrong. It's just that you left so suddenly yesterday that it surprised me." What Linda didn't add, however, was that she had feared that Tom was running away from her.

"It's okay, kiddo. I'm on top of this case now. I'll probably be here for a couple more days—three, tops. Then I'll head right back."

"Where are you staying?"

"I'm in a motel in Arlington, just outside D.C." He read off the name and phone number.

Linda recorded the information and then asked a new question. "You'll be staying there the whole time?"

"I don't know, maybe. But I might move around. I'll call."

"Okay." Linda then paused as she looked out the window. The late afternoon sky was dark and there were whitecaps on

Lake Washington. "Tom, what's it like back there? Is it really cold like the TV news says it is?"

"Yes, it's freezing and I'm not used to it at all."

"Is there a lot of snow?"

"Not a lot, but enough to make it difficult to get around in." Tom paused before continuing. "So what's it like back home? Still raining?"

"Yes. And it's getting windy too. A big storm's coming in tonight"

Tom decided to change subjects. She had never answered his first question. "So, tell me, how have you been doing?"

"Good."

"You feeling okay—any more of those headaches?"

"Everything's under control. I even went into the office for half a day today. It wasn't bad."

"Great! That's just great!"

"And later this week, Bill Sullivan and I are taking a new client out to lunch. I'm actually looking forward to that."

Tom felt a sudden release of pressure. *She's really coming around. She's going to be okay after all.* "That's just wonderful, honey. I can't tell you how pleased I am to hear that."

"Well, you just hurry back here. I miss you."

Tom smiled. "I miss you, too."

Linda and Tom continued to exchange small talk for a few more minutes. He then called home. Keely told him all about a finger-painting project she and her classmates were working on in school. The ten-minute father-daughter talk was a real morale booster for Tom.

He was now sitting cross-legged on his king-size bed, a map of the metropolitan Washington area laid out in front of him. Resting on the bed next to the map was a three-inch-thick phone directory. It was opened to the Yellow Pages under the listing of Recreational Vehicle Parks. There were numerous listings.

Tom was busy plotting the location of each RV park. His next task was to locate all of the local mobile-home parks. There were dozens of those listings too.

During the next couple of days, Tom planned to visit every transient facility he could find in the metropolitan Washington area. Come hell or high water, he was going to find Stan Reams.

FORTY

BACK IN TOWN

THE FBI AGENT STARED THROUGH THE WINDOWS OF HIS OF-
ice while he sipped from a coffee mug. It was raining and
he gray-black clouds that hugged the peaks of the surrounding
igh-rises raced across the windswept cityscape. It was a typ-
cal Seattle winter storm—wet and wild.

Charlie Larson wasn't ready for the lousy weather. He and
eanette had just returned from an extended Hawaiian Islands
acation. They had left Seattle the day after Christmas. It was
heir first trip without the boys and his first real vacation in
early five years. They'd had a ball. The tropical climate was
erfect. They had spent a week on Oahu, seeing all of the
ourist sights. The rest of their trip had been spent on Maui.
They had rented a condo on the beach near Lahaina. The water
vas warm and it never rained. Despite Charlie's ebony skin,
e even managed to get a little sunburned.

Today was Charlie's first day back at the office. There was
foot-high stack of correspondence waiting for him on his
lesk. He had just started to read a staffing memo when a
roung woman walked into his office. Special agent Virginia
Wong had been with the bureau for five years. She was Char-
ie's assistant, the second-in-command of the antiterrorism unit
or the Seattle office.

"Welcome back, chief," she said, smiling.

"Hiya, Virginia."

"I trust you and Jeanette had a good trip?"

"Fantastic. Hawaii's more beautiful than I thought."

"Yeah, I know." Virginia inched closer to his desk, still
tanding. "I'd like to hear all about it but first there's some-
hing I need to brief you on."

"Of course—have a seat," Charlie said gesturing to one of the chairs by his desk.

"Actually, I was hoping you'd come into the conference room. I've got everyone there."

Charlie leaned forward. *What the hell's going on?* he thought. "Everyone?" he asked.

"Yep. It's pretty important."

"Okay, let's do it."

It was almost 1:00 P.M. and Tom Parker was running out of steam. He had started his search just after sunrise. So far he had visited two RV parks and one mobile home park, but no one had recognized the photograph of Stan Reams. And none of the park managers reported any recent arrivals from California.

Tom was sitting in his Jeep Cherokee. He was parked at a Kentucky Fried Chicken restaurant in Alexandria, working on one of the Colonel's specials. The food was tasty yet he hardly noticed. The map marking all of the campgrounds, RV parks and mobile home facilities surrounding Washington was sitting on the passenger seat. Although many of them were closed for the winter, plenty remained open. *Good Lord,* Tom thought, *this is going to take forever.*

Just a few blocks from where Parker was eating lunch, Stan Reams was walking out of a shopping mall walk-in medical clinic. He had just been fitted with a cervical collar. And in his coat pocket was a prescription for a muscle relaxant.

His replacement pickup, with its brand new bed-mounted trailer hitch, was parked in a lot near the clinic. As he opened the cab door, he paused before climbing in. "I'll be damned," he said, "it's working." The neck brace was a bit like wearing a straightjacket but he didn't mind. The collar helped support his head, relieving the stressed muscles in his neck. Already the pain was beginning to subside.

Charlie Larson was now sitting in the conference room, three doors down the hallway from his own office. It was still mid morning and he was in the middle of a briefing by his staff. He sat at the head of the table, Virginia at the opposite end.

Six other agents sat on the sides—four men and two women. The entire counterterrorism unit was assembled.

Charlie could hardly believe the story his second-in-command was describing.

"You mean we're now actively searching for the Russian uranium?"

"Yes," Agent Wong replied. "NEST has a full-scale operation underway."

"When did all of this happen?" Charlie asked, shaking his head. He was dumbfounded at what Virginia had just reported. One of the nation's most dangerous terrorist threats was now occurring and he had been left completely out of the loop while in Hawaii.

"It all started just before Christmas—the day after you started your leave. We thought about contacting you but the director vetoed that idea. He said he didn't want your vacation ruined."

Charlie nodded. "Who's running things on our end?"

"Paul Trasolini. He's the task force agent-in-charge."

"Good man. Do we know anything about who might be behind this mess?"

Agent Wong checked her notes before answering. "Charlie, it could be any one of a number of groups: Middle-East fundamentalists, IRA extremists, drug merchants, even our own white supremacy or militia factions. We're checking every known threat."

"That's all we've got?"

"Yes. At least that's all Washington has told us. We're just in an advisory mode up here. The alert in Southern California was called off a couple of days ago. NEST is now concentrating its efforts on the East Coast. Right now they're conducting a major search in Miami and the surrounding areas."

Larson turned away from Wong, glancing at a wall-mounted map of the United States. He ran his right hand repeatedly over his scalp. It was like he was trying to smooth out his naturally curly hair. He was unaware of his action; It was an automatic response to the building stress. His worst nightmare was now materializing in broad daylight. *Damn! Terrorists with the Bomb! God help us!*

Charlie turned back to face his assistant. "Other than trying to detect the radioactive materials, what the hell else are we doing? There must be some other leads. What about the Mexican operation?''

"Trasolini's task force is continuing to track down the Mexican connection. He's certain that the bomb materials passed through an organized crime syndicate based in Guadalajara.''

"That's where the boss man was exposed to the radiation?''

"Yes. Rodriguez. We now have positive confirmation that he died from radiation poisoning.''

"And the Russians confirmed that the stuff was smuggled out of Vladivostok and then most likely off-loaded in Puerto Vallarta?''

"That's right.'' Agent Wong paused momentarily to again check her notes. "The Russians don't know how it was transferred but they suspect that an outsider may have been involved. Trasolini's fairly sure he's an American, but we haven't been able to ID him yet. All we've got is a photo supplied by the Russians.'' She handed Charlie a copy.

Charlie's reaction was instantaneous. His eyes widened in awe.

Everyone else in the room noticed their boss's reaction.

"What's wrong?'' Virginia finally asked.

"This man,'' he pointed to the photo, "I know who he is!''

Linda Nordland was sitting at her office desk. Her health had improved dramatically. Her eyesight was almost back to normal. She could actually concentrate without having to worry about triggering another headache. And she was finally used to her short hairstyle. The scars in her scalp were completely hidden by the new growth.

Linda had been in the Nordsoft building for almost an hour now. She had come in just after lunch. After briefly chatting with one of her senior programmers, she had retired to her office. The company was about to launch a massive development effort for a new product line. Her approval of the final plan was required before it could be implemented.

She was halfway through the business plan when her intercom buzzed. She was surprised at the interruption. She had left specific instructions with her secretary that she was not to be bothered. Linda pushed the intercom's "transmit" switch. "Yes, Pat. What is it?''

"I'm sorry to bother you but the reception desk is in a panic right now."

"What are you talking about?"

"There are two FBI agents in the lobby and they're demanding to see you."

"FBI? What in the world do they want?"

"I don't know. They won't say anything, other than they want to see you immediately."

"Okay, send them in."

Linda unconsciously reached for her purse. As she started to check her makeup, her mind wandered. *What could the FBI want with me? The company hasn't done anything wrong.*

"Ms. Nordland, I'm very sorry to barge in on you like this, but I really didn't have a choice," said Charlie Larson after he had introduced himself and Virginia Wong. Charlie was sitting across the desk from Linda. Virginia was on his right.

"Please, just call me Linda. Tom's told me so much about you that I feel like I've known you for years."

Agent Larson smiled. "Thanks. We go back a long ways."

Linda returned the smile. "Now, what can I do for you?"

"Do you know how I can contact Tom? We've tried his office but his answering service only knows that he'll be out of town for several days. They have no idea where he went."

"Tom left a couple of days ago. He's on the East Coast, in the Washington, D.C., area."

Charlie stiffened. "Do you know where in Washington he's staying?"

"He called me last night at home. He was staying at a motel somewhere around there. I think I've still got the number at home someplace."

"Can you get that for me? It's important that I contact him—immediately."

"Certainly. I'll call my housekeeper right now and have her find it." Linda reached for the phone. Before dialing, however, she looked straight into Larson's eyes. "What's all this about? Is Tom in some kind of trouble?"

"No—not at all. But we think he might have some information that will help us on a case we've got."

"Oh, okay," Linda said, relieved as she dialed.

The phone was answered on the third ring. "Hi, Tina, this is Linda." A slight pause. "Could you please check the notepad by my desk? I need you to give me a telephone numbe that's on it.''

Linda turned to face Charlie. ''This will just take a second she's in the kitchen.''

Charlie nodded.

''Yes, that's it. There should be a phone number for Mr Parker—'' Linda stopped in midsentence. ''When did he call?''

The two FBI agents listened intently to the one-way conversation.

''Did he leave a number?'' Linda asked. ''All right—give me the other one.''

Linda wrote down a series of numbers.

''Okay, thanks, Tina. But if he calls back while you're still there, please make sure to get his new phone number for me It's very important.''

Linda hung up and turned to face Agents Larson and Wong ''Bad timing. Apparently Tom called the house about twenty minutes ago, spoke with my housekeeper. He told her that he planned to head home late tomorrow evening or early the following day. Once he has a confirmed flight he'll call back.''

''He didn't say where he was staying?''

Linda shook her head. ''Tina didn't ask and he didn't volunteer anything.'' She handed Charlie the sheet of paper with the telephone number. ''This is where he was last night, but you might not find him there. I now remember him saying something about moving around and that he might be staying at another motel tonight.''

''Okay, we'll check it anyway. But if he does call you, will you please tell him to call this number?'' Charlie wrote a special telephone number on the back of one of his cards ''That number will connect directly with me, wherever I might be.''

''Sure, I'll give that to him.'' Linda hesitated. She still wasn't completely comfortable with the FBI's sudden interest in Tom. ''Does this have anything to do with what Tom's doing back East?''

''What do you mean?''

''Well, this case that Tom's working on—is the FBI involved too?''

Agent Larson now had a tough decision to make. He didn't want to hurt Linda. He was well aware of the trauma she had suffered. But a lot of lives were now at stake. He had no choice.

Charlie turned to face Agent Wong. "Virginia, can I have the file, please?"

His assistant handed over the thick file folder. Charlie opened it and removed the photograph, the one he had obtained for Tom after tracing the suspect's fingerprints from the lighter.

Charlie handed the photo to Linda. "We're after this man. He's a suspected terrorist and we think Tom might be tracking him too."

The blood drained from Linda's face as she stared at Stan Reams. *Oh, my God!*

The director of the FBI and the president's national security advisor were meeting in the FBI's Hoover Building. It was early evening. A light dusting of snow coated the streets and sidewalks surrounding the building.

The two men, both in their late fifties, were sitting on the couch in the director's office. The room was too warm. They had removed their suit jackets.

"So you now suspect that it might be one man?" asked the NSA as he thumbed through a thick FBI file folder. Although he was still in the Navy, the four-star admiral was on a temporary assignment to the White House. It was his job to advise the president on all matters that affected the security of the nation.

"Yes," replied the FBI director. "The man definitely has the skills to pull it off."

The admiral continued to leaf through the file folder. It was a duplicate of Charlie Larson's file. He was increasingly concerned about the file's contents. "This guy worked on the Stealth Bomber?"

"That's right. Specialized in radar-evading composites. Apparently, he put everything into his company, counting on the B-two program to go into full production."

"He must have lost his shirt when Congress slashed the project."

"Yep. He eventually went bankrupt."

"Jesus, do you think this guy's looking to get even?"

"We don't know. Our agent in Seattle, who uncovered all

of this, is on his way here right now. I'll be briefed later this evening. Maybe I'll know more then."

The national security advisor shook his head as he stared at the photographs. One came from the Department of Defense's Top Secret file on Reams' company. The other was a duplicate of the snapshot provided by the Russians. The same man was pictured in both photos. "Do we know anything about the woman?" He was referring to the second photograph, which pictured Reams and Irina.

"The Russians claim she's the one that stole the uranium from the weapons plant. Apparently she's dead, though."

"Do we have any idea where this guy might be?"

"None. We don't have a clue. All we know is that there's a private detective based out of Seattle who's been searching for him. That's how we stumbled onto Reams in the first place."

"How'd that happen?"

"It has something to do with an attempted kidnapping of an American businesswoman in Mexico. The PI thinks Reams is the culprit. That's why he's tracking him down. He contacted our Seattle office for help a couple of months ago."

"Does he know about the nuclear connection?"

"No. Our Seattle agent is convinced that the PI has no inkling about what this Reams character is really up to."

The presidential advisor again stared at the photos. "Russians, Mexicans, kidnapping, murder, stealing enriched uranium. Good Lord, this stuff's right out of one of those Tom Clancy novels. You sure no one's jumping to conclusions here?"

"It's all for real, I'm afraid," the FBI director said.

"So, what's NEST doing now?"

"There's a full-scale search starting up in the Seattle area and we're checking Los Angeles again. There's a chance that Reams intends to seek his revenge locally. He's lived in both areas."

"Are you still checking Florida?"

"Yes, but it looks like a dead end."

"Where else could this nutcase be?"

"He could be anywhere, even around here. All we know is that the detective from Seattle is somewhere around here right now. It's possible that there's a connection."

"He's in D.C.?" asked the NSA.

"Yes, we're trying to locate him right now to find out what he's doing. From what we understand, he's here working on some other case, but we've got to confirm it."

"Damn—then it means that this Reams character could be around here too. With a bomb."

"Yes, but we don't think it's very likely. NEST has hundreds of remote sensors scattered throughout the District of Columbia. They're permanent installations. If any nuclear materials were brought in, we'd know about it. So far, everything's clean."

What the FBI director didn't add, but what the admiral was well aware of, was that a small truck or car could drive into the capital loaded with a nuclear weapon. The sensors might detect the escaping alpha particles and neutrons as it headed into the city. However, it was unlikely that NEST, the FBI or the Secret Service would have enough time to react. If the bomber was intent on suicide, he could detonate the device anywhere inside the District and accomplish his mission.

"What do you suggest that I tell the president?" asked the NSA.

"I'll know more in the morning. Right now I think it would make sense to brief him about the risks. He'll have to make the final decision."

"You know he won't cancel it—not on what we've got so far."

"Yeah, I know."

FORTY-ONE
D-DAY

IT WAS A FROSTY MORNING. THE EXHAUST FROM THE pickup's V-8 blasted out of the tailpipe like a jet engine. The plume rose ten feet into the air before dispersing.

Stan Reams eased the automatic gearshift lever into drive

and the Ford inched forward. The powerful engine hardly noticed the load from the huge trailer.

Stan slowly wove his way through the narrow driveway of the RV park until he reached the manager's office. He pulled off to the side and parked. He was feeling like a million bucks. He had had a long, restful night of sleep and when he woke, his neck wasn't nearly as sore as the day before. The medication had helped, allowing him to get by without the cervical collar.

He opened the cab door and stepped out. He left the engine running.

"Well, good morning, Stan," said the female manager as he walked into the office. "Looks like you're all ready to shove off."

"Right. I'm all set."

"You still heading to Florida?"

"Yep. I just wanted to come in and settle up my account before hitting the road."

"Okay, just a sec while I check the books." She reached for a ledger under the counter.

The woman was in her late fifties. She lived alone in another trailer located behind the office. She made it her business to know everyone in her park.

"Ah, here it is," she said. "Looks like I owe you your damage deposit back."

"Right."

"Okay, just hang on. I've got to go back inside to get your money."

"Fine."

As soon as she left, Stan turned to his right, searching. He found what he was looking for a few seconds later. He walked up to the wall and began studying a gas-station map of Virginia. It was tacked to the wallboard.

Stan couldn't remember the exact location of the hillside clearing. It had been nearly dark when he started back for Oakton on the day of his visit and his own map with the location marked on it was still inside the cab of the wrecked pickup.

He used his right index finger to trace a path along one of the major arterials that led to the base of the Bull Run Mountains. He then spotted a familiar landmark. *There's Signal Mountain. It must be right about there.* He pointed with a finger to an area just southeast of the 1,300-foot hilltop.

"You thinking about heading over to the Bull Run area?" asked the manager. She was now standing behind the counter. There was a wad of cash in her right hand.

Stan turned, startled at the woman's sudden return. "Maybe. I was thinking of taking in some of the sights before heading south. Aren't there some Civil War memorials near there."

"Yeah, there's all kinds of them but I don't know how much you'll be able to see. Most everything's closed up for the winter over there."

"You're probably right, but I think I'll head over and take a look-see anyway." Stan looked back toward the map. He almost had the route memorized. A moment later he again turned to face the woman. "Well, I guess I'll be going." He then spotted the cash in her right hand. "That my deposit?" he asked.

"Yep."

She handed over the hundred dollars.

"Thanks a lot. You got a nice place here."

"You're welcome. Come back and visit us again."

"Maybe I will."

Two minutes later Stan climbed back into the cab of his truck.

The manager watched the Ford F-250 and its long trailer pull out of the park driveway and then head onto the frontage road. She was a little mystified at Stan's interest in the distant foothills. *For a guy who's supposed to be heading down to Florida, he's sure taking a hell of a detour.*

Linda Nordland and Bill Sullivan were lunching together in Linda's office. It was a quarter past one o'clock. Bill had just returned from a two-day business trip to San Jose.

The Nordsoft executives were sitting at a small circular conference table in one corner of the office. Linda had a salad; Bill was working on a clubhouse sandwich. He had just reported on his meeting with a competing software-development firm. Nordsoft was proposing a joint venture with the Silicon Valley–based firm on the development of a new CAD product.

Linda had her eye on the California company. If this JV was successful, she might try to acquire it.

"That's just great, Bill," Linda said.

"Well, thanks. I'm real pleased with the deal we cut. We'll both make good money on it."

Bill took a bite from his sandwich before changing subjects. "I understand we had a visit from the FBI yesterday. What was that all about?"

Linda's face went neutral. Bill noticed. "What's the matter, Linda?"

"They were looking for Tom."

"Tom! What for?"

"I'm not sure but they seemed desperate to find him."

"Where is he?"

"Back in Washington."

"The capital?

"Yeah."

"What's he doing there?"

"He told me he was working on some case . . ." she hesitated ". . . but I really think he's trying to track down the man who hurt us. One of the agents is a friend of Tom's and he showed me this picture . . ."

For the next few minutes, Linda repeated the high points of her conversation with the FBI agents. Sullivan was mesmerized by the story.

"But you don't know for sure if Tom's tracking this guy or working on some other case?"

"That's right. All I know is that his FBI friend, Charlie Larson, was going to try and track him down back in the Washington area."

"You mean he flew back there just to find Tom?"

"Yeah, I guess so." Linda reached for her purse. "He gave me his card with a special number on it. I'm supposed to have Tom call him whenever I hear from him. But he hasn't called yet."

Dammit, what's going on here? Sullivan wondered. *Why would Tom run off to Washington so suddenly.*

And then it hit, like a pail of ice water in the face. He recalled his conversation with Tom at Thanksgiving. *The credit-card trace—the guy must have used the damn credit card!*

Ten minutes had passed. Bill and Linda were now talking on a speakerphone. Charlie Larson was on the other end of the line. He was sitting in an office in the FBI's Hoover Building in the capital.

"Do you know the name of the man at the bank that Tom was working with?" asked Larson.

"No," replied Sullivan. "He never mentioned it."

"Okay. We'll check it out from here." Charlie paused as he prepared to take a new tack. "Ah, Linda, I assume you never heard from Tom last night?"

"That's right—he hasn't called back. And I take it you haven't found him yet, either?"

"Correct, we're still looking. Anyway, if he should contact you again, please tell him to call me ASAP—use the same number. It's really important."

"I will."

Charlie Larson didn't waste any time checking out Bill Sullivan's tip. Within twenty minutes of his call, Special Agent Virginia Wong was on her way to the federal courthouse in downtown Seattle. The judge was waiting. He issued the warrant and she immediately left for the headquarters of the local bank in question. She walked; it was only a few blocks from the courthouse. An advance team of agents was waiting for her in the lobby of the high-rise.

The bank's cooperation was instantaneous. Tom Parker's contact was produced within minutes. The man was utterly confused when Agent Wong grilled him about the computer surveillance work he had done for Parker. The technician told her everything that he knew, including the name of his counterpart at the bank's parent firm in California.

A similar operation was then unleashed in downtown Los Angeles. Armed with a duplicate copy of the federal warrant from Seattle, FBI agents descended on the bank's corporate headquarters. Every scrap of paper and computer file regarding the credit card in question was produced. That's when all hell broke loose back in Washington, D.C.

From a conference room in the FBI building, Charlie Larson was talking with a senior agent in L.A. The agent had just called Charlie to report on the investigation.

"You mean that card was used, there, just a couple of days ago?" Larson said. He was clearly astonished.

"That's right, sir. We traced it to a hospital in Fairfax." The man read off the name and address.

Larson recorded the information on a slip of paper and, with his hand held over the phone's transmitter, he called out to a nearby assistant: "Steve, check this out ASAP."

The man took the slip of paper and sat down at a nearby computer terminal.

Charlie uncovered the speaker on the handset. "Okay, Russ, good job. We're going to check it out from here. If you come up with anything else, call me right away."

"You got it, sir."

Larson hung up and turned to face the agent who sat behind the computer terminal. "What ya got?" he asked, waiting for the answer.

"It's a real address all right. Checks out as a hospital."

"All right, get your coat. We're going for a ride."

The drive to Fairfax was a nightmare. All of the bridges across the Potomac were plugged with homeward-bound commuters. The arterials bisecting Arlington were just as congested. The hordes of vehicles trying to escape the District of Columbia, combined with the icy roads, resulted in dozens of fender benders. Everything moved at a snail's pace.

Finally, at a quarter to seven, Charlie Larson and a team of FBI agents rolled into the hospital's parking lot. Charlie led the way to the emergency room.

"Is this the patient?" asked Charlie as he held up a photograph of Stan Reams.

The physician studied the photo and then looked up. "Yes. He's the man I treated."

"How badly hurt was he?"

"He was banged up pretty good—he had a nasty concussion."

"Could he function normally?"

"What do you mean?"

"If he took off on his own, would he be able to get around all right? Drive a car, that kind of thing?"

"Yeah, I guess so. He'd have a sore neck for a week or so but that really wasn't his problem."

"You mean he was hurt some other way in the accident?"

"No. It had nothing to do with the accident. He's . . ." The young doctor stopped. "I don't think I can say any more. That's getting into privileged information."

Larson almost lost his temper. A nuclear bomb might be loose somewhere in the nation's capital and the doctor was worried about violating one of his professional canons. "Look, Doc, I understand your reluctance to talk about your patients, but we've got a real serious situation here. We believe this man is a terrorist and he may be planning to kill a lot of people. You've got to tell me everything, and right now."

The doctor stared at the floor. Everyone else stared at him. And then he gave in.

"Okay, okay. I'll tell you." The physician paused to think out his next words. "The patient is very ill. He has a massive brain tumor and it's possible that he knows nothing about it. If it isn't treated immediately, he'll die. There's no question about that."

"Brain tumor?" asked Agent Larson. "Just what kind of effect would that have on him?"

"Hard to say for sure. But I imagine that he's suffering from migraines. He may even have convulsions. All kinds of things could happen."

"How about his sanity—would that affect it?"

"Sure, a tumor like that has the potential to cause all kinds of mental problems."

Holy shit, thought Larson. *The guy's really a nut after all.* "Thanks for your help."

The army of agents filed out of the building and headed for the parking lot. Charlie grabbed the secure phone in his car when he climbed in. A couple of seconds later he was linked to the NEST crisis team in the Department of Energy building. He was speaking with Agent Trasolini.

"Paul, everything's starting to fit together now. We just found out that this guy Reams has got a frigging tumor growing away in his skull. The doctor said it could easily make him crazy."

Good Lord, thought Trasolini, *we're dealing with someone who's insane.*

It was one thing to track politically motivated terrorists. To a degree they were predictable, and they usually worked within a group. This offered additional opportunities for infiltration and capture. However, a single individual, bent on carrying out a mission of mass destruction, might be impossible to stop. The Unabomber was a perfect case example. It had taken the FBI almost twenty years to find the disgruntled academic. He had used simple pipe bombs to terrorize the nation. But now they were facing a threat thousands of times greater: a madman with a nuclear weapon and the technical skills to use it.

"Maybe he's really the one behind all of this?" Trasolini offered.

"Yep, I'm beginning to think so."

"Have you had any luck locating that private detective friend of yours?"

"No, we still don't know where he is. We tracked down where he rented a car but the police haven't spotted it yet."

Trasolini didn't respond for a few seconds. He had to make another huge decision. "Okay, Charlie, I'm calling a full regional-wide alert. Nothing's been detected yet, but I'm not taking any chances."

"Good. Right now we're heading out to the local state-police station. I'm going to try and find out some more about the accident that guy had. It might lead to something."

"Okay, keep us posted here."

"Will do."

Trasolini hung up the phone and turned to face the crisis-management team. Every man and woman in the room had been listening to his side of the conversation. "Okay, people," he said, "this is the real thing. I want the D.C. area saturated. Get those NEST people moving as soon as they touch down."

Trasolini had anticipated the turn of events earlier in the day and had already recalled several of Cathy Schalka's teams from other areas of the country. They were now airborne, converging on the District of Columbia.

Major Yuri Kirov was sitting in the lobby outside the FBI-NEST command center. The search team that he had been observing in New York City and then Florida had just returned to Washington. Three additional chartered jetliners, carrying the rest of the nuclear search teams, were now landing at Andrews Air Force base. Within an hour, all 535 nuclear detectives would be scattered throughout the Washington metropolitan area.

The Russian security officer leaned back in his chair and lit up a cigarette. No one seemed to care about his smoking at the moment.

To Yuri, the unfolding drama was almost surreal. Five minutes earlier, Agent Trasolini had briefed him on the situation with Reams. He could hardly believe the news. *All of this death and misery because one man was going insane!*

It seemed impossible, yet it was happening.

Tom Parker was bored stiff as he drove along the western shoreline of the Potomac River. He had spent the entire day visiting RV and mobile home parks located east and north of D.C. The previous day he had scoured the countryside west and south of the capital. But there had been no sign of Stan Reams or his fifth wheel trailer. He was beginning to believe that he was on the proverbial wild goose chase. Yet he wasn't ready to quit. Tom had a new lead. At his last stop, he had learned about a new park that had opened earlier in the year. It hadn't been listed in the yellow pages. It was located back in the Fairfax area, near Oakton. It would take him about forty minutes to reach it.

The director of the FBI didn't bother to consult with the national security advisor or to telephone in his request. Instead, he presented himself personally at the White House. The president's chief of staff met him in the lobby.

"I'm sorry, but the president can't be disturbed. He's still working on his speech."

"Look, Matt, I know that. That's why I've got to speak with him."

"You'll just have to wait until he's ready. Then I'm sure he'll see you."

The director was almost beside himself. He took the man to the side, away from the secretary's desk. "I haven't got any time to screw around here. I must see the president, now." He paused for effect. "We think there might be a lunatic running around Washington with a nuclear device and that he intends to use it—possibly tonight."

"Oh, dear God," replied the chief of staff. He thought for a moment before continuing. "All right, come with me."

* * *

The FBI director had the president's full attention as he described the threat. ''You mean you think this character's somewhere in the vicinity right now?'' asked the president.

''Yes, sir. We're looking everywhere inside the Beltway.''

''And NEST—what are they doing?''

''We're saturating the District with radiation detectors. They're supplementing the other permanent monitors. If there's a device within a ten-mile radius of here, we'll know about it.''

''Good. Sounds like you have everything under control.''

''For the time being. But we can't predict anything with this character. We think the threat is remote but just to be safe I'd like you to consider postponing your speech tonight.''

The president's gaze bored into the director's eyes. ''You want me to cancel the state of the union speech?''

''Yes, sir. Just give us a day or so and we'll track this son of a bitch down. Then it'll be safe.''

The president shook his head. ''I can't do that. Everything's been set for weeks.'' The president was steadfast in his response. He was going to announce a series of new spending and tax proposals as part of his speech. Once again the nation was floundering from a severe recession. His own party, as well as the majority of the electorate, was counting on his leadership to guide America back to prosperity. If he were to cancel the state of the union speech, his credibility would plummet.

''Sir, we can handle it easily. All we have to do is report that you took ill suddenly, like a case of food poisoning—something like that. Your doctor can cover for you and then we'll fly you up to Camp David—just to be safe.''

''What about the Congress?''

''We could immediately start flying out key members of the congressional delegation along with your Cabinet. If it's done discreetly, the press won't pick up on it.''

''And the rest of Washington?''

''There's no time for a mass evacuation. If that were to occur the bomber might just decide to detonate it anyway.''

The president shook his head again. ''No. I'm not going to do that. Unless you can conclusively prove that there's a real threat—not just a theory—then I'm going on as scheduled.''

''But—''

"No buts about it. Can you imagine what would happen if it gets out that I deserted Washington, along with a handful of senators and representatives, all of us trying to save our own collective butts, while we left everyone else behind? God, the press would crucify me."

The director didn't reply. He had lost.

The president looked down at his wristwatch. It was almost seven o'clock. "There's two hours before my speech. If this guy really exists, you'll have to find him before then because I'm not calling it off."

"Yes, sir."

The sun had dropped behind the ridge a few hours earlier. The sky was velvet black and there was snow and ice everywhere. The air temperature was hovering just above twenty degrees.

Stan Reams didn't mind the cold or darkness. He was toasty warm inside his trailer. The portable propane heater worked fine. Before heading up the hillside road to the campsite he had filled the empty tank at a nearby country store. The fuel supply would last several days, if needed. And there was plenty of light too. His built-in Honda generator was purring away.

Stan didn't have any trouble finding the dirt roadway that led to the hillside site. However, a few more inches of snow had accumulated on the ground since his first visit. As a result, towing the trailer up the steep grade was a slow process. The chains he had installed on all four tires of the all-wheel-drive Ford made the difference. He arrived at the clearing just before ten o'clock. That gave him the remainder of the morning and all afternoon to set up. Everything was ready now. There was nothing else to do but wait.

It was dark inside the trailer. The only light came from the TV. Stan was tuned in to a local station. The ABC anchorwoman was reading the news: "And later tonight the president will deliver his state of the union message. It is expected that he will announce a series of proposed federal spending cuts and sweeping tax rollbacks. All of these measures will be designed to stimulate the nation's sluggish economy. They reflect a total repudiation of his predecessor's policies. Whether or not he can convince Congress to act remains to be seen. Nevertheless, an ABC-Gallup poll released today shows overwhelming nationwide support for—"

Stan hit the remote-control button. The Sony blinked off, leaving him in darkness. He had heard it all just a few minutes earlier on CBS.

Stan didn't care about the new president or the positive changes that were now taking place in Congress. It just didn't matter. The system that had destroyed his business—his life— was still in place. And its core was just thirty-five miles away.

Stan looked through the trailer's window. From his hillside perch, he could easily see the atmospheric glow. Reflected light from metropolitan Washington lit up the distant horizon like the aurora borealis. The fluorescent sheen was spectacular in the frosty, crystal-clear evening sky.

FORTY-TWO
CLOSING IN

WHEN TOM PARKER TURNED INTO THE DRIVEWAY OF THE RV park in Oakton, he was exhausted. It was half past seven in the evening. It was his last stop of the day and then he'd find a motel. The following day he planned to visit the Baltimore area to complete his search. If he found no sign of Reams by then, he'd call it quits and fly back to Seattle.

Tom pulled up his Jeep Cherokee next to the office and stopped. He was glad that he had rented the four-wheel-drive vehicle. Half of the parks he drove through were covered with snow and ice.

The manager watched the stranger approach her office. He was bundled up in a parka. Thick plumes of breath marked his trail.

Tom walked up to the steps and opened the door. The warmth of the office spread over him like a tropical tidal wave. "Hi, there," he said as he spotted the older woman. She was standing behind the counter. There was a large console television in the corner of the room. It was tuned to CNN; the volume had been muted.

"What can I do for you?" she asked.

"You the manager here?"

"Yes."

"Good. Maybe you can help me. I'm looking for a man who might be staying in your park."

"You a cop?"

"No. I'm a private investigator. Name's Parker, Tom Parker." Tom opened up his wallet and flashed his Washington State investigator's license.

She adjusted the glasses on her nose as she scanned the document. None of the other park managers Tom had visited had bothered to check his credentials. "You're from Seattle," she said. "What the heck are you doing out here?"

Tom slipped his wallet back into his trousers hip pocket. He then removed a photo from his parka. "I'm trying to locate this fellow. Goes by the name of Reams, Stan Reams. But he might be using another name."

The woman accepted the color print, holding it under a lamp on the counter for a better view. Her reaction was immediate. "Oh, yeah. He was here. Checked out this morning. Nice guy."

Tom's heart skipped a beat with the news. "He was here?"

"Yeah. Rented slot forty-two, down by the pond."

"How long did he stay?"

"About a week. Came up from California."

"And he left today?"

"Yeah, around eight this morning." She paused to study Tom's face. *He's certainly attractive.* "Why are you looking for him, anyway?"

"His family's trying to locate him. He's got an inheritance coming but he has no permanent home address so they can't notify him. I've been following him around for a month now." Tom had used the same story all week. No one questioned it.

A month! she thought. *There must be some serious money involved in that inheritance.* "Well, I'm sorry you missed him."

"Do you know where he was going?"

"Florida, St. Pete area. At least that's where he said he was planning to end up. But I'm not so sure he's headed south yet."

"Why not?"

"Well, he said he was heading over to the Bull Run area first. He mentioned something about checking out some Civil War sites."

"The Bull Run area?"

"Yeah." She walked over to the road map that was tacked back onto a wall. "It's right in this area. About twenty to twenty-five miles away."

"Are there any RV parks out there?"

"A couple. One at Haymarket, another at Gainesville. They're both kind of located near Lake Manassas."

Tom nodded, remembering. He had visited both RV parks the previous day. *But could he be there now?* Tom wondered. "Ah, he didn't happen to mention where'd he be staying tonight, did he?"

"You mean like at one of those parks?"

"Yeah."

"No. He didn't say anything about that."

"Any other place out there where he might stop off at . . . a state park, campground, that kind of thing?"

"No, not this time of year but if he found an area he liked, he'd probably just pull off to the side of the road and set up camp. His rig's well-equipped and that new truck of his has four-wheel drive."

"Oh, yeah, the truck—can you describe it?" Tom asked, remembering Reams' first vehicle from the wrecking yard. It would never run again.

"It's one of these big Fords with an extended cab. Supercab, I think they're called. Brown with white trim. Four or five years old. He picked it up a day or so ago." She paused for a moment. "Too bad about his first one, though. I'll bet it was some kids."

"Kids?" Tom was confused.

"Yeah. It was stolen when he was in Tyson's Corner, shopping. Took it right out of the parking lot in broad daylight."

Tom just nodded. *This guy really does cover his tracks.* "Well, thanks a lot for your help. I appreciate your time."

"You gonna check those parks, see if he's camped out there?"

"Yeah, I'll take a run out there tomorrow morning."

"Good luck."

"Thanks."

Five minutes later Tom was on a road heading west. He was pumped up. He wasn't about to wait another day. *All right, Reams, you just sit tight tonight. I'm on the way*!

After Parker left, the trailer-park manager settled into a chair by the TV. She flipped off the mute, restoring the sound. The CNN anchorman was in the middle of his narration. He was speaking with a reporter who was broadcasting live from the steps of the Capitol building. The screen was focused on the twenty-eight-year-old reporter. Her teeth gleamed in the camera's lights. Her golden-blond hair shimmered. She was in high profile, knowing that millions across the nation were watching.

"Well, Bill, it sure looks like it's going to be a full house tonight. The White House reports that all one hundred senators and all but two representatives will be in attendance. Congressman Miles is still in the hospital and Congresswoman Sanchez is attending a funeral in California."

The Atlanta anchor's face flashed onto the screen. "How about the president's Cabinet? Will everyone be attending?"

The camera homed in on the pretty face again. "All but one, Bill. As you know it's government policy that at least one of the president's key advisors remain out of Washington during the state of the union address. Should something happen to the Capitol, God forbid, then there will be someone to carry on the government." For just an instant the woman glanced down at her notes. "This year it's the Department of Commerce's turn. Secretary Allison left this afternoon for Japan. She's in San Francisco tonight. Tomorrow she'll fly to Tokyo for a week of meetings with trade officials."

"What's it look like for the rest of the guests?" asked the anchor. The screen remained centered on the woman.

"Ah, it looks like the House chamber is really going to be packed. The entire Supreme Court will be there as well as a number of appellate court judges. All of the Joint Chiefs—and the chairman, of course—plus dozens of other generals and admirals from the Pentagon."

The anchor's image reappeared just long enough for him to ask another question. "I understand there's quite a Hollywood contingent showing up as well."

"There sure is. So far Tom Hanks, Jane Fonda and Steven Spielberg have already arrived. A long list of others is expected to attend, but we haven't spotted them yet.'' The woman broke into a smile. ''As you know, Bill, the president is extremely popular with the entertainment industry and they are here to honor him and offer their support.''

Once again the anchorman's image filled the television screen. ''Well, I'm sure he appreciates their efforts very much. Now, Wendy, if you'll stand by, we'll get back to you shortly. Right now we need to take a break.''

The Honda commercial was just beginning when the manager hit the channel selector on the remote. The screen switched to the Wrestling Channel. Two hairy giants were pounding away at each other in mock combat. *Ah, this is more like it,* she thought. *It's all BS, just like that state of the union crap, but at least these guys are entertaining.*

''How long will it take to get there?'' asked Charlie Larson. He was sitting in the passenger seat of a government-issue Ford sedan. The car was speeding down an arterial from Arlington, heading west. Larson and his team had just left a Virginia state-police office.

''About fifteen minutes, sir,'' replied the driver. The thirty-two-year-old FBI agent had been with Larson since early morning, picking him up at National Airport and then accompanying him throughout the long day.

Charlie turned in his seat, looking through the back window. The headlights from a twin of their Ford followed behind. There were three FBI agents inside. ''Looks like Chafe and his boys are still behind us.''

''Yes, sir. They'll keep up with us.'' The driver paused. ''Ah, sir, about that guy the state patrol was talking about, do you think he's the one from Seattle—your friend?''

''Could be. Parker's been known to masquerade as an insurance adjuster before. It could very well have been him checking up on the accident.''

''Then it sure sounds like he's tracking this Reams fellow.''

''Yep. I'm betting on it.''

The driver turned for an instant to look at the senior agent. ''Do you think he has any idea what Reams is up to—I mean the missing uranium and all that? Do you think he's trying to stop him from using it?''

Charlie shook his head. ''No, Steve, not at all. Tom wants revenge. I'm almost certain of it. I've seen him do it before.''

"Revenge?"

"Yeah, Tom's got a score to settle with our man Reams. That's why he's here."

The driver waited for Larson to continue the story but there was only silence. He desperately wanted the puzzle solved. He had been around long enough, however, to know when to quit probing. He would have to wait.

Charlie sat quietly looking out the passenger window. The dark countryside raced by but he wasn't paying any attention to it. Instead, he was thinking back to three years earlier. That's when his dear friend's life had been so horribly upended.

Tom Parker had been away for almost a week when he flew back into Seattle late that Friday evening. He had been working on a child-abduction case where a former Bellevue resident had kidnapped his son from his ex-wife. Tom found them hiding out in a suburb of Los Angeles.

Tom drove straight home from the airport. At that time he was living in Seattle's Leshi district. The Parker residence was a two-bedroom cottage, about 1,400 square feet. Tom, Lori and Keely had moved in about a year earlier. Although the one-story building was tiny, it had a wonderful view of Lake Washington and a spacious backyard. Both he and Lori had worked liked coolies to accumulate enough for the down payment. It was going to be their dream home.

Just recently Tom had hired an architect to begin planning a major expansion. They would soon need more room; Lori was two months pregnant.

The hair on Tom's neck stood up the second he found the front door ajar. Lori never, ever left it unlocked when he wasn't home. Tom had made home safety a crusade. Their affluent, upscale neighborhood was ripe for burglaries.

While standing on the porch, he opened his suitcase and removed his revolver. He then walked into the living room. It was a quarter to one.

The room was blacked out. He took a few steps forward and then collided with something. He tumbled to the carpet but managed to hang onto the .38. After picking himself up, he searched for a wall light switch and then flipped it. *Oh, my God,* he thought as he scanned the living room.

It was an absolute disaster. All of the furniture had been

turned over, the wall shelves knocked down and the paintings and photographs ripped from the walls.

Tom ignored the mess, heading straight for the bedrooms. Keely's room was first down the hall. He rushed inside. It hadn't been touched. His beautiful daughter was sound asleep in her pink PJ's, her favorite teddy bear lying by her side. Tom let out a sigh of relief as he backed out.

And then he found Lori.

To say that Tom was horrified would be a gross understatement. Words could never describe what he felt when he found his murdered wife.

Charlie Larson was still working out of Houston when Lori Parker was murdered. He flew in for the funeral and then spent a week coordinating with the Seattle police and the local FBI field office. It was the least he could do for his friend.

It only took a few days of lab work to confirm the crime-scene findings. Lori's murder fit the same profile as the others in California and Nevada. The two men, code-named by the FBI as the Gemini Killers, had murdered seven other women over the course of several years.

The serial killings almost always followed the same method of operation. The FBI theorized that the two men would stalk their potential victim first, probably from a shopping mall or similar public place. After selecting a target, they would follow the woman to her residence. And then, after hours of surveillance, checking to make sure she was alone, they would force entry into the house or apartment.

Gemini One raped the victim while Gemini Two preferred sodomy. DNA tagging absolutely confirmed those wretched acts. And when they had finished, they always left the same barbaric calling card. It was their trademark.

The murderers routinely ransacked the home before leaving, stealing anything of value. They also left plenty of forensic evidence behind: fingerprints, semen deposits, pubic hairs and, on two of the victims, bite marks on the buttocks.

But it wasn't enough.

No one—not the FBI, the various California and Nevada police jurisdictions or the Seattle PD—had an inkling as to who the killers were. All they could do was add Lori Parker's name to the list: Victim Number Eight.

By the time Charlie returned to Houston, Tom was already

tracking the killers. He had abandoned all of his other cases and, like a man possessed, spent every spare moment searching for Lori's murderers.

But it was all for naught. As good as Tom was, and as motivated as he was, he found nothing concrete. Every lead soon dried up. And like with all the other victims, the forensics evidence obtained at the Parker residence provided nothing new. The Gemini Killers remained at large.

Charlie kept track of Tom over the months, periodically calling him. Tom would never say much, only that he was still looking. To find out what was really going on, Charlie would check in with the local FBI office. The federal investigation of the serial killers remained in full force. But, like Tom, they were no closer to identifying the Gemini Killers than to solving the murder of Jimmy Hoffa.

Eventually Tom moved out of the Leshi home, renting a Queen Ann condo. The memories were too horrible for him to stay in the tiny house. Besides, he needed the money from the sale. His business was in a shambles and there was no life-insurance money.

Tom netted almost fifty thousand from the sale. The lot that the house sat on was worth much more than the structure itself. The new owners tore down the cottage and replaced it with a three-story contemporary.

The money from the sale kept Tom going for another year. He spent most of it trying to track down the killers.

Agent Larson continued to stare blankly out the car window into the blackness. He ignored the driver sitting beside him. His thoughts remained focused on Tom. Charlie was not aware of how sick his friend had become until it was nearly too late. Two years earlier, Tom's clinical depression had progressed to the point that it was wrenching him apart. Anything could have happened. And if Alice Parker hadn't intervened, using Keely as a wedge, Tom might never have survived. *Thank God for his mother!*

But now it was starting all over. The signs were all there: the brutal assault on Linda, Tom getting shot, the tracing of the credit-card purchases and now his sudden trip to Virginia. Charlie was convinced that Tom was hot on the trail of Stan Reams.

Charlie's thoughts about Tom continued to cascade: *Slow down, buddy! Back off! Let us find this turkey! You don't know what you're dealing with!*

Charlie feared for his friend. Tom Parker didn't have the slightest inkling of what he had stumbled into. The nationwide hunt for the nuclear terrorist was now rapidly converging on the capital and its surrounding communities. Thousands of police, federal agents and military personnel were being mobilized. If Tom was anywhere near Reams when they found him, he could be swept away like a leaf in a hurricane.

FORTY-THREE
JOE'S PLACE

THE U.S. ARMY BLACKHAWK HELICOPTER WAS PATROLLING the countryside west of Fairfax. It was one of a dozen helos that were flying over the Washington metropolitan area. The Blackhawk was the farthest west of the capital. It was assigned to search a sector that stretched from the Potomac River southward to Reston.

Major Yuri Kirov sat in the cargo compartment of the helicopter. He was accompanied by two NEST technicians, both DOE employees from Los Alamos. They were busy monitoring the boron trifluoride neutron detector and the germanium gamma-ray detector. The highly sensitive instruments had drawn a blank so far. Nothing but background radiation was being detected as the helicopter flew a few hundred feet above the ground.

The Blackhawk's crew chief, a burly sergeant with ebony skin, sat next to the Russian officer. They both wore helmets with built-in intercoms. It was noisy inside the compartment.

"You in the Russian Army?" asked the NCO.

"No. I'm really more like what you would call an intelligence officer."

"Oh, you must be one of those KGB guys."

"Well, not quite. The KGB doesn't exist anymore. I'm part of what is now called the Federal Security Service."

"Sounds like a cop."

Kirov smiled. "Yes, in a way that's what I am."

The sergeant nodded, accepting the answer. His eyes then focused on the two nuclear technicians at the far end of the cargo hold. "You think they're going to find anything with those high-tech gadgets?"

Kirov raised his hands, signaling his doubt.

The sergeant again nodded. "Yeah, me, too. This whole thing sounds like a cluster-fuck to me. There's no bomb out there. Someone's just screwing with us, pulling our chain—that's all it is."

The sergeant didn't want to believe what his aircraft commander had told him at the start of the mission. His entire family—wife of sixteen years, five children, mother and father, and his brothers—lived in Washington, D.C. To think that they might all be incinerated within the next hour or two was incomprehensible. He simply refused to believe it.

While the sergeant sat back in his canvas seat, lost in thought about his family, Major Kirov couldn't help but think about what had brought him halfway around the world. *All of this for just sixty kilos of metal. Incredible!*

The strongest nation on earth was being held hostage to the specter of an unimaginable horror. And there was virtually nothing anyone could do about it. Kirov was convinced that the Americans would never find the weapon—until it was too late. And then a lowly Russian engineer, driven over the edge by her addiction, would forever earn her place in the history books. By default, the late Irina Sverdlova was about to change the world forever.

Tom Parker was hopelessly lost. It was his overconfidence that did him in. The day before he hadn't had any difficulty finding the RV parks near Lake Manassas. It had been bright and sunny. But tonight, in the blackness, it was another world. Nothing looked familiar, and there was no traffic on the country road.

It was his own fault. He hadn't bothered to look at his map after leaving the RV park in Oakton. *Dammit*, Tom said to himself. *This whole thing is crazy. Screw Reams. I don't care anymore. I quit*!

Tom pulled over to the shoulder and stopped. He then flipped on the dome light and pulled the map up. The road map came with the car, compliments of the rental agency. Unfortunately, it wasn't nearly as detailed as the one back in the RV park's office.

After studying the map for a minute, he tossed it back onto the passenger's seat. He was convinced that the road he was traveling on wasn't shown on the map. *Now what do I do?* he wondered.

Tom waited a few more seconds before turning off the dome light. *The hell with it. I'm just going to keep going. Somehow I'll get back to civilization.*

The Cherokee charged forward into the darkness. He hit the brights. The halogen high-beams lit up the snow-covered roadway for a hundred yards. The thick ice-coated trees that guarded each side of the road created a tunnel-like appearance. It was like driving into an Arctic hell.

Stan Reams was outside the trailer. The temperature had dropped another couple of degrees. He didn't mind, though. He was dressed for it.

Stan was standing on a fold-out ladder next to the drone. The aircraft was on its launch platform, just a hundred feet north of the trailer. It had taken him only four hours to put it together. His weeks of planning and testing had paid off. His machine was ready to fly. All systems were go.

Stan was making one last adjustment to the warhead. It was already sealed up inside the fuselage. He was checking the detonating circuits. He had constructed two independent mechanisms to insure that the warhead would explode: the primary and the backup.

The primary detonator was radio-controlled. At the transmission of a three-part code from the trailer, the drone's computer would activate the firing circuit. The detonation process would start with a small burst of direct current from four D-size batteries linked in series. The electricity would surge through the dual wires that led to the two blasting caps. The tiny caps, each one filled with pentaerythritol tetranitrate, were secured to several feet of detonating cord. The det cord, more

PETN packed inside a tubelike protective casing, was neatly coiled around eight ounces of claylike C-4. The plastic explosive was then molded into the firing chamber directly behind the U-235 projectile.

When the caps fired, the detonating cord would explode. The resulting shock wave would then ignite the C-4. Like a cannon, the force of the blast would shear the retaining screws and rocket the uranium plug down the two-foot-long barrel into the U-235 target core.

Should the primary detonator fail, the backup system was designed to insure that the warhead exploded. The device had only two parts: a twelve-gauge shotgun shell and a heavy steel spike.

The lead pellets in the shotgun shell had been removed, replaced with an extra charge of gun powder and PETN. The shell was mounted inside the forward end of the warhead compartment, right behind the firing chamber containing the C-4. A tiny hole in the casing exposed the brass rim. Lined up with the center of the shell was the working end of a two-inch galvanized-steel nail. The blunt end of the thick nail was welded to the steel bulkhead that separated the warhead from the drone's camera compartment. There was about an inch gap between the nail and the shell's rim.

The backup detonator was designed to explode on impact. The metal cylinder containing the warhead was not rigidly bonded to the inside of the drone's fuselage. Instead, foam blocks on both ends held it in place. During the rocket-assisted launch, the rear-mounted foam padding would compress, cushioning the warhead from the acceleration force. Alternatively, during deceleration—as in a collision—the entire bomb casing would slide forward, carried by its momentum. The foam at the forward end of the compartment would be crushed, slamming the exposed end of the shotgun shell into the stationary nail. The nail would function as a firing pin which, in turn, would fire the shotgun shell. The det cord would then explode, igniting the C-4. The rest of the reaction would occur pro forma.

To further insure the detonation process, Stan had constructed a device designed to trigger the nuclear release. The initiator consisted of two thin metallic disks, one radioactive and the other nonradioactive. One disk was glued to the inside of the stainless-steel tamper, aligned with the hole through the U-235 target core. The other disk was fixed to the impact end of the uranium bullet. Separately, the two disks were benign. But when hammered together under the massive impact force of the plastic explosive, the two different metals would fuse together, resulting in an avalanche of neutrons. The extra neutrons would bombard the cascading U-235 chain reaction, guaranteeing the nuclear detonation and boosting the weapon's energy release.

A wafer of beryllium was fused to the uranium plug of Stan's weapon. It had been originally installed by the Russians when the warhead was assembled so Stan did not need to replace it. The other disk, radioactive polonium 210 in the original Russian weapon, had not been recovered when the U-235 was stolen. Consequently, Stan had been forced to find a substitute. He ended up using an amalgam of plutonium and americum, both extracted from hundreds of smoke detectors.

Stan aimed his flashlight one last time at the open warhead compartment. Everything checked out. He closed the hinged lid and then began to seal up the compartment, using a socket wrench to seat the four stainless-steel anchor bolts.

After finishing, Stan stepped off the ladder and slipped under the aluminum launch cradle. He used a flashlight to check the rocket's ignition circuit. He had purchased the solid-fuel motor from a Bay Area firm that catered to ultralight and glider enthusiasts. The rocket motor was imported from Europe. It had been designed to catapult manned gliders into the air.

Stan was now standing a dozen yards from his creation. Illuminated by a gas lantern sitting on the ground, the pewter-black craft was a vision of beauty to his engineer's mind. *Perfect!*

He started walking back to the trailer, whistling. Not once did he think about the evil he was about to do. His mind was far too diseased to distinguish between good and bad. He was focused on just one thought: *Fly, baby, fly!*

Charlie Larson and the four other FBI agents who had accompanied him all afternoon were back in Fairfax. They were now in the middle of a standoff.

The guard dog refused to cooperate. He snarled and barked

while running back and forth along the inside edge of the ten-foot-tall chain-link fence. The Doberman was trained to attack any stranger who tried to enter the auto-wrecking yard.

Agent Larson had a perfect view of the pickup truck. The pole-mounted floodlights in each corner of the lot lit up the storage area like a Las Vegas casino. Charlie was standing next to the locked fence gate. The smashed-up Ford was just a dozen feet away but it might as well have been on the other side of the Potomac.

"You know, Charlie," commented one of the agents, "that damn dog isn't going to let us in."

"Yeah, I know."

"What are we going to do?" asked the agent.

"Did Wilson have any luck locating the owner?"

"No. No one's answering at the number listed in the phone book—just a recorder. It's a small outfit—only one tow truck. The owner's probably out working another accident right now."

Charlie checked his watch. It was a quarter past eight o'clock. "I've got no choice. We're running out of time."

"You want me to do it?"

"No. This is my case. I'll do it."

Charlie slowly removed the .357-caliber Smith & Wesson from his shoulder holster. *God, I hate this,* he thought as he moved the revolver into firing position. He pulled the hammer back and aimed at the animal, sighting through an open link in the fence. The dog was now stationary, about ten feet away. He would try for a head shot; he didn't want the animal to suffer.

Charlie was just starting to squeeze the trigger when a vehicle pulled off the frontage road and blasted onto the yard's gravel driveway. The distraction saved the Doberman. Charlie holstered the pistol and turned around. A second later he was caught in the glare of the approaching headlights. He raised his right hand to shield his eyes.

The truck came to a screeching halt just a few feet away from Charlie. The driver's door exploded open and a huge man jumped to the ground. The African American carried a Louisville Slugger in his right hand. His arms looked like ham hocks and his eyes were burning with anger. "Get the fuck away from my property," he screamed, "or I'm gonna knock the shit outta ya."

One of Charlie's assistants started to draw his weapon but Larson stopped him. Charlie then stepped toward the intruder. "Hey, buddy, how about putting the bat down? We're not trying to steal from you."

The tow-truck driver glanced at the black man who had just spoken and then focused on the four white men who stood behind him. They were all caught in the glow of the Dodge's headlights. The intruders were clean-cut and dressed in suits. It was not what he had been expecting. *Geez, these dudes don't look like thieves.* "What the fuck you all doing here?" he finally asked.

Charlie reached into his breast coat pocket and produced a wallet. "I'm Charles Larson, FBI. These men are with me. Are you the owner of the yard?"

"Yeah," replied man as he reached for the wallet. He stared at the photo ID for a few seconds before looking into Charlie's eyes. "FBI? What the hell have I done?"

"Nothing. We're not looking for you." Charlie turned to the side and pointed. "We just need to take a look at that Ford pickup over there. We're conducting an investigation and believe there might be some evidence in or on the vehicle."

The man handed the wallet back. "You just wanna look at that piece of junk?"

"Yes. But we're kind of in a hurry so could you open the gate and call your dog off, please?"

The man tossed the bat inside the truck cab and then started to walk toward the gate. "Follow me," he said as he passed next to Charlie.

While Charlie and another man examined the contents of the cab, the other agents probed the exterior of the F-250. One man had the hood up and was using a flashlight to check the engine compartment. Another one had slipped on a pair of coveralls and was working under the rig. The third man had removed a small stainless-steel box from a briefcase and was holding it over various sections of the truck body.

The agents completed their inspection in just fifteen minutes. All five reassembled on the right side of the wrecked truck. The yard owner and his dog remained on the other side. "Okay, boys," Charlie said, "what's it look like?" He turned to the agent who had checked the engine. "Bill, you first."

"Everything looked normal in the engine compartment. Nothing out of place there."

"Russ?"

"Standard running gear. Tranny's leaking oil—probably the result of the accident."

Charlie nodded and turned to the third man. "What did the Geiger counter say?"

"Really looked pretty clear, but it's hard to say. There was a slight increase in output near the end of the truck bed, but it's so close to background that I can't say for sure. There could have been something there."

"Like inside of a towed trailer?"

"Yeah, it's possible."

"Okay," Charlie said. "Now, here's what we found." He produced a packet of registration and vehicle warranty papers. There was also a bundle of maps.

"We gonna take this stuff back and check it out in the lab?" asked one of the agents.

"No. I want to do it here. We haven't got time to go back." Charlie looked toward the tow-truck driver. "Sir," he called out, "would you mind if we went into your office for a few minutes. We need a table to lay out some documents so we can check them."

"Yeah, why not," he said as he started walking toward his tiny office. The dog followed in his footsteps.

Charlie Larson didn't notice it the first time he scanned the map but one of the others did. The X mark was faint but nevertheless it was there. It had been made with a pencil. The mark was the only clue they could find; there was nothing else.

"What the hell good is that?" asked an agent. "It could mean anything."

"I don't know," answered Charlie as he looked up, making eye contact with the agent. "Where is that place, anyway?"

"That looks like it's near Signal Mountain, part of the Bull Run hills."

"How far away is that?"

"Oh, twenty-five, thirty miles or so, as the crow flies. Something like that."

Charlie Larson didn't have any idea of what to do next. He was stumped. "How long would it take to drive out?"

"Tonight?"

"Yeah."

"Oh, man, I'd say at least forty-five minutes, maybe an hour or more if the roads are iced up."

Charlie again checked his watch: 8:37 P.M. *Goddamn! We're running out of time.* "Okay, here's what we're going to do. Steve, I want you to get on the horn and get us . . ."

While the FBI agents worked inside the warm office, the yard owner remained outside in the cold. He didn't mind, though. He was busy looking over the battered Ford pickup. *What in the world is so special about you?* he wondered.

Joe's Place wasn't much more than a wide spot in the road. And it seemed like it was in the middle of nowhere. There were no neighboring businesses or nearby homes, just a lot of tall iced-over trees and snow-covered thick brush. But to Tom Parker, it was a godsend.

Tom walked into the country store. He wore a thick blue parka and a black wool cap. He was rubbing his hands together, blowing on them with his warm breath.

"Hi, there," Tom said when he spotted an elderly man standing behind the counter.

"Good evening," replied the proprietor and the store's namesake.

Tom walked to the counter. "Say, I hope you can help me. I seem to be a little lost."

"Just a little lost?"

"Well, no. I'm lost, big-time. I don't know where I am."

"Well, then, how about telling me where you want to go."

"I was heading for Haymarket when I screwed up and took the wrong exit off I-66."

"Well, you're not far off. It's just a couple of miles from here."

Tom grimaced, now really embarrassed. "I don't know what I did, but I sure got turned around on these side roads. Your store's the only thing open around here."

Joe nodded. "Yep. We don't get many visitors this time of the year. Come springtime, though, that will all change."

"Yeah, I bet it's popular with the tourists all right. Must be a lot of Civil War history to see."

"That there is." Joe paused as he looked the stranger over. "You up here looking for land?" he finally asked.

"No. Why do you ask?"

"We still get a few speculators looking around here. They talk about building fancy subdivisions with golf courses."

"Golf courses—way out here?"

"Ever since they tried to put in the Disney park, real estate people have been looking the area over real good. I guess they think it still has potential."

"Disney park? What are you talking about?"

"The Disney people were going to build a new park, near Haystack. But it's dead now."

This was all news to Tom. "You mean they were going to build a Disneyland around here?"

"Yeah, something like that—it was supposed to have a Civil War theme."

Tom shook his head. "Man, I bet that would have changed this area."

"Yeah, but we stopped 'em good. They won't be back."

Joe and his neighbors had helped kill the theme park. He liked things just the way they were. He didn't want his backyard turned into another Orlando or Anaheim.

Tom leaned against the counter. His hands were now warm. "Say, you wouldn't happen to have a map that I could take a look at."

"Nope, I ain't got one. Some tourist stole it a couple of months ago. But I'll tell you how to get back to Haymarket."

"Great."

Tom listened carefully and took copious notes. He wasn't about to lose his way this time. His goal was to check the RV parks in Haymarket and Gainesville, and then, assuming he struck out, he'd find a motel somewhere and hit the sack. He was frazzled.

"Gee, thanks a lot," Tom said. "I really appreciate your help. Let me reimburse you for your time." Tom pulled out a five-dollar bill and laid it on the counter.

Joe pushed it back. "Thanks, but there's no need for that."

Tom smiled as he took the bill back. "Well, thanks again."

"You're welcome. Have a good trip back home."

Tom was about to walk out the front door when he had a new thought. He turned back to face the store owner. "Say, Joe, I could use some gas. Are your pumps working?"

"You betcha. But I gotta go reset 'em first. They're the old kind and don't have any of those fancy computers that do everything for you."

"No problem," Tom said.

Joe grabbed his coat and a key ring with a wood label on it that read "Pumps."

The Jeep Cherokee took twelve dollars of unleaded. Tom could have easily made it back without filling the tank but he wanted to buy something from Joe. It was the least he could do.

"You sell much gas this time of the year?" Tom asked as he handed Joe the cash. They were both standing next to the pump.

"It's not bad. I got my regular customers and once in awhile someone like you will come along. Even in winter we get people traveling around in their RVs and trailers. A lot of them stop by here to fuel up."

RVs and trailers? thought Tom. *Well, why not?* "Anyone like that up here today?"

"Today?"

"Yeah." It took Tom just a moment to invent a new story line. He didn't think Joe would buy the inheritance cover. "The main reason I drove out here tonight was that an old buddy of mine was supposed to be touring around here. I thought he might be staying at one of the RV parks."

"What's he driving?"

"A Ford pickup with a trailer."

Joe shook his head. "Didn't sell no gasoline or diesel to anything like that. Just a couple of Winnebagos, traveling together." Joe paused as he remembered something else. "But now that I think about it, I did have one guy stop by early this morning. Didn't need any fuel for his pickup, but he took ten gallons of propane. Said he needed it for his heater."

"He was towing a trailer?" Tom asked.

"Right. One of those long ones—the kind that have the hitch in the truck bed."

Tom's interest perked up. "You mean a fifth wheel?"

"Yeah, that's what it was. A big Fleetwood. And it was

kind of a strange setup. His truck had Virginia plates but the trailer had California ones."

Tom's heart beat faster as he reached inside his jacket. He removed the photo of Stan Reams and handed it to Joe. "That the guy?"

Joe stared at the photograph. The light by the pump was poor so he moved a few feet closer to the storefront doorway. There was a fluorescent fixture over the threshold. "Yep," he said, "that's the one. But he looks a little older than in the photo. He's a friend of yours?"

Tom was beside himself right now. All thoughts of giving up vanished. "Yeah, we were in the Army together. Served in Germany. Did he happen to say where he was going?"

Joe handed the photo back. "Nope. He didn't say much at all. Only talked about how cold it was and that he wanted to make sure he had enough propane."

"He must have been heading to one of those RV parks." There was hope in Tom's voice.

"No. I don't think so." Joe hesitated. "He was headed in the other direction—north."

"North?"

"Yeah, I watched him head down the road. Went about a quarter of a mile or so and then turned off to the left. There's an old gravel road that leads halfway up the hillside there. I think he might be camping out up there tonight."

"Just up the road?"

"Yes." Joe pointed toward the right. "Just head that way and keep your eyes open. Look for an old cattle crossing by the road. That's where it starts. If he really stayed up there you should be able to find him. You can't get far off the road because of the trees and brush."

Tom reached out to shake the man's hand. "Thanks. Thanks a million."

"You're welcome."

FORTY-FOUR

FLY, BABY, FLY!

THE HOUSE CHAMBER WAS OVERFLOWING. DOZENS OF MEMbers of Congress milled around in the tiny assembly area that fronted the podium. They were joined by numerous appointed officials from the executive branch, legions of journalists and an army of admirals and generals. Hundreds more sat in the benches and chairs that covered the lower gallery. The multiple tiers of the upper gallery were also overflowing with dignitaries and assorted guests. It seemed like everyone who was anyone in the government was in attendance.

The din from several thousand voices, all speaking at once, was crushing. It was like a distant, steady thunder. And the air was thick with anticipation. You could almost taste the tension.

At precisely 9:04 P.M., EST, the roar inside the House chambers began to subside. "He's here," was whispered repeatedly throughout the vast auditorium, passed on from person to person.

All eyes were focused toward the back of the chamber, at the head of the main aisle. The walkway led straight to the podium. And then, without any warning, a small man wearing a nondescript black suit stepped from behind a hidden door next to the aisle. The House doorkeeper had once been a Marine drill instructor. His voice was in fine form as his announcement boomed throughout the assembly: "Mr. Speaker, I present the president of the United States!"

The entire assembly, every man and woman, except for those in wheelchairs, rose to greet the president. The ovation was deafening.

The president walked slowly to the Speaker's lectern, shaking hands all the way. His face was glowing. He was an attractive man, tall and slim. He had a strong face with a chiseled, gently weathered look to it. Most women found him handsome.

This was the president's first state of the union speech. The previous year his predecessor had resigned and then, as the vice president, he had automatically assumed the presidency. The transition had been a whirlwind, but his feet were now solidly planted on the ground. He was ready to lead the nation. He was about to make the speech of his life. He could hardly wait.

The president walked up to the lectern, setting his typed notes on the oak podium. He then turned and shook the hands of the Speaker of the House and the recently appointed vice president, now serving as president of the Senate. The two men were presiding side by side in the pulpit that was located immediately behind and above the podium. The cheering and clapping continued as the president turned to face the joint session of Congress.

The president was almost ready to begin. Only one final item of protocol remained.

The Speaker of the House's voice thundered throughout the chamber. "Members of Congress, I have the high privilege and the distinct honor of presenting to you the president of the United States!"

Again thunderous applause. It would continue for several minutes. In the interim, the television network anchor teams that surrounded the House chamber took the opportunity to make a few final editorial comments to their viewing audiences. Once the president began to speak, they would remain mute until his delivery was completed.

The president cleared his voice and then, for the third time, he raised his hands, signaling that he was ready to begin. This time the crowd complied. The decibel level dropped like a falling brick.

The president smiled as he looked into the television cameras. "Mr. Speaker, Mr. President, members of Congress, distinguished guests, my fellow Americans, tonight we have come together to . . ."

Stan Reams smiled at the electronic image of the president of the United States. Stan's long odyssey was finally over. He reached up to the Sony and flipped the channel selector from the local NBC affiliate to another channel. The screen filled with static.

Just before the president began to speak, the NBC anchorman had reported that the speech was scheduled to last forty-one minutes. The president would never finish.

Tom Parker stared through the windshield. He was leaning forward in his bucket seat. His fingers were locked onto the steering wheel. The radio was off but the heater fan was on full. Warm air blasted through the defrost vents, drowning out the engine.

The headlights of the Jeep Cherokee lit up the road but it was still hard to follow. It was covered with almost half a foot of snow. If the wheel tracks hadn't been there to mark the hidden gravel surface, he would have driven off the roadway several times.

Tom was almost a half mile from where he had turned off the main county road. After traveling along a flat grade, the roadway turned to the left and then began to snake its way up the hillside. He was now climbing the flank of the slope, creeping along at about five miles per hour.

As Tom drove into the unknown, his thoughts were focused on one goal: *Reams, if you're really up here someplace, I'm going to find you. And then you're going to pay!*

Stan Reams made one last check of the drone's optical guidance system. The camera was now switched on, temporarily powered by a twelve-volt car battery resting on the ground. The void into which it was staring filled the Sony television screen with a bluish-green tint. The camera's night-vision lens sensed the overhead starlight, using the weak natural background light to amplify the images of reflecting surfaces. Because the drone was pointed up at a thirty-degree angle on its launching frame, there was nothing to see through the camera but the clear night sky and a scattering of stars.

Stan peered out a trailer window. The gas-powered Coleman lantern, still sitting on the frozen ground near the rear of the launching frame, lit up the drone.

Stan turned back to face the control panel. It was finally time. A moment later he reached forward and flipped the remote start switch. The drone's gas-powered engine exploded to life.

The TV camera's image vibrated on Stan's monitor. The motor was cold and it shook the entire fuselage, including the camera housing. He let it warm up.

While waiting, Stan reached up to his control panel and flipped another switch. It was the timer. The drone had approximately fifty minutes of fuel aboard, almost twice as much as might be needed. A flashing red light and an obnoxious buzzer would be activated in forty-eight minutes, providing Stan with a two-minute warning before the fuel supply was exhausted. If the drone hadn't reached its target by then, he would have to improvise.

It took almost a minute before the vibration smoothed out. Stan then flipped another toggle switch on his control panel, switching the TV camera's power source from the exterior battery to a tiny generator that ran off the aircraft's engine. The television screen blinked for just an instant during the changeover.

Stan next began to increase the power. Despite the growing vibration from the whirling propeller blades, the TV camera's image remained clear. When the engine power level reached 100 percent, he took one last look at his remote sensors. *Everything's in the green,* he thought. And then, without further thought, he hit the launch button.

The rocket motor ignited and half a second later the restraining clamps on the launching frame released their hold on the drone. The twelve-foot-long aircraft blasted off the cradle in a blinding fury of white light. Exhaust from the rocket's plume knocked the lantern over, extinguishing its flame.

The noise of the rocket echoed down the hillside, like a thunderclap.

"Fly, baby, fly!" shouted Stan as he watched the drone climb into the heavens.

Although Tom Parker was a couple hundred feet downslope from the launch site, he was almost directly under the drone's flight path when it accelerated overhead. The twenty-foot-long flame that blazed a trail through the night sky was visible for miles around. It looked like a comet.

The sudden light startled Tom. He slammed on the brakes

and the Jeep skidded on the slick surface. Before he could react, it slid off the road and plowed into a shallow ravine.

When the four-by-four stopped moving, Tom rolled down his window and looked down the hillside. He could see the torchlike flame as it continued eastward. And then it disappeared. The intense light was extinguished in a blink of an eye. *What the hell was that?*

The U.S. Army Blackhawk helicopter was twenty-two miles to the east when the drone launched. The flight crew watched the erie light climb into the heavens for fifteen seconds before it disappeared.

"Damn, what the heck was that?" asked the pilot over the cockpit intercom.

"I don't know, Skipper," replied the copilot. "It kind of looked like a flare to me."

"That wasn't any flare. Too damn powerful." The pilot paused before again keying his mike. "You get a fix on it?"

"Yeah, I'm working on it now. Just a sec." The copilot was entering data into the aircraft's navigation computer. He was attempting to determine the origin of the UFO. By projecting a range-finding laser beam from the Blackhawk to where the light had been observed, the computer could estimate its approximate location.

"Holy shit!" the copilot said as he studied the computer's digital readout.

"What?" asked the pilot.

"That thing, whatever it was, it took off near our target coordinates."

"Son of a bitch. Something's really going down after all."

"What do you want to do?"

"Get that FBI guy on the cabin intercom."

Charlie Larson and four other FBI agents were seated in the cargo compartment of the Blackhawk. Major Yuri Kirov and the two NEST technicians assigned to the helo were also sitting next to the federal officers.

The Blackhawk had picked up Larson and his crew in the parking lot of the auto-wrecking yard. They were heading west toward the Bull Run Mountains. The mission was a long shot; the map recovered from Reams' vehicle was the only clue the search team had to work with.

"Larson here," Charlie said after the helo's crew chief handed him his own headset. There weren't enough intercom units to go around for everyone aboard.

"Ah, this is the pilot, sir. I just wanted to let you know we just spotted something funny up here. Looks like we had some kind of an aircraft launch to the west."

"What the hell are you talking about, Captain?" Charlie Larson was confused.

"We don't know what it was—only that something definitely blasted off. Looked like a frigging rocket launch to me, sir. Lit up the whole countryside for about ten to fifteen seconds before it fizzled out."

"A rocket launch?"

"Yeah, I saw lots of 'em during Desert Storm. You don't forget something like that."

"Where'd this take place?"

"Our nav computer says it took off close to those map coordinates you gave us."

A chill swept down Charlie's spine as the Army captain's words struck home. "How close?" he asked.

"Plus or minus twenty meters."

Mother of Christ, thought Charlie. "Where's it heading?" His voice was now frantic.

"We don't see it anymore but we're estimating that it headed east, almost due east."

Charlie reached into his jacket pocket and removed the map he had recovered from Reams' smashed-up pickup truck. After unbuckling his seat belt and kneeling on the aluminum deck, he unfolded the map and placed it on the floor. While one of his agents held a flashlight, he placed his finger on the map's X mark. He then slowly moved it east. A few seconds later he reacted: *Oh, my God!*

The projected flight path of the drone was lined up directly with the capital.

Charlie keyed his lip mike. "Captain, I've got to talk to my people in D.C. right now. Every second counts."

"Hang on, sir. We'll patch you right through."

Another chill engulfed Agent Larson as he waited for the radio connection to be completed. He was scared. An airborne intruder was bearing down on the nation's capital and there wasn't much time left to stop it.

It had happened before—twice. In 1974, a disgruntled soldier from nearby Fort Meade had landed his stolen helicopter on the White House lawn. And twenty years later, a man intent on committing suicide crashed a Cessna into the White House, right below the presidential living quarters. Both incidents had caught the Secret Service by surprise. There just hadn't been enough time to react.

The previous close calls had resulted in much tighter aerial security around the capital, especially during a key event like tonight. *But will it be enough?* wondered Charlie.

The drone flew into the night sky. When the roaring solid-fuel rocket engine expended its energy and fell away, the robot aircraft had reached a height of 400 feet.

The tiny gasoline engine was now pushing the drone through the frigid air at a modest ninety miles per hour. The engine was so quiet that it was barely audible on the ground. And it was also impossible to see. The fuselage and delta-shaped wings were painted black and there was no visible exhaust. To reduce its thermal output, the exhaust ports were concealed within the wing roots. The hot gases were vented with the cold-air intake vents before discharging to the atmosphere. Stan Reams had learned much from the design of the B-2 Stealth.

The drone was currently flying entirely on its own. Its GPS-linked computer was following a preprogrammed route designed by Reams. Every few seconds, the receiver computed the drone's earth coordinates by interrogating signals from a fleet of overhead satellites. The onboard computer then compared the real-time coordinates to those stored in its memory. If the drone strayed from the flight path, the computer would adjust the control surfaces until it returned to the right course.

Stan had used a U.S. Geological Survey map to log in the latitude and longitude for each key milestone of the flight. The coordinates of the final destination, however, had been logged in electronically. He had completed that task the first day after arriving in Virginia. He had crossed the Potomac, parked his truck in a pay lot, and then walked to ground zero.

While standing in the center of the expansive stone walkway, directly under the center of the dome, he had removed the handheld GPS receiver from his coat pocket. He had then punched in a few keystrokes. That's all it had taken. The exact earth coordinates of the target were then locked into the device.

Stan had anticipated that the drone's launch might be observed so he had directed it to fly a serpentine path to evade any hostile aircraft that might be dispatched to intercept it. Instead of heading due east, toward the capital, it would first fly south. After six minutes, it would then turn northeastward. About eighteen minutes later, it would again automatically change course, this time heading almost due east. At that point, Stan had the option of allowing the drone to continue on its own or taking manual control. If the weather had been bad, he would have let it fly itself all the way to the target. But tonight atmospheric conditions were perfect. He would pilot it in himself.

The night-vision camera mounted in the drone's nose compartment relayed the digital images it observed back to the antenna mounted on the trailer roof. The encrypted televised signal wasn't crystal-clear but it was more than enough to get the job done.

Stan Reams stared at the TV screen. The reflected glow of the various towns and villages that the drone was now flying over was clearly visible. Later, when he eventually took control, all he would have to do was keep the drone aimed toward the capital lights and he would be home free.

FORTY-FIVE
SHOWDOWN

THE AIRSPACE AROUND THE CAPITAL WAS CLOSED. NO CIVILian aircraft of any kind were allowed to enter or operate within the twenty-five-mile radius of the restricted zone. National Airport, Dulles International, Baltimore, and all of the private fields that ringed Washington were temporarily closed. No departing or inbound flights were allowed during the ninety-minute closure period.

The only aircraft allowed to fly were military. And tonight there was an armada of jets and helicopters in the restricted airspace. Four F-15 supersonic fighters from Langley Air Force Base patrolled high over the District of Columbia. They flew in pairs, loitering over the capital at 10,000 feet and 30,000 feet. Armed with infrared-seeking and radar-guided missiles, the Eagles could shoot down any hostile high-flying aircraft.

Six U.S. Army Apache attack helicopters defended the lower elevations. They orbited the capital in a series, following a slow racetrack pattern that stretched from Andrews Air Force Base in the south to the city of Kensington in the north. Equipped with missiles and powerful chain guns, the Apaches were a formidable force. Their infrared night-vision targeting systems and companion laser designators could destroy land or air targets several miles away.

On the ground, teams of Secret Service agents and U.S. Army Rangers surveyed the city from the rooftops of a dozen federal buildings. Besides their individual firearms, each two-man team was equipped with a shoulder-mounted Stinger antiaircraft missile. The portable weapon could knock down a jet airplane or helicopter within a three-mile firing radius. The tiny missile, only sixty inches long, homes in on the hot exhaust gases of an aircraft's engine. Like a marijuana-sniffing dog, the Stinger is relentless in its pursuit.

Aiding both the airborne and ground-level defenses was a powerful radar surveillance system. The primary transmitter was located at Andrews Air Force Base. It repeatedly swept the skies over the District of Columbia, continuously tracking the Eagles and Apaches. Portable radar units were also deployed throughout the Capital Beltway. The truck-mounted phased-array radars covered the holes in the Andrews coverage. The result was an integrated search web that saturated the District of Columbia's airspace with radar energy.

And linking everything together was the command radio network. The multimillion-dollar battlefield-tested system allowed the Army general responsible for protecting the capital to instantly talk with any element of his command. The F-15s could be vectored to a radar contact within just a few seconds.

The Apaches could be similarly dispatched to check out a suspicious low flyer or a possible ground target. And finally, any one of the Stinger teams could be directed toward an approaching target, allowing time for the missile's infrared seeker to lock onto the target.

As powerful and sophisticated as the capital's air-defense system was, it was totally unprepared to deal with the threat that was now approaching from the west. For all practical purposes, Stan Reams' tiny drone was invisible to the barrage of electronic sensors that inundated the airspace surrounding Washington, D.C.

The president was fourteen minutes into his speech. His voice was smooth and steady. The words flowed effortlessly. He was in fine form.

The applause and standing ovations were lasting a lot longer than the president's handlers had planned. They were now predicting that the speech would run about four minutes over. They were all ecstatic about the reception he was receiving.

Stan Reams was hunched over the television monitor. He had shut down all of the extraneous lights inside the trailer. It allowed him to concentrate on the images on the screen.

The drone had just completed the first leg of its flight. It automatically changed course near Lake Manassas and was now following Interstate 66, heading toward Fairfax. It was only a few hundred feet above the roadway.

When the aircraft angled left, the image on the television screen underwent an enormous transformation. The greenish atmospheric glow of Washington lit up the horizon like it was daytime. Each second, the light intensity of the distant city increased on Stan's TV screen. The cold, crisp night air provided for extraordinary visibility. He probably could have guided the drone without the night-vision lens.

Tom Parker had a clear view of the darkened trailer. He was about a hundred yards away. The rising sliver of moon provided just enough light to reveal its presence. The trailer was still hitched to the Ford pickup.

After running the Cherokee off the road, Tom had set out on foot, following the winding hillside road. It had taken him nearly ten minutes to reach the clearing. He was now breathing hard, a combination of the road grade and apprehension.

Tom stopped and knelt in the center of the snow-covered road, lowering his body profile. The same moonlight that illuminated the trailer could just as easily broadcast his presence.

The trailer appeared to be abandoned. He couldn't see any lights from inside. However, he could hear a muffled mechanical noise. It was coming from the trailer. It took him a few seconds to make the connection. *Generator,* he thought. *So, somebody's home after all!*

Tom reached into his coat pocket and removed the Smith & Wesson. By instinct, he flipped open the chamber. The short-barrel, Detective Special .38 was fully loaded. He carried two extra speed loaders in another pocket, just in case.

The open terrain around the trailer made it difficult to approach. In order to reach it with the least chance of detection, Tom decided to work his way along the brush line that surrounded the clearing. He would then drop down the slope, heading for the truck. Once at the pickup he would use it as a screen until he decided how to enter the trailer.

Tom began slowly walking toward the west. His shoes made a crunching sound as they compressed the snow.

"How far away are we now?" asked Charlie Larson. The FBI agent was wedged into the tiny cockpit crawlspace.

"Just a couple of minutes away," reported the pilot. "Right now we're scanning the airspace to the west with our FLIR unit." He was referring to the helicopter's forward-looking infrared camera system.

"You spot anything?"

"No. Nothing. There's no other aircraft around here."

"Well, what the hell did you see, then?"

"Don't know—maybe it was some kind of fireworks."

"All right, when you get a visual on the ground coordinates with your camera, let me know. I'm still waiting for orders so you'll have stand off until I get an okay."

"Understood."

The senior Secret Service agent responsible for the hundred and fifty men and women that were currently guarding the president was beside himself. He was standing in a small office area located just behind the Speaker's podium. The president was only twenty feet away but the agent couldn't see him directly. Instead, he watched through one of a dozen surveillance cameras that viewed the House chamber.

Although the agent was staring at the color monitor, his mind was elsewhere. He had a phone glued to his right ear. The caller on the other end of the telephone line had just ruined his evening.

"I know this sounds crazy," Paul Trasolini said as he sat at his desk in the nearby Hoover Building, "but all I can tell you is that we now think that there might be some kind of aircraft heading for the capital. One of our senior agents just called in from the field. He's in an Army chopper somewhere west of Fairfax. Our guy's recommending that you evacuate the president immediately."

"How the hell can he recommend that? I haven't heard anything from General Adams!"

"Apparently they witnessed some kind of launch a few minutes ago, about thirty-five miles out. Whatever it is, it appears to be coming in from the west, heading for D.C. We don't know how fast it's moving so it could be on us in just minutes."

"Well, get the damned Air Force after it."

"We are. They're looking right now. But if they can't stop it, it might get through. That's why we think you should evacuate now."

"Jesus, you want me to yank the president off the podium, right in front of millions? You think I'm crazy?"

"Look, it's your call. I know all of this is thin, but what if it's true? The damn thing could be carrying an atomic bomb."

Atomic bomb! thought the Secret Service agent. He had been briefed on the latest terrorist threat but had never really believed the speculation about the nuclear weapon. What really worried him, however, was the specter of terrorists filling a small plane with conventional explosives and then crashing it into the Capitol Building or the White House. Worst yet, when the flight restrictions over D.C. were lifted after the speech, a jumbo jet preparing to land at National or Dulles could be diverted during the last stages of landing. Within just a few seconds it could be over the capital, piloted by the ultimate *kamikaze*. Novelists had been predicting such events for years. The fiction-based threats were legitimate; an aerial assault on the capital headed the Secret Service's list of horrors.

"All right, dammit," the Secret Service agent said, "I'll do it. Tell your people we're executing Plan Bright Star right now."

He slammed the phone down before the FBI task-force commander could respond. He turned to one of his aides. "Tell Marine One and Two to start warming up. We're going airborne in ten minutes."

"Yes, sir," replied the woman. She then picked up a radio handset and began issuing orders to the Marine flight crews.

The huge presidential helicopter and its backup twin were already parked on the lawn near the southeast wing of the Capitol Building. Although the president had been transported from the White House to Capitol Hill by limousine, the Marine choppers had been flown in just after his speech started. The Secret Service left nothing to chance, and even though the risk of an attack during the state of the union address was remote, they had planned for every conceivable event. That's why Operation Bright Star had been conceived.

The plan called for the emergency evacuation of the president, vice president, all key Cabinet advisors, and the senior congressional leaders. All total, twenty-six men and women, plus assorted Secret Service agents and Marine guards, would be loaded aboard the choppers and whisked away from the capital. Marine One, with the president and half of his Cabinet, would fly north to a U.S. military base located near Raven Rock, Pennsylvania. The secret fortress, simply identified as Site R, is buried inside a mountain near the Maryland border. It serves as a backup to the Pentagon's National Military Command Center.

Marine Two, led by the vice president and filled with congressional leaders, would head west toward White Springs, West Virginia. The evacuees would take shelter in a giant bunker complex located under the Greenbrier Hotel. The massive underground facility had been built in the late fifties to protect the entire congressional delegation during a nuclear war.

The Secret Service agent unconsciously straightened his tie and ran his right hand through his hair. He was about to make history. The television cameras would forever record his image.

The F-15 pilot stared blankly at his radar screen. He was approaching the target sector at 600 miles per hour, swooping down from the northeast. His wingman was a quarter of a mile behind.

The pilot keyed his microphone. "You pick anything up, Billy?" he asked.

"Negative, Skipper," replied the wingman. "All I've got is that Army chopper."

"Yeah, same with me. I don't think there's anything out there—at least at an altitude that we'd see it."

"Roger. If there's something down there, it's too close to the ground for us to see it."

"Okay, let's make one more pass and check that projected flight path. Maybe we'll spot something."

"You got it, Skipper."

The F-15s turned to the right and began to prepare for another radar search. It would be a waste of time. Although the F-15s' look-down, shoot-down radar was one of the best ever made, they were looking in the wrong area. Besides, even if the drone had been scanned by the fighters' radar, the pilots wouldn't have been able to distinguish the drone from the background clutter of the ground. The special carbon-based composite materials covering the drone soaked up radar emissions with a thirst that rivaled a dried-out riverbed.

Tom was now kneeling next to the left front wheel well of the F-250. He had just pulled the glove off his right hand and placed his bare skin against the radiator grill. It was ice-cold. *He's been here for a long time*, he thought.

Tom slipped the glove back on and dropped onto all fours. He then began to crawl along the side of the truck. When he passed under the forward end of the trailer he reached into his pocket and removed the pistol. He inched forward a few more feet. The din of the generator masked his movements.

Tom slowly stood up and peered into one of the windows. He was expecting to see a blacked-out interior. Instead, he saw the blue tint of a television screen. And sitting next to it was a man who had his back to Parker. *What the hell's he doing?* wondered Tom.

Stan Reams spotted the approaching lights of a town through the television screen. "That must be it," he said to himself. He used a pencil to cross off the name from his flight-path checklist.

So far, the flight was proceeding as planned. The robot aircraft had just reached the halfway point. The drone had been airborne for fifteen minutes.

Stan reached forward to his control panel and flipped a switch. A moment later, the radio transmitter broadcast a three-part coded message to the aircraft. The tiny microprocessor inside the drone recognized the signal and activated the arming circuit. The warhead was now armed. It would explode when Stan triggered the last switch on his panel.

The F-15s patrolling over the target area didn't spot the drone but one of the ground-based portable radar units deployed outside of Fairfax did. The return was fuzzy, just a stray reflection from one of the spinning plastic propeller blades. It lasted only a few seconds. But that's all it took.

The technician manning the radar scope radioed in his report to the command center at Andrews. Almost instantaneously, new threat warnings were broadcast to all units. There really was something out there.

The Capitol Building was in a panic. People were scurrying around in a daze. No one could believe what they had just witnessed.

The Secret Service agent had approached the president right in the middle of his announcement concerning a proposed tax rollback. The agent stepped onto the podium and whispered into the president's left ear, cupping his hand to cover the message.

The president was visibly shaken at the news. He had turned, wanting to speak into the microphone, but the agent had persisted. With his hand firmly clasping the president's arm, the agent had escorted him off the platform. Similar interruptions were taking place throughout the vast auditorium as key officials were rounded up.

The ABC anchorwoman was stunned at what she had just witnessed and she was letting her viewing audience know how she felt.

"Ladies and gentlemen, something extraordinary has just occurred. The president has just left the House chamber, escorted by a contingent of what must have been Secret Service agents. And as soon as he was spirited out of the chambers, the vice president, the Speaker of the House, the Senate majority and minority leaders, and most of the Cabinet were similarly removed."

The woman stopped speaking as she tilted her head to the side. She was receiving new information over her earphone. "And now I've just been informed by one of our correspondents that two Marine helicopters are outside of the Capitol Building. Apparently, they're waiting to pick up the president and the others."

Tom crawled alongside the trailer until he reached the door. He stood up, pressing his body against the aluminum skin of the trailer. With his pistol in his right hand, he tested the doorknob. It moved. *Good,* he thought. *It's not locked.*

Tom took a deep breath and shut his eyes. His heart was pounding inside his chest. *Calm down,* he told himself. *All you need to do is surprise the bastard. Once you've got the drop on him, he'll give up.*

Tom took another breath. *Good. That's it,* he said to himself. *Keep it together now. You can pull this off—just think positive.*

He focused on Keely, and then Linda. It helped calm him. It was like turning down the volume dial on a radio. Suddenly, all of the fire and rage that had driven him for so long had mellowed out.

The realization that he was about to fulfill his goal was taking its toll. Tom had no idea what he would do with Reams once he captured him. The steadfast determination that had led him to seek the man for so long was now lukewarm. *Maybe I'll just beat the prick silly and call it a day.*

Tom opened his eyes and had just started to turn the knob when it happened. A vision of Lori's pretty face flashed through his mind. It was there for just a second, but that's all it took.

He pulled the comforter away, exposing the back of her head and naked shoulders. Her rich golden hair was fanned out across her back, as if displayed in a magazine advertisement. Her arms were extended outward across the mattress, each wrist bound to the corner of the bed frame by a necktie—his ties. And her life fluid had invaded everything. By now it had congealed into a gooey carmine ooze that corrupted the once-milky-white bedding.

Like in a slow-motion movie, he reached forward with his hand. He gently brushed the golden locks aside, baring the vicious wound that would forever be fused into the core of his essence.

The Gemini Killers always slashed their victims' throats in a trademark fashion: a single deep slice, clear to the bone.

Tom dropped to his knees. The bile in his gut surged upward. He covered his mouth but he couldn't stop the tide.

He was now on all fours, right below the entryway to the trailer. The patch of snow under him had turned a greenish-brown, stained by the contents of his stomach. And his .38 was lying on the snow a couple feet away.

Tom's head was spinning as he tried to regain his strength. He started to reach for the revolver when another wave of nausea tore through his belly. *Oh, God, he's going to hear me puking!*

But nothing happened. Stan Reams could not hear Tom Parker. The generator noise had masked the retching. Besides, he was too busy to notice. He had just taken manual control of the drone, shutting off the satellite navigation system that had worked so perfectly. Stan now wanted the pleasure of driving the drone right into the target. Like the graphic videos from Desert Storm, where the onboard camera systems followed the missile or smart bomb right into the target, he was going to savor the last few minutes of the flight.

Two minutes had passed since the final spasm. Tom was now standing, the pistol in his right hand. He shook his head and then took another deep breath. The awful taste in his mouth and the foul odor flooding through his nostrils helped purge his thoughts. The burning images of the flashback had faded. He was back in control.

His heartbeat began to race as he prepared to enter the

trailer. He was scared—not for himself, but for what he might do. He was now ready to kill; he *wanted* to kill.

Stan Reams never heard the door open. He was too engrossed by the camera's image. The drone was entering the outskirts of Arlington. The Capitol was visible in the background. He could see the tall spire in the foreground. It was lit up with an army of floodlights. He made a small adjustment to the joystick control, altering the drone's heading by a few degrees. *Perfect,* he thought. And then he smiled. *It's going to happen. It's really going to happen!*

"Freeze, motherfucker!" yelled the voice.

Stan was so startled that his heart skipped a beat. He jerked his head up, looking over the TV in the direction of the voice. He could just see the silhouette of a man standing inside the open doorway.

"Who are you? What do you want?" Stan yelled. He started to push his chair away from the table.

"Don't move, Reams," Tom Parker commanded.

Stan froze in place, moving only his eyes. *He knows who I am!*

Stan looked at the detonating switch on the nearby instrument panel. A plastic guard covered the stainless-steel lever. The guard would have to be removed before he could throw the switch. He looked back at the intruder. "What do you want?"

Tom carefully inched forward, his pistol fixed on Reams' chest. With his free hand he searched for a wall switch. The interior of the darkened trailer was crammed full of electronic equipment and there were wires everywhere. He didn't want to trip on any unseen object. Besides, he had to make sure if it really was *him.*

Tom finally found a switch and flipped it. A light next to Reams lit up the room.

Reams stared at the invader for a few seconds before reacting. "You!" he finally said.

"That's right, you prick," Tom replied, smiling as he made a positive ID. "And now that I've got you, you're never going to forget me again."

New images cascaded through Tom's head: Linda lying on the hotel-room floor, her scalp ripped open, blood everywhere.

And then he remembered the searing pain from the bullet that had bored into his leg.

The man who sat in front of Tom Parker had brutally attacked Linda and himself, and then left them both to die. Tom desperately wanted to pull the trigger. It would be so easy—one shot, right between the eyes, and it would be all over. No one would find the body for days. By that time Tom would be long gone. He could get away with it. And it would make up for so much bitterness, so much frustration. Revenge could be the sweetest justice of all.

But Tom Parker wasn't ready to pull the trigger—at least not yet. He wanted more answers.

Tom inched his way toward Reams, gripping the pistol with both hands. "Tell me," he said, "what did you do to Dave Simpson?"

"Who?"

"Dave Simpson. The man who was staying in the hotel. What happened to him?"

Stan was about to respond when he felt the vibration. The din of the generator had masked it but now it was increasing at a prodigious rate.

Tom sensed it too. It was more than a vibration. The sound was a familiar one. *Chopper,* he thought.

And then a blazing light flooded the interior of the trailer. A second later a mechanical voice boomed from the heavens. "This is the FBI. You are surrounded. Come out with your hands up. Now!"

Reams took one last look at the TV screen. The drone was on a beeline over a densely populated residential area. The Capitol was still in the distance. *Too early to detonate.* He reached forward. His own pistol was in a drawer under the tabletop.

"Stop!" yelled Tom as he spotted the movement. An instant later he fired. The brutal report of the pistol blast temporarily stunned Tom. He hadn't ever fired a weapon in such confined quarters. His ears were ringing.

The bullet grazed Stan's shoulder but it didn't stop him. He had his Beretta out before Tom realized what had happened.

Reams fired wildly, spraying half a dozen nine-millimeter slugs at Parker. One round caught Tom in the gun hand. The bullet didn't actually hit his hand, but rather slammed into the heavy metal frame next to the revolver's chamber.

Tom's pistol literally tore itself apart from the impact. Fragments of lead and torn steel ripped into his fingers, shredding the glove. He cursed while simultaneously dropping to the floor.

Stan Reams stood up, now momentarily stunned by his own wound. He turned to examine his shoulder. Blood poured from the tear in his shirt. He then looked back at the television screen. He smiled. *Another couple of minutes and it'll happen. Then they'll pay for . . .*

Reams' thoughts were interrupted when he heard the intruder thrashing about on the floor. He leaned over the table, his automatic pointed toward the floor.

Tom was on his side, clasping his good hand over his bleeding fingers while frantically moving about. He was trying to find some kind of weapon that he could use to protect himself.

Stan smiled as he aimed. It would be a head shot. He didn't have time to toy with the man.

Stan started to squeeze the trigger.

He never finished.

The shot came from the side, through the closed window. Charlie Larson was seven feet away when he fired. The window shattered as the round bored through it.

Reams flopped to the floor. The .357 slug tore through his side, ripping apart his lungs and heart.

FORTY-SIX
FISSION

"TOM, YOU ALL RIGHT?" ASKED THE VOICE.

Tom Parker was on the trailer floor. The air stunk of cordite and sweat, and blood dribbled from his torn hand. He looked up. He could hardly believe what he was seeing.

"Charlie, is that really you?"

Agent Larson was almost straddling Tom. His gun was still drawn, aimed at the corpse that had once been Stan Reams.

"You hurt bad?" asked Larson.

"I don't think so but my hand sure hurts like hell." He started to pull himself up when Charlie leaned forward and grabbed an arm.

"So, this is the guy you've been tracking from Mexico."

"Yeah. I was going to bring him in tonight but he got the jump on me at the last . . ." Tom stopped as the shock of Larson's sudden appearance finally registered. "Charlie, what the hell are you doing here? You're supposed to be in Seattle."

"It's a long story. But it turns out we've been tracking this jackass, too. We think he's . . ." Charlie's voice petered out when he finally noticed the television screen. He could see it just out of the corner of his eye. "Son of a bitch," he yelled.

"What?" asked Tom.

Charlie didn't reply as he moved closer to the TV set. He wanted to vomit. "Oh, sweet Jesus, it can't be!"

Tom moved to his side. The image on the screen was startling. The 550-foot-tall spire was illuminated like a Christmas tree. "Hey," Tom said, "isn't that the Washington Monument?"

Charlie Larson was too stunned to answer. *Oh God, what do I do now?*

"Charlie," Tom said, "what the hell's going on?" Tom was in the dark about everything.

Larson pointed to the TV screen. "It's gotta be a drone—a pilotless aircraft. There's a camera on it and it's sending back live video of where it's going."

"But what does that—"

Charlie cut Tom off before he could finish his question. "There's a goddamn atomic bomb aboard that thing. The president's giving his state of the union speech tonight. Reams is trying to wipe out Washington."

The horror on Tom's face echoed how Larson felt.

The two soldiers standing on top of the Lincoln Memorial were ready. Their Stinger was warmed up and its heat-seeking sensor probed the airspace to the west, across the Potomac.

They hadn't detected anything yet but they couldn't fire even if they had. They were ordered to stand down for the next few minutes. Marine One and Marine Two were now airborne. The president's helicopter was cutting across the Capitol grounds, heading northwest toward Site R. Until it was safely out of range of the antiaircraft missile, the missile operator couldn't fire. Similar orders had been issued to the eleven other missile teams that ringed the Capitol. The risk of accidentally shooting down the presidential helicopters was too high.

The sergeant holding the Stinger on his right shoulder had his eye glued to the optical site. The luminous screen began to flicker. "Hey," he called out to his companion, "I'm starting to pick up something."

"Where?"

"I'm not sure, but I think it's dead ahead."

"Well, keep your finger off the trigger. We've still got to wait another two minutes before we can do anything."

"Yeah, I know. Anyway, it ain't much of a reading. Can't lock onto anything. It's probably some kind of venting across the river."

"Right."

A half a minute later, the drone crossed over the Potomac, passing just a hundred feet over the Lincoln Memorial. The heat output from the vented engine was so well diffused that the Stinger's IR sensor was never able to lock onto it. It continued to tell the operator that something was there, but the heat signature was too weak to process.

"What the fuck was that?" yelled the observer as the whining noise passed overhead. Neither man saw the black body as it raced by.

The missileer spun around, trying to aim his Stinger at the strange sound. But he still couldn't achieve missile lock.

The drone was moving eastward at a mile and a half per minute. It was flying blind, responding only to the last heading and altitude settings transmitted by Stan Reams. It would barely miss colliding with the narrow spire of the Washington Monument. But as it raced over the Mall it wouldn't miss the Capitol Building.

The drone was heading toward the central dome. It would

impact the cupola slightly right of center, about thirty feet below the bronze statue of a woman. Lady Freedom was a symbol of America's strength. But she was powerless to stop the evil that was bearing down on her.

"How the hell do you turn this thing?" screamed Charlie Larson. He and Tom Parker were now standing by the control panel, directly in front of the television screen.

The drone had just whisked past the Washington Monument. It was seconds away from colliding with the Capitol Building.

Tom's eyes darted from console to console. There were radios, video enhancers and a host of other electronic components that he couldn't identify. But there was one item he was familiar with. The joystick control was still sitting on the table, directly in front of the TV.

Without saying anything Tom grabbed the control, using his uninjured hand. He studied it for a moment. There were four arrows on it, one at each major heading point, like on a compass. Tom had taken a few introductory flying lessons years earlier but he had never bothered to get his license. Nevertheless, he remembered enough from his training to recognize that the hand control looked a lot like a miniature version of an aircraft control column. Push the column forward and the plane would dive, pull it back and it would climb. Tilt it left or right and the plane would bank in that direction.

Tom pulled the stick back a few degrees. The reaction on the TV screen was almost instantaneous. The drone pulled up.

"Son of a bitch," shouted Charlie, "you moved it!"

"Yeah, I think I can fly this thing—like a real plane." Tom then banked it to the right.

They watched the aspect angle of the TV monitor change as the drone turned south, away from the Capitol Building. Two seconds later it raced past the southwest corner of the building, clearing the dome by fifty feet.

Charlie slapped Tom on the back. "You did it—you saved Washington!"

Tom grinned as he continued to hold the hand control. His euphoria was short-lived as reality set in. The drone was still flying over heavily populated areas.

"What the hell do we do now?" Tom asked.

"We're going to let the Air Force have the thing. They can shoot it down or let it land. I don't want anything more to do with it."

Tom was about to reply when a new voice broke in. The trailer was now packed with other passengers from the helicopter. There was a trace of an Eastern European accent in the voice. "Mr. Larson, I think you should have your man continue to fly the drone straight out to the ocean. If you try to land it or shoot it down, it might explode."

"He's right," answered one of Los Alamos scientists. The NEST operative had a Ph.D. in nuclear physics. "We've got to get that thing to the ocean. If it blows over any populated land areas, it'll be an unmitigated disaster."

Charlie Larson faced Kirov. "Major, how much damage could that thing do?" he asked.

"It has a nominal yield of around eighteen kilotons."

"What the hell does that mean? In English, man!"

"It's roughly the same size as the device you used on Hiroshima."

"Damn!" replied Charlie.

"God Almighty," Tom gasped. He was absolutely stunned at what was happening.

Tom remained fused to the seat in front of the TV screen. He had been remotely piloting the drone for almost eighteen minutes now. But something had just happened. He had lost his frame of reference. He had no idea where the drone was heading. It was as if he were flying inside a blacked-out room. All he could see through the camera's lens were a few very dim specks of light in the distance.

"What happened?" asked Larson.

"I don't know. One second it's moving along okay—I can see the ground and all of the lights ahead. The next moment, nothing."

One of the FBI agents straining to view the screen figured it out. "Hey, it must have crossed onto the bay."

"What?" Tom asked.

"Chesapeake Bay. It's a giant bay that stretches from Baltimore to Norfolk."

"Geez, that's right. How far to the ocean?"

"It's still eighty miles or so to the east—that thing's got to cross the rest of Maryland and then Delaware before it'll reach the Atlantic coast."

"Shit," Tom said, now recalling the local geography. "It could run out of fuel before then."

Just as he spoke, a red light began to flash on the instrument panel and a buzzer sounded. The warning devices were linked to the clock built into the panel. The low-fuel warning had just been activated.

"What the hell's that racket?" asked Larson.

Tom leaned forward. He could barely make out the word "fuel" below the flashing light. It had been scratched onto the metal facing with a pencil. Tom turned toward the FBI agent who had been educating him about the Chesapeake.

"Quickly, man, this thing could go down any second. We're never going to make the ocean. Where's the widest part of the bay?"

The FBI agent closed his eyes, creating a mental image of Chesapeake Bay. He had spent most of his summers sailing on the waters of the vast estuary. "Turn toward the right side of the screen. That should take it toward the main part of the bay."

Tom executed the turn. The screen still remained blank. He hoped he had turned it in the correct direction.

The drone continued to fly for ninety-five seconds before it ran out of fuel. The engine sputtered and stopped. Power to the onboard radio transmitter had been supplied by a tiny generator on the engine. Without the generator, the transmitter stopped broadcasting its coded video signal.

Charlie Larson was the first to comment when the TV screen blinked to a solid sheet of static. "Hey, what happened?" he asked.

Tom wiggled the joystick. No response. He then reached up and slammed the TV monitor. The snowstorm continued. "I don't know. It's like the thing just went dead."

Major Kirov was the first to make the connection. "I think it's going down, gentlemen!"

The drone was almost 1,200 feet above the bay when the engine stopped. It had been gradually gaining altitude ever since Tom took control. He deliberately favored the climb setting on the joystick, preferring to keep the robot high up to avoid potential obstructions.

Without power, the nose-heavy drone angled downward. The aircraft's wings didn't provide a lot of lift but it still had enough forward momentum to maintain a steep glide path. It would remain airborne for almost a minute.

The seven men inside the trailer remained huddled around the static-filled television monitor. The air was thick with anticipation. Everyone had a bad feeling, especially the FBI agents who were based out of the capital headquarters. Most had relatives who lived in communities bordering the Chesapeake. It would have been easy for the G-men to lose control, knowing that their loved ones might be incinerated any second. But they all remained stone-faced. They were professionals.

All eyes were focused on Tom Parker. He was speaking to Charlie Larson.

"Charlie," Tom said, "what the hell do we do now?" He unconsciously jiggled the joystick, hoping the TV screen would come alive again.

"Jesus, I don't know. Was it still over the water when the TV quit?"

"I think so but I really don't have a clue as to where it was."

One of Larson's men spoke up. "Maybe it already crashed—that's why the screen blanked out."

"Hey, yeah," replied the African American helicopter crew chief. "That's gotta be it—it must have already gone down and it didn't blow up! The damn thing's a dud. It's going to be okay, after all."

Smiles started to replace frowns on the faces of the others. There was a ray of hope.

Tom and Charlie remained neutral, unsure of what to think.

Only one man suspected the worst. Major Kirov quickly scanned the tiny trailer compartment. The nearest window on the exposed side was a few feet to his right. He backed away and turned his head from the opening.

At 9:59 P.M., the drone slammed into Chesapeake Bay, about one-half mile offshore of Maryland's western shoreline.

It was traveling at 120 miles per hour when it hit the water surface.

During the first instant of contact, the warhead casing slid forward inside the fuselage, just as Stan Reams had designed. Its momentum crushed the foam shock absorber, triggering the backup detonator. The exposed end of the casing impaled itself on the steel spike. The shotgun shell fired. The C-4 exploded.

The soup-can-size uranium projectile accelerated down the steel tube as fast as a rifle bullet. A microsecond later it entered the U-235 target core. Assembly.

The beryllium disk fused to the tip of the bullet smashed into the wafer of plutonium and americium glued to the base of the tamper. The resulting bombardment of extra neutrons supercharged the critical-mass reaction. Supercriticality.

A hundred millionth of a second later, 132 pounds of enriched uranium began a catastrophic transformation. Fission.

The fission process consumed only about one percent of the assembled U-235 mass before the reaction tore itself apart. But it was more than enough to do the job. Detonation.

"Gentlemen," Kirov called out, "I think it might be a good idea to move away from the—"

The Russian security agent never finished his warning. He was preempted. The eastern horizon came alive with a man-made hellfire. The trailer filled with a light brighter than a dozen noonday suns.

"Cover your eyes," someone screamed.

It was too late. The nuclear flash was long gone by the time the first man reacted.

Only one man was temporarily stunned by the brilliance. The helicopter crew chief had happened to be looking toward an eastern-facing window.

Kirov started for the door. The others followed right behind.

Tom was the last one out. His companions were all standing by the trailer, looking toward the east. No one spoke.

The night sky was responding to the nuclear fireworks. The spectators were too far away to feel the effects of the shock wave but they had just been inundated with the delayed roar of the blast. The hellish thunder shook them all to the core. And then there was the rising fireball. It was a sight that could never be forgotten.

When the warhead detonated, a huge block of Chesapeake

Bay underwent a monstrous transformation. The fireball, its initial core temperature reaching 50,000,000 degrees, obliterated almost a square quarter mile of bay waters near Columbia Beach, Maryland. The nuclear fire consumed 4,000 tons of seawater and muddy bottom in a tiny fraction of a heartbeat.

Just a few seconds after the detonation, the expanding bubble of superheated gases, steam and radioactive debris skyrocketed into the night sky, reaching a height of fifteen thousand feet. As the fireball advanced into the heavens, the companion shock wave from the air blast spread concentrically across the bay, racing over the water surface. It slammed into the western coast of Maryland with the impact of a hurricane.

Like the atmospheric shock wave, gigantic water waves radiated from the detonation point. The waves, created by a combination of the blast and then bay waters collapsing back into the void, moved like *tsunamis*. Less than a minute after the warhead exploded, the first train of ten-foot-high rollers began to pound the nearest shoreline.

Tom Parker and Charlie Larson were now standing side by side, about a dozen yards away from the others. They were still looking toward the east. Several minutes had passed since the awful detonation. Except for a violet glow—remnants from the decaying fireball—the distant horizon was almost blacked-out. The night air was freezing but neither man noticed. They were still overwhelmed.

"Do you think it landed in the bay?" Tom finally asked, breaking the silence.

"Dear God, I hope so," Charlie said. He paused for a moment. "But if that thing blew up over a city, a hundred thousand people may have just been incinerated."

Photographic images of the victims from Hiroshima and Nagasaki flashed into Tom's mind. He again felt sick to his stomach.

FORTY-SEVEN

AFTERMATH

THE SUN ARCED LOW ACROSS THE CLOUDLESS SKY, BATHING everything in glorious tones. The indigo bay waters stretched to the east for miles. A foot of snow covered the coastal uplands, blanketing the ground in a sea of white. And there wasn't the slightest breath of a breeze; it was dead calm along the Chesapeake.

The helicopter flew southward, parallel to the shoreline. The heavy beat of its rotors broke the early morning silence. The giant U.S. Navy Sea Stallion was capable of ferrying a platoon of Marines, but there was only a handful of passengers aboard. Like the flight crew, they all wore moon suits. Aluminum tanks strapped to their backs provided a constant supply of air to their helmets. Built-in, electrically heated undergarments protected them from the frigid temperatures inside the aircraft.

Although the radiation-exposure garments were not really needed, the nuclear-warfare experts at the Pentagon had insisted that they be worn anyway. There was no way they would take a chance now, not after what had happened just two days earlier.

When the warhead exploded, much of the Eastern Seaboard of the United States went into total panic. The deafening blast was heard as far away as New York City, over two hundred miles to the north. The initial nuclear flash was observed even farther away, its brilliance radiating into the atmosphere as if it was a miniature sun.

Millions had been watching the president's speech when he was so hurriedly rushed away from the podium. And then they watched awestruck when the TV news cameras focused on the two gigantic presidential helicopters sitting on the lawn behind the Capitol Building. As the rotors whirled at high idle, the Marine guards and Secret Service agents herded the dignitaries aboard with uncommon speed.

None of the network anchors understood the risk. It wasn't their fault, though. No one knew what was happening because events were transpiring too fast. After the helicopters disappeared into the night, the news teams at the Capitol Building were left completely in the dark. No one from the government had yet made any attempt to explain the president's sudden departure. Consequently, the airwaves were ripe with speculation and rumor. One anchorman reported a story that an assassin was loose in the House chamber. Another report said that a truckload of Middle East terrorists were fighting it out with Marine guards at the White House. The wild talk continued for over fifteen minutes and then it stopped—suddenly.

During the early phase of the explosion, the electromagnetic pulse (EMP) from the detonation raced into the atmosphere at the speed of light. The high-energy burst covered the frequency spectrum from infrared to several hundred megahertz. By itself, the pulse was not a great threat. However, when it came into contact with a cable or an antenna, the pulse induced huge current and voltage spikes. This often resulted in disaster for any non-EMP-protected electronic circuit. Power lines and telephone cables, televisions and radios, personal computers and video-game boards, automobile engines and jet airliner navigation systems—almost any modern electronic device linked to a power source or antenna—could burn up in a flash of sparks and flame.

When the invisible EMP zoomed across the District of Columbia, it shorted several of the operating remote television camera systems in and around the Capitol Building. As a result, half of the live network broadcasts from Washington were terminated without warning, filling millions of TV screens across the nation with sheets of static.

An instant before the television signals were lost, the nuclear flash blinked. Most people inside their homes near Washington thought it was a lightning strike and were not yet concerned. Some could taste the lingering aftereffect of the brilliance—it tasted of lead—but thought nothing of it. About two minutes later, however, everything changed.

The roar of the nuclear blast was crushing as it sped across the nation's capital. To those within fifty miles of the detonation, the noise sounded like a million train cars smashing together simultaneously. Farther away, it sounded like thunder from hell.

The horrendous racket, combined with the useless TVs, confirmed the worst fears of those who resided in and around the District of Columbia—something horrible had just happened.

The Sea Stallion was flying along the western shoreline of Maryland at an altitude of 600 feet, cruising at a modest thirty knots. While most of the helicopter's observation team remained in the cargo hold, looking out the portholes and the open aft cargo doorway, one team member was in the cockpit, occupying the copilot's seat.

It had been a long time since the national security advisor had been on the flight deck of a helicopter. Nevertheless, he felt at home. After spending thirty-plus years as a Naval aviator, he could fly just about anything.

The four-star admiral wasn't piloting the Sea Stallion today, though. He left that up to the twenty-eight-year-old lieutenant in the right-hand seat. Instead, his job was to observe and report. And that's just what he was doing.

The Sea Stallion was in direct video/audio link with the president of the United States, using an EMP-protected military satellite in geosynchronous orbit to relay the real-time televised signals. The president was now at Camp David, having heloed in from Site R the previous afternoon.

The color TV camera was mounted just under the nose of the Sikorsky-built helicopter. The Naval officer could control its field of view with a hand control. A portable display unit located in the cockpit also allowed him to see the same images that were relayed to the president. All transmissions to and from the aircraft were encrypted, ensuring maximum privacy.

"Well, Mike," asked the president, "what's your assessment so far?"

"We were very lucky, sir. Very lucky. It appears that the damage along the shoreline isn't quite as bad as we had first estimated. I'm sure the bay waters absorbed a lot of the blast effect."

"Well, I don't know about that," the president said. "Those

waterfront houses on the bluff you flew over a few minutes ago looked pretty bad to me."

"They were, sir. That area was one of the worst. Those homes all took direct hits from the blast shock wave. We've observed pockets like that all along the shoreline—within a five-mile radius of the detonation point."

"What about the fires?"

"Many of the houses and other buildings that were nearest to the blast caught on fire from the thermal radiation release. So far, we've counted one hundred sixty-eight affected structures. They all burned to the ground."

The president remained silent for half a minute, continuing to study the television images. He didn't want to ask the next question. He finally gave in. "Mike, what's the latest count on casualties?"

"So far, FEMA estimates a total of nine hundred ninety-two deaths and over five thousand wounded, many seriously."

"My God! I didn't realize it was that bad."

"I know, sir. The casualty reports are really starting to come out now as more emergency crews make their way into the damaged areas. Overall, it's just a mess down there."

Most of the deaths had been caused by collapsing houses. First, the atmospheric shock front had slammed into the light-framed structures, many already burning from the initial thermal release. A few seconds later, hurricane force winds had hit. In many instances, that one-two combination was enough to rip a building off its foundation. But those houses located too close to the water's edge were hit with another barrage. The waves ran up the beaches and overtopped bulkheads, assaulting the expensive residences with a massive hydraulic punch.

In addition to the victims inside the destroyed homes, scores had been caught out in the open. The resulting flash burns were hideous. Those who were not killed outright were left with horrible burns. In many cases, the radiant heat had fused clothing directly to skin.

Besides the obvious blast and thermal damage, there was enormous collateral damage to the local infrastructure. Hundreds of trees were blown down, blocking roads and knocking out power and telephone lines. Landslides along the bluff areas dumped a few houses right into the bay. And the ground shock was so violent in some areas that an untold number of water and gas lines broke.

"Was there much of a problem with EMP?" the president asked.

"Yes, locally. From what I understand, about half of the car and truck engines within ten miles of the blast zone won't start. Same thing goes for TVs and radios. Their electronic components were fried real good. It's not quite that bad in D.C., though. Several of the network TV cameras are still out of service, but some of the local stations are up and running. Many vehicles are working, too."

"What about our military equipment? That okay?"

"Yes, sir. No problems there. Andrews is just fine. All critical components there were hardened years ago. Even Patuxent NAS came out okay."

"Good. That's good news. Now, have we had any luck locating that missing French yacht?"

"No, sir. I'm afraid we haven't found it yet. It was supposed to be heading up to a private waterfront estate near Annapolis, but no one's heard a peep from it since before the incident. It doesn't look too good."

"Then it must have sunk?"

"Maybe, but so far we haven't found a trace of the hull. The Coast Guard and some of our units from Norfolk have been running sonar searches along the bottom but nothing's showed up so far."

"Damn. What happened to it then?"

"It's beginning to look like the yacht was passing near the impact point when the warhead exploded. It was probably outside the main channel, taking a short cut across the bay somewhere near Columbia Beach. If that happened, then it may have been caught in the fireball—vaporized. There would be nothing left."

"Dear God!" A short pause. "How many?" The president's voice sounded weary.

"They were having some kind of party aboard. There were sixty-two passengers and crew on her, sir."

"Oh, no! Sixty-two more lives, all gone in a flash!" The president paused again. "Thank the Lord, Mike, that there wasn't a jumbo jetliner nearby when that thing went off—we could have lost another three hundred people."

"I know, sir."

The com line remained silent for half a minute before the president spoke again. "Mike, what's the fallout situation look like now?"

"The bottom areas around the blast point are still lethal, of course. And we've got some problems to the east. But overall I think we came through okay. The wind saved us."

Most of the severely contaminated airborne debris had been blown out into the Atlantic by a southeasterly flowing wind. Once out over the ocean, the radioactive elements trapped in the clouds would slowly settle out as the winds flowed eastward. However, there were still a number of local hot spots on the mainland located immediately downwind of the detonation point. The heavier contaminates had dropped out of suspension before reaching the ocean.

The radioactive contamination was principally confined to the eastern shoreline of Chesapeake Bay, south of Cambridge. Much of the poisoned area was located on the Blackwater National Wildlife Refuge. The Department of Energy had already evacuated all of the inhabitants of the privately owned properties that surrounded the refuge. They wouldn't be able to return for years.

"I'm glad to hear that, Mike. One less thing to have to worry about now."

"Yes, sir." The admiral paused as a new thought developed. "But, sir, if the wind had been blowing from any other direction, then we'd have had a much more serious situation."

"Yeah, I know what you mean," the president replied. "I don't want to even think about what would have happened if that crap had blown over Washington or Baltimore."

Or Virginia Beach or Norfolk or Newport News, thought the Naval officer. There were dozens of coastal communities along Chesapeake Bay that could have been forever tainted by the by-products of fission. Radioisotopes like strontium-90 and cesium-137 are biological time bombs. If ingested into the human body, they will come back to haunt their victims years later.

It was the fear of fallout that really panicked the Washington metropolitan region. Within just an hour of the blast, all major freeways and arterials surrounding the capital had been plugged solid with just about any vehicle that would start. It seemed that everyone wanted to escape. Most were heading west, trying to put as much distance between them and ground zero.

Gridlock had paralyzed the region until late the following afternoon. At that time, the Department of Energy had broadcast a radio bulletin over the National Emergency Alert System, informing the citizens of the District of Columbia and nearby communities that the danger from the nuclear fallout had abated. It was safe to return home.

The helicopter approached a sixty-foot commercial tugboat that was grounded at the base of a rocky bluff. "Ah, Mr. President, here's another one of those small craft that was apparently hit by the shock wave." He zoomed the camera lens on the pilothouse. "See how the windows are all blown in? Looks like definite blast damage to me. It must have been caught out in the open."

"Did the crew make it ashore?"

"We don't know. The Coast Guard reported that the hulk was found washed up on the rocks yesterday. But no one knows what happened to the crew."

"Well, I sure hope they made it."

The airborne observer didn't comment. He just looked out over the windscreen and aimed the camera at the approaching shoreline. It all looked the same now—miles and miles of coastal bluffs, intertidal marshes and sandy beaches. A moment later he finally keyed his mike. "Ah, sir, I think that's about all we're going to see for now. We can head across the bay to the eastern shore and make a run over the Blackwater area if you'd like."

"No. That's okay. I've seen enough." He paused. "You know, Mike, you are right. As bad as all this is, we were extremely lucky. If that warhead had exploded on land, it would have been a real catastrophe."

"No doubt about that. The water detonation saved us. Short of reaching the ocean, those guys in that trailer couldn't have found a better spot to dump the damn thing."

"I know. I'm very grateful for what they did."

"Sir, is it true that the FBI is still holding to the single-man theory?"

"Yes, all the evidence points to just the one man."

"The guy who worked on the B-two?"

"That's the one."

"Good Lord. If one man—working alone—could do this . . . ," The officer shook his head in disbelief. ". . . What about all those terrorist groups out there? If those bastards get hold of enriched uranium or plutonium—"

"Mike, we can't ever let this happen again."

"But how are we going to stop it, sir? The Russians are having a hell of a time trying to control their own nuclear materials. And then we've got all of those third-world nations like Iran, North Korea, Pakistan and India with their own atomic bomb programs. Just what the hell are we going to do?"

"I don't know, Mike. But somehow we've got to find a way. We'll never get a second chance."

EPILOGUE
THE PROPOSAL

THE MOUNTAIN AIR WAS CRISP AND COOL. THERE WERE JUST a few clouds skirting the nearby peaks on this spring day. The view of the distant lake was like a postcard. It was the perfect setting.

The outdoor deck of the mountaintop ski lodge wasn't crowded yet. Lunch wouldn't be served for another hour. The man and woman sat off to one side, away from the others. They were each sipping from steaming mugs full of hot chocolate and a splash of whiskey.

Tom Parker and Linda Nordland took in the incredible vista with genuine awe. It was their first clear day in the Austrian Alps. The area had been socked in with thick clouds during the previous four days of their visit.

Tom looked across the table, stealing a brief look at his love.

Linda was enjoying the view, unaware of Tom's gaze.

She looks wonderful, he thought. He then closed his eyes. *Thank you, Lord. Thank you for saving her!*

Linda had been renewed, born again. Her spirits had never been higher. The headaches had disappeared and her vision was finally back to normal. She was going to be just fine.

Tom opened his eyes and turned to once again take in the vista. He too was awed. "This is really some view from here," he commented.

"It's positively wonderful," Linda replied.

"A good day to be alive." He then took another sip from his mug.

Linda turned back. "How's your hand with this cold?" she asked.

"Not bad. It really feels okay." He set the mug on the table and then flexed his right hand. The lacerations had healed but his doctor had warned him that the tendons might be stiff for months.

Linda locked onto his eyes. "You know, Tom," she said, "Jeanette told me what really happened." She paused. "You were very lucky that madman didn't kill you."

"Is that what you two were talking about at the airport?" asked Tom.

Charlie Larson and his wife had driven the couple to Sea-Tac Airport, helping to launch their monthlong vacation.

"Yes, she told me the whole story. I'm sure glad Charlie got there in time."

"Yes. I owe Charlie my life. I'm indebted to him forever."

"So am I," Linda said. "So am I."

Linda waited a few more seconds before again speaking. "Promise me, Tom, that you won't take a chance like that again. I don't know what I'd do if I lost you."

Tom nodded. "Don't worry. I learned my lesson. I'll take it easy in the future."

"Good. And so will I. No more vendettas—for either of us."

Tom didn't respond. He turned away, looking toward a mountain peak. He still had a score to settle. He was at peace with it—for now. The horrible dreams and flashbacks had abated. But the underlying wound continued to fester. *Someday,* he thought, *I'll find 'em. And then they'll pay!*

Linda surveyed Tom's face as he looked away. He was

there, but then he wasn't. She had seen the look before. *You poor man. It must be horrible to remember what they did.*

A month earlier, Tom had finally told her the whole story about Lori, except for the dreams where Linda had become the victim.

He's thinking about it again. I've got to help him forget. Linda shifted position in her chair. It was time to change subjects. "Honey, have you given any more thought to that invitation?"

"What?" Tom asked, turning back to face Linda.

"You know, from the president."

"Ah, geez, I don't want to do that. It's all a bunch of hype."

"But you earned it, darn it. You can't turn it down."

"You really think I should go? I didn't do anything."

"You didn't do anything! Are you nuts? If you hadn't stopped Reams when you did, Washington would have been incinerated. Everyone there would have died. And the rest of America would have been mortally wounded."

"But all I did was fly that stupid thing for a few minutes."

"Of course you did! You piloted it away from land. If it had landed in one of those suburbs around the capital, hundreds of thousands, if not millions, would have died. You're a national hero, Tom Parker, whether you like it or not."

"Yeah, I guess so. But what about all those people living along Chesapeake Bay?" He paused to take another sip from his mug. "I'm sure they're not too happy about what happened."

"They can rebuild their houses. That wouldn't have happened if it had exploded on land."

"Maybe. Anyway, there isn't going to be any fishing or oystering there for a long time."

"A small sacrifice. We'll send 'em some salmon and clams from Puget Sound."

Tom laughed. "Right—that's a good idea."

Linda again locked onto Tom's eyes. "Then you'll go?"

"Go where?"

"To the ceremony. If we leave next Monday, we'll arrive in plenty of time."

"But it's right in the middle of our vacation."

"We can fly back the next day. We'll go on the Concord—my treat. It'll be a blast!"

Tom shook his head. "Hell, I didn't even vote for the man."

"But he's going to present a medal to you—and Charlie—at the White House. There'll be thousands there!"

"I don't know. I'd just like to forget about the whole thing."

"Tom, please don't tell me that you're going to turn down the award. Please don't tell me that."

Tom would never admit it to anyone, but he was flattered by the president's gesture. Linda had been hounding him for weeks about it. He finally surrendered. "Okay, okay, I guess I'll go."

Linda's face broke into sunshine. "I'm so proud of you. It'll be wonderful."

"Do we need to confirm it or something? I never committed to being there."

"Don't worry about it. You don't need to do anything."

"What do you mean?"

"It's already been done."

"What?"

"Matt Barrett, the White House chief of staff, called yesterday, when you were out getting your skis fixed. I assured him that we'd be there."

"What about Keely and Mom?"

"It's already been taken care of. They'll be there waiting for us."

Tom shook his head. "So I'm that predictable, after all."

Linda didn't say anything. She just beamed.

Tom smiled back. He had a surprise of his own. His trip to the ski shop the previous day had been a ruse. He had really gone to a specialty jeweler. At first he was going to buy a diamond, but then he found the perfect emerald. It had cost him five grand, but he didn't care. He had more than enough left over from the sale of the Corvette.

He reached into his parka jacket, retrieving the tiny ring case.

Linda's eyes lit up as he placed the gift-wrapped box on the table.

"You know, honey," he said, "remember that little chapel we saw in the village the other day?"

"Yes," she replied, her heartbeat accelerating with anticipation.

"Well, I was thinking that we could . . ."

AUTHOR'S POSTSCRIPT

To all of the wannabe A-bomb makers that are out there in the real world, beware. Certain elements of the nuclear device depicted in this novel, along with its delivery system, have been deliberately altered and/or omitted. If you try to copycat the weapon's design, you might zap yourself or have a dud on your hands.

JEFFREY LAYTON is a professional engineer. He lives in the Pacific Northwest. He is the author of *Blowout*, also published by Avon Books.

STUART WOODS

The *New York Times* Bestselling Author

GRASS ROOTS
71169-/ $6.50 US/ $8.50 Can

When the nation's most influential senator
succumbs to a stroke, his brilliant chief aide
runs in his stead, tackling scandal, the governor
of Georgia and a white supremacist
organization that would rather see him
dead than in office.

Don't miss these other page-turners from
Stuart Woods

WHITE CARGO   70783-7/ $6.50 US/ $8.50 Can
A father searches for his kidnapped daughter in the
drug-soaked Colombian underworld.

DEEP LIE   70266-5/ $6.50 US/ $8.50 Can
At a secret Baltic submarine base, a renegade Soviet
commander prepares a plan so outrageous that it just
might work.

UNDER THE LAKE   70519-2/ $6.50 US/ $8.50 Can
CHIEFS   70347-5/ $6.50 US/ $8.50 Can
RUN BEFORE THE WIND
70507-9/ $6.50 US/ $8.50 Can

SEALS
THE WARRIOR BREED

by H. Jay Riker

The face of war is rapidly changing, calling
America's soldiers into hellish regions where
conventional warriors dare not go.
This is the world of the SEALs.

SILVER STAR
76967-0/$5.99 US/$7.99 Can

PURPLE HEART
76969-7/$5.99 US/$7.99 Can

BRONZE STAR
76970-0/$5.99 US/$6.99 Can

NAVY CROSS
78555-2/$5.99 US/$7.99 Can